WHAT I PROMISE YOU

LIZ TOLSMA

BARBOUR
PUBLISHING

Published by Barbour Publishing, Inc., 1810 Barbour Drive, Uhrichsville, Ohio 44683, www.barbourbooks.com

Our mission is to inspire the world with the life-changing message of the Bible.

 Member of the
Evangelical Christian
Publishers Association

Printed in the United States of America.

DEDICATION

In remembrance of those the world forgot.

"They called me and I went. I did not think much of it.
It was fortunate to be able to do what had to be done."
<small>ELISABETH EIDENBENZ</small>

"What we have done for ourselves alone dies with us; what we
have done for others and the world remains and is immortal."
<small>ALBERT PIKE</small>

And the King shall answer and say unto them,
Verily I say unto you, Inasmuch as ye have done it unto one
of the least of these my brethren, ye have done it unto me.
<small>MATTHEW 25:40 (KJV)</small>

GLOSSARY

FRENCH WORDS

Allons-y - *Let's go.*

alors - *The people in France I asked had a difficult time translating this word, but I heard it all the time. Generally, it means now, then, next, so.*

arrêt - *stop*

au revoir - *goodbye*

bonjour - *hello*

boulanger - *baker*

Camp de Rivesaltes - *transit camp first opened in 1939 for Spaniards fleeing the revolution, then used by the Vichy and Nazis as a transit camp for Jews and other political prisoners who were taken to Drancy and then to Auschwitz.*

ça va - *very informal, multipurpose word, but its general meaning is "okay." It can be asked as a question and can be given as an answer to that question. Equivalent of asking "How are you?" and the response being "I'm fine."*

Ce n'est pas vrai - *That's not true.*

centime - *1/100 of a Euro*

C'est un musée - *It's a museum.*

C'est vrai - *That's true*

Comment vas-tu? - *How are you? (informal)*

De rein - *you're welcome*

domaine - *winery*

enchanté - *Nice to meet you (masculine); Enchantée (feminine)*

en Francis - *in French*

et - *and*

excuse-moi - *excuse me*

Gare de Perpignan - *Perpignan train station*

grandmère - *grandmother*

grandpère - *grandfather*

Je ne comprends pas - *I don't understand.*

Je ne sais pas - *I don't know.*

Je suis désolé - *I'm sorry (masculine); Je suis désolée (feminine)*

Je t'adore - *I love you; literally, I adore you.*

Je t'aime - *I love you (informal)*

Juifs - *Jews*

La Maternité de la Paix - *Peace Maternity Hospital*

madame - *missus*

maman - *mom*

merci - *thank you*

merci beaucoup - *thank you very much*

mère - *mother*

mon - *my (masculine); ma (feminine)*

mon ami - *my friend (masculine); mon amie (feminine)*

mon chéri - *my dear (masculine); ma chérie (feminine)*

mon coeur - *my heart*

mon doux garçon - *my sweet boy*

mon fil - *my son*

mon petit - *my little one (masculine)*

monsieur - *mister*

non - *no*

Nous l'apprécions - *We appreciate it.*

Où se trouve la maternité? - *Where is the maternity hospital?*

oui - *yes*

pains au chocolat - *flaky pastry wrapped around a log of soft chocolate*

père - *father*

Père Noel - *Father Christmas, Santa Claus*

Puis-je vous aider? - *Can I help you?*

Que faisons nous aujourd'hui? - *What are we doing today?*

s'il te plaît – *please (informal)*

s'il vous plaît – *please (formal)*

Soyez silencieux – *Be silent.*

TGV – *(pronounced TAY-ZHAH-VAY) – acronym for Train à Grande Vitesse, literally "train of great speed." High speed train that operates all over France.*

toilettes – *toilets*

GERMAN WORDS

Fräulein – miss

Halten Sie – stop

Schnell – fast

CHAPTER ONE

22 August, 1955
Elne, France

They say every building has a story, an unwritten history contained within its structure. Walls hold secrets, burying them deep into their cores, into darkness that is never meant to see the light of day, nothing but faint whispers of what has been, what might have been, and what will never be known.

If this building in front of me could tell a tale, what would it be? One of sorrow and overwhelming pain, fear and insecurity, even horror? Or would it be one of joy and peace, safety and rest, a haven?

If I open the doors, I might release bright children's laughter that echoes in the high-ceilinged rooms, a music that tinkles like chandeliers on a morning breeze. But if I throw open the windows, the eyes into the building's soul, I might discharge crying and screaming.

Perhaps it is best to leave the building alone, crumbling, sinking into the rocky ground, the past buried in the ruins of the place. Unspeakable events that unfolded within are best never disturbed, like a coating of dust on furniture that would choke someone if they dared to run a cloth over the surface, releasing a consuming cloud.

Perhaps it is best to allow the past to be lost to time. Then again, maybe it is a past that is worth the remembering, like photographs dug from deep within an attic trunk, rediscovered and restored.

There are overgrown gardens, coneflowers and black-eyed Susans and lamb's ears that have gone wild and intermingled with the lawn, a tangle of color and grass that only needs a bit of weeding and taming to return them to their former glory. Others have been consumed by briars and brambles that pierce the tender skin of any hand that attempts to control them, so that only a bulldozing will set it right again.

And what of the building before me? What secrets and stories and laughter and pain does it contain?

I know. I know only too well.

CHAPTER TWO

15 July, 1942
Perpignan, Vichy France

Somewhere in the distance, crickets sang their night song. From underneath the window, a cat meowed a pitiful plea, likely wanting to be let in to sleep, out of the heavy, damp night air. Otherwise, the world was still and quiet, tucked in slumber as a beam of moonlight streamed through the thin bedroom curtains.

Noémie Treves snuggled deeper into her husband Levi's strong embrace. For a moment he stirred, adjusting to her new position, then he settled down. His light snore, so familiar to her, added to the comforting coziness of the night.

She touched the place where their child slept. Or perhaps the little one was awake. Because it was early in her pregnancy, she had yet to feel the baby move within her. What would it be like when the child actually fluttered? What a wondrous moment that would be. One to look forward to. One to embrace.

If only *Maman* were alive to experience this with her. To guide her in what to expect.

Still, she had Levi, and for now, they were at peace. Their small city was as safe as it could be in the midst of a war that embroiled the entire world. Though the Nazis controlled the northern part of France, here in the South, they were in no immediate danger. The Vichy didn't care for Jews like them very much, but at least they weren't arresting them in great numbers and shipping them away to Poland.

Oui, there were whispers about Jews in the city disappearing off the streets—not in great numbers, but a few. Whispers of what was happening just a few kilometers away in Rivesaltes. When it had been a camp for Spaniards fleeing the civil war, it was bad enough. Rumors swirled like leaves in the wind about how much worse it was now that it was full of Jews and those who opposed the Vichy regime.

She shoved away the thoughts of conflict, of men killing each other with guns, of airplanes dropping their deadly bombs on innocent civilians, of people wearing yellow stars disappearing from the streets, never to be heard from again.

People who were taken because of her.

All these concerns and regrets continued to creep in, no matter how she worked to put them away, to keep them on a high shelf where she couldn't reach them. They tore her heart to shreds and ate at her very soul. Why had she been so naive? So trusting? Too trusting?

She had blood on her hands, blood that would never wash away.

Once she had forced herself to close the lid on that box, she worked to bring to mind happier thoughts. She and Levi had so much good coming their way. They had settled in this charming town in the balmy south of France. He worked hard in the vineyards and olive groves and provided well for her. And now they were expecting the amazing gift of a child.

What more could she want? Oui, she would be happy to be working again, creating beautiful stained-glass creations, but that was not possible now. Staying alive was their main concern.

As long as the Vichy remained in power and she and Levi kept themselves as much out of trouble as possible, they had nothing to fear. Life could go on as normal as possible despite the rationing and blackouts. They were minor inconveniences compared to the horrors many were experiencing in other parts of Europe.

The news that the Vichy were ramping up their arrests to placate the Germans was nothing but saber-rattling. It had to be. For over two years, they had lived here in peace. She prayed that would never change. If nothing else, they had the Spanish border not too far away.

As she stared into the darkness softened by moonlight, her eyelids fluttered and were almost shut when the cold, wet nose of her sweet little dachshund Tchin touched hers. Though the dog's body was tiny, the entire bed shook as she wagged her tail. Noémie reached over and pulled the squirmy animal into her arms and whispered into her soft ear. "Go to sleep, my sweet nugget. You may snooze all day, but I have work to do."

Levi tightened his grip on her. "What's going on?" His voice was heavy with sleep.

"Now see, Tchin, what you've done? You have the entire house awake." She reached behind her and stroked Levi's beard-covered cheek. "I'm sorry, my love. It's just this dog who thinks it's time to play."

"Wait until the baby comes. I guess it's a good thing we're getting used to waking up in the middle of the night. Great practice for when we become parents."

"Still, you need your rest. We all do because, as you say, our days of sleeping through the night are numbered." She tucked Tchin underneath the covers, up against her chest, then reached behind her to claim a kiss from Levi. "Go back to sleep."

He kissed her with fervor. "You make that difficult."

"Enough. You won't be any good for work in the morning, and how will I explain the bags under my eyes when I go to get bread?"

"That you have a husband who loves you."

"Good night, Levi." She kissed his hand and rested with her back against his chest. Warm. Protected. Loved.

A drum beat interrupted her half slumber, at first distant and slow, then faster and nearer, harsher, demanding.

She blinked her eyes open. The thumping wasn't a drum. Fists pounded at their door. She bolted upright, Tchin jumping from the bed and running toward the entrance, yipping and yapping for all she was worth.

Levi shrugged into his robe and slippers and shuffled to the door. Noémie raced after him and grabbed him by the arm just as he was about to turn the knob. "Don't." She kept her voice quiet but insistent.

"Why?"

The pounding came again, its rhythm and intensity the same as the throbbing of her heart. "Open up." Though spoken in French, the words

15

were harsh and strict. Gendarmes. French police who worked for the German puppet government.

"That's why. Maybe if they think no one is home, they'll go away and leave us alone." Moments ago, she had been so confident of their safety. But the saber-rattling wasn't a false narrative.

It was true.

Though they had done nothing, those with the power and authority to arrest banged on their door.

Levi bent and kissed the top of her head. "*Ma chérie,* I only wish that were possible. Even if, by some miracle, they went away now, they would be back."

"Then we'd have time to hide or get away." She had to make him see that they had to buy a few hours, a few days to escape.

"They will question us and release us. Or resettle us. That's what I've heard." He stroked her cheek, sending a shiver down her arms.

"I've heard about *Camp de Rivesaltes.* That isn't a place I want to go. No one does."

The pounding continued. "Open up, or we will kick in the door!"

Levi turned the lock and pushed the door open. He had barely cracked it when the gendarmes flung it wide and poured in. Before Noémie could even register what was going on, a burly officer with a scruffy mustache grabbed her and wrenched her arms behind her back. Pain shot to her shoulders, and she gasped.

Levi lunged for her, but another soldier, this one even bigger than the one holding her, punched her husband in the gut, then in the face. He crumpled to the ground.

"Levi!"

When she attempted to go to him, the one holding her tightened his grip on her wrists, surely bruising them. She swallowed back the salty tears that had built in her eyes and her burning throat.

Levi's guard pulled him to a standing position. "Pack. You have five minutes. One suitcase each. Now."

Noémie changed and threw everything she could manage to fit into her one brown bag while Levi did the same. Before stepping out of their sanctuary, Levi came to her and took her in his arms. "*Je t'adore,* Noémie.

Je t'adore. Never forget that, no matter what."

"Je t'adore, Levi, *mon coeur*. My heart." Before she was ready, the guards entered and grabbed them again then shoved them toward the doorway. They herded them down the winding staircase, three flights, and out the door to the narrow, shop-lined street.

At this time, all was usually quiet, but now the hum of truck engines broke the stillness of the night. Up and down the street, lights shone through the cracks in the shutters. Their neighbors, their fellow Jews, emerged from their homes, many dressed in their nightclothes, in the clutches of the police. Along with Levi and Noémie, they were forced into the backs of the trucks.

There was *Monsieur* Charpac, the tailor from across the street and Monsieur Furtado, the man who owned the anchovy and sardine shop at the end of the road, both with their wives and several children. Levi helped *Madame* Krivine, the jewelry maker, in, and she sat on the hard wood bench beside Noémie. "This is our worst nightmare coming true."

All Noémie could do was nod and rub her belly where her child grew.

Madame Krivine shifted closer to Noémie as more men, women, and children climbed inside. Levi was still helping them aboard. "Do you think they'll treat you better because of your condition?"

"I hope that will be the case."

"Then you're delusional. They take pity on no one."

A gunshot echoed off the hundred-year-old buildings, and Noémie jumped. "Is there a fight on the street?"

"Someone resisted them, and they don't let such a crime go unpunished." Madame Krivine pulled her coat tighter and sat up straight, her once-smooth skin now crinkled. "Don't give them the satisfaction. You're a statuesque woman. Stand tall and proud. They want to humble us. Stay proud and strong."

Strong. Oui, Noémie could do that. Had to do that. She'd been strong when leading the glass factory after Papa died, taking over and being in charge of men old enough to be her father. Standing firm on her proposals and changes.

But this was something entirely different. What would Camp de

Rivesaltes be like? Were the stories about it true?

A moment later, Levi squeezed in between her and Madame Krivine. He drew Noémie close, and she leaned against his shoulder. Her rock. Her strength. She drew on it now as she drew on air. "Don't leave me." He'd been with her and had encouraged her when she was alone in the world and facing the daunting task of heading up a company of fifteen employees.

"I'm not going anywhere." Levi kissed her temple. "As much as it's in my power, I'll stay by your side and protect you and our child. If I can help it, I won't allow them to hurt you."

The truck lurched forward, flinging them all to the side. Noémie almost ended up in Levi's lap. She clung to him as they began their trip to. . .

Who knew where the Germans were going to take them. Camp de Rivesaltes was only a guess. Who knew what was going to happen to them. Who knew what fate awaited them.

Many of her acquaintances would say Hashem knew everything. Some of her Christian friends had told her that in their Bible, Hashem knew every hair on their heads and every sparrow that fell from a branch. With a sigh, she rested against her husband.

If only it was true. But if He knew everything, He would stop this carnage.

Soon they left Perpignan behind and came to the country. The road was narrow and bumpy. When they hit a rut, she and Levi bounced in unison, sometimes pushed against the truck's canvas top. Because it was bound tightly, they wouldn't fall out.

Theirs wasn't the only truck. Through the opening at the back, she spied others following them. Maybe two or three, it was difficult to tell. How many were there?

Levi leaned over and whispered into her ear, loud enough so she would hear over the engine noise. "Will you promise me something?"

She nodded. "Of course. Anything for you."

"If something happens to me, take care of yourself and our child. Don't let anything happen to the baby. Even if I don't survive whatever lies ahead of us, do everything you can, whatever you have to, in order to live. To give life to our little one."

She shushed him with a kiss. "Don't speak like that. We are both going to be fine. We'll raise him and the others that we are blessed with and grow old together. We'll go home to Mulhouse and wander the cobbled streets between the half-timbered houses and watch the sun rise over the Rhine. Life will be good. You'll see."

Levi pulled her closer, and together they endured the ride. Even though it wasn't very long, she was stiff and sore by the time the brakes screeched, signaling an end to their journey.

Hopefully it was the end and there wasn't anything else awaiting them.

A moment later, a German soldier flipped down the tailgate. "Out, out, all of you. Now! *Schnell. Schnell.*"

The others who had been crowded into the truck with them scrambled for the exit and jumped to the ground. Levi held her back so they were the last to get off. He helped her down and took her by the hand.

Bright lights illuminated the scene in front of them. As far as the eye could see, white concrete barracks stretched across the barren plain. The wind whipped her skirt and tangled it around her legs. A deep chill settled in her bones.

Guards with German shepherds surrounded them, the dogs' ears pricked as they barked and growled. Noémie stepped closer to Levi's side.

"Get moving!"

Though no one knew where they were going, they advanced as one, like a wave on the sea.

Then they stopped, and a tall soldier shouted commands at them through a megaphone. "Two lines. Make two lines. Women to the left, men to the right."

There was no way she was going to be separated from Levi. She grasped his hand tighter.

"You have to let me go." His words were firm, his voice steady. How could he remain so calm when she trembled from head to toe?

"I can't." Her strength seeped from her limbs, and her legs shook. "How will I do this without you by my side?"

"You are a strong woman. You've endured much more. You will survive this." As Levi spoke, a soldier approached and pulled them apart. Though she held to Levi with all her strength, she was no match for the well-muscled Nazi.

They marched Levi away and forced her in the opposite direction. "Levi, je t'adore!"

The wind swept her words away, and Levi disappeared from sight.

CHAPTER THREE

18 August, 1942
Camp de Rivesaltes, Vichy France

Little by little, Noémie shrugged off sleep and rolled over in bed. She reached for Levi but came up empty. Was he up already? Had she overslept?

Fatigue tugged at her, and she struggled to remain awake. Perhaps if she pulled away the quilt, she would rouse. But instead of a quilt, all that covered her was a thin blanket.

Oui, it was summer. No quilt needed. But this bed wasn't soft, and there was no cotton mattress. Only this one, filled with filthy, bug-infested straw.

What was going on?

She forced her eyelids open. In the semidarkness, she made out a long room with beds stretching from one end to the other on each side. Was she sick and in a hospital ward?

Then like a tsunami, reality crashed into her. This was no hospital. And Levi wasn't nearby.

This was Camp de Rivesaltes. And she was a prisoner.

Every morning since they had been here, the same scenario repeated itself. Every morning, the same realization slammed into her, a physical force that struck her.

Was that what it was like for those she might have saved? She could have spared them this. They could be waking up in their beds in England, preparing for another day's work or play.

Now she was receiving her just punishment for her crimes.

The familiar morning sickness greeted her as she awakened. By now, it should be gone, but just the thought of the thin rice gruel the guards served them every morning and evening sent her stomach soaring and diving. She pushed it down. At four months along, she only had a slight bump.

"You'd better get up and get moving." Hannah, a dark-haired woman who occupied the bed next to Noémie, passed her and slapped her on the bottom of her feet. "Roll call soon."

Though Noémie curled into a ball, not willing to face the day in front of her, Hannah would have no part of it. "You've been here a few weeks, and you know how this works. If you don't show up, it's the rest of us who pay the price. I'll carry you out there myself if I need to."

Noémie couldn't help the smile that crossed her face. A woman after her own heart. "I'll move faster if you leave me alone." And if the awful morning sickness would pass.

Hannah tipped her head to the side and studied Noémie. She held out her hand and assisted Noémie to her feet.

The room spun, and she barely kept the bile that was rising in her throat from spilling out of her mouth. She had to fight with all she had to keep herself and her child safe.

"Are you okay?"

Noémie nodded. "I will be. Just give me a minute."

"A minute isn't something you have. If you need extra time, you have to get up earlier."

"Earlier than this?" She pointed to the sky, light pink streaks barely visible through the cracked window.

"You can lean on me if you need to." Hannah was certainly built large enough to carry both of them.

"*Merci*, but I need to stand on my own two feet here."

"That's for sure."

"Then I will." Noémie took a deep breath and straightened her spine. Without too much in her stomach, there was little chance she would vomit. All she had to do was ignore the nausea.

Easier said than done.

At least she didn't have to get dressed. Any items she'd had were soon stolen. She hadn't washed her dress in weeks because she'd learned her lesson the hard way.

She followed Hannah and several dozen or so women out the door and into the warm, late-summer morning. Once more, the wind from the plain whipped at her uncombed hair and her rumpled dress. The gale never stopped, often knocking over the wobbly carts they used to distribute the rice.

Thankfully, Levi had insisted that she wear her sturdy boots, even though she would have much preferred her cooler peep-toe pumps. The ground was rough and rocky, and she would have turned an ankle in them.

She and Hannah took their places next to each other, keeping the rows and columns straight, just the way the German-controlled gendarmes liked them.

Because Noémie had spent all her life in the French and German area of Mulhouse, she was well aware of this characteristic. One that Maman often employed herself. Noémie was also conditioned to be that way.

As she stood waiting for her name to be called by the large-boned woman with narrow eyes and ruddy cheeks, she snuck glimpses of the countryside surrounding them.

Not that there was much to see. Barracks surrounded them, but their section in particular was fenced off with barbed wire. That was new since yesterday. If the rumors were to be believed, the Nazis pressured the Vichy government more and more. And the Vichys were bending to the German will.

Beyond the fence lay desolate wilderness, nothing but grass dried by the summer's heat and drought and a few scrubby bushes and trees. The Pyrenees mountains rose against the horizon, blue and gray against the early-morning sky. On the other side of the craggy rocks lay Spain. Freedom. Was there a way to escape? A way to get out of here and make it to safety?

Yet these mountains were also a barrier. Another fence, hemming them in. The terrain was steep and rocky, not easy for a pregnant woman to cross, especially with no supplies.

Hannah elbowed her in the side, drawing her attention away from the magnificent yet confining mountains. "Don't look there. They'll know what you're thinking. And in your condition, you would never make it. Your chances are better here."

"*Soyez silencieux!* Be quiet! No talking is allowed." The muscular woman in charge directed her cold stare right at Hannah then flicked it in Noémie's direction.

For the rest of the agonizing hour or so, as the sun rose over the plains, Noémie stood as still as possible, her feet sweating in the heavy boots. Even though her stomach was still queasy, she managed to keep its very few contents inside. One small victory.

At last they were released, and Noémie and Hannah headed toward the barracks together.

What about Levi? Had his morning been similar? It had been a while since she'd seen him, had been able to speak to him and touch him. And with the fences, it would be more difficult. She would have to keep a watchful eye on the guards.

Hannah nodded toward the new fencing. "Perhaps if we are model prisoners, they'll set us free. Perhaps life won't be so hard for us if we do what they tell us."

From someone who, from all appearances, was a fighter, it was strange she would talk about being a model prisoner. "Why do you believe that if we obey, we'll be saved?"

Hannah stared at the smudgy mountains on the horizon for several long minutes. "I just do. You have to trust me." Her voice wavered, a crack in her invincible facade.

Noémie leaned closer to Hannah and kept her voice to a whisper. "Have you attempted to escape?"

The screech of young children's voices saved Hannah from answering. As if some bell only they could hear had rung, they poured from their barracks and toward a woman just entering the block from a different part of the camp.

She opened her arms to the children and embraced as many of them as she could. Instead of civilian clothes, she wore a pale blue nurse's uniform with a white apron over it and a white cap on her head.

Something about her manner, her easy smile, the way the children responded to her, drew Noémie to her. Every day, she held herself back from running to *Fräulein* Reiter's arms along with the children.

With the self-sacrificing nature of Fräulein Reiter, a volunteer from the Swiss Children's Aid and Red Cross Aid to Children who voluntarily lived in the camp, it was sure to be a place of safety and comfort.

She'd been there for almost a year and had managed to get a good number of children away from this cesspool. If Noémie were Catholic, she'd be nominating Fräulein Reiter for sainthood.

That invisible pull, that tug on Noémie's heartstrings, was now too urgent to ignore. She followed the stream of children but stood at a distance as they interacted with the nurse.

"Hello, my lovelies, hello. How are you all today?"

A chorus of sweet, high voices answered the question while Fräulein Reiter laughed, her eyes dancing with light.

"What have you brought us today?" A brown-haired boy, no more than eight, posed the question.

Fräulein Reiter hushed him and cast a glance at the guards near the fence. "All in good time. No reason to be impatient. Shall we go inside, out of the wind, and see what there is?"

"Fräulein Reiter, did you see that Beryl and Margot are back?"

She spun to the slender girl behind her, a curl escaping the yellow kerchief on her head. All the sparkle and light fled her eyes. "Back?"

"Oui, they came in a truck last night from the home they'd been living in."

Two girls, about eight and ten years old, mirror images of each other, stepped forward, heads bowed, holding hands. Noémie gasped. Beryl and Margot de Carcassona, along with their parents, had been neighbors of theirs in Perpignan. They'd disappeared a few weeks before the roundup in which Levi and Noémie were taken, and no one knew what had become of them. Strange that she hadn't run into Madame de Carcassona in the camp. She moved toward the children.

As soon as they spotted Noémie, they raced to her, and she gathered the girls to herself. Oh, how delicious it was for her thirsty soul to hold them. "Why are you here?"

Beryl gazed at her, a shower of tears dampening her pale cheek. "They said that Maman and Papa are being moved to another camp and that we had to come here so we could go with them."

"*Non*." Fräulein Reiter shook her head so hard that she had to hold her cap on her head. "They assured me you would stay at the children's home. I won't allow it. Who took you?"

"Gendarmes." Margot shook in Noémie's arms. "They said we had to come with them or Maman and Papa would be in terrible trouble. The matron at the home didn't know what else to do. She didn't have any other choice but to send us with them. So here we are." Another cascade of tears followed.

"That home is Swiss territory. Neutral. They can't enter and take who they like. Unacceptable. The Vichy may be caving to Nazi commands, but I never will." She peered at the girls who stared at their battered, dust-covered shoes. "Don't worry. Nothing will happen to you. I'll make sure you're safe. Let me speak to the camp commander about this right away. We'll get it straightened out."

A collective groan rose from the other children.

"Now, now, you'll have to wait for our classes today. Sometimes we don't get what we want right when we want it."

Never had children been more able to understand the truth in that statement. Still, it was a shame the little ones, so happy to be with Fräulein Reiter, who had experienced so much hurt and disappointment in their short lives, had to endure even a second more of it.

Noémie turned her attention to Fräulein Reiter. "Can I do something?"

"Perhaps. I've appreciated your assistance these past few weeks." She turned to the gaggle of children. "Would you like it if Madame Treves is with you for a little while?" Fräulein Reiter's words were warm, like a spring sunbeam.

"Oui! Oui!" Like a wave rolling into shore, the children moved toward Noémie, almost knocking her to the ground with their enthusiastic hugs.

"Merci." Fräulein Reiter reached into her bag and passed Noémie a small sack. "A little something for them." With that, she was off, out of the enclosure that penned the Jews in like they were pigs.

A little boy with the biggest eyes ever to grace a child's face took Noémie by the hand. "Come on. Let's go to school. Fräulein Reiter is nice. And you're nice too."

For the first time since the gendarmes had pounded at the door and roused her and Levi from their slumber, Noémie laughed. *"Merci beaucoup.* I love your enthusiasm for school. More children should be like you. What do you say you lead the way, and we'll get started."

Soon the boys and girls were seated on the cool concrete floor of one of the barracks, eating the rolls that were in the bag Fräulein Reiter had left with her. Some of the children were nothing but skin-covered skeletons. Most of them slept on wooden beds and scratched the lice that crawled in their hair.

Hannah came with her. "Though Fräulein Reiter manages to get food and bring it to us, there is never enough. And if the children have come from other camps, they may not have had as much to eat there as the children here do."

"Which isn't much." Noémie's morning sickness had passed, and she was more than ready for a substantial meal.

"Never is."

How would she be able to carry her pregnancy to term in such conditions? What would become of her and her child? "And what does it mean that children who had been taken out of here are back? I know those girls."

Hannah shrugged. "Fräulein Reiter worked to get them to a Swiss orphanage in the east, to save them. I can't say I'm not worried about them sending the two here and telling them they're to be transported elsewhere with their parents."

"Can she save them again? I know she's a force to be reckoned with, but that's a tall order."

Hannah shrugged. "There's no guarantee any of us will survive."

CHAPTER FOUR

22 August, 1955
Elne, France

The dry, brown grass crunches underneath my white pumps as I meander around the building. At the back sits an old, rusty swing set, the wooden seats rotted away long ago. Still, the squeaks of the chains and the squeals of the children reverberate in the air.

Almost as if no time has passed at all.

The bare dirt where children's feet scraped the ground to bring them to a halt is now overgrown with thistles and weeds. A vine entwines itself around one of the swing set's legs, tenacious in its grip on the play equipment's frame.

Oh, the careless days of childhood. And how fast reality robs kids of that innocence.

I continue my trek around the building, peering upward into one of the second-story windows, almost believing that a child, dark eyes large in a round face, stares back at me. But then the image fades, and all that remains is a broken pane, the wind howling through the remaining shards of glass.

What was once glorious is now dreary and faded. Old before its time. But the years have this way of running away from us, and we chase after them with open arms in a desperate attempt to hold on to them.

They always manage to elude us.

CHAPTER FIVE

June 2, 2022
Chicago, Illinois

The white-lettered green highway sign proclaimed that I-90 to Chicago's O'Hare airport was the next exit. Caitlyn Laurent's stomach clenched at the sight of it, but this was the only way.

Mom sat in the back seat with her because Dad was driving and her grandfather, Pops, always got the front. Mom turned to her and smiled, the slight crow's feet around her blue eyes crinkling. "We're almost there."

All Caitlyn could do was nod. This was the best way to outrun the memories and the nightmares. Escape them. If she got far enough away, perhaps they wouldn't haunt her.

Before she got to her destination though, she was going to be sick. This wasn't how her life was supposed to turn out. Not at all. She and Lindsey were supposed to be missionaries for a few years, return to the States, get jobs at a hospital somewhere warm, like Florida or Arizona. Anywhere but cold, snowy Illinois. They were going to meet handsome doctors, have a double wedding, and experience pregnancy and child-birth together.

Lindsey would never get to do any of those things. And Caitlyn was headed across the Atlantic to fulfill the dream they had imagined, into a world she knew nothing about and was not prepared for.

But ready or not, the time had come. She couldn't stay here a minute more. If she did, she might go crazy. Might lose her mind.

Soon, Dad had parked the car, and he, Mom, and Pops walked into the terminal with her. She checked her one oversized bag. There was still plenty of time until she had to go through TSA and to the gate, so they found a grouping of chairs and sat together. All the restaurants and shops were on the other side of security.

Mom swiped away a tear. Caitlyn had shed so many over the past few months that she had no more left. Dad crushed her in a side hug. "We're going to miss you so much."

"I'll miss you too, Dad." She squeezed him back. Her parents had been so supportive through everything she'd experienced. They'd done all they could to help her heal. But nothing pulled her from her fear or her pain. This was the last resort. And if she could do some good in the process, all the better.

"I pray this is the right move for you, that going away isn't going to make things worse." Mom's voice cracked, and she pinched her nose like she always did to regain her composure. "Anyway, you're going to be a great nurse, and the missionaries on the field are going to love you."

"If I make it through training first. Especially French." She and Lindsey had been French buddies. Without her best friend to speak to, she hadn't touched the language in six months. Hopefully it wouldn't be too painful, that the memories of them talking to each other and cracking up over their mistakes wouldn't overwhelm her.

"You'll do great." Mom reached into her purse for a wad of tissues. "Don't doubt yourself. Be confident, and you'll do fine."

Pops, his white hair thin on top of his age-spotted head, patted her hand. "You're going to be so close to where I was born, in Perpignan, France. Did you know that, Pam? Mark can tell you all about it."

"Maybe I'll get to go there." More often these days, Pops confused her for Mom. They had recently sold his house, and he was living with them until they found a memory care center for him. That didn't help his recollections. He lived in the past.

"My mother had a hard life. I'd love to see a picture of the maternity home where I was born. Go there for me and take one, okay?"

She patted his hand back. "Okay, Pops, I will."

"I'd like to know more. I can't remember much."

"I'll find out for you. I promise."

"You're a good girl, Pam. I'm glad Mark married you."

All Caitlyn could do was nod.

Mom continued to dab away the tears. "Just give us a call or text when you get there so we know you're safe. We're going to miss you so much. The house will be empty without you. You've been a blessing to us your entire life."

By this time, Caitlyn couldn't handle any more. If she heard one more kind or encouraging word, she would crack into a thousand pieces, unable to be put together again. She jumped to her feet and grabbed her backpack from its place on the floor by her feet. "I'm going to get going. I just want to be sure I can find my gate and relax a little before the flight."

She didn't miss the quirking of eyebrows that passed between her parents. Before they had much time to react, she hugged and kissed both of them as well as Pops and headed toward the line in front of the TSA security desks. It wasn't until she was sitting on a bench putting her tennis shoes back on that she stopped a moment and inhaled to calm her racing heart.

This was happening. She was leaving home just weeks after graduating college, boarding a plane for Barcelona, and training to become a missionary nurse.

You're running away.

Going to another continent won't erase the memories.

At some point, you're going to have to come to terms with what happened.

The voices of her friends, her parents, even her counselor, echoed in her brain. They were right, no doubt about it. But she couldn't face the memories, the terror of the incident, at this moment. Putting an ocean between herself and Lindsey's grave might help her to right herself, get her feet back underneath her so she could come to terms with what happened.

Time healed all wounds, right? Wasn't that what they said? That and a little distance was just what the doctor ordered. Or what she ordered for herself.

She couldn't go to church one more Sunday and face Lindsey's parents. Each time, it wrenched a little more from her heart until she was dry inside. As shriveled as an old woman.

Maybe this time away would moisten and soften her heart. Funny that she would be going to the mission field when God had never felt further from her than He did now. But it might be just what she needed. If she spoke to others about the Savior and told them how He had promised to never leave or forsake them, then maybe she would come to believe it again herself.

Or maybe she would just end up walking away from God once and for all. She didn't want to, but if she found she had nothing left to give Him, if He'd taken everything away from her, what choice would she have?

A Starbucks Frappuccino and a bag of nuts from one of the concourse shops shored her up. Just as she was making her way in the general direction of her gate to await boarding, someone from behind called her name.

"Caitlyn. Hey, wait up."

She didn't have to turn around to know who it was. The strident voice that could carry above the din in the crowded concourse could belong only to Marissa Newsome.

The last person on the planet she was in the mood to have a conversation with.

But she'd been brought up with manners, which dictated that she turn around and paste a smile on her face and work to make it as real as possible. "Marissa. What on earth are you doing here?" Good. Caitlyn had managed to keep the sarcasm from her voice.

The skinny blond, with a designer bag and high heels that had no place in an airport, approached. Oh, if Lindsey could only see this. What she would have to say about Marissa.

"Mercy and I are off to Europe for our gap year. She's in the little girl's room right now. Anyway, we're going to hit all the sites—London, Paris, Rome, Vienna. It's going to be the time of our lives before we have to settle down and get jobs. Ugh." She pulled her long hair away from her face. "I don't even want to think about that. For twelve glorious months, we get to be free and live life a little. Ben wanted to get engaged, and I thought about it, but I decided to have one last adventure. Though I have this feeling he's going to surprise me with a proposal in

Paris. Can you imagine?"

She couldn't. At this precise moment, she just couldn't.

Marissa eyed Caitlyn up and down and scrunched her nose just a tiny bit. "Where are you off to?"

"Barcelona."

"By yourself?"

"Yes." If she kept to one-word answers, maybe Marissa would leave her alone.

"Wow, I can't imagine jetting off by myself. I can't imagine my parents allowing it. Then again, I suppose without Lindsey, you don't have anyone to go with you."

That was the straw that strained the camel's back just about to the breaking point. "If you must know, I'm going there to train to use my nursing and French skills on the mission field."

"Oh." Marissa's mouth fell open just for a second. Then she cocked her head and pasted on her own smile. "Good for you. What a wonderful thing to do. I'm sure your parents must be very proud of you. I hope you have a good time and don't get malaria or anything."

"Enjoy your trip." Caitlyn leaned against the cool wall opposite a bank of windows overlooking the tarmac as Marissa flounced away, her hair swinging along with her hips.

Caitlyn had to stop using barbs like that as a defense mechanism. So said her counselor. But with all the thoughts and feelings swirling inside her midsection, the words had slid past her lips. Marissa was not the person to allow past the wall she'd built to protect her very fragile heart. Maybe someday someone would breach it, but not her and not today.

An hour later, Caitlyn was situated in the aisle seat with economy-sized legroom, packed in for the eight-hour flight to Spain. An older couple was seated to her right. The woman swiveled in her seat as best she could with a seatbelt on. "And what are you going to be doing in Barcelona, my dear? Did I tell you that you remind me so much of my granddaughter?"

Caitlyn explained the reason for her trip.

"Well, isn't that wonderful." The older woman turned to her husband. "Larry, this delightful young lady is on her way to be a missionary.

Can you believe that the Lord dropped her practically into our laps? And here I thought this was going to be a boring trip with no one to talk to. Larry isn't the biggest chatterbox in the world, but I love him nonetheless. Fifty years this spring. The European trip was a gift from our family, a lifelong dream of ours come true."

All the encouragement the woman—a Mrs. Monroe, Caitlyn discovered—needed to continue her prattling was an occasional smile and a nod now and then. No wonder her husband wasn't very talkative. She had more than enough to say for both of them.

If only it were Lindsey sitting beside her. They would have so many laughs. Lindsey would have loved going to Spain. It was close enough to France that they could have traveled there on weekends and rekindled their love for the country first instilled in them during their semester abroad.

Caitlyn didn't care if Mrs. Monroe was proud of her or if Mom and Dad were proud of her. All that mattered was if Lindsey would have approved.

And she would have. She would have been in the seat right beside Caitlyn, who blinked away tears at the thought. Marissa and Mercy would have had nothing on the fun Caitlyn and Lindsey would have had. No matter what disasters struck, Lindsey always had the best attitude about them. She called them grand adventures and laughed them away.

Even above the roar of the jet's engines, Caitlyn could almost hear her best friend's sparkling giggle. Lindsey was such a ball of energy, they would have never sat still for a minute. Every day was another to be lived to the full.

That was the one point of consolation Caitlyn had in this entire, sordid mess. At least Lindsey had lived her life on her terms. She drank in every single one of the few minutes she'd had on this earth. She'd delighted in the small things. Nothing was too slight for her to exclaim over. No one she met went without a hug or a boost of confidence.

With Lindsey beside her, Caitlyn had been unstoppable. Had believed she could do anything.

Without her, she could barely pull herself out of bed each morning. Some days, she didn't even bother to get dressed. Lindsey would have scolded her and told her to get moving, but Lindsey wasn't here anymore to do it.

Caitlyn closed her eyes, the thrum of the engines and the slight bounce of turbulence a rhythm which lulled her almost to sleep.

Oh Lindsey, it should have been me.

CHAPTER SIX

22 August, 1955
Elne, France

After exploring the back of the house for a while, I return to the main entrance, once a bustling place, people coming and going, children spilling from its doors to the fresh, sun-splashed day, just a hint of sea salt in the air. Voices full of hope, joy, and anticipation. Lives with so much promise.

And in the amount of time it takes to snap my fingers, those delightful laughs turn into a sound I shut my mind to.

I had hoped and prayed that the house wouldn't tell me those stories. Not today. They're not what I need to hear now. Those tales are still too fresh in my mind, the wounds they left behind too tender to touch. The knife continues to cut, to scar my heart.

I thump on the trunk of a fallen tree. The wood is soft, in the process of returning to dust. *Earth to earth, ashes to ashes, and dust to dust; in sure and certain hope of the Resurrection to eternal life.* But if I have learned no other lesson in my life, I have learned that there is nothing sure or certain in this world.

Peace and tranquility, joy and love, laughter and singing are temporary. Fleeting. Mortal, like every human being.

The inside of the house, once bright and alive, is now dark and dead.

Too many of the voices that once rang down the halls and into the glass copula have been silenced forever.

CHAPTER SEVEN

18 August, 1942
Camp de Rivesaltes, Vichy France

Though the barrack's concrete floor was bare and cold, Noémie sat on it, her legs tucked underneath her, the children in a ring around her. After they had eaten their meager rolls, they had recited their lessons for her, from the smallest to the tallest. The oldest in the group couldn't be more than ten or twelve.

She didn't ask where the older ones were, and no one volunteered.

Some spoke in French and others in German, but somehow, they managed to understand each other. Being from Mulhouse in the Alsace region, Noémie understood both languages.

"Je t'aime, Madame Tre...Tre..." A blush crept over the pale face of a six- or seven-year-old girl with the most wonderful dimples.

Once again, Noémie laughed. "You may just call me Madame T, and I like you too. Now, who wants to hear a story?"

Amidst the chorus of cheers, one young boy, no more than six, raised his hand, and she called on him. "It's not scary, is it?" His dark green eyes shimmered with unshed tears.

Noémie fisted her hands. When the gendarmes arrested her and Levi, that was terrible enough. Frightening beyond measure. How must it have been for one so young? At least the mothers and children weren't separated here, though there were likely some without maternal care. "No, not scary at all. I only tell happy stories."

This earned her a grin, and she got down to the business of telling the children about the ugly duckling and how she turned into a beautiful swan.

Before she finished, Fräulein Reiter scurried into the room, her cap gone, her once-pinned hair now wild about her face. She made a weak attempt at smoothing the flyaway strands. "Beryl and Margot, come with me now."

The two girls stood.

"We have to hurry before they come and take you to the trucks that go to the train."

Beryl wept while Margot supported her sister.

Fräulein Reiter went to them. "Hush, now. We can't have you making a ruckus. You must be quiet, and if you are, all will be well. Trust me."

Probably not an easy order for the girls.

"Hurry, hurry, there isn't much time." Fräulein Reiter turned to Hannah and Noémie. "Madame Treves, will you come with me? The girls know you best. Hannah can stay with the other children. I need your help."

"Of course." Noémie stood and brushed off her dark wool skirt then followed Fräulein Reiter and the de Carcassona girls from the building.

They hurried along the uneven, rocky path. "There is a truck leaving soon for the train station in the village of Rivesaltes. The girls will not be on it, not if I have anything to say about it. Are you agreed?"

"Of course." Never again would she fail to do what she could to protect others. Noémie struggled to keep pace and grabbed Beryl by the hand as she lagged behind.

Fräulein Reiter turned to them, even as she continued pumping her legs. "You'll hide in the storage warehouse until it's safe to attempt an escape. You need to keep them as quiet as possible. Not a sound. The guards will search for them and will be thorough, but I'll do everything in my power to keep them away from the warehouse. Is that clear? Do you have any questions?"

"I'll watch over them. You can depend on me."

Fräulein Reiter nodded in time to her rapid footsteps. "I knew the moment I laid eyes on you weeks ago that you would be of great help to me. Merci. These girls are counting on you."

"What about Maman and Papa?" Margot, her brown braids swinging against her back, strode alongside Fräulein Reiter.

"Don't you worry about them." Fräulein Reiter's voice didn't wobble. "I promised them I would take care of you, and so I shall. And so will Madame Treves. There's no need for alarm, if only you are quiet. Do you understand how important that is?"

Both of the girls nodded, and Noémie squeezed Beryl's hand to give her an extra bit of reassurance.

They came to the warehouse, another long, narrow concrete building just like the barracks. Fräulein Reiter conducted a quick scan of the area, slipped a key from her pocket, and unlocked the door. The four of them entered, and she turned the lock behind them.

Most of the building was empty. Their footsteps echoed against the solid walls. In the far corner sat a pile of burlap bags filled with what looked like potatoes, judging by their lumpiness. "This is where we store the food. You can hide underneath them. Be very still and quiet, and when the guards have finished their search, I'll come and get you. Be prepared, as it may be a while."

Noémie, Beryl, and Margot sat in the corner, backs against the cold concrete, and Fräulein Reiter arranged the burlap sacks over and around them.

"Not a sound now. I'll be back." Her footsteps faded, and the door clicked shut behind her.

A heavy stillness fell over them. Beside her, both of the girls trembled. The weight of the sacks and how they were stacked around them prevented Noémie from rubbing their backs or offering the girls any type of comfort. She couldn't speak or sing to them. All she could do was be near them.

As the moments lengthened to minutes and then hours, Noémie's legs cramped. What on earth was she doing here? How had life changed in such a short space of time? In once-upon-a-time land, she had been a business owner and successful in what she did. First she lost her company, Papa's company, and then her home, then her freedom.

This was the right thing to do though. These girls, not yet women, needed help, someone older than they were who could take care of them. Whispers around camp spoke of transports leaving for Drancy and then to Poland.

Poland. The word carried as much fear with it as if someone had said hell.

Maybe that's what this was. Hell on earth. A gateway to Sheol.

Noémie's back ached. She had to use the latrine.

"Maman." Beryl's voice reverberated in the building's emptiness.

"Shh." Noémie kept her reply as soft as possible.

"I want to go with Maman."

Noémie had no choice but to answer her. Isn't that why Fräulein Reiter wanted her here? She was making up for her past sins. "Your maman wants you to stay where she knows you'll be safe. You don't want her to worry, do you?"

"Non."

"That's good. When she returns, she will find you, and you can go home. For now, you must be apart, but she would want you to stay strong until then. Can you do that for her? And for your papa?"

"Oui." Both girls answered the question.

"Then we must be quiet."

Time continued to tick away. By now, lunch and dinner must both be over, if there was any food to be had at all. No one had come to the warehouse for any. Hopefully, Hannah would watch out for Noémie's tin cup, so that it wouldn't be stolen. If it was, she would have no way to get her rations and would go hungry. From now on, she would keep it with her at all times.

In this time and place, tin cups were more valuable than gold or diamonds.

Maybe Fräulein Reiter had forgotten about them, or maybe something had happened to prevent her returning. By now, the guards must have been able to search the entire block. It was large, but they had a big enough force to be able to cover all the grounds by now.

Just about the time she was ready to get up and try to figure a way out of there, the door squeaked open.

Margot moved, and Noémie managed to nudge her in the side. She froze.

Fräulein Reiter would have called to them if she was able. Instead, it was a deep male voice that barked orders. "They couldn't have gotten away. They have to be here somewhere."

For several moments, Noémie's heart forgot how to beat. All that was in here was the few sacks of food. In no time, the guards would move them and discover her and the girls cowering in this corner.

Her throat burned and threatened to close. Poor Levi. He would be devastated to hear what happened to her. And maybe proud too. He would declare that she would give the coat off her back in a snowstorm. That might be an exaggeration, but someone had to help these girls.

They had almost made it. This must be the last building the guards were searching. For so long, they had held out. Though she was raised as a nonreligious Jew, this was the time to pray. *Hashem, You parted the Red Sea and used Elisha to raise the young boy to life. If You can perform such miracles, You can save us. I pray that You would protect us. I pray that You would deliver us as You once delivered us from Egypt.*

She sat without moving a muscle, hardly daring to breathe or blink. Her heart pounded in her ears. Any moment now, they would make their way to this side of the warehouse, move the bags, and discover her and the girls.

Was there anything she could do to keep them safe? To prevent them from being taken away on the transport? Maybe she could create some kind of distraction. If she pretended to stumble and twist her ankle, would the guards stop? Could she tell the girls to run then?

As fast as the thought entered her head, she ushered it out. The guards had weapons and were big and strong. Two young girls couldn't outrun either the men or their bullets. All she would be doing would be sentencing them to death.

All three of them.

She needed a different plan. But what? What could she do? Though ideas swirled around her, none of them were viable. All of them carried too many potential risks, ones she wasn't willing to take. Not with the lives of someone else's children.

Each idea was nothing more than the whistling of the wind. Fräulein Reiter wasn't here, and there was no way Noémie would be able to speak to her. Even if she could, there was no guarantee that she would know what to do to save the girls.

And so, Noémie forced herself to relax and wait for the gendarmes to arrest them. At least the girls would be reunited with their parents. Though their parents had wanted a different outcome for their children, they would be together in the end.

What would they do with her?

She slammed the door on that thought. No use in trying to guess what the Vichy had in mind. No use in dwelling on what that might be. If only she could have said one last goodbye to Levi.

Footsteps approached. The time had come, and an amazing peace rushed over her. Inexplicable but real nonetheless. Wherever the guards took her, whatever they did with her, she wouldn't be alone. Some said that with Hashem, one never walked alone.

"They must be in with the supplies." The man who spoke those words, his voice as deep as a canyon, was close by. Any moment, light would hit their eyes. Maybe they would find her first and leave the girls undiscovered.

That was it. That was the way she could protect them. If she could get out of her spot and stand without uncovering Beryl and Margot, they would be safe.

She tensed her leg muscles, ready to come to her feet.

CHAPTER EIGHT

22 August, 1955
Elne, France

Even though the August sun is strong and high in the sky, bathing my head in its light, I shiver. Rubbing my arms doesn't rid me of the chills. Why?

This place used to be warm. It radiated light. Love and laughter spilled from the doors and windows. Everyone who came here was touched, forever changed by it in some way or another. All these years later, it still affects me. The light draws me the same today as it did then. I'm not the same person I was when I first walked through those doors.

That's what this building's purpose was. To transform people. To envelop them in an embrace that spoke to them of joy and peace. Security. A place where they could allow their true selves to shine.

A gust of wind picks up just then, blowing my skirt against my knees. The breeze whistles through the cracked windows, an eerie melody, the song stolen from this place.

Yes, this building used to sing. Oh what a sweet, sweet song it sang. I close my eyes and listen for it again. Though it's faint, it's there. Not completely lost. I blow out my pent-up breath and allow the soft music to carry me away.

For a moment, there is no present, only past. A past that was glorious. But times have changed. Nothing is the same anymore. In a flash, the song flees my brain, slamming me back to the present.

I swipe away a tear trickling down my cheek. No time for weeping.

This wasn't a place of sadness. Not most of the time, anyway. Every now and again, a sliver of darkness would invade, but hope always outshone it.

And then the fear set in, sweeping away all that had been established here. The sun was eclipsed by craziness, and in an instant, the light was cut off from this place. It was no more.

Will it ever be again? I have no idea. Who would bring the light and joy back here? I'm weary. Too scarred to do the job myself, or I would. They stole the fight from me.

I used to have it. So much of it that I swore no one would ever conquer me. But what happened within these walls and on these grounds ripped the fight from my heart. Ripped my heart from my body.

They never gave it back. Some would say that I'm allowing them to win, even all these years later. Perhaps I am. But when you have fought so long and so hard with every ounce of energy that you have, and then they come and blindfold you so not even a sliver of light penetrates the darkness, you're helpless.

Hopeless.

Perhaps that's the biggest thing they robbed me of. My hope. So many found it here. For a while, I did too. And I relished it. I dispensed it like *Père Noel* dispenses candy.

Many walked out of these doors with the hope they had discovered here.

But it was here that I lost mine.

CHAPTER NINE

July 1, 2022
Barcelona, Spain

Hey, are you ready for our trip to France?" Caitlyn nudged her friend and roommate, Elissa, as they walked the street between the school and their apartment building. Overhead, the Barcelona summer sun was strong in skies as blue as the Mediterranean.

"I've been packed since Tuesday. Well, except for my makeup and hair products." Elissa's ponytail bobbed in rhythm with her steps.

Caitlyn raised and lowered her eyebrows. "I haven't even started, though I'm excited about the trip." The first thing she'd been excited about in months. "I can't wait to see the place where my grandfather was born. It's cool that I ended up at a school so close to where he was."

"I just want to eat some good French pastries."

"Hey, wait up for me."

Caitlyn turned. Aiden Klein jogged to catch up to them. "Have you even started packing yet, Caitlyn?" He shook his head, as if he already knew the answer. Then again, he probably did. A couple of weekends ago, they had gone to Toulouse with a group of other students.

"I'll be packed in twenty minutes."

Aiden rubbed the top of his head, mussing his mass of blond curls. "I dare you. Especially since that's about all the time we have until we have to leave to catch the train."

"Don't worry. I'll be ready."

"I doubt it."

"Oh, you've seen nothing yet."

"I double dare you."

"I don't even know what that means, but I accept the challenge. See you in twenty minutes." She took off on a sprint. The adrenaline that pumped into her body lifted her spirits.

Aiden called after her. "And if you forget anything, you lose."

Whatever. She'd never run away from dares, and she wasn't about to start. She hustled up the stairs to her closet-sized room, grabbed her suitcase, and threw in a pair of jeans, a couple of shirts, some shorts, and a cute dress.

Exactly eighteen minutes and thirty seconds later, she stood outside of the apartment, her backpack loaded with all the necessities of a three-day trip. In other words, not much.

Aiden was waiting at the bottom of the steps, his brown backpack slung over his shoulder. She'd learned enough from traveling in France on her semester abroad that packing light was key. There often wasn't room on the train for a great deal of luggage. And if she had to cross the tracks, it was a pain to carry a heavy bag up the stairs, across the walkway over the tracks, and back down.

"Well, well, well." Aiden glanced at his watch. "I'm impressed. But do you have everything? Shoes, pants, socks, shirts, underwear?"

"Knock it off." For the past few weeks, she'd been trying to work out if he was flirting with her or if he acted this way with everyone. To this point, she hadn't made up her mind. "Let's just get going. Where's Elissa?"

Just then, the door behind Caitlyn opened, and Elissa exited with two roller bags. She hadn't learned how to pack efficiently yet. Aiden grabbed one of them from her.

"Let's get going." Caitlyn made her way down the sidewalk. "The last thing we want to do is miss the train."

A short time later, the metro deposited them at Barcelona Sants station, bustling with passengers. Two areas were roped off for security, the rest of the large building filled with waiting areas, shops, and restaurants. They breezed through security then grabbed a snack from the café.

Aiden sipped his Coke then turned his attention to Caitlyn. "So what is it you hope to find out about your family from this trip?"

"Well, I know my grandfather was born at a maternity hospital there, so I'd be interested in finding out what it was like. What it looked like, where the nursery was, who took care of him. That kind of thing. And he wants me to take a picture of it."

"Interesting."

"He doesn't know much about his mother's and father's histories. They never talked about their pasts. All they would say is that the war was hard on them, and they lost many friends, but that's about it. I know many Jewish children were born there, so I'm assuming we're Jewish, though my great-grandparents practiced Christianity."

"Well, this will be good practice for our French."

Elissa picked the tomatoes out of her salad. "I'm nervous about that. When we went to Toulouse, I bombed. I couldn't remember a thing, and I had a hard time understanding them. You'd think after all these years of studying the language, I'd be more proficient."

"You'll get the hang of it. We should only speak French to each other. That will help."

"Ugh." Elissa pushed the rest of her salad away. "I'm beginning to think I should be a missionary in England, not Senegal."

"Hey, don't get discouraged." Aiden cleared his throat and switched to French. "Soon, you'll be speaking like a native."

Je ne comprends pas. I just don't understand. I'm going to take my tray back and find a restroom. People are queuing already."

Since they had assigned seats, it didn't matter if they were first in line or last to board.

"What's gotten into her?" Aiden continued the conversation in French.

Je ne sais pas. I think she's nervous and freezes when she's forced to speak to a native. It's not the easiest language in the world." She sipped her water. "It's too bad my great-grandparents only spoke English once they came to the States. If they had spoken French, I would have learned it as a child, and it would have been so much easier."

"That's interesting that they didn't."

Caitlyn downed the last few drops. "They wanted to become as American as possible. I understand why they would do that, but at the same time, I would think they'd want to keep some of their culture."

Aiden stood and collected both his tray and hers. "I understood about ninety percent of that. You have the best skills of any of us."

Caitlyn shrugged and leaned against the garbage can as they waited for Elissa.

"Thank you for asking me to come on this trip with you," he said.

"Of course. We traveled together the other weekend."

"This one is different. More personal. I can understand bringing your roommate, but including me was nice of you. I like spending time with you."

Oh, maybe he did think of their relationship as more than friendship. They'd only known each other for a month. And once training ended, she'd be a nurse in Africa and he'd be a pilot, flying all over the world.

Elissa saved the day by joining them. "Okay. Sorry for my little anxiety attack there. Let's do this. I won't get better at French if I don't practice."

"En Francis, s'il vous plait. In French."

"Fine."

An hour later, they had left the bustling city of Barcelona behind and were crossing the Pyrenees. The views were beautiful, of purple mountains rising in the distance, the Mediterranean sparkling in the summer sunshine, the terraced vineyards rising from the plains. Caitlyn pressed her nose against the window and drank in the sights.

They had taken this trip before, or at least part of it, when they'd visited Toulouse. But they didn't stay in Perpignan, didn't visit the maternity hospital in the area. This time, it was all about her family's history. She would walk the same streets as her great-grandparents. Maybe she could even find out where they'd lived.

And she would see where Pops had been born. He didn't know much about his parents' pasts, but he did know about the maternity hospital. For whatever reason, that was what he talked about the most.

And now that dementia was robbing him of all those beautiful memories, it would be wonderful to give him one more. Yes, he would soon forget it, but for one precious moment, he would have it. And they could share it over and over.

She had only six months or so until she left for Africa, so this needed to be a priority when she wasn't in class. The training was rigorous, preparing them for life on the field, honing their language skills, giving them the tools to share the gospel. Right now, though, this quest took priority.

Aiden leaned over. "A Euro for your thoughts."

"That's very expensive. I thought it was supposed to be a penny."

"Fine. A *centime* for your thoughts."

"They're worth much more than that."

"You're a difficult woman to please." He was so close to her now that his warm breath tickled the back of her neck. She had to admit it wasn't an unpleasant sensation.

Focus, Caitlyn, focus. "This is my homecoming, you know. There's this connection I have with this place. I can't quite describe it, but it's like I belong here. When we step off the train and stroll down the streets of Perpignan, I might walk past a cousin of mine and not even know it. There's this need I have to plug in here."

"I don't want to see you get your hopes up only to be disappointed. You don't know how much information you're going to get."

"I know. The maternity home might not have even kept records from the time. It was so long ago. All the children born there are elderly. Many of them have probably passed away. Still, it's hard not to wish. For Pops' sake, I want to do this. To at least tell him where he came from. This is for him. If nothing comes of it, he'll be none the wiser. If I discover more about his parents, then maybe I'll be able to make one of his last days happy. Does that make sense?"

"Perfect. And count me in. I love a good mystery."

"You grew up on the Hardy Boys?"

"How old do you think I am?" His voice dripped with mock indignation.

Elissa piped up from the seat across the table from them. "At least fifty, if not sixty."

Aiden narrowed his eyes. "Haha."

The rest of the trip flew by as fast as the scenery outside the window. Soon they pulled into the Perpignan station. Of course, they had to cross the tracks to get into town, but thankfully, Perpignan was large enough to have elevators. They went to a below-ground level, through a tunnel, and up the elevator to the street. Next time they went somewhere, Caitlyn would have to pack for Elissa.

At last they emerged from the train station, the road that led perpendicular to it stretching as straight as a ruler in front of them, sweeping into the city.

She turned and gazed over her shoulder. The sign on the beige stone building with arched doorways across the front proclaimed it to be *GARE DE PERPIGNAN*. Simply, Perpignan Train Station. Had her great-grandparents and her grandfather come through this station? What had it looked like at the time they'd been here?

Aiden and Elissa headed down the street toward their rental for the weekend while Caitlyn held back. Despite what she'd told Aiden, she couldn't leave here without answers.

CHAPTER TEN

22 August, 1955
Elne, France

Wind and rain and cold have worn away the steps, and the mortar that held the bricks together has crumbled. Oh, the feet that ran up and down these steps, some small, some large.

Some running to, some running away.

And then there were the boots that marched up the stairs, a sound I cannot recall without a shudder.

The sun on my back today allows me to push that memory far, far away so that it will not disturb me. The sun is the same one that warmed our backs as we worked in the garden, growing the vegetables that would keep all of us, especially the youngest and weakest, healthy. And give hands purpose and meaning, minds occupation, hearts a moment of peace, not dwelling on what was or what might be.

For a moment, I hesitate, unsure of what I should do, then move down the steps once more until I discover a patch of sand where grass should grow. No one is watching, not as they did in those days, so I plunge my hands into the dirt, allowing the crumbling ground to sift through my fingers, warm. Life-giving.

Much like the house in front of me. Life-giving not just to mothers but also to children. To all who frolicked on the grounds and labored in the garden plots. To all who worked and lived and played and loved within its walls.

I close my fist around the remaining dirt in my hands and press them to my chest. Will that be enough to impress this place on my heart forever? For this will be my last visit here. There is no doubt about it.

Then again, this pretty, pale peach building reaching its glass and metal ceiling into the cerulean sky has always been a part of my soul. Of who I am. It shaped me and changed me in ways I could never have imagined when I first stepped foot on the grounds.

I dust off my hands on my dark skirt, then dust off my skirt. What has come over me? The pull, the allure of this place. This sanctuary.

But I haven't much time for woolgathering today. Oh, I could stand here forever and drink in every inch of the property and replay each memory over and over in my mind, but there isn't time. The clock ticks away the minutes and the hours, incessant.

In those bygone days, time stood still. It dragged at a painful pace, each moment an eternity, some filled with joy, many filled with pain.

I make my way over the uneven ground toward the house once more. A chunk of concrete falls away from the crumbling steps as I climb them. At the landing, I pause and cast my gaze over the view. The grass is sparse, much like it was all those years ago, trampled by the same little feet that traipsed up these stairs, laughter on their lips, brightness in their eyes.

CHAPTER ELEVEN

18 August, 1942
Camp de Rivesaltes, Vichy France

Noémie held her breath. The weight of the burlap sacks crushed her shoulders. How were the children holding up? This load must be so much for them to bear.

Any moment now, the solider who stood in front of them would move the bags and discover them hidden here. She was ready to give herself up, ready to do whatever she had to do to keep these two precious lives safe. This time, she wouldn't fail. She also had to convince the guards that Fräulein Reiter wasn't involved. Her work in the camp was too important.

"Gentlemen, I trust you've completed your inspection and have found nothing, just as I said would be the case." Fräulein Reiter's voice, so strong and sure, was muffled only a little by the potatoes.

"We have to finish our search in here."

"Oh, those potatoes are moldy. Not very pleasant. If you move them, the smell will be terrible. Come, now. I believe the transport is ready to leave." Her heels clicked across the floor until they stopped just in front of Noémie. "You don't want to miss it."

The gendarme sighed but moved away. Maybe Fräulein Reiter dragged him away. Even with the little Noémie knew about her, it was plausible.

As soon as the door shut, Beryl wiggled. "Can we get out now?"

"Shh." Noémie's heart had yet to return to a normal rhythm. "We don't know if they'll come back. We must stay here until Fräulein Reiter returns and lets us know it's safe."

"But I want to get up."

"I know. You must be quiet though. They could still arrest us."

That was enough to hush Beryl. How difficult it must be for them, their parents likely being herded into the truck and driven off to who knew where. If Noémie could, she would rub her belly where her child lay. Their mother's heart must be shattering at the thought of leaving her girls. Then again, she'd made the choice months ago to send them away for their own well-being.

Still, they had been in her care, taken away, returned, and now she was leaving them. Maybe one day very soon, all four of them would survive this madness and be reunited. Perhaps it would be the same for herself and Levi and their unborn child. He deserved the chance to get to know their son or daughter.

And their son or daughter deserved the chance to be born, even into such a crazy world as this.

Just when her legs and shoulders were screaming in pain, the door opened again and heels clacked on the hard floor. "They're gone."

Fräulein Reiter. Noémie's heart finally slowed as Fräulein Reiter moved sacks of potatoes, while Noémie and the girls did what they could on their side, their limbs stiff and sore from hours in the same position. As soon as they broke through, Noémie inhaled a breath of sweet, clean air. Or as clean as the air could be inside Rivesaltes with its open latrines.

The two girls stretched then stumbled forward and latched onto Fräulein Reiter's legs. "Where are Maman and Papa?" Margot stared at her with her big, brown eyes.

"I want Maman. Please, don't take me away from her again."

Fräulein Reiter lifted Beryl into her arms and cast a glance at Noémie as if pleading for help in explaining an inexplicable situation.

Noémie's legs wobbled for a moment before she stepped forward and rubbed both girls' backs. "I know how much you want to be with your parents right now, but that isn't possible. This is only until it's safe again for you all to be together. As soon as that happens, your maman and papa will come for you. They want you to be big, brave girls and to wait for them. To do everything that Fräulein Reiter says. Can you do that?"

Beryl swiped away her tears. "I'll try."

"We will do it." Margot stepped away from Fräulein Reiter and straightened her spine. "We have to do it for Maman and Papa." So young to have to be so grown-up.

Fräulein Reiter set Beryl on her feet. "You and your sister stay here while Madame Treves and I go collect your belongings. Is there anything I need to gather?"

"We already have them together, remember?" Margot crinkled her nose.

"Of course. How silly of me. We'll be back soon. Stay quiet and hide again if you hear the guards."

Both gave solemn nods before Noémie and Fräulein Reiter left the building. As soon as they were outside, Fräulein Reiter nodded to Noémie. "Merci for all you did for those two. It was very brave of you to take care of them."

"I could do no less. I've known them ever since Levi and I moved to Perpignan. Not only that, but with my child due in about five months, I imagined how I'd like someone to take care of my little one if I wasn't able to be there for him or her."

Fräulein Reiter clapped her hands. "That's perfect. The Lord above sent you here at this time for this reason, I'm sure of it."

Noémie furrowed her brow. "What do you mean?"

"Beryl and Margot can't stay here, of course. If the Vichy discover that they were in the camp all this time, they will be in grave danger."

As would Fräulein Reiter herself.

"There is a maternity home not far from here where the director, Eleanore Touissant, has taken in both children and pregnant women in order to hide them and help get them to Spain. I should be able to take you there without too many problems, I hope, and it would provide the perfect cover for the girls."

Noémie's mouth went dry. "But my husband is here. I can't leave him." She wasn't about to run away and desert him. Whatever lay in front of them, they would face it together.

Fräulein Reiter shook her head. "You are going to have a baby. A helpless child who can do nothing to ensure his or her survival. Is your husband young?"

Noémie nodded, the churning in the pit of her stomach ramping up.

"Is he strong?"

Again, she nodded.

"Who needs you more?"

Noémie turned in circles several times. What a question for a veritable stranger to ask. Who needed her more? They both did. And she needed both of them. There was no questioning it, no debating it. It was unthinkable that she would be forced to choose between the man she loved and the unborn child she adored. "That's a question that has no right answer."

"What about the girls' parents? What about their choice?"

"I don't know how they did it." Noémie sighed. "I've never been a mother before. This is our first baby. I don't know how I'll ever allow my child out of my sight, not even for a second."

"Come with me." Fräulein Reiter led the way outside and to a barracks Noémie hadn't been in yet. From it came mewling, like a litter of tiny kittens.

Noémie stepped inside, her eyes adjusting to the dim light. When they did focus, she took a sharp breath.

Babies, no nappies on their bottoms, lay in wood cribs, no mattresses or sheets, their stomachs bloated, flies swarming around their faces. Scattered among them were several children of different ages lying on crude mats. Two women moved among them, comforting the ones who were crying. Noémie turned to Fräulein Reiter. "What is this? Why are they like this? Why don't you take them to the maternity home?" She had to turn away from the scene.

"Most of these infants came here in this condition. There is nothing to be done to save them. This is the fate Monsieur and Madame de Carcassona want to spare their daughters, especially if they become ill. There isn't enough medicine to treat them, even with all that the Swiss send us. Not here and not at the home. There are too many. As heartbreaking as it is, we can't save them all. I'm giving you the chance to keep your child from ending up in this situation."

"But how could they let them go?"

"They did it out of love for their daughters. There is nothing in this world like a parent's love."

"So you are a mother then? You understand?" Noémie dragged her attention back to the scene in front of her.

Fräulein Reiter shook her head. "God has blessed me with neither a husband nor children. But I don't have to be a mother to grasp what that kind of love is like. All I have to do is think about how my own parents loved me and all they sacrificed to make sure I was happy and healthy."

Noémie picked up one of the babies, so tiny, so fragile in her arms. "I suppose. But how are the girls' parents giving their children over to an uncertain fate?"

"Because if their daughters stayed with them, their fate would be this."

Goose bumps broke out on Noémie's arms. "You don't know that for sure."

"I truly believe that very few of the children who are taken from this place to other camps, to places in Poland, will survive. How could their parents do anything but protect Beryl and Margot? A difficult choice, to be sure, but one that wasn't so hard in the end. To give your offspring the best chance they have at life is the greatest gift you can give them."

A weight settled on Noémie's chest, and she had a difficult time drawing in a deep breath. Levi would tell her to go. He wouldn't even hesitate with his answer, and not because he didn't love her. Just the opposite.

But what if they never saw each other again? When they married, they became one flesh, one flesh that now was bringing new life into this world. A child who needed both mother and father. That was what was best for this little one.

But not guaranteed.

She rubbed her throbbing temples.

Fräulein Reiter touched her shoulder, jarring her from her musings. "You will love *La Maternité de la Paix*. Madame Touissant is wonderful. She and the staff there will care for you, keep you safe, and help you when it comes time for your child to be born."

"That's still five months away. Can't I wait to go?"

In the distance came the roar of engines. The transport leaving for Drancy and places beyond. Places no one wanted to think about.

"If you do, you risk being sent away. What will the Nazis do with a pregnant Jewish woman?"

Another place Noémie refused to allow her mind to wander to. "Can Levi, my husband, come as well?"

Fräulein Reiter shook her head. "I'm sorry. Only women and children. You understand."

It would be too dangerous with men around. They couldn't claim they were just helping women to have a healthy delivery. So Levi would stay here. Or more likely, would be taken to the Rivesaltes train station a few kilometers away and then even farther away from there.

And Beryl and Margot, snatched from the Vichy's clutches not just once but twice. A third time, and they wouldn't survive. At last, she gave the tiniest nod. "I'll go on one condition. Please arrange one more visit for me with my husband. Somehow get him to the fence that separates us and allow us to say goodbye. We need a plan to find each other once this madness ends."

"Of course." Fräulein Reiter also nodded. "I understand. But just a few minutes. No need to alert the guards."

She needed to say no more about what would happen if they caught Noémie and Levi talking. Such interactions were forbidden. But one chance to say farewell was worth it. To touch Levi's hand through the wires.

Noémie returned to her barracks, her case tucked away so no one could steal it. Once she had ensured that her few remaining items were folded and in their proper places, she left the barracks wearing her winter coat, even though the evening air was still very warm.

Then she sat on her case, beside the barracks but away from the guards' eagle eyes, and waited for Fräulein Reiter. Minutes ticked away. Precious minutes. They had to get the girls away from here as soon as possible. No one could discover that they hadn't left on the transport.

The wind, ever-present on the plain, blew her hair into her face. She should have fixed it before she closed her valise. Sitting under sacks of potatoes surely mussed it. Levi shouldn't have to see her like this.

No sooner had she opened her suitcase and found her brush than Fräulein Reiter came around the corner. "He's waiting for you."

"But my hair."

"If he loves you the way you say he does, it won't matter a bit to him."

Still, it was important to Noémie that she look her best. She took a minute or two to fix her hair. There was no getting around the fact that she didn't have any lipstick. She'd done all she could to make herself presentable to her husband.

Because this could be the last time they saw each other.

CHAPTER TWELVE

When Noémie spied Levi's tall, slim form at the fence, she ran toward him, choking back a sob. She approached, and they locked fingers through the spaces in the barbed wire fence. The dim, dusky light was just enough to show the bags under his eyes. His clothes, once so perfectly tailored to his physique, now hung on his frame.

She rubbed his thumb. "I had to see you."

He nodded. "I've missed you."

"I hate being separated. How are they treating you?"

"I'm fine. There's no need to worry about me. My concern, however, lies with you. Are you well? Have they hurt you? When I got word that you wanted to see me, I thought maybe something had happened. Is the baby well?"

"There's no need to fret. I'm fine. This isn't a luxurious Parisian hotel, but I haven't been mistreated. The baby is doing well. Still making me sick in the mornings."

This brought a slight smile to his lips, cracked from the dry air and incessant wind.

"I have an opportunity to escape and go to a maternity hospital not far from here. It's run by a Swiss woman. We're taking the de Carcassona girls that one of the aid workers saved from today's transport. But I don't want to go without you."

"They'll never believe I'm a pregnant woman." He chuckled, and the sound of it relaxed her shoulders.

"*C'est vrai.* So true. What am I to do?"

"You're to go. Remember, live life with no regrets." He confirmed what she already had decided. "Staying here puts you and our child at great risk. There's no doubt they'll eventually clean the camp out and send us all somewhere worse."

"Non. Don't say that. You'll be fine. Keep your head down. Don't make waves, and they won't send you on a transport. Fight to stay here, so that when I come back, you'll be waiting for me."

"In these days, you don't make promises. You only hope for the best. That's all we can do."

Such defeat in his voice tore the skin from her chest and exposed her heart. "Don't say that. Tell me you'll be here when I return with our child, when this craziness comes to an end, and I'll be able to bear this separation. It can't be long, especially not with the Americans joining the fight."

"We have no idea how long it will be. But when the war is over, we'll meet at our little home in Perpignan. Go there, and if I can, if I'm alive, that is where we'll be reunited. The three of us." He dropped his gaze to her middle.

"Levi, I. . ."

"There are no words." He had been brought up as a religious Jew, and he crooned a Hebrew blessing over her, giving her a measure of peace and confidence.

By the end, tears soaked her cheeks and dripped onto her thin dress.

Then a searchlight arched overhead, illuminating the gathering darkness. He pulled away from the fence. "We have to go before we're caught. Take care of yourself and of my child. Remember, always, that I love you. I'll never stop."

"Neither will I. Until we meet again." Her throat closed, and speech was difficult, but she had to get the words out. "Je t'adore, Levi. You're my heart and soul. No matter what, nothing will change that. You will always be my love."

The brilliant light circled in their direction. Levi motioned her away. "Go, go." Then he turned and scurried toward one of the men's barracks.

She backed away from the light and waited until Levi disappeared inside the rectangular structure. How long until they were reunited?

She shook herself, picked up her case, and turned for her own quarters. If she focused on getting the girls to the maternity hospital and having a safe and healthy pregnancy, the time would pass. Still slowly, for sure, but it would pass. When they were old and gray, they would laugh about the small drop in a bucket this time was.

She returned to the warehouse and the girls to wait for Fräulein Reiter to arrive to spirit them away. For some reason, she wasn't at all afraid. There were no butterflies in her stomach, and her hands didn't shake.

Strange. She should be frightened. So much could go wrong. It only took one Vichy collaborator to turn them in and destroy their lives. Yet, as she sat in the corner, a girl on each side of her, she even managed to doze.

The door creaked, and Noémie was instantly awake.

Before they could dive for the pile of potato bags, Fräulein Reiter's voice sounded in the darkness. "Come on. We must go now. It's morning, and the bakery truck will be here soon. Hurry. There's little time to lose."

By the time Fräulein Reiter finished speaking, Noémie had stood and grabbed her bag. All she owned in the world.

Together they tiptoed from the building. Fräulein Reiter hadn't shared the details of the escape with Noémie, so that she couldn't be questioned and give away secrets. But as the sun streaked the eastern sky pink, before any rays peeked above the horizon, a truck pulled through the open gate, driving into the block and backing up to the storehouse.

Men spilled from one of the barracks, some of them still pulling on their pants as the guards shouted for them to move faster. They crossed the fence and formed a line, bucket-brigade style, and got to work emptying the truck of its precious cargo, little of which was likely to find its way to the bellies of the Jewish prisoners.

She strained for a glimpse of Levi but couldn't make him out in the faint predawn light.

A tug on her arm drew her attention away from the line of men. Fräulein Reiter motioned to her, and the two of them along with Beryl and Margot swung around the back of the line, opposite where the guards stood watch making sure none of the prisoners helped himself to a bite of breakfast.

They crouched low as they duck-walked along the line toward the idling truck. As they approached the vehicle, Levi came in sight. He was the first man in the queue, taking the baguettes from the person in the truck and passing them along.

His eyes widened as they locked on her, but he otherwise kept his expression neutral. She worked hard to do likewise. While Fräulein Reiter went and distracted the guards, Levi handed the girls into the truck.

Then he turned to her and grasped her by her waist, firm yet gentle, the way he had always been with her. With a kiss on her cheek and a squeeze of her hand, which she returned, he lifted her over the tailgate and into the truck.

A moment later, Fräulein Reiter hopped aboard, and Levi closed the door, blocking him from her view once again.

"Move toward the back." As Noémie and the girls did so, Fräulein Reiter knocked on the back wall, and the driver took off so fast it jolted Noémie and sent her crashing into the side of the truck.

The driver honked the horn but didn't slow. The darkness of the vehicle's interior prevented her from shooting a glance Fräulein Reiter's way. "What's going on?"

"He knows to ignore the guards so they can't search the truck. François is a good man. Don't worry about a thing. He'll keep us safe. He's done this before."

Was she saying that for Noémie's benefit or to keep Margot and Beryl from being scared? Whoever she spoke to didn't matter, because Noémie managed to take a deep breath. They were out of the gate. Away from the prison.

Still, she left a piece of herself, the other half of her soul, within that fence. In those miserable conditions. He was strong. He would do whatever he had to in order to get back to her and his child. She had to trust that.

But how was she supposed to get over this horrible ache in her heart?

Just then, Fräulein Reiter, who was seated beside her, patted her hand. "I know you'll miss him. Separation is never easy on a couple, and it's especially difficult when you're expecting your first child. I pray you'll have peace and comfort. With Jesus beside you, you're never alone."

Hoping Fräulein Reiter wouldn't take it as an affront, Noémie pulled her hand away. Hashem or Jesus or whoever was up there—if anyone was—wasn't doing anything about the mess here on earth. Fräulein Reiter was wrong. He had left them. Abandoned them. That was no kind of God she wanted to know.

Oui, she prayed every now and again, but more out of habit and superstition than out of hope that her prayers would change anything.

They bumped over the road, often not slowing. The truck climbed from the plain, the engine working harder as they ascended. Away from Camp de Rivesaltes. Away from Levi.

Non. Better to focus on what was ahead. A safe place to live. A warm bed. Care for herself and her child.

Margot and Beryl would be free from danger as well. As long as the Vichy continued to turn a blind eye to what was happening inside the maternity home, they wouldn't have to worry. It was difficult enough for Noémie to be separated from her husband. How much worse it must be for these young girls to be away from their parents.

She would look after them and make sure someone was there in the middle of the night to comfort them. Together, the three of them would face what was in front of them with grace and courage and thankfulness they had escaped the horror that was Rivesaltes.

And they would look forward to being reunited with their families once this craziness was over.

After a while, the truck turned and slowed. The bumpiness increased, jostling all the passengers. They must be down a side road. Perhaps nearing the maternity home. François stopped and tooted his horn.

"We're here. We just need to wait for Madame Touissant to come and open the gate." A brightness filled Fräulein Reiter's voice.

Beryl spoke for the first time since they left the camp. "Will Maman and Papa be here soon too?"

"Non." Margot's word was short. "Remember, we can't go with them. This is where we'll be safe. This is what they want for us."

The girl's steeliness would serve her well in the next months and maybe even years. A steeliness Levi often told Noémie she possessed.

Well, with what she'd gone through in her life, it was essential. If not, she would have crumbled to the ground to be licked up by the dogs.

Outside there was a creak, and the truck moved forward again, soon coming to a halt with a screech of brakes. Several moments later, the driver opened the doors and the early-morning sun streamed inside. Noémie blinked away the darkness and reveled in the light.

No sooner had he helped her down than she was wrapped in a warm, motherly embrace. "I heard you were coming, and I'm so glad you're here. Merci for helping with the girls." The woman released Noémie, taking the scent of vanilla and cinnamon with her. The fragrances of home.

"I'm glad to be here." Her words were mostly true. "I'm Noémie Treves."

"Eleanore Touissant. And this must be Margot and Beryl de Carcassona." Madame Touissant greeted each of the girls, and they gave her shy half smiles.

"Merci for allowing us to stay here. It's very kind of you." Margot clasped her hands in front of her.

"Merci." Beryl slid closer to her older sister.

Madame Touissant's smile was as bright as a summer's day. "You're going to love it here, especially if you enjoy babies and small children. And there are plenty of mothers to go around. We all look after each other. Come with me. I'll show you where you'll be sleeping, and you can put your things away."

Madame Touissant led them to a house that stood on a hill overlooking a small village and the rolling Pyrenees foothills. Here and there, vineyards and olive trees dotted the landscape. The building itself was pale peach and had four wings radiating from the center. Noémie gazed upward and spotted a glass conservatory at the very top of the building.

From inside came the cries of infants and the laughter of toddlers.

A place to call home.

But would it be safe? Was there anywhere anymore where someone like her was truly protected?

CHAPTER THIRTEEN

22 August, 1955
Elne, France

I stand on the mansion's threshold, facing the house's large, carved oak double doors, my heart pounding in my chest, my mouth as dry as the dirt I had just held in my hands.

What memories will greet me inside? Will I be able to stand the weight of them?

The rusty doorknob creaks as I turn it, the door sticking a little but finally giving way on a squeaky hinge with a bit of pressure. As soon as I step inside, the musty odor of mold tickles my nose, and I sneeze. The large, open foyer welcomes me. How many did it welcome? Hundreds. So many. Almost too many to count. A place of warmth. Home. Security.

I sigh and breathe in the musty scent of age. Once, so many years ago, the odors of vanilla and cinnamon and yeast had permeated the entire building. Fragrances that would make my stomach rumble. Now, nothing but mold and mildew and rotting wood.

Spiders have draped cobwebs like bunting in almost every corner of the open entryway. If the sun weren't shining, the atmosphere might be creepy, but it's not to me. I can see what it once was in my mind's eye.

The wallpaper with tiny pink rosebuds is now yellowed with age and peeling. In the past, it brightened this space and welcomed everyone who entered. It has lost that quality, now a sad reminder of what used to be.

The black, light red, and white mosaic floor, once sparkling, is now faded and dulled with age and dust. Still, it brings a smile to my face.

Heels clicked against it, and bare feet slapped it.

Floors that had been so shiny that they had reflected light from the chandelier above are now dull and covered in scratches. I turn my gaze upward. Dust darkens the light's crystals.

How many exclaimed over its beauty and the brightness it brought to an otherwise dark world. It was the focal point of the entry, the first thing people noticed when they stepped inside.

I find the switch and flip it on, but no light comes from the bulbs. Either they burned out long ago or else there is no longer any electricity to the building. Probably the latter. A heaviness settles on my chest.

I lean against the wall, still sturdy despite the cracked and chipped plaster. For a moment, I stare upward, three stories to the glass dome some long-dead architect designed. Even that is covered with dirt and spotted from years' worth of rainwater.

Resting there, I listen for the voices, for the stories contained within. So very, very many of them, each different in their own way.

What about the ending of those stories? Some were happy while others were not. Joy and tragedy mingled together for many. The wind whips up, and the house creaks, almost as if it's attempting to give me the answers I seek.

The front door squeaks, and I jump around to see who's come, but there's no one. Only the breeze blowing it farther open. No one coming. Not anymore.

They used to, almost every day, sometimes a few at a time, sometimes several at a time. But they arrived for shelter from the storm raging just outside these walls.

Their voices cry to me in the wind, begging for relief. Begging for help. So many. Too many.

The remembrances are strong and powerful. Perhaps too much for me to handle. Perhaps it would have been better for me to stay away as I have all these years and allow the memories to remain buried, perhaps in one of the holes the children dug in the sand.

But I need to hear these stories again, to make myself believe that I didn't fabricate them. That they aren't some vivid dream or imagination.

One glance at the door, a beam of sunlight falling across the threshold.

Beauty inside. Beauty outside. Beauty wherever the eye roamed, even in places where no one else saw that beauty.

Beauty in the midst of ugliness. The worst ugliness to ever cover the earth. Even then, a tiny glimpse of heaven.

No, I need to do this, before it's too late. Before each of these walls, each of these beams, crumbles to dust and the world remembers no more.

CHAPTER FOURTEEN

July 2, 2022
Perpignan, France

The morning sun peeked through the east-facing window, poking Caitlyn awake, though snuggling under the thick duvet and enjoying the view of hundred-year-old buildings from her bed all day would be perfectly acceptable to her.

She rolled over and stared at Lindsey's picture on the brass and glass bedside table. Next to the photograph sat Caitlyn's Bible. She should open it, should read a chapter. A few verses, at least. But she couldn't. Couldn't bear to hear the words of judgment and condemnation contained within. Yes, peace also. Her head accepted that. Her heart wouldn't allow her the comfort.

Across the apartment, floorboards creaked, and someone turned on the kitchen tap. The humming of a hymn reached Caitlyn's ears. That must be Elissa. Only she was so chipper at this time of the morning. The first line of the hymn floated unbidden into Caitlyn's mind. *"Whate'er my God ordains is right."*

She closed her mind to the words, to the music, jumped from bed, and headed straight for the shower. A good dose of hot water and floral-scented soap washed the past and the music away. She picked the flowy flower-dotted maxi dress in an attempt to brighten her mood. Anything that helped.

Like the shot of caffeine that Elissa poured her as she sat at one of the bar stools in the tiny European kitchen. "That'll put hair on your chest."

Elissa cocked her head.

"Come on. Don't tell me you never heard that saying."

"Can't say that I have."

"Well, I have." Aiden came down the steps from the lofted bedroom, still pulling his shirt over his head. "And since I'm pretty lacking in that department, you'd better pour me a cup too."

Caitlyn's face heated at Aiden's words. She could almost hear Lindsey's comment to that in her head, and the temperature in her cheeks rose further.

Elissa, however, took no notice of him. "So, what's on the docket for the day?"

"En Français, s'il vous plaît." Caitlyn took another fortifying sip of what passed for coffee. The French and Spanish both liked it too strong for her taste.

"I don't know how to say that in French."

"Say what you do know."

"*Que faisons nous aujourd'hui?* Did I ask what we're doing today?"

"Don't doubt yourself so much. You've got this." Caitlyn pulled up a website on her phone. "Look, I found this great tour, *Le Petit Train de Perpignan.* The Little Perpignan Train. It takes you all over the city and should be a great way for us to get our bearings. And maybe we can talk to the people who run it and see what they can tell us about an old maternity hospital here. There's one in Elne, but Pops was specific that he was born in Perpignan."

"That sounds like a plan." Aiden downed his miniature cup of coffee in a single gulp and smacked his lips. "You're right. I feel the hair growing already." His pale blue eyes gleamed at his own joke.

Both Caitlyn and Elissa suppressed their laughs. Aiden leaned over her phone. "What time is the next tour?"

"In half an hour."

Elissa picked up the cups from the counter. "Then we'd better get going if we're going to make it. *Allons-y!*"

"Yes, let's go." Caitlyn slipped on her comfy tennis shoes, and soon they were in the warm, sunshine-filled morning. A soft breeze blew, and the most wonderful odors of yeast and chocolate danced in the air. *Live my life for me.* Lindsey's voice filled her head.

I will. They first made their way to a boulangerie and grabbed some croissants and *pains au chocolat.* The pastry surrounding the middle rod of chocolate was so flaky, it melted in Caitlyn's mouth. There was no denying that this was far better than what she could get in an American grocery store.

A short time later, they were seated on the little train, headphones on that would translate the tour from French into English. While trying it all in French would have been a great challenge, missing out on an important detail in her search might prove disastrous. Besides, Elissa begged them to so she wouldn't be the only one with headphones.

While the tour was interesting, the whole time they traveled down the ancient roads in the Arabic quarter, by the church of St. John, and through the historic city gate, the guide didn't mention a maternity hospital.

When they returned to the small kiosk that served as the starting and stopping point for the tour, she handed the headphones to the guide, thanking him as she did so. *"Où se trouve la maternité? C'est un musée."*

"No maternity hospital that is a museum. Not in Perpignan."

Caitlyn's shoulders sagged. Perhaps it had been brought to ruins years ago and the information she had about it was wrong. Her fault for not researching its existence better.

"In Elne."

"Excuse-moi?"

"Elne. Two train stops away. One is there."

"That's the only one in the area? None in Perpignan? Not even an old one from the Second World War?"

The guide shook his head then turned to a couple who spoke in rapid Spanish, asking to purchase tickets for the next tour.

Pops had always told her that he'd been born in Perpignan. Could it be that he had it wrong? That his mother told him wrong? Or perhaps his confusion had started long before anyone in her family had realized it.

"I think it's worth a trip there to check it out."

Aiden's voice at her shoulder sent her jumping.

"Sorry. Didn't mean to scare you."

"It's fine. I was thinking about something. I guess it couldn't hurt.

And it would be another adventure. Look, there's a restaurant that's actually open." One weird thing about France that she'd learned while studying here was that one could only eat out between noon and two and then from seven thirty until ten or so.

They took a seat at a round street-side table and browsed the menu. Once they'd ordered a pizza and salads, Aiden got back on his phone and started the research he was so good at. Much better than either Caitlyn or Elissa.

"Here it is." He passed his phone across the table.

Sure enough. La Maternité de la Paix in Elne. And not far, just like the tour guide said. "Why would my grandfather say he was born in Perpignan though? That doesn't make any sense."

Elissa popped a tomato into her mouth, chewed it, and swallowed. "Maybe he couldn't remember the exact town but knew it was in this region."

A logical enough explanation. And since Pops wasn't here right now, it was the one Caitlyn had to accept.

Aiden leaned back in his chair. "So tell us about your grandfather. He must have an interesting story to send you digging into his past like this."

"That's just it." Caitlyn sipped her water. "All he's told me is that he was born in a maternity hospital in Perpignan in 1942 and that his mother was Jewish."

"Not a good time to be Jewish." Aiden leaned forward.

"Definitely not. His parents survived the war and came to the United States soon afterward. But I don't know anything else about his birth or if his family was in a concentration camp or what happened to them between 1942 and 1946. So I don't have much to go on."

"It's something. You might be able to look up online if your family was in any of the camps. And now we might have pinpointed the maternity hospital, so maybe someone there can tell us something. This is fun. I always love a good mystery. My favorite TV show when I was a kid was *McGyver*."

Elissa laughed. "You're just a nerd, Aiden."

"I'm out to lunch with two lovely ladies in France. You tell me how much of a nerd I am."

This elicited a smile from Caitlyn. And then a pang in her heart.

Soon afterward, they paid the bill and headed to their rental, the late afternoon gentle and soft. She drank in the sights of the homes built on top of the old city wall, their neat pastel-painted exteriors in stark contrast to the old, dark stone beneath them.

They followed the main road until they came to a huge metal sculpture of a silver chair with a red caricature of a man sitting in it. That was their cue to turn down a street lined with small shops, restaurants, and homes.

Once they reached their temporary residence, Caitlyn changed into some comfortable leggings and an oversized T-shirt. The bed invited her to plop into it, close her eyes, and shut the world away.

She turned before she could give in to temptation and headed into the small living area. The French doors stood open, and Aiden sat on the balcony overlooking the little side street.

"Hey there. Anything interesting going on?"

"Just people-watching. It's kind of a pastime of mine. So, yeah, I basically am a nerd, but it's fascinating to imagine where these people are coming from and where they're going. What their stories are."

"I get it. No one travels the same path in life. Stories are interesting. I guess that's why I'd like to find out more about Pops. He didn't seem to know his own past other than the town he was born in, and now I'm not sure if he knew even that much."

Aiden turned and rested against the balcony's railing. "So what's yours?"

"My what?"

"Your story. What brought you to Barcelona and the mission field?"

"Nursing. Ever since I was very little, or so my mother tells me, I always wanted to be a nurse. While other little girls changed their minds from day to day, from ballerina to princess, I had my future planned out for myself." With Lindsey's help. She and Lindsey had played nurse every chance they had when they were young.

"There had to be some kind of drive behind it."

"I don't know. Just something God planted deep in my heart." A heart that hurt so much right now, it might never heal. She had to change the subject before she broke down in tears in front of one of the nicest guys she'd ever met. "And how about yours?"

"I'm an open book. Ask me anything you want."

"Why a pilot? Isn't that dangerous?"

"There's a little bit of danger inherent in everything we do, including walking down the stairs or crossing the street."

A fact Caitlyn was all too well aware of.

"Actually, I've always loved to fly. My grandparents were missionaries, and sometimes we'd visit them on the field. I got to see up close and personal what the work was like and hear their stories. See what God was doing in the lives of people not so very different from you or me."

"That's very cool. My friend and I went on a mission trip to Senegal when we were in college. Said we'd always go to the field together and work as nurses. It didn't work out." Caitlyn swallowed hard. Several times. She couldn't break down in front of Aiden, or she would have to tell him everything. And she wasn't about to do that.

"That's too bad. At least you're making your dream come true."

All Caitlyn could do was nod.

"I sense a hesitation there."

Great. Aiden had to be a sensitive guy to boot. "The dream feels different now somehow. I need to figure out if this is the route I want to take or if God has a different plan for me." That was the trouble with Him. He was always changing her plans. Everyone's plans.

"I think you'd make a fantastic missionary."

Really? Even when she was having doubts about her relationship with God? "What makes you say that?"

"You're nice, and genuine. Anyone can see that. And something about you, something I can't quite put my finger on, tells me that you understand a lot about people and how to reach them. You have a way of connecting with others and really caring about what they have to say."

A slight tingle raced across her fingertips. "That's the nicest thing anyone has said to me in a very long time." And the warmth it produced throughout her was a welcome relief from the cold in the depths of her soul.

"Then it's a shame no one tells you anything like that." He reached out and touched her arm, warm and soft, and just the thing that might burst the dam she'd so painstakingly built.

Instead of allowing him to see that, she turned and fled to her room, slamming the door behind her a little too hard.

CHAPTER FIFTEEN

July 3, 2022
Perpignan, France

Caitlyn stood bleary-eyed at the small kitchen counter, working to operate the petite coffee maker, when the soft click of a door sounded behind her and the steps to her right creaked under Aiden's weight. She couldn't bear facing him this morning with the way she'd acted last night, but there was no escape.

He came alongside her, almost brushing her arm. "Good morning."

She mumbled in reply. It was all she could do to hold herself together.

He touched her shoulder, and she sidestepped out of his reach.

"I'm sorry. For whatever I did last night, whatever I said that upset you, I apologize. I shouldn't have pushed. I won't do it again, not until you're ready to talk, if you ever are. We don't know each other very well yet, and I pushed you beyond what you were comfortable sharing."

Why did he have to be such a nice guy? It would be much easier for her to keep her distance if he were an idiot. But no, he had to go and be all sympathetic and even apologize. She'd been led to believe that guys like him didn't exist anymore. Of course, she and Lindsey had always fantasized that they would meet and fall in love with two of the few good ones left, but that was before. . .

"Thank you. I appreciate it." She dropped the K-cup she held in her shaking hand.

Before she could retrieve it, he swooped in and picked it up. "Let me."

She went and sat on the sofa, staring out the window at the street below. A bus stopped and a few passengers entered, off to their jobs most likely. Living normal lives.

Aiden stepped in front of her and handed her a steaming cup. "I think it's extra strong, which makes up for it being in such a small mug."

For the first time since yesterday, she allowed the corners of her mouth to turn up. "You give it too much credit to call it a mug. But I'm used to it. You can't imagine my great joy when I discovered a Starbucks near where I was studying during my semester abroad. Finally, I was able to have a decent-sized cup. My friend and I started singing 'I Saw the Sign.'"

Aiden laughed. "Did you know that makes you as much of a nerd as I am?"

"What, the song?"

He danced around the apartment, flapping his arms and singing. "I saw the sign, and it opened up my mind. I saw the sign."

Caitlyn had to hold her sides, she was laughing so hard. No guy she'd ever known would have dared be that goofy in front of a girl. She struggled to draw in a few breaths. "That's taking nerdiness to a whole new level."

He hummed a few more measures before finishing the dance with a flourish.

"Yeah, now I see that you don't need coffee at all. It would be a very, very bad thing for you." Caitlyn relaxed against the back of the couch. "I love France. When I left, I vowed to return."

"And look, dreams do come true."

"Some of them."

Aiden stared at her for a second, then shrugged. "Of course. We can't all be astronauts or cowboys or princesses. Can you see me with a tiara?"

She gave another good, long laugh. "But you'd be gorgeous."

He dropped a curtsy. "Thank you, ma'am. I'll take the lie."

There went her smile again. How did he manage to tease it out of her when very few others could?

They chatted for a few more minutes before Elissa emerged from her room. They purchased SNCF train tickets for very little money on their phones and were soon on their way to Elne. In no time, they had arrived. Europe did get it right when it came to public transportation.

Caitlyn pulled up the map on her phone, squinting as she studied it. "Okay, according to this, the hospital is about a kilometer in that direction." She pointed to the west. "We follow the A612 road over there to the hospital. So does everyone have their water bottles filled? Are we ready to set off?"

Elissa shook her head, her dark hair swinging with the motion. "You make it sound like we're striking off to the wild jungles of South America. We're going a kilometer. That's less than a mile, you know."

"Whatever." By this point, she could hardly wait to get going. To snap a few pictures of the place where Pops was probably born and tell him more about his beginnings. Help him get the true story about where he came from.

It should be an interesting day. Her melancholy slipped from her shoulders like a cloak, and by concentrating on this, she left her problems behind for a while. Desperately needed relief.

They hadn't strolled too far, however, before the buildings that comprised the small town gave way to scattered dwellings and woodlands. The road narrowed into a two-lane highway with an almost nonexistent shoulder bordered by a deep ditch, traffic zipping along in both directions.

"Here comes a truck!" Elissa scurried to the side, and Caitlyn and Aiden followed.

"Suck in your butt!"

Caitlyn hurried to comply with Aiden's order, digging her nails into his upper arm as she clung to him, her heart speeding along faster than the TGV high-speed train. She held her breath, only releasing it once the wind created by the passing truck subsided and stillness returned to the countryside.

"Well, that was quite the adventure." Aiden opened his arms wide and gave a belly laugh.

"I'm sorry. I guess I didn't research this enough. This is crazy. Maybe we should go back to the station and see if we can get a taxi."

"In this little town?"

"We might be able to."

Elissa pulled her along. "Come on. It's not that far. If we walk fast, we'll be there in no time. Long before a taxi would ever make it to pick us up."

But who knew what could happen in that amount of time? Then again, Elissa had a point. They would have to walk back along the road, facing the same perils, if they waited for a ride. They might as well get going to the maternity home as soon as they could.

They got good at dodging the vehicles that passed them, even zig-zagging from one side of the road to the other when possible. And it wasn't too long before the sign came into view on the side of the road, almost hidden by brush. LA MATERNITÉ DE LA PAIX.

At last they turned off the highway and onto a gravel road, wooded on either side, leaving behind the busy road, the scene growing more tranquil with every step. Just about the time a bead of sweat developed on the side of Caitlyn's face, a beautiful pale peach building rose up from a manicured lawn. Topping it off was a glass dome that sparkled in the summer Mediterranean sunshine. "Wow."

"Look at this place." Elissa took a few steps closer. "This is amazing. It's not a hospital but a mansion."

"It sure is." Caitlyn led the way to the side of the building. "Why would my grandfather, a Jewish boy during the war, be born in a place like this? I'm sure they couldn't afford to stay here."

Aiden's footsteps crunched beside her on the gravel. "No, I read on my phone last night that this was used to hide Jewish children and their mothers. Almost six hundred babies were born here."

Wow. "I'd whistle if I could. And look at this gorgeous stone porch with these fancy railings and steps." The stairs swept down both sides of the balcony, a grand show for a spectacular building.

"I think the entrance is over here." Aiden pointed to a more modern door, its sleek steel and glass gleaming in the light.

"Wait. Let me get a few pictures for Pops." Caitlyn snapped as many as she could from as many angles as possible. Once she finished, they made their way inside, through the door Aiden had pointed out.

"*Bonjour.*" The young man behind the desk greeted them in the bouncy, cheery way the French had.

"Bonjour." She returned his exclamation with an equal amount of good-naturedness and continued the conversation in French. "Three tickets, s'il vous plaît."

They each put down a few Euros, and the man gave them a booklet in English. Caitlyn groaned. "I hoped my French was good enough that you wouldn't detect an accent."

"It is very good, but not perfect. You are from England?"

"The United States."

"Not many from the United States come here."

"Actually, maybe you can help us. I believe my grandfather may have been born here during World War II. Do you have any records of the babies who were delivered in this hospital?"

"A list of them is on one of the displays upstairs, but there are no family names."

She crinkled her forehead. "Why not?"

"Eleanore Touissant, the nurse who opened and ran the hospital, didn't want anyone in danger. The names would tell they were Jewish. But she wrote them down and hid them so one day they would know who they were."

"Oh." Caitlyn deflated. How many boys named Steven would there be on that wall? Hopefully not too many. It wasn't really a French or Jewish name.

"Look at the exhibits and read what is there. If you have other questions, I will try to answer."

"That's very kind of you. Merci."

The three of them headed across the lobby, the floor tiled in a pretty black, mauve, and white pattern made to resemble flowers. She again got out her phone and snapped pictures of everything, including the beautiful floor. Pops would want to see every bit of this place.

They made their way to a curving stone staircase accented by scrolled iron railings and climbed to the second floor. Caitlyn drew in a deep breath. Her great-grandmother may have been here and given birth to Pops in one of these rooms. Imagine that.

They wandered through the exhibits, learning more about Eleanore Touissant and how she established the hospital for refugees fleeing the Spanish Civil War in the 1930s and then used it to house and hide Jewish women and their children in the following decade.

On the walls of the large, old rooms hung pictures of children. A group of them splashing each other in a huge metal tub. Several of them running in the yard. One newborn, hands fisted and eyes shut, sleeping in a blanket-lined basket.

Could that child be Pops? Or maybe he was the little boy sitting on the step, tears running down his face as someone tended to his scraped knee. She studied each picture for any clue that one of the subjects might be Pops or his mother.

Nothing.

They moved into another room, this one with the same displays filled with photographs and captions and explanations of what life was like during the days the mansion operated as a maternity hospital. Again, though she studied each word and picture harder than she had ever studied for any test, she found nothing that might possibly be about her family.

Then, from the other side of the room, Elissa squealed. "I've found it."

"What? You've found Pops?" Caitlyn hurried around the corner to where her friend stood.

"No. The list of names. And the curator was right. No last names. Only first names and last initials. But they are sorted by year, and they do list the date of birth, so maybe you'll be able to figure it out that way."

"Maybe. Pops was born in 1942. November twentieth. Is there a Steven L.? That would be him." She hugged herself as she stepped to the list of names, finding the surrounding dates with little problem. The trouble was that there was no Steven L. And no November twentieth either.

Aiden joined the girls. "What did you find?"

"Nothing. Nothing at all. This isn't making sense. His name should be here. This is the only maternity hospital that's a museum around here. That's what the train operator said."

"We can ask the guy at the front desk about that. Don't give up." Aiden handed her the water bottle she'd left on the bench in the room's corner. "There are any number of possibilities why he's not listed. It will just take more digging."

The trouble was that they didn't have much time to dig.

CHAPTER SIXTEEN

22 August, 1955
Elne, France

If only these walls could talk.

If only they could laugh and sing and dance.

A little handprint still marks the white paint. I touch it in reverence, as if touching the letters marking out the name on a gravestone. From deep within me wells a sigh, and pain squeezes my heart, my very soul.

Just to recapture those days, even for a brief moment, would be utter joy. Light upon light shattering the blackest darkness.

The music of the voices that once filled this place now fill my head. They could overwhelm me, but instead, I allow them to comfort me and bring me peace. For a brief time, in a crazy world, there was a pocket of sanity.

> *Chante rossignol, chante,*
> *Toi qui as le cœur gai*
> *Tu as le cœur à rire,*
> *Moi je l'ai à pleurer*

The meaning of the words comes to me, unbidden, and tears streak down my cheeks.

> *Sing, nightingale, sing,*
> *Your heart is so happy.*
> *Your heart feels like laughing,*
> *Mine feels like weeping.*

We laughed as much as we could. This little corner of the world, this small plot of land, for a time, was where joy flourished. While the world wept, we laughed.

Perhaps we were naive. Perhaps we should have wept more.

Farther down the wall is the marking of a crayon, half gone with repeated washing and with age. If only it hadn't been scrubbed. This was someone's mark, someone's signature that they had been here, that they had existed.

Though I attempt to only allow the happy words of the song into my head, the last line, the one about weeping, is the one repeating. Over and over.

I force myself to move on, not touching the crayon mark, so I don't erase any more of it. It's a testimony. A witness. Once it's gone, so is the voice of the one who created it.

In the unswept corner of the room lies a small wooden train car. I pick it up and brush away the dust and dirt. Years ago, it was red, but now it's faded to rust. My lips curl upward at the memory of someone making chugging and whistling noises in imitation of a train, the tracks not far from here.

"Train, train!" a child would yell at the sound of the whistle, and then everyone would run to the window, their noses pressed against the glass as if they could catch a glimpse of it down the road and behind the trees. Every time the whistle blew its deceptively cheery noise, the scene repeated itself.

Some child must have missed this toy when they left it behind. Perhaps they cried themselves to sleep the first few nights without it. Poor little one, denied the comfort of the harmless toy.

I wipe the image and the tears from my eyes. Instead, I picture a group of small children in a circle on the floor, the entire wooden train, held together by magnets, making its circuit of the group, each one adding their own distinctive chugging or whistling or braking imitation.

If only those happy voices hadn't been silenced.

CHAPTER SEVENTEEN

19 August, 1942
Elne, Vichy France

Noémie sipped a warm cup of chamomile tea in the large, bright dining room, beside several other women in her same position. Most were further along in their pregnancies. A few held their infants in their arms as they ate.

Though the other women were kind and welcoming, she remained detached from them. So much had happened in the past few weeks. Not that long ago, Levi was across the dining room table from her as they enjoyed the morning together. And then everything changed so fast. They lost their home and almost everything they owned. For the second time. The gendarmes took them to an awful, strange place. And before she was barely acclimated there, she again found herself on the move.

This time without her husband.

What was he doing this morning? Was he missing her as much as she was missing him? The hole in her heart, the one where he fit, grew in size each passing hour.

She didn't dare allow herself to think about how long, if ever, it would be before she could see him again. Right now, her focus was on their child. He or she was all that mattered.

The small woman next to Noémie, a tiny baby in her arms, leaned over. "I don't believe I caught your name, but I know you came in with the two young girls yesterday, didn't you?"

Noémie nodded.

"Word has been getting around about what you did for them, of your amazing courage. I'm not sure I could be so strong in the face of such terror."

"I only did what any mother would." Noémie shifted in her seat. "In fact, it's Fräulein Reiter who deserves the credit. All I did was follow her orders."

"Still, I shudder to think what could have happened if you'd been caught."

No doubt the consequences would have been severe. A chill raced down Noémie's spine. But she couldn't have left those defenseless girls by themselves, not with their parents boarding a train to parts unknown. Last time, she'd allowed sheer terror to stop her from doing right. Not this time. Not ever again.

"Were you scared?"

Noémie had come to this place to get away from the horrors of Camp de Rivesaltes, not to talk endlessly about it. "I'm sorry. I don't believe I caught your name."

"Oh." The young woman's fair face flushed as red as the stripe on the French flag. "That wasn't very good etiquette on my part. I'm Salomé Duval, and this is my son, Paul. I started blathering about the girls and forgot all about my original question. But forgive me if I don't ask yours. I doubt there has been time to change it."

"What do you mean, 'to change it'?"

"We all get new names, Gentile names, to protect our identities. Is your husband still at the camp? Mine is, as far as I know. Of course, we don't get information from there very often. Sometimes when Fräulein Reiter comes, we might hear a word or two. If you're lucky, a passed note, but that's unusual. It's too dangerous for her to be caught ferreting women and children out of the camp with correspondence in her possession."

Wow, Salomé could talk once she got going. "My husband was there when I left yesterday. I expect it will be some time before I hear anything more."

"You never know. You're already one of the lucky ones, getting to come here so early in your pregnancy. Most of us weren't spirited out of the camp until it was almost time for us to give birth. Maybe they'll end up sending you back, though I hope not. I really like you."

Sent back? That thought hadn't once flitted across Noémie's mind. Then again, it would make sense. They required room here for those closer to labor. She was taking up precious space intended for women who truly needed the services this maternity home offered.

What punishment would she receive upon reentering the camp? She'd escaped, after all. They wouldn't be kind to her. Not in the least. She might well lose the baby. She might well lose her life.

Her skin prickled.

The tea, which just moments before had been so soothing to both her stomach and her nerves, was now bitter. She pushed it away.

"Morning sickness? I was so glad to be done with that." Salomé took a big bite of eggs. Eggs. Imagine that. Where did they get such a delicacy?

Then again, Noémie wouldn't be able to eat a single bite. Not the way her stomach was jumping around like a toddler on a playground.

"Madame Treves?" Margot was at her side, pulling on her cardigan's sleeve.

"Bonjour, ma chérie. How are you doing?"

"Missing Maman and Papa, though it's nice here. We're getting used to being away from our parents. We just pray for the end of the war so we can be together once again. Even when I get married, I'm going to live next door to Maman and Papa."

Oui, these children would carry the scars of this war with them for the rest of their lives. Noémie touched the spot where her own child grew and breathed a prayer that he wouldn't be faced with such permanent effects. Perhaps by the time he entered the world, peace would once again have a foothold.

"Anyway, Madame Touissant would like to see you. I can take you to her office. I wonder what she wants to talk to you about."

Noémie excused herself, rose, and followed Margot toward Madame Touissant's office. "She probably wants to assign me some chores while I'm here so that I don't get bored and so I can earn my keep."

"Will we have to do chores too?"

"I imagine that everyone has to help in one way or another."

"I just don't want to wash dishes. I really, really hate doing them."

Noémie chuckled. "Then I'll volunteer for that so you won't be forced to play in the sudsy water."

"Merci."

By this time, they had climbed the winding marble staircase to Madame Touissant's private chambers on the second floor at the back of the house. Noémie knocked on the door, and Margot scurried away.

"Come in."

With shaking hands, Noémie turned the knob. This conversation wasn't going to be about chore assignment. This was going to be about her return to Camp de Rivesaltes. The sickness in her stomach had nothing to do with her coming child. She entered the room, the weathered floorboards creaking under her feet. "You wanted to see me?"

This morning, Madame Touissant wore her hair in braids wrapped in a crown around her head. Though she wore no makeup, her face glowed with happiness and health. How could she be in such a good mood when she was about to send Noémie back to the horrors of the camp? Perhaps she had done it so often that it no longer affected her. Or maybe she was putting on a good front so she didn't upset Noémie. "Have a seat, s'il vous plaît."

Noémie took her place in a hard, straight-backed chair across the small desk from Madame Touissant and clasped her hands together to make their shaking less obvious.

"Don't be nervous. I truly don't bite." A genuine warmth lit Madame Touissant's brown eyes.

Noémie slid forward on her chair. "Don't send me back, I beg you. Though I do want to be with my husband in the worst way, I don't know what the guards would do to me if I returned. I don't like to imagine the tortures waiting for escapees."

"Who told you we were sending you back?"

"Salomé."

Madame Touissant pressed her lips into a thin line and nodded. "Of course. I should have known it would be her. That woman is sweet and wonderful but couldn't keep her mouth shut if she were in a room filled with millions of flies. Don't pay any attention to her. We aren't in the habit of sending back anyone who has escaped Rivesaltes."

"Merci beaucoup. I can't tell you how relieved I am to hear that." Noémie blew out a breath.

"Of course. That's not why I wanted to speak to you. Instead, I wanted to thank you for what you did for Margot and Beryl. It takes a special woman to put herself in such a position."

"I once had the opportunity to escape and help many others flee, but I didn't take it. If I regret anything in life, that's it. This, in a small way, is my partial repayment of that debt." Her throat burned, and she shoved away the memory.

"You can't live your life looking over your shoulder. Keep your eyes focused on what's in front of you."

The kind words settled in Noémie's heart even as her throat swelled shut. Still, she owed her employees, Levi, and even her child a great deal for her mistakes. "Do you have children of your own?"

Madame Touissant furrowed her brows, and her eyes darkened, just for a moment before she schooled her features. "Non, I do not."

"Still, I'm sure you become attached to the children here and want the best for them. Why else would you set up a maternity hospital and put yourself at risk if you didn't care about the littlest and most helpless of the human race?"

"You're right. I was the oldest of thirteen children, so I often found myself as more of their mother than their sister."

"And you would do anything for them. Even give your own life."

"Of course."

"That's all I did for Margot and Beryl. They deserve a chance at life, as much as my own child does. All I did was protect them. And I wasn't very brave. I was terribly frightened the entire time we hid in the warehouse. And not just of the guards."

Madame Touissant gave a hearty laugh. "Rats are the only creatures I fear more than Germans or collaborators."

Noémie joined in the laughter.

"I feel we shall be very good friends, Madame Treves. I've had that feeling since you walked through the door holding the girls' hands. I sense something special in you. Something very special God has planned for your life."

Here was the first thing she and Madame Touissant disagreed on. How could any of this be a special time in her life, something that Hashem would use for good? Not with all this hatred. Not with all this animosity toward her own people. Not when countless Jews were slaughtered in the streets and died in camps like Rivesaltes.

Without a knock at the door, a young boy, probably not even two years old, burst into the room. "Elle, Elle," he cried as he flung himself into Madame Touissant's arms.

"Javier, what can I do for you?"

Strange that his name was Javier. With his light brown hair and green eyes, he didn't appear Spanish. Then again, these were the days when one didn't ask too many questions. Didn't delve too deeply into someone's heritage.

Madame Touissant kissed both of the boy's round cheeks. "Have you been a good little boy?"

"Oui, oui."

"If you keep doing that, you'll grow to be a fine, strong young man."

He reached up and claimed another kiss from Madame Touissant. "Je t'aime, je t'aime."

"And I love you too, *mon chéri*."

The tot held out a train engine he clasped in his hand. "Look."

"Oh no. What happened?"

"Broke."

"It did break. *Je suis désolée*."

He babbled something or other that Noémie didn't catch, but Madame Touissant knew the meaning. "Jorge did that?"

Javier nodded.

"He must be very sorry. Why don't we go and see what the others are doing? I'm sure the nurses are wondering where you've gone off to." Madame Touissant set the boy on the floor, took him by the hand, and turned to Noémie. "Come along. I'll give you a tour, and then I have a special job here for you. One that will require a lot of hard work, dedication, and discretion."

"Are you sure? You don't know me."

"I know you. People tell me I have this innate sense about others, that I can see right into their souls and know what kind of people they are. I'm not so sure about that, but I am able to read people pretty well.

"Plus Fräulein Reiter told me what you did for your employees in Mulhouse. You're someone who wants to help and who has the skills and ability to do so. Someone she could trust with the lives of Margot and Beryl is someone I can trust."

Noémie wiped her hands on her skirt. Hopefully, she would be up to whatever task Madame Touissant was giving. At least she wasn't going back to Rivesaltes.

Not for the time being.

CHAPTER EIGHTEEN

Madame Touissant led Noémie to a small room behind the sweeping marble stairs on the second-floor landing. The space was so tiny it must have been a storage closet at one time. Tucked away in here, though, was a desk befitting the room's diminutive size, on top of which sat a typewriter. There was a wooden chair on rollers and a tall, skinny filing cabinet.

That was it.

Noémie turned to Madame Touissant. "What's this?"

She led the way, motioning for Noémie to follow. Once they had both squeezed inside, Madame Touissant pulled the metal chain on the bare bulb that lit the room and shut the heavy oak door. The walls came closer, and Noémie inhaled deeply several times to keep from bolting right through the closed door.

"Are you going to be okay? I never thought to ask if you were claustrophobic. If you are, perhaps I'd better find someone else."

"Non, I'm fine."

"Good, because I'd like you to stay. What we do here is very important."

"Giving shelter and protection to innocent women and children is one of the most important things in the world."

Madame Touissant nodded. "There's that. But we can't protect them if they walk around with identification papers that read *Noémie Treves* and are marked with a large *J*."

In the room's dimness, Noémie couldn't make out the other woman's expression, but this must be what Salomé had been talking about.

"The Vichy now have it in their minds to cooperate with the Germans, or at least placate them, by shipping Jews east. The Nazis are pressuring them more and more. Every day, I hold my breath, waiting, wondering if this will be the day or the evening or the night when we're raided and everyone is arrested. When that happens—it's inevitable—we have to be prepared."

"So you falsify names." The fog around Noémie was clearing.

"Oui. Fräulein Reiter told me you used to run a business, and since the last woman with this job was returned to Rivesaltes, your arrival was providential."

"So you want my help."

"If you're willing. It's not without its risks."

"I was the child who stood on the roof, a hay bale below me, convinced I could fly." Only once, when the Germans had come, had she been paralyzed with the fear of the unknown.

"Good. That's wonderful to hear. Sometimes we don't get many admissions. Other times, we have several in a day. We sometimes have multiple babies born within hours of each other. Why don't you have a seat?"

Noémie followed Madame Touissant's instruction.

"Push in as close to the desk as you can. It's good that you aren't too far along in your pregnancy."

Again, Noémie did as she was asked.

Madame Touissant scooted around, bent over, and lifted several floorboards. Then she drew out a stack of papers. "This is what could get us into trouble."

"What are those?"

"The real identity papers of the women and children who come here. We fill in forged identity papers—don't ask where we get them from—and then we type cards with both their real and falsified information so that someday we'll be able to reunite any who are separated."

They wouldn't lose their true identities. Her shoulders relaxed.

"If, God forbid, anything should happen and the mothers and children are separated, we'll have a record. They can return here and find out as much information as possible. We want to be a place where families will be reunited after this awful war ends."

That was a thought that had never crossed Noémie's mind. What if she was separated from her child? Goose bumps broke out on her arms. May that never be.

For the next fifteen minutes or so, Madame Touissant showed Noémie what the job involved. Mostly typing and filing, filling in records. Much easier than running a factory and well within her capabilities. The musty dustiness of the little room sent her sneezing, but she listened to everything Madame Touissant said.

"There now. Do you think you understand what I need you to do?"

"Oui. This should be no problem."

"I knew it wouldn't be. Now comes the most important part. At least for today."

From her spot in front of the typewriter, Noémie glanced at her. "What might that be?"

"You need a new name."

Of course. If all the other Jewish women and children were receiving Gentile names, why wouldn't she? But she wriggled in the chair, and her mouth went dry. Renaming herself would be like turning her back on her people and her culture. Everything she had ever known would be wiped out in a few typewriter keystrokes.

Madame Touissant touched her shoulder. "I understand what that means and how difficult it must be for you. It's the only way, however, to keep you, your child, and everyone else here safe. Margot and Beryl will also receive new names. You can reassure them that this is for their good and that their old names will not be forgotten. Of course, you must never tell them how that will be—you must never tell anyone that—but you can give them that hope."

A small, brief nod was all Noémie could manage. This renaming sucked the life out of her, straight from her heart. Who would she be?

Non, this was ridiculous. Inside, she would remain Noémie Treves. She would always be Noémie Treves. No black-inked typewriter letters would change her essence, her being. Even if the world forgot who she was, she would never forget who she had once been. Who she would always be.

She straightened her spine and took up her position at the typewriter.

"Do you have a name you'd like to suggest?"

"It might be better coming from you. That way, you'll be comfortable with it."

"I suppose you're right." Noémie nodded. But what should she choose? Growing up, her family had a very kind neighbor. Hélène. "Hélène Etu." The last name came from the *boulanger* she once knew who always gave her a small roll when she came in the morning with Maman to purchase the day's bread.

"Then type it up. It's a pleasure to meet you, Hélène Etu."

"Likewise, Madame Touissant." If that was even her name.

A short time later, she brought in Margot and Beryl, and they picked their new names. Marie and Beatrice. They didn't question the change at all but chose new identities without much thought or any complaint. They skipped off together, holding hands, their old identities now typed onto a card and filed under the floorboards.

After a few hours in the tiny room, her work now completed, Hélène—that was how she had to think of herself so she would answer to it without hesitation—headed outside for a breath of fresh air.

The early-afternoon sun was strong, and she lifted her face to relish its warmth. Soon enough, the winter winds would blow. She had a heavy coat but had been planning and saving to purchase a new one this year because hers had seen better days. Now she was forced to deal with what she had. For the time being, it was best to enjoy the outdoors as much as she could.

Was Levi still in Rivesaltes? Could he lift his face to the same sun? Or had he been transported to Poland, a place where she imagined there was no light, only darkness.

That was what became of countries controlled by Hitler.

No light. No joy. No peace.

Just utter, deep darkness.

And then the laughter of children floated on the soft breeze that teased her hair.

How was it that this one place, this small plot of land on a hill, was a spot of brightness, a pinprick of happiness?

She turned to discover Madame Touissant passing through the door, a group of children running ahead of her, an infant in her arms. Hélène hurried to her. "Let me take the baby. You have your hands full."

"Merci. I can keep the baby. The children are a joy though. I never want to hush them or keep them shut up in the house. Innocent little ones, that's what they are, and they deserve the best life can offer them. They deserve the chance to survive and thrive."

Noémie—Hélène—peered at the little boy, his eyes wide even though he nestled against Madame Touissant's shoulder. "And who do we have here?"

"This is Étienne. He likes to take in all the action. I've never known a child so bright at such a young age, just a few months old." She kissed his brow, a motherly gesture. There was no doubting that she loved each and every one of these children.

Étienne lifted his head from Madame Touissant's shoulder and whimpered, squirming in her grasp. She nestled him against her and jiggled him. He soon quieted. In just a few months, Hélène would cradle her own child. Part of her and part of Levi. Her heart ached with missing him. He should be here to share in every step of this pregnancy.

To push away the pain, she focused on Étienne. Madame Touissant handed him to her so she could spend time with the other children. Hélène walked with him and talked to him and jiggled him when he got fussy. Meanwhile, Madame Touissant played tag with the children, her hair somehow remaining in its braids, coiled around the top of her head. Though she ran and chased, her cheeks didn't even flush.

One by one, the children dropped out of the game, panting on the grass that they pulled and threw at each other. Strange to think that in a few years, her own child would be into the same antics.

Since Levi wasn't there to relish this time with her, she would do her best to remember every detail so that when they were reunited, she could tell him everything. So that, even though far away, he wouldn't feel like he'd missed out on anything.

By the scent of the infant in Hélène's arms, it was clear that Étienne needed to be changed. Most all of the children had retired to the grass, so Madame Touissant called for them to go inside. Hélène followed.

"Where is Étienne's mother? I'd like to take him back to her." She'd never changed a diaper in her life, but there was no way she was going to admit that. She was her parents' only child and had never been exposed to infants nor been expected to change one.

Madame Touissant shook her head, her usual smile fading from her lips. "She cannot care for him."

"What do you mean? Is she sick? Is she. . .?"

"It's best you not know."

Something terrible must have happened to her. That was the only way she would ever allow herself to be separated from her child. Hélène leaned against the wall. "But I believed this to be a safe place. One where we would be protected, out of the eyes of those hunting us. Isn't that why we all have new identities?"

Madame Touissant sighed and rubbed her bloodshot eyes. "Our work isn't perfect, much as we wish it. Sometimes they raid us and arrest women just for sport. Just because there are rumors in town regarding what goes on here."

Though the sun streamed through the window and pooled at Hélène's feet, an icy chill ran through her. "How can that be?"

Madame Touissant shook her head. "People talk. They know, or they think they know, and they talk. And when the Nazis put the pressure on the Vichy to cough up more Jews, they visit us. It doesn't matter to them, as long as they make their quota and keep their overlords happy. Keep the power and control they have."

"What do we do when they come?" Noémie locked her knees to keep from sinking to the floor. "Is there a plan to hide or run or something?"

"Look around. There are too many to hide. We do our best, say our prayers, and leave the rest up to God."

That wasn't a very good plan. There had to be a better way.

CHAPTER NINETEEN

22 August, 1955
Elne, France

I move down the hall that follows one side of the open staircase on my right, two doors on my left, and step into the first one, the pale pink paint even paler, washed out by the sun. The weight on my shoulders lifts, and I draw in a deep breath. This is better. Much better. A happier, cheerier room.

I throw open the tall windows, allowing the wind and the fresh air to blow inside, to sweep away the mustiness and the sadness that intermingle. For several minutes, I stand at the window, leaning out from time to time for a better look at the yard. To my right is a flat patch of green grass where the children played tag until they petered out and lay among the dandelions.

To my left, red and orange and yellow butterflies flit over the patio where the mothers and nurses set baskets covered in mosquito netting, the babies inside snoozing in the sun or reaching out to try to catch a buzzing bee. Sweet, innocent lives.

In the distance, the church bell tolls, ringing out the time for all to hear. It has done so for centuries, since before the sarcophagi containing the bones of saints were placed in the crypt. Even before the elaborate carvings were etched onto the columns to tell the story of the Christ child.

This land, this place, lay witness to so much, some of it good, some of it not. Do the buildings whisper to each other after dark, when the residents are tucked in bed and snoring away the night? Do they recount what they have witnessed over the course of many generations? Or do they hold their secrets close, not willing to share either their griefs or their joys?

Sometimes it is better not to know. To remain in oblivion, innocent of current events. So it was for the infants and children, those unspoiled and untainted as of yet by the cruel, harsh world. The walls may or may not speak, but the adults never did.

As a chrysalis protects the tiny life contained within it until it becomes a full-grown butterfly, so was this place. One that nurtured and harbored but never gave up the truth to those whom the truth would crush.

Because that's what the truth does, oftentimes. Like a millstone about the neck, it can sink a person into the depths so that they can never return to the surface for even a gulp of air. So it is better for events to go unrecorded, for memories to be lost to the ages, for recollections to be buried under the sands of time.

I stretch my back, inhale once more, then close the windows before leaning against the faded wall. "Never tell. Promise me that you will never tell what you saw or heard. For I vow that I never will."

CHAPTER TWENTY

July 3, 2022
Elne, France

Flanked by Aiden and Elissa, Caitlyn dragged her way down the maternity hospital's wide, winding stairs. None of them said much on the way to the first floor. She'd come to France with such high hopes of finding Pops' birthplace and discovering his background. Of getting to know a little more about him.

What a fool she had been to think it would be as simple as walking into the hospital-turned-museum where he must have been born and find his name on the wall. To unlock all the long-held secrets within a matter of minutes or hours.

They reached the bottom of the staircase, and Aiden bumped her arm. "Cheer up and don't give up, no matter what. You really want to find out about your grandfather?"

"Of course."

"Then you have to be relentless and pursue this all the way to the end. Do you think your grandfather would even be alive today if his mother had given up?"

She stopped and stared up, through the stairwell to the glass dome above them. A shaft of light beamed inside and landed at her feet.

No one in her family was a quitter. Pops wasn't. Neither was Dad. Even when they'd had rough times in life, like when Dad had declared bankruptcy, they didn't throw in the proverbial towel.

She gave Aiden a small smile, just a hint of a grin. It wouldn't do to make him think that he was the one responsible for helping her to feel better. If he had a crush on her, that would only encourage him. "Thanks for the perspective. You know, the docent at the front desk said to ask if we had any more questions. Well, now I do, so I'm going to see if I can find out anything from him."

"That's the spirit." Aiden took off marching down the hall, the two girls following him, both of them giggling.

Elissa shook her head. "Whyever did we agree to bring him along on this trip?"

"Beats me. But he's here, so I guess we have to put up with him."

"Or leave him on the side of the road."

"Nah." Caitlyn hurried to catch up with Aiden. "He's like a cat. He'd just find his way home again."

Elissa had to stop because she was laughing so hard, but Caitlyn kept going. "Aiden. Wait up. This is my grandfather. I want to be the one to ask the questions."

"Of course, milady." He swept a grand gesture and, once again shaking her head, Caitlyn approached the young man behind the desk. "Excuse-moi?"

"Oh, you are done? You found what you were looking for?"

"No. In fact, I have more questions." She went on to explain that not only hadn't she found Pops' name, but she hadn't even discovered his birthdate.

"Sophia is here. She will know much more. She can talk to you. Come with me. I will show you to the conference room, then I will go get her."

"Merci beaucoup." Maybe Aiden had been wise after all. She was about to give up too fast. This would take time and would involve meeting just the right people. Sophia could be that person.

The three friends followed the docent down the hall, his rubber-soled shoes squeaking on the tiled floor that Caitlyn would duplicate in her own home someday, down another set of stairs hidden behind a door, and into a basement conference room with a large table, several upholstered chairs, and buzzing fluorescent lights.

Caitlyn plopped into one the chairs. She'd been on her feet for a couple of hours, and it was good to sit down.

The docent popped in after several minutes, three water bottles dripping with condensation in his hands. "Maybe you are thirsty. The weather is warm, no?"

"Merci." They each accepted a bottle, and Caitlyn downed hers in less than thirty seconds.

At least this room was cool. They could be grateful for small favors.

Elissa lifted her long, dark ponytail and cooled the back of her neck with the water bottle. "So, Caitlyn, how do you think you did on that last quiz?"

Caitlyn shrugged. "Okay, I guess." It would have been better to have Lindsey there, helping her to study. Only because of Lindsey had she managed to graduate with honors. Without her tutorials and flashcards and constant quizzing that really bothered Caitlyn at the time, she would have been somewhere in the middle of the class. "How about you?"

"It's all review of what we learned in school, so not too bad. At least I hope not. You know, as soon as you go thinking you've aced a test, that's when you fail."

"True. So you actually had community health in college?"

"Yep. You didn't?"

"It was offered, but I didn't take it." That was because it was offered the last semester of her senior year. When Lindsey wasn't there to help her. She'd only gotten to graduate by the graciousness of her professors who understood and made accommodations. Because she did well on her practicums, they passed her.

"Weren't you thinking about becoming a missionary nurse at the time? You said you had been planning this for a while."

A bitter retort, like an unswallowed pill, lay on the tip of her tongue. Thankfully, a young woman with straight, bobbed brown hair entered the room, and Caitlyn pushed the reply down her throat.

"Bonjour. I'm Sophia. Claude tells me you have some questions about someone who was born here." She pulled out the chair at the head of the table and sat, setting several manila folders in front of her.

"Oui. *Mon grandpère* was born here in 1942. At least, that's what I believe. I didn't see his name listed on the wall upstairs. The man at the desk said they only used last initials, but his first name wasn't there."

"That's correct. Madame Touissant changed both the first and last names of the children born here and of their mothers to protect them from the Vichy and Germans. You see, most of them were Jewish."

"That's what I understood." Caitlyn slid forward on the seat.

Sophia opened a folder and sorted through several papers. "Madame Touissant did everything she could to protect those children, absolutely everything. Sure, the Vichy and Germans had an inkling she was hiding Jews, but they couldn't prove it."

Aiden capped his water bottle. "And that was enough for them to leave the residents here alone?"

"Non, not really. Madame Touissant wasn't able to save everyone, but she was able to save some."

"But that doesn't explain mon grandpère's birthdate not being on the wall." Caitlyn clasped her hands in her lap.

"What is it?"

"November twentieth, 1942."

"Ça va. A few days before the Germans closed the hospital. Maybe they didn't have time to make a card."

"I suppose that's possible. He's positive he was here at some point."

"Even with how crazy it was then, trying to evacuate everyone, there should be a card for him. Madame Touissant kept very good records, and he would have been listed. I have some cards, so maybe that will help. Some of the residents took theirs after the war. And I have some of the real identification papers."

Caitlyn brightened. There was hope that they still might find proof that Pops was born here.

"You have seen all the exhibits?" Sophia straightened the papers.

"We have."

"Since you come all the way from America, or so Claude tells me, and since you believe your grandpère was born here, let me show you what others don't see."

"That would be fabulous." Caitlyn was the first one on her feet. "I'm excited to discover whatever I can. You never know where there might be a clue."

"That is very true." Clutching her folders, Sophia led the way from the room and up the stairs. "You wait here while I drop these in my office, and then I will show you around." She disappeared down the hall.

"See." Aiden leaned against the wall with his arms crossed. "You never know what nuggets we might find on this tour. And Sophia could prove valuable. She might know something that would help you and not even realize she possesses that information."

Once again, Aiden had a point. "I'm going to stay optimistic that she might be able to shed some light on Pops for me."

"Wouldn't it be cool if she had a picture of him?" Elissa dug in her backpack and pulled out a couple of granola bars. She handed one to Aiden and then Caitlyn.

"That would be nice. I don't have any photographs of him until after he came to America. His parents always told him that their pictures were destroyed in the war."

"That's so sad." Elissa crunched on her own bar then sipped her water. "Imagine losing everyone you know, every possession you have, and having to start over again in a new culture."

"That's so sad." The sweet and salty snack hit the spot after their long morning, and Caitlyn took another bite, chewing for a moment. "Unfortunately, that's nothing new," she said after she swallowed. "I took an international relations class in school that studied migration patterns. Over the centuries, millions have been forced out of their homes and have had to make lives elsewhere. Just think of the Arabic women coming to Spain and Southern France now because of how they're treated in their homelands."

On that sobering thought, they finished their bars just as Sophia returned from her office. *"Alors.* Let me show you around." She led the way upstairs to a door almost hidden in the wall on the second-floor landing.

"I didn't even see this when we were up here." Caitlyn stood beside Sophia.

"Most people miss it, but it was the most important room in the entire house." She pulled out a set of keys and unlocked the door then tugged a string to illuminate a bare light bulb. The closet-sized room was empty.

"I don't understand." Caitlyn frowned.

"This was a secret office where some of the women worked. It was probably here the mothers' and children's identities were changed. In the early 2000s, when the building was undergoing renovations, we discovered loose floorboards, and underneath, some papers and cards. This is where they hid the records."

"Do you mind if I take a look inside?"

"Of course not."

Caitlyn was the only one who entered. The room was so small that maybe one other person would have fit with her, but that was it. The musty odor tickled her nose, and she sneezed. "I can't imagine working in here all day."

"Someone who wasn't afraid of small spaces did it. And someone who believed in freedom. If they were discovered, the gendarmes would shoot them."

Caitlyn sucked in her breath. "Wow. I can't imagine." For several minutes, she stood in silence, in awe of the woman or women willing to risk their lives to save the lives of others.

Sophia broke the silence. "Je suis désolée, but I don't know your name."

"Caitlyn Laurent."

Sophia's mouth dropped open. "You said Laurent?"

"Oui."

"Oh my. Oh my. There is something I must show you."

CHAPTER TWENTY-ONE

Caitlyn's arms tingled at Sophia's announcement. Something about being a Laurent. Maybe she would get the answers she sought.

Or not. She worked to temper her expectations to avoid disappointment. Life was filled with them. If anyone knew that, it was her. She reined in her smile and nodded. "I'd love to see whatever you have to show me."

Sophia's green eyes shone. "Come, then."

They followed her back to her office. The top of the desk was littered with papers and folders and stray pens. Her computer screen was black. She opened a drawer in one of the several gray metal filing cabinets in the room and pulled out a number of papers then woke up her computer.

When she sat in her chair and rolled it to the desk, it creaked. With no other chairs in the room, Caitlyn, Aiden, and Elissa stood.

"Laurents are very famous here."

"Really?" This might be better than Caitlyn had anticipated.

"Did you see that small castle on your way here? I don't know which direction you came from."

"From Perpignan."

"Then from the train window about halfway between the two towns."

Elissa rocked back and forth. "I remember it. I took a class in medieval history in college, so it caught my attention as being very old."

"It is. The Laurents lived there for hundreds of years. Up until the second Great War. Aime Laurent, the head of the family and owner of the castle at the time, disappeared."

Like a Macy's parade balloon at the end of Thanksgiving Day,

Caitlyn deflated. "I've never heard of Aime. My grandpère is Steven, and his father was David."

"Hmm." Sophia tapped her nose. "Maybe if I look more, I'll come up with something. Maybe he was a cousin. I have studied the castle quite a bit, just interested in history and Aime disappearing during the war."

Aiden slid his hands into the pockets of his jeans. "We should visit the château. Maybe we could find out more there. It's very possible that you're related to someone who lived there at some point."

"But how can that be? My great-grandmother was Jewish."

Sophia glanced up from her computer. "She might have been, but if you are a Laurent, your great-grandfather wouldn't have been."

Caitlyn shrugged as a wave of exhaustion overtook her like a steaming locomotive. "Maybe we can see the castle another day. Why don't we go back to Perpignan, get something to eat, and regroup?"

"If you give me your information, I can call or text you with anything I might find."

Caitlyn scribbled the details on a piece of paper Sophia gave her. There was no way she'd find it in the mess on her desk, but at least she had it. She also put Sophia's information into her phone. Outside again, Caitlyn snapped a few more pictures of the building and the surrounding countryside before they headed toward the station.

Aiden and Elissa managed to get a good distance in front of her. The traffic on the road was picking up as it was time for people to head home from work for dinner.

A black car roared toward her at a high rate of speed. It was small, much like the car on that dreadful night.

And Caitlyn froze. She couldn't move a muscle. Darkness dropped over her like a blanket, and all she could make out were headlights. Just tiny dots on the horizon, but they got big so fast.

Her heart skipped several beats then raced like crazy. She couldn't breathe. Her ears buzzed and sweat broke out over the goose bumps covering her.

It was going to hit them. The car barreling in their direction was going to slam into them, and there was nothing Caitlyn could do about it. Her muscles refused the commands her brain sent to them.

All she could do was watch in horror, like a bystander. She should turn the wheel or step on the gas or the brake or something. But she was strapped in the passenger seat.

Then something hit her in the middle of the chest, and she tumbled down the embankment and came to rest on her back, staring into the sunny blue sky.

"What in the world were you doing?" Aiden sat beside her, picking grass from the knees of his jeans.

Her tongue couldn't form a single word. Instead, she shook from head to toe, silent sobs wracking her body.

A moment later, Aiden wrapped her in a hug and held her tight against himself. She couldn't stop the tremors that coursed through her.

"Shh, it's going to be okay. You're fine. You're fine."

The words, Aiden's, sounded as if he were speaking through an empty wrapping paper tube. They did nothing to halt the trembling.

For a long time, she sat on the side of the French highway, Aiden holding her, never letting go. At one point, a car stopped and the person inside spoke to Aiden, but the driver was soon on his way.

"Just take some deep breaths."

After a few minutes, she was able to do what he said.

"Good. Keep it up. In and out. In and out."

Several more minutes passed before her shaking stopped, and she managed to push herself out of Aiden's grasp. "Thanks. I don't know what came over me."

He raised an eyebrow as Elissa handed Caitlyn a water bottle. "If I hadn't pushed you out of the way, that car would have hit you. Why didn't you move?"

"I got scared and froze." That much was true.

"You couldn't jump out of the way?" Elissa pushed a strand of hair behind her ear.

Caitlyn shook her head.

"Are you okay? I didn't hurt you when I pushed you, did I?" Gone was the usual teasing glint in Aiden's eyes.

"No. I'm fine. Just let me drink a little more water, and we can go." She took several more gulps, and, with Aiden's assistance, came to her feet.

"Are you good?"

She nodded. "I probably just need to eat."

"Great. I'm starving." Elissa pulled out her phone and did a quick search. "There's a restaurant not too far into town that looks like it's open now. We can head there." She scrambled up the hill and turned in the direction of the village.

Aiden clasped Caitlyn by the hand and helped pull her to the roadway, but before they started their trek, he touched her cheek. "If you ever want to talk about it, I'm willing to listen. You just give me the word."

"Thanks, but I'm really fine."

"You're not, and I know it. But I won't push. I just wanted to offer."

Elissa had gone to take a shower, and Aiden sat on the balcony overlooking the Perpignan street, people coming and going, some by bus, some on bikes or on foot, and some in cars. Fresh out of the shower herself, her hair still wrapped in a towel, Caitlyn pulled out a chair at the tiny table across from him and sat.

"You look like you feel better."

She glanced at her old gray shorts and oversized blue hoodie. "I guess I do. Listen, thanks for what you did for me today. I really appreciate it, and I feel like I owe you an explanation."

He held up his hands. "None required. Like I told you, if you want to talk, I'm ready to listen. If not, no big deal."

"You don't think less of me because of it?"

He gazed at her. "Why would I? I've seen panic attacks before. My sister gets them, so they don't phase me. They're scary, but they have to be scarier for you than me."

"Yeah. I can't breathe or move. That's why I couldn't get out of the way of the car. I owe you my life, and to me, that's a pretty big deal." She tucked her legs underneath her.

"Someday when I'm locked in a tower, I'll let down my long, golden hair, and you can come rescue me. Then we'll be even."

Caitlyn couldn't help but smile and giggle a little bit. "How do you manage to do that?"

"Do what?"

"Cheer me up. Make me laugh, even when I'm upset or down."

"Just a gift, I guess. Mom says I've been a goofball from the very beginning, just like my dad, so I come by it honestly. To be fair, I really like to hear you laugh, so I try to do it as often as possible."

Heat rose in her face, and it probably didn't have anything to do with the warm shower she'd just had. "Thanks. I need to hang around you more."

"I hope so."

My, it was rather hot out here. "Yeah." She turned her attention to the few people who strode the street at this time of night, some stopping for kebabs at the Arabic restaurant across the street, some strolling and peering into the darkened shop windows.

"And I mean it, Caitlyn. Whenever you're ready, if you ever are, I'm a good listener. Whatever it is that has you panicking like you do, I can handle it. But no pressure."

"I appreciate it."

But if she couldn't even think about it, how could she ever talk about it?

CHAPTER TWENTY-TWO

22 August, 1955
Elne, France

The wind picks up and races through the cracked windows, producing a whistle. Though the noise might grate on others' nerves, it doesn't bother me. To me, it is the whistling of children, a chorus of loud screeches and puffed-out air. Oh, what a crazy, wonderful cacophony it was.

And how lovely that it echoes in this place, throughout the years, despite all that has happened.

I sit on the staircase's bottom step, the marble cool underneath my hands, even seeping through my wool skirt.

Echoes, echoes, so many echoes, in each and every room and up and down the halls. In a way, they haunt me. They won't leave me alone. That's why I'm here. To try to find some peace at last.

In another way, though, they comfort me, despite all my losses. So many. Too many to count. Only the Almighty knows how many. Even I have lost track. If those echoes go away, I will be left hollow, just a shell of the woman I once was.

I push away a strand of gray hair, another sign of the advancing years. Just as time has ravaged this place, leaving it crumbling and in disrepair, so too has time ravaged me. The storms of life have taken their toll, and it shows.

I shake my head. No use in getting morbid. Sentimentality serves no purpose. I rise and climb to the second-floor landing. The door remains, though scuffed and scarred. Age has darkened the brass, the patina not without its charms. I turn the handle, and the door gives way with a loud groan, an old lady protesting being disturbed.

Nothing remains inside. What had been here is gone. Looted, more than likely. The mustiness is strong as ever. Stronger, even, because the door hasn't been opened in years. The memories rush at me like a flash flood, and I slam the door shut to hold them inside.

For several minutes, I stand against the sturdy plastered wall until my heartbeat regains its normal, slow rhythm. Opening that door was a mistake. How much better to remember the light and love than the pain and heartache.

CHAPTER TWENTY-THREE

1 September, 1942
Elne, Vichy France

The harsh summer sun beat down on the dry, cracked ground so that sleeping was uncomfortable.

Even had the weather been cooler, she still wouldn't be able to sleep well. Because Noémie—Hélène—didn't know where Levi was. If he was alive or dead. Whenever Fräulein Reiter returned, bringing more pregnant mothers and children with her from Rivesaltes, Hélène pounced on her, begging for more information.

Fräulein Reiter's answer was always the same. "I don't know. I asked, but no one has seen him."

She feared he'd left on one of the transports to places unknown. How long until she had any information on his whereabouts? Until she could sleep through the night without rolling over on the narrow bed and reaching for her husband?

Long ago, her tears had abandoned her, the well of them dried. It was good that the store of them wasn't replenished. She could go about her daily tasks without having to stop and swipe away a stray tear or two. On the outside, at least, she could remain composed and keep working at her tasks.

The typing tied up several hours a week. Each time she completed a new identification card, she slipped the original into its hiding place. The gendarmes could raid them at any moment. Just because they were French didn't mean they would leave the residents here in peace.

Hélène would never forgive herself if any of the mothers or children were taken away because she had left papers lying about. So she was meticulous. It consumed time and filled her days. Absolved her of her guilt. Each paper she typed, each one she filed away in the hiding spot, was another one saved.

But it still wasn't enough. It would never be enough. No matter how many she helped save here, she couldn't bring back the others. Could never undo what she had done.

Or hadn't done.

When not locked in the storage room, she spent much of her time in the nursery, rocking the babies who were there without their mothers for one reason or another. She did her best not to dwell on why they were alone. Instead, she nestled them and sang to them and held them close to her chest.

Étienne, with his bright green eyes and his always-ready toothless grin, was one of her favorites. No wonder Eleanore also had a special place in her heart for this boy. In the not-too-distant future, Hélène's own child would coo and smile just like this one.

Today she stood on the wide stone balcony overlooking the grounds. Just below her, children ran about, throwing dried leaves at one other, shouting. Like children should.

Like they all should.

She rubbed her belly, now a visible bump beneath her clothing. In the evenings, she let out the seams on the few dresses she had. Soon Madame Touissant would have to loan her some larger dresses to accommodate the growing child.

Soft footsteps approached. She might not have even heard if the person hadn't stepped on a board that squeaked. She turned to find Madame Touissant exiting the doors onto the balcony, Étienne in her arms.

"It's a lovely afternoon."

"Oui. I'm glad it isn't quite as hot as it has been, though it's still plenty warm."

"Be thankful that you will enjoy most of your pregnancy in the coolness of the fall and winter. The women who spend the summer in their final months are the most miserable."

Hélène shrugged. "Children are a blessing no matter what time of year they come." New admittees had come today and left her stuck in the closet for quite some time. Fräulein Reiter took as many as she could, but not too often. The large turnover in guards at the camp helped. Before they could suspect what she was doing, they were transferred to other camps or to the front.

Hélène rubbed away a headache pounding at her temples. "How is everyone getting settled?"

"Fine. They'll adjust well. No lice this time, which is a blessing."

"That it is. Perhaps living conditions at Rivesaltes are improving."

Madame Touissant squeezed her shoulders. "I love that about you. You're an optimist. Do you ever get tired or discouraged?"

"All the time. Maybe I don't show it, but I do. And what a funny question coming from you. You're the one with the unflagging energy and the sunny disposition. Do you ever grow weary of the work?"

Madame Touissant sighed and jiggled Étienne as she stared at the blue sky. "If I'm honest, I do all the time." Then she returned her attention to the children's game in the yard, gesturing toward them. "But I keep going for them." She squeezed Étienne. "And for him. For all those who can't help themselves. For you and for your child. If I say that I love the Lord and that I care about others but sit in my comfortable, safe home in Switzerland, what good is that?"

Hélène nodded. But what she wouldn't give to be in a cozy home in Zurich or Geneva or anywhere in neutral Switzerland right now. "Maybe someday we will all be able to be in our homes, safe and protected."

"Someday, oui. When the Lord returns. Until then, Jesus said there would always be the poor and needy among us." She surveyed the scene for a moment more. "Did Fräulein Reiter bring any news of Levi?"

Hélène shook her head. "If she had, you would have heard about it."

She chuckled. "Of course. How silly of me." She leaned on the sturdy stone railing. "Watching and waiting is the hardest, isn't it? The not knowing about a loved one."

Hélène studied her friend, her fine features, her upturned nose, her square chin all in profile, dark against the now-dusky sky. "I often wonder if Levi is out there, watching the sun set as I am, or if his soul has taken flight to Sheol."

"I'll pray that Fräulein Reiter will bring word soon, that you will have the answers you crave, not only for yourself but also for your child."

Hélène swallowed the lump in her throat. "This little one deserves to know his father."

From inside came the whimpers of an infant, followed by humming, and then silence.

"They will come, won't they?"

Madame Touissant turned to her, her brow furrowed. "Who?"

"The gendarmes. They'll come to arrest us. Part of me is willing to go if it means being reunited with Levi."

"You have no guarantee of that." Madame Touissant gripped Hélène's upper arm and lowered her voice. "What you saw at Rivesaltes was just the tip of the iceberg compared to camps like Drancy and those in Poland and Austria. You don't want to go there. Levi wanted this for you. A chance to live."

"Are we living, or are we merely going through the motions of life?"

"Listen."

A chorus of children's voices floated on the gentle breeze, words indistinguishable but joyful. Above them, a flock of birds twittered, and the train whistle blew in the distance.

"What do you hear?"

"Life."

"Ah, a very good answer. And you're right. Life. It has its mountains, its valleys, and its plains, but it continues forward, ever forward. Sometimes it is good, sometimes it is wonderful, sometimes it is painful. All of it is a gift from God. We dare not take a single breath without acknowledging that He granted it to us. And when we are presented with the opportunity to live so that we might serve our families and others, we must grasp it with both hands and hang on to it, even through the gale."

"I'm trying. Sometimes, though, it's so difficult."

"What is right is not always easy."

How well she knew that.

From the corner of her eye, she caught sight of someone else approaching. A man, tall and broad-shouldered with a confident stride, his hair slicked back, not a strand out of place, and perfectly pressed clothes.

Madame Touissant smiled as he approached the balcony stairs. "Monsieur Laurent, how good to see you. It's been a while."

Sunshine broke out on the man's face. "I've been busy, you know." He climbed the steps then kissed Madame Touissant on both cheeks. "The work never ends."

"That's true. I was just taking a minute to enjoy some fresh air and listen to the birds and the children."

"Something we should all take time to do." He turned to Hélène. "I'm Aime Laurent."

She studied her feet, avoiding meeting his eyes. "No—Hélène Etu." "*Enchante.*"

Heat rose in her cheeks. Thankfully, Madame Touissant came to her rescue. "Madame Etu came to us from Rivesaltes."

Hélène snapped her gaze up. "Madame Touissant."

"Don't worry. We can trust Monsieur Laurent. Even if everyone else does, he will never betray us. He's been here since the beginning, since I came to establish this hospital to help Spanish refugees."

"Trust is a difficult commodity to come by these days, so I don't blame Madame Etu. I have to prove myself to her."

"My baby is coming in a few months." Why did she blurt that out? It was none of his business what her condition was.

"Congratulations." He left it at that, not pushing or questioning where her husband was. If he was familiar with Rivesaltes, he likely knew.

"Merci." She nodded to him. "Excuse-moi. I'm going to see if they need any help in the nursery." She turned to Madame Touissant. "Do you want me to take Étienne with me?"

She shook her head, and Hélène dashed from the porch and into the safety of the hospital.

Monsieur Laurent unsettled her, and there was no explanation for it.

Salomé wandered down the hall, her son in her arms, and stopped short of Hélène. "What's wrong?"

She touched her flaming cheeks. "I just met Monsieur Laurent."

"Oh, he's the nicest man. I'm surprised you're just meeting him now. Perhaps he's been away on business. Once you get to know him, you're going to like him."

"But I have a husband."

"Not like that. He's kind to all the women here."

"He's a womanizer?"

"Of course not." When her infant fussed, Salomé jiggled him. "He's just a good man, one who wants to help, who does whatever he can to protect us and to make sure we have everything we need."

"Oh." Hélène touched her chest where her heart pounded. "That was so stupid of me. I don't know what just came over me."

"Pregnancy, that's what. There were days I couldn't remember my first name."

"I understand that. Between carrying this child and everything that's happening in the world and to my family, sometimes adding another thing to think about is too much."

"I was going to take Paul outside for a little stroll and some fresh air. Why don't you join us?"

"I was just on the balcony. Right now, I'm in the mood for some baby snuggling."

"Enjoy, then. I'll see you at dinner."

They parted ways, and Hélène continued down the hall until she came to the large room that served as a nursery. Fine, gauze-like mosquito netting covered blanket-lined baskets that circled the room. Nurses moved between the makeshift cribs, picking up crying babies or sticking bottles in their mouths, propping them with blankets.

She entered and was drawn right away to a bright little boy with a head of dark hair. He alternated between sucking on his fingers and playing with his feet. "Bonjour, Jacques. *Comment vas-tu?*" As if he could tell her how he was.

He giggled for her, and she lifted him from his basket and snuggled him in her arms. "There we go. You're such a good boy that you don't get the attention the screaming babies do. How about you come and sit with me, and we'll play a little game?"

Jacques gurgled, which she took for his approval, and she found an empty rocker where she played peek-a-boo with him.

Salomé had informed her that Jacque's mother was taken back to

Rivesaltes just a few weeks after his birth. Though they did all they could to keep mothers and children together, they weren't always successful. And who knew what her fate might be? When all this was over, Jacques, if he survived, could well end up an orphan.

A pain shot through her chest. Who would take care of these children, the ones the Vichy and Germans were doing everything in their power to eliminate? And what if she got sent back to the camp? What would become of her child?

Jacques tugged at her hair and brought her back to the present. No use in worrying about something that may or may not happen. Madame Touissant had told her that fretting too much wasn't good for her baby. Instead, she focused on the child on her lap and continued the game with him.

All of a sudden, Salomé rushed into the room. "They're here! They're here!"

The nurses scrambled, picking up some of the youngest and most-obviously Jewish children and covering them with blankets.

"Who's here?" Hélène rocked Jacques, now crying because of the commotion.

"The gendarmes. It's a raid. Hashem, please don't take me away from my baby."

Hélène's entire body went numb so that she couldn't rock anymore. The cards she'd filled out had to protect them, right?

One thing was for sure. She had to find Margot and Beryl and make sure they weren't taken yet again.

CHAPTER TWENTY-FOUR

With her pulse pounding in her temples and her heart beating as fast as her feet across the floor, Hélène returned Jacques to his basket and the care of the nurses and sped from the room, praying that she wouldn't run into any gendarmes along the way.

She didn't. Instead, she encountered another one of the blue-clad nurses herding the older children inside. Some were only toddlers, thumbs in their mouths and tears in their eyes because they had to stop their games. Hélène scanned the stream of children but didn't see the two girls.

The nurse tugged along a reluctant three-year-old. "If you're looking for Marie and Beatrice, I'm not sure where they are. They said they had to come inside and use the restroom. That was not too long before the gendarmes showed up."

"I'll find them." Hélène could hide with them in the closet, with the door locked. That way, she'd also be able to safeguard the typed cards and identity papers, the ones with the women's and children's true names. She hurried toward the facilities on the ground level. The gendarmes weren't there.

The girls must have gone to the restrooms they used on the third floor where their dormitory was. Hélène was careful not to slip on the smooth steps but did take them two at a time and called for the girls when she knocked on the water closet's door. They didn't answer, and when she peeked inside, it was empty.

Where could they be?

Men's voices mixed with those of Madame Touissant and the other female staff members downstairs. The gendarmes were loud and harsh enough that, even though Hélène couldn't make out the words, there was no doubt they were upset and demanding something. Women? Children? Both?

She rubbed away a shiver and entered the room where the girls slept, keeping her footsteps light and her words soft. "Margot. Beryl." She used their true names so they would trust her. "Where are you? It's Madame Treves. I'm going to take care of you, but you have to come out so that I can."

Boots thumped on the stairs. The police were coming. If she didn't find the girls soon, they wouldn't be able to get to the closet in time. Already, it might be too late.

Silence, at least from the girls.

She was just about to leave and search a different room, when a small voice called. "Madame—"

Hélène dropped to her knees on the worn wood floor. Sure enough, the sisters huddled together underneath one of the beds, Margot's hand clamped around her sister's mouth.

"Come out, come out. I'm going to take care of you."

Margot shook her head. "They'll take us away, just like they did before. And we aren't going back to that awful camp."

"I'm not going to let that happen." Hélène's mouth was so dry, she had difficulty speaking. "But that's why you have to come with me, and you must come right away."

"I'm scared." Because Margot had released her grip, Beryl could speak at last.

"I know, but I won't let anything happen to you. Come now, come on. Allons-y." Hélène held out her hand, and Beryl reached for it. Margot crawled out by herself.

Though she longed to take the girls in her arms and comfort and calm them, there wasn't time. Instead, she nudged them forward. From her vantage point on the open stairwell, Hélène spied the gendarmes entering one of the dormitory rooms on the floor below. "Hurry, hurry. But be quiet."

The three of them flew down the steps, Hélène fumbling for the key in her dress pocket. She grasped it just as they arrived at the closet. The soldiers were still occupied in the room they had entered earlier. With her hands shaking the way they were, it took a few extra precious seconds to insert the key and turn the lock.

The girls entered the stuffy room, and Hélène followed, locking the door behind them. Now that they were tucked away, she drew the sisters to herself and hugged them tight. All three of them trembled.

She stroked their long, loose locks, soothing herself in the process. Beryl whimpered. "I'm scared of the dark."

"Shh. I'm here." Hélène clung to Beryl, who returned the tight embrace. She didn't dare say more. Any noise, any sound, might draw the attention of the gendarmes.

Though she dug her fingernails into her palms, her breathing came fast and furious. Surely they would hear even that noise and discover the closet. Margot buried her face in Hélène's dress and soon soaked the material with her tears.

Hélène bit her lip to keep it from trembling and to stave off her own weeping. At this point, it would do no good. For the sake of these two, she had to be strong and brave, even though her legs might as well have been made of pasta.

Ages might have passed as they crowded inside the too-warm closet, as still as statues and even quieter than mice. None of them even so much as squeaked.

Then boots clomped nearby, and the floorboards creaked underneath the men's weight.

No, no. They couldn't be discovered. She wouldn't allow them to take Margot and Beryl away yet again. As it was, the girls had already lost everything. Hélène wouldn't allow them to lose their security here or their lives.

Never again.

Her child fluttered within her, perhaps sensing her absolute fright. Still holding Margot and Beryl close to her, she didn't have a free hand to comfort her own little one. Instead, she rocked just a little bit from side to side and took as many deep breaths as she could. If she shook too much, she would only frighten the girls more.

The footsteps stopped outside the closet. "What's in here?"

Madame Touissant answered, her words calm and sure. "Nothing but mops and brooms, monsieur. At least that's what I believe is in there. I lost the key about two years ago and haven't been able to find it. I should get a locksmith here, but the war is making everything difficult. It was easier to buy more brooms and store them elsewhere."

Hélène bit the inside of her cheek. Would the gendarme believe Madame Touissant's story? While it might be a little farfetched, it also had the ring of truth to it, possibly because they did have to remove the cleaning supplies to make way for the desk and typewriter.

How had Madame Touissant even known they were in here? Maybe she didn't. In all likelihood, she wanted to keep the men as far away from the records as possible.

A bead of sweat raced down Hélène's spine.

"I want this door opened." The gendarme's voice was deep and commanding.

"As I explained, monsieur, the key is missing. I have no way to access this room. If you'll come along, I'm sure we can find a cup of tea for you to enjoy before you're on your way."

"Non. I don't want tea. I want to see in here."

While she had never been a woman to pray, she had prayed more in these past few weeks than ever, and now Hélène lifted more pleas heavenward. One plea for protection after another. Begging Hashem to save their lives, to blind the men's eyes, to make them go away and never come back.

A strangled cry came from Beryl. Hélène covered the girl's mouth. If the man heard, he would break down the door and take all three of them to Rivesaltes.

The poor girl had been through so much in her eight years, arrested and separated from her parents, shuttled from one safe house to another. She had to hang on for just a while more. Madame Touissant would convince him to leave. She had that way about her.

"Now!"

The man's shout startled all three of them, and Hélène bumped into the desk when she moved. Madame Touissant coughed, probably to cover up the sound. *Please, please, please.*

"What was that?" His voice deepened another step or two.

"I'm sorry, sir. Allergies."

"Not that, you imbecile. The sound from inside the closet. I demand you get that key immediately and get this room unlocked. Otherwise, I'll be forced to shoot it open." A gun cocked. "Now, what will it be?"

A bullet aimed at the doorknob would strike Beryl in the back. Hélène worked to reposition herself so she would take the shot, but she couldn't do it without bumping the desk again. The space was too small for the three of them to maneuver.

"Fine, fine, I'll do another search for the key. Let me think where I might have put it. I always kept it in the kitchen on a hook near the door with all the other keys. Perhaps it fell behind the stove. Would you be good enough to come with me and help me move it? I can't do it on my own."

"I'm not going anywhere." A tiger's roar would be softer than the gendarme's voice. "Go, go. And you'd better come back with it. I'm running out of patience."

"I'll try to hurry. Like I said, I may have to move the stove, and it's a big, heavy old thing."

"LaMarche, take the truck and get the others out of here. I'm ready to be finished. I think we have what we came for, but first I need access to this room. I won't allow anyone to keep me from seeing what I want to see. Who knows where they could be hiding their *Juifs.* I'll bring along any I find."

The tap of Madame Touissant's heels and the clomp of the soldier's boots faded away as they descended the stairs. How long would she be able to hold this one off? Eventually the man would get into the closet, one way or another.

Hélène's weak knees threatened to give out, but she had nowhere to lean. The girls must be getting tired too. A rivulet of sweat dripped its way down the side of her face.

What had become of her? Once the owner of a business, now hunted like a dog. All the money, all the prestige her family had worked so hard to earn got her nothing in the end. The Vichy and Nazis meant to strip everything from them until the Jews were no more.

They treated their dogs better than they treated women and children. Human beings who deserved a right to live, to work and laugh and play. Her unborn child deserved to take a breath of air, to feel the sunshine on his face, to see his parents' shining eyes. He or she was as worthy as any Aryan child.

Wasn't he?

Of course. They might steal every shred of dignity she ever had, but they would never take her humanity. Would never humiliate her so much that she would lose who she was.

"Well, did you find it?"

How much time had passed while Hélène was busy musing? Must have been quite a bit for Madame Touissant to be returning from the kitchen. She would have stalled as long as possible.

"Non, it wasn't there. As I told you, we scoured this place from top to bottom in search of it. But I beg you, please don't shoot at the door. You'll ruin it, and you'll frighten the babies. I don't think you want a slew of screaming infants."

"I have ways of taking care of them too." The man's breath must have been visible for how cold his words were.

"I will get a locksmith from town as soon as possible, and then I welcome you to investigate this room. You'll be disappointed to only find buckets and cleaners."

"I'm not leaving until I have seen the inside." He cocked his weapon once more.

Hélène did her best to cover Beryl's side with her arm. If the bullet had to first pass through Hélène, perhaps the damage to the girl wouldn't be as severe.

Hashem, hear me. Hear me. Protect us. Take care of us.

"I'm finished with your stalling tactics. Stand back, unless you want to be shot as well. That would be just as easy for me."

Then the retort of a gun rang in Hélène's ears.

CHAPTER TWENTY-FIVE

22 August, 1955
Elne, France

As I step away from the closet that once held most of the secrets of this place, a dark stain on the wood floor catches my eye. My breath whooshes from my lungs, and the sound of gunfire echoes in my mind.

I bend and brush my fingertips across the stain. My throat burns, and my eyes water. More tears. Will they ever stop?

The same, age-old question that plagued us in those days too. Will it ever stop? The pain, the hurt, the death. We saw so much of it, too much of it. Even the young ones weren't shielded from it, though we tried with all our might to protect them, to allow them to believe that the world was a good and happy place.

But some of them, surely, were left with the same scars we adults still bear. The nightmares that plague us, the memories that assail us and leave a trail of goose bumps along our arms.

With the back of my hand, I swipe away the moisture in my eyes. There were too many innocent victims then. None of us deserved what happened to us.

Then again, there were some who did receive the justice they deserved. I'm called to forgive and to remember the past no more, but that is fine to say. It's another thing to do. So, so hard to do. Impossible, really. How can I turn my mind off? The pictures of the past come unbidden. And I am helpless to shut them off.

Like how this stain came to be. An unnecessary shedding of blood.

All of it was unnecessary, commanded by a singular madman. I grasp my chest as a pain radiates from the center of it down my arms. Pain at all the loss, not only within these walls but also without.

Only with a series of deep breaths do I manage to ease the tightness.

The Almighty has His purposes, and His ways are unsearchable. Perhaps when I die, I will understand. Right now, I do not. There is no comprehending the suffering and death we experienced, even within this house, this bit of sanctuary. It was not always a place of safety or of rest.

I squeeze my eyes shut and push away the image of the bleeding body that once lay here.

Yes, there are many things I want to remember.

There are also many things I long to forget.

CHAPTER TWENTY-SIX

July 3, 2022
Perpignan, France

Caitlyn clutched her phone and pressed it to her ear as Mom spoke to her from the other side of the Atlantic.

"Honey, honey, just calm down. Take a deep breath."

Caitlyn struggled to comply with her mother's instructions. The incident today had been too close of a call, sending unwanted memories surging through her. "I, I, I'm trying." Her breath shuddered. "It's so hard."

"I know, sweetheart, I know. But it's going to be okay."

"How?" Nothing would ever be okay again.

"Time will pass, and you'll move on with your future. You can't stay stuck in the past forever. Nothing good ever comes of it. Yes, there are beautiful memories to be cherished, and those are what you should hang on to. But let the rest go. Give your burdens to God."

"It's not that simple."

Mom was silent for a moment. She was a sympathetic crier, so she likely had to compose herself. "Nothing about this is simple, and I can't even imagine what you're going through. If I could take this burden from you, I would. But I can't."

"I should have seen the car."

"You say that over and over, but that's not true. You weren't driving. It wasn't your responsibility. It wasn't even Lindsey's. It was the other driver's."

"How can I forgive him for what he did?"

"That's difficult. All I can say, and I know this sounds trite, is that God's ways are perfect and unsearchable. We may never know the reasons for what happened this side of heaven. But we trust. It's all we can do."

"How?" Why couldn't anyone give her any answers? Her pastor at home couldn't. Mom couldn't. Her professors and her counselor at school couldn't.

"You have to release the pain and give it over to God. That's all I can tell you. Pray, read the Bible, and allow God to work in your heart. Are you doing that?"

"I'm at missionary training. It's kind of compulsory." Caitlyn winced at the sarcasm in her own voice.

"Not for a school project or because it's expected of you, but because you want to. Remember that summer you broke your leg and had to spend most of it in a cast? You didn't think it would ever heal, but it did."

This was more than a broken leg, but she wasn't going to get any help from Mom. It wasn't that she didn't mean well or that she didn't try. There were no answers, really. "Okay, Mom."

"Do you promise to spend more time with the Lord and quiet yourself before Him?"

Caitlyn sighed. "Yes."

The pause was so long that she thought she'd lost the connection. Just as she was about to hang up, Mom cleared her throat. "I love you, sweetie. And if you need to come home, if you need to take more time to heal, that's all right. No one will blame you. Your mental health is what's most important right now."

"Thanks, Mom. I can't do that, but I appreciate it."

For a long while after they hung up, Caitlyn sat on her narrow, squeaky bed, staring out the window at the building across the street with multipaned French doors and small balconies enclosed by wrought iron railings. Used tissues littered the bed, a testament to the emotional call with Mom.

Mom, who only wanted to help, who loved Caitlyn and tried to do her best for her.

Mom, who didn't understand and never would.

A light knock sounded at the door. "Caitlyn, are you okay?"

Great. Aiden. The exact person she didn't want to see right now, not in her state with disheveled hair and red eyes. She swallowed hard and cleared her throat. "I'm fine." She kept her voice as light and happy as possible.

"Are you sure? I didn't mean to eavesdrop, and I didn't hear anything, but I thought I heard crying."

"I thought you didn't hear anything."

"I meant words."

"I'll be right out." With a single sweep of her arm, she deposited all the tissues in the trash can. She pulled out her makeup and dabbed a little under her eyes to erase the tear tracks then ran a brush through her hair. Not great, but enough to be passable for tired and not a wrung-out dishcloth.

Aiden was sitting in the office chair in the alcove right outside her room. She stepped backward. "I thought you weren't eavesdropping."

He held up his hand. "I promise I wasn't. I just came in and heard some noise from your room and was worried. No crime committed, I assure you. Are you okay?"

"Great." She threw in a smile for good measure.

He held up a bag. "Crepes. Both savory and sweet."

"Oh, count me in." Though how she'd manage to get any into her stomach and make them stay there was beyond her.

They made their way to the kitchen. "You don't have to pretend, you know."

She pulled several plates from the cabinet above the dorm-sized refrigerator. "Pretend about what?"

"That you're okay. That something isn't bothering you. There's no shame in showing your feelings."

"Ah. Well, I am showing feelings. Happiness at getting crepes to eat, in France no less. What more could I ask for?"

"Are you homesick?"

She gripped the plates for all she was worth and pursed her lips. At last, she managed to turn to him without the false grin but without tears either. "Remember that you promised not to push?"

He nodded, a half-smile playing with his lips.

"I appreciate your concern, I really do. It's nice of you. It's great to know there's someone looking out for me when I'm thousands of miles from home. But I'm okay. I had a good talk with my mother, and it's fine."

Aiden opened a drawer and pulled out a couple of forks then withdrew the containers from the bag. "I know a hint when I hear one. I won't push you, but remember that whenever you're ready to talk, I'll be here, ready to listen."

"That means a great deal to me, it really, truly does."

He gave her hand a squeeze then opened one of the containers. "Oh, these are the sweet ones." He went to close the lid, but she stopped him.

"No you don't. Life is short. Let's eat dessert first." She grabbed a fork and sliced off a piece. Nutella. Delicious. She allowed the sweet, chocolatey, nutty goodness to linger on her tongue. Just one bite, and her appetite returned with a vengeance. "That is the best. Nothing like having a crepe in France."

"Did I hear crepe?" Elissa emerged from the bathroom, a towel wrapped around her head.

Caitlyn held up her fork, another piece of the crepe stabbed on the end of it. "Nutella."

"Yes, please." She pulled up a stool to the small peninsula, grabbed one of the forks, and dug in.

As they moved through the dessert crepes to the savory ones filled with chicken and pesto, the conversation was light, and they bantered with each other. A little of the heaviness in Caitlyn's heart lifted. The flashback from the morning was nothing more than a temporary setback. If she powered through, she could make it.

Nothing would be easy, but she would make it.

She had promised Lindsey.

And she had promised Pops. "I wish we could go to the Laurent château on this trip. I, unfortunately, blew that opportunity."

Aiden shrugged. "I think we have time tomorrow before we have to catch the train. It shouldn't be too far of a walk, or we could hire a taxi to take us there. Too bad they don't have Ubers here."

Caitlyn raised her hand. "I vote for the taxi."

Elissa did the same. "Taxi for me."

"Okay, taxi it is then. Elissa, it would be good practice for your French if you called and got it here."

"Ugh." She chewed on her crepe for a minute. "Okay, but you have to help me write out what I'm going to say. And I'm going to have you both on speaker with me so that if I get something wrong, you can correct me. Since we don't have too long, we don't want to have to hunt down our driver."

"If you don't mind my not helping you, Elissa, I'm going to journal what we learned today before I forget. I want to keep this all straight in my head so I can accurately report it to Pops." Caitlyn slid from the stool. *"Merci pour les crêpes."*

"De rien." Aiden grabbed a sheet of paper and a pen from the counter and got to work on the script for Elissa.

Once inside the sanctuary of the bedroom, Caitlyn flopped on the bed and sighed. What a day. Her thoughts and emotions were all over the chart, and she was exhausted. She pulled the leather-bound journal from her backpack beside the bed and scribbled down the information they'd gleaned from the museum.

Maybe the Laurent angle would prove to be a dead end. Maybe she wouldn't be able to find any information on Pops or his family at all. She rolled over, stared at the white plastered ceiling, and sighed yet again. These days, she did enough of that. She had to think positively, focus on the good. That was what her counselor would tell her.

Well, the good was that they had more information than they did this morning. That was a plus. She understood the system. Another good was that they knew where the Laurents had lived. At least some of them. And they had the time, at least according to Aiden, to visit it tomorrow before their train took them back to Barcelona.

In addition, she'd had a good conversation with Mom. The one constant, steady presence in her life. Caitlyn really shouldn't have bit Mom's head off for just trying to help her, but Mom always understood and forgave her.

She picked up her phone and shot off a text, apologizing for her bad behavior. Not fifteen seconds later, three dots appeared, followed by Mom's reply.

Don't give it a second thought. I'm always here to help. That's my job as a mom. Take some time for yourself and don't pressure yourself too much. Healing will come. Lean on the Lord and on His promises. I love you so much and am so proud of you. I pray for you every day, all day.

The message warmed Caitlyn's heart and even bubbled a giggle from her chest. Mom was a little old school when it came to texting. Complete sentences. Every word spelled out. No emojis other than the occasional heart or smiley face.

Mom's face was the first one she'd seen when she'd awakened in the hospital after the accident. No matter how long she lived, she'd always carry that image in her brain, the look of concern and love spelled out in Mom's soft smile and teary eyes, Dad hovering over her shoulder.

After knocking, Elissa entered the room and plopped on the bed beside Caitlyn. "How are you doing after today's ordeal?"

By now, she should be used to such questions. She'd answered them about a thousand times since the accident. "Fine. Sorry to scare you. I don't know what came over me. Just a small panic attack, I guess. The shower helped. I feel a million times better now. And I talked to Mom while you were in the shower."

"That's good. I have to admit, I'm a little homesick. Wish I could call my mom, but she's probably too busy with Brynn's volleyball games. That's been her primary focus since Brynn made the league."

"I'm sorry about that. It must be such a bummer."

Elissa shrugged and pulled a long dark hair from her navy blue sweatshirt. "I've gotten used to it."

"Next time I FaceTime Mom, you can join the conversation. She's a pretty good listener, and I have it on good authority that she's emptied out her piggy bank to send a care package that should be waiting for us at school."

"Now you're talking. I love care packages." Elissa squeezed Caitlyn's shoulder.

"Thanks."

"Hey guys." By the volume of his voice, Aiden must be in the office right outside their door. "You have to come see what I found."

CHAPTER TWENTY-SEVEN

22 August, 1955
Elne, France

I am tired. So very, very tired. Being back here, walking among the memories, touching them, seeing them, has sapped my energy.

But I'm not ready to leave. I'm not ready to let them go, to open my hand and allow them to blow away on the wind. For now, for a little while longer, I need to have them with me.

For so long, I fought against these memories, fought against coming here and reliving every one of them. But it's time. Time to allow myself to walk backward and to reminisce.

There are so many though. All the time I was here. The remembrances can't be soaked up in a single swipe of the sponge.

So why am I resting? There are more rooms to explore, more walls whose stories I long to hear and then beg them to be silent forever.

I move across the hall, the floors creaking beneath my feet. Oh, how often in those days did little feet make these boards sing the music of life? How long have they been silent, not tread upon?

Silence. That was the worst. When the place fell into absolute silence. Not the contented silence of peaceful sleep but the uneasy silence of disaster hanging over our heads.

Too often it happened.

The room I wander into now contains the squeaks and squeals and cries of the youngest residents. Those without anyone else to care for them. The least of these. And my heart loved every one of them.

Within these walls are countless lullabies, the sounds soft and melodic and soothing, just as they were meant to be. I rock back and forth, caught up in those songs once more. Hushing colicky little ones, comforting those who were frightened and alone.

Too many of them.

And some born too soon.

Some who contracted illnesses.

Some who died.

I swipe away a tear that manages to escape from the corner of my eye. That shouldn't have happened. The cries and the giggles cut too short. Silence filling the empty spaces they left.

Silence that permeates my being and has me holding my hands over my ears to block it out.

I hug this wall, still cool and smooth, and allow myself to weep for all who were lost. Many of them. Even one was too many. They all deserved life. Deserved the chance to laugh and cry, to dance and sing, to love and lose.

They are still here though. Not physically or even spiritually, but just here in the memories held inside. In the secrets hidden within this place.

I weep until all my tears have dried, and I'm left more exhausted than when I entered the room. Yet, even in their silence, they deserve to be remembered. They may not have had much life, but they live on inside of me. Inside of others they touched in their short days here on earth.

This is part of why I came. To remember those the world may have forgotten.

CHAPTER TWENTY-EIGHT

1 September, 1942
Elne, France

Hélène's ears rang, and the odor of cordite and sulfur hung in the air. She couldn't breathe and had to bite her tongue to keep from crying out.

She stifled Beryl to keep her whimpers from drawing attention. Apparently, the gendarme wasn't above using his weapon. Madame Touissant had tried her best to protect them. Anytime now, a bullet would pierce the door and one of them would be hit.

Perhaps even die.

"Madame Touissant! Are you all right?"

Hélène released her breath. That voice was masculine. And one she recognized. Monsieur Laurent? He was here?

"I'm fine."

"He didn't hurt you?"

"Thanks to you, not at all."

"I couldn't allow him to get into that closet. It's a shame to have stained my floors, but I had no choice. And with the way you were stalling, I deduced there must be someone hiding in there."

"Oh my, oui." Her keys clanked, the lock rasped, and the door handle turned. Soon, a shaft of light reached into the darkness and drew out Hélène and the girls. The children all but fell into Madame Touissant's arms.

After a few minutes of blinking to adjust to the sudden flood of sunshine, Hélène stretched her arms and rubbed her belly where her unborn child fluttered. Still there. Still alive. Still well.

Margot and Beryl clung to Madame Touissant. "We were so scared, but Madame Trev—Etu kept us safe. She wouldn't let us cry and told us we would be okay." Margot's little voice was childlike and mature all at the same time.

"Then you ought to thank her."

And they charged at her, hugging her again, squeezing her hard. "Merci, merci."

"De rien. You're welcome. I would do anything for you. But we have to stop having to hide together, isn't that so? I'd rather play a different game with you."

The girls laughed a little bit before sobering.

Madame Touissant stood in such a way as to block their view of the bleeding body on the floor. "Go to the kitchen and find out what the cook has for you." The soft, spicy scent of turmeric drifted to Hélène's nose. Likely paella for dinner, without the shrimp or mussels. Where they were still getting spices like turmeric was beyond her.

The children descended the stairs, their steps slow and hesitant, as if they were old ladies. In a way, maybe they were. The war had aged them all, especially the young, who were forced to grow up far too fast. They had lost their innocence and their wide-eyed wonderment at all the world offered.

Monsieur Laurent stood to the side, and Hélène approached him. "I believe I have you to thank for my life."

"Think nothing of it."

"Is this truly your home?"

He nodded and chuckled. "After a fashion. The château on the hill is mine. Years ago, when Madame Touissant approached me about using this as a hospital, I purchased it and donated it to her organization. The gendarmes know what I do here, but my family has been in power in this area for hundreds of years. Right now, they don't dare cross me. One of these days, that will change."

"How are you managing to stay so calm?"

"Nothing but the Lord."

So Hashem gave him peace? She furrowed her brow and shook her head. "I'm not sure about you, but again, I thank you for saving my life and the lives of the girls. Without you, I don't know what would have become of us."

He motioned toward Madame Touissant. "She is more than capable of handling situations like this."

Did that mean she also had a weapon hidden somewhere?

"Right now, we have a bigger problem on our hands." He stared at the lifeless body of the gendarme. "We have to bury him and clean this up before they return to search for him."

"The first place they'll look is on the grounds. You have to take him away from here." Madame Touissant's face had lost all its color.

"Oui. Help me move him now, and tonight, I'll go to one of the olive groves outside of town and bury him."

Hélène stepped forward, careful to avoid the body. "And what are we to tell them when they come back? Where are we to say he's gone?"

For a long minute, Monsieur Laurent studied the ceiling. "That's an excellent question. Instead of burying him, perhaps I can stage it to appear as if he had an automobile accident."

"And the bullet hole in him?"

"It will be a fiery car crash."

"I think that's about all we can do. That and pray that the Lord will blind his colleagues' eyes." Madame Touissant bowed her head for a moment, but her hands trembled as she clasped them.

Monsieur Laurent turned to Hélène. "Take the rest of the children downstairs and give them their lunch. Madame Touissant and I will take the body to my vehicle."

Hélène went to gather the children but stopped at the top of the stairs and turned to him. "*Au revoir. Et merci beaucoup* once more. I would be dead if not for you."

"Non. God is the one who truly protected you. I was only His instrument. But I'm thankful neither you nor the girls came to harm."

Monsieur Laurent nodded at Hélène and turned toward Madame Touissant. "Let's take care of this."

Hélène heard no more as she gathered the children together on the first floor and sent them down another level to the basement where there was a large dining room with a table big enough to accommodate everyone. They didn't eat like kings, and flour was getting more difficult to procure, but they weren't starving like those in Rivesaltes.

A good fifteen minutes passed before all the mothers and the children who were old enough to eat had their noon meal in front of them. Once she finished passing out the food, Hélène swayed, and Salomé steadied her. "Let's get you in a chair with your feet up."

Katrine, one of the nurses, left her place at the table nearby and took a quick look at Hélène. "Can you bring some bread and water to us?" she asked Salomé. "Madame Etu is unwell."

Salomé clucked. "We all are after that visit. The worst yet. I have to take some bottles upstairs, and then I'll come back to get the bread."

"I can get it." Katrine headed in the direction of the kitchen.

A few moments later, she returned with a slice of buttered bread and a glass of water. "Merci." Hélène's voice shook. Perhaps she was going into shock.

Salomé returned and knelt beside Hélène. "How are you, really and truly?"

"I have to say that I was terribly nervous with the man right outside the door. Any bullet he shot would have pierced Beryl in the side. I did what I could to protect her, but in the end, it wouldn't have been enough." It was never enough.

"It was clever of you to lock yourself in the closet. That was quick thinking."

"But it has put Madame Touissant in an awful position. We can't leave the typewriter and papers in there. The closet must be full of mops and brooms the next time the gendarmes show up."

"You're right. We'll come up with a plan as soon as possible. Perhaps we'll have to move everything into her office and hide the papers elsewhere in case of another raid."

"Do they happen often?"

"More and more of late." A frown pulled down the corners of Salomé's mouth. "The Germans are putting increasing pressure on the Vichy to turn over the Jews at a faster pace. If the French want to stay in power, they have no choice but to do their master's bidding."

"What do you mean? They always have a choice. Always. There's always the choice to do right or wrong." Why had she said that? She was a fine one to talk. Her stomach clenched at her own hypocrisy.

Salomé nodded. "We know that. We understand that. They don't. To them, power means more than human life."

"Nothing is worth more than that." Her throat burned.

"Evil blinds them to such a truth. That's why it's evil."

Hélène leaned against the back of the chair, fatigue tugging at her, coaxing her to sink into her bed and sleep.

Salomé must have sensed this, for she helped Hélène to stand and led her up the stairs in the direction of her room. "Go and have a rest. It's been a long, trying day. For your child's sake, you can't let yourself get run down and sick."

They met Madame Touissant and another woman on the second floor working to scrub the blood from the worn boards. She glanced up when Hélène passed by. "Are you ill?"

"The implications of what almost happened are hitting me. I just need a nap."

Salomé held her by the elbow even as her lightheadedness increased. Madame Touissant dropped her scrub brush into the pail of water. "An excellent idea. I believe we may be going to Rivesaltes tomorrow for another delivery, so you will have more cards to type."

"Is that why Monsieur Laurent was here?"

"The less you know, the better off we all will be. Just believe me when I tell you that you can trust him. In fact, we depend on him, as he proved himself today."

Hélène nodded, too tired to say anything more.

"Go to my room and shut the door." Madame Touissant nodded in the direction of her private quarters. "It will be quieter in there, though I can't claim that the bed will be softer."

Hélène flashed Madame Touissant a small smile, and she and Salomé headed in the direction of Madame's room. So kind to allow her a quiet place to be alone and to sit with her thoughts. To sift through all that had happened.

It was the closest she'd come to returning to Rivesaltes as a prisoner. For her child's sake, she had to remain a free woman. That was the only way her baby would have a chance at life.

She clicked the door to Madame Touissant's room, shut it behind her, and moved deeper into the space. Oh, how quiet and peaceful it was. The children's voices and infants' cries were muted in here, almost like she was underwater. A moment to unwind. To let the balm of aloneness work in her soul.

She slipped off the oxfords Eleanore had given her from a charity box and settled on top of the cot, not so different than her own in the dormitory, the blanket soft but not as cozy as the one she'd left on the bed the night she and Levi had been arrested. After a bit of doing, she managed to find a position that was comfortable, and she allowed her eyelids to slide shut.

Each of her tense muscles relaxed, and the world around her slipped away.

The next thing she knew, she was back in their apartment in Mulhouse, in bed beside Levi. He snored just a little—not enough to disturb her. Instead, it was the music by which she slept each night.

In his sleep, he murmured, "Help me. Help me."

At least, that was what it sounded like. His voice was muffled, and his words weren't clear.

"Help me. Help me." Louder and stronger now.

But all around her was dark. She couldn't see him. Couldn't find him when she reached for him. "Levi. Levi!"

"Help! Don't let them take me! They took the others. Don't let them take me!"

"Levi! I won't. I'm coming. Just wait for me."

With a start, she woke up, bolting upright, her heart hammering against her ribs and her eardrums. She untangled herself from her sheets and hugged her legs as the nightmare faded.

"I'm coming, Levi. Wait for me."

CHAPTER TWENTY-NINE

7 September, 1942
Elne, Vichy France

Though the din of voices enveloped Hélène throughout breakfast, the croissant was like cotton in her mouth, and the awful coffee substitute did nothing to help wash it down. She couldn't eat, couldn't force it past her throat.

Salomé slid into the chair beside her, Paul on her hip as always. While she chewed on her first bite of her yeasty baguette, she studied Hélène. Not able to bear the scrutiny, Hélène turned her attention to the pastry in front of her, pulling apart the flaky layers.

"What's wrong?"

Hélène shook her head.

"You can tell me."

Another headshake.

"Come on. Let's go for a walk. It's not too warm this morning, and we can talk."

There was no point in arguing with Salomé. Sooner or later, she'd pull the story from Hélène, so she might as well get it over with. Maybe she'd feel better if she talked about it.

Salomé left Paul in the care of the nurses, and the pair met near the front door. The wind blew, though that was nothing new. The dried lawn crunched underneath their feet as they strolled, the grass brown from lack of rain. At least the sun was shining and bathed Hélène's face.

Salomé said nothing, but her presence calmed Hélène and brought a measure of serenity that had fled with the dream. The silence wrapped around her and slowed the thudding of her heart. At last, she was able to take a deep breath. "I had a dream."

They strolled a few more paces. "More like a nightmare. It was awful, and that's why I'm having a difficult time talking about it." Overhead, a bird twittered, its song joyful and upbeat.

"You can trust me. I want to help you if I can. We all have nightmares, so you aren't alone in that. All of us have been through so much."

And who knew how much more they had left to endure before the waking nightmare would end? "I dreamed about Levi. At first, it was wonderful. We were together and so very, very happy. It was like our life before the Nazis came. Peace. Joy. Everything you could want in a marriage."

"So you two are very much in love?"

"Very much. Oh we disagreed, much like any couple. He would like me to be a better cook, and I wish he would pick up his socks from the floor, but nothing big. He was kind and supportive of what I wanted to do. He was proud of how I ran the factory, though that all changed soon after the Germans invaded."

"That's wonderful that he was always there for you." Salomé sighed and stared into the distance for a moment.

When she returned her attention to Hélène, Hélène continued telling her about the dream. "Then it all changed. They came, just like they did in real life. They broke down the door and dragged my husband away. Though I tried so hard, there was nothing I could do to keep them from separating us. That's when I woke up."

"How awful. Like you were reliving the arrest all over again."

"It was so true to life. But the dream left me with such a bad feeling. Very different from our arrest. Like it meant something else, something more than a retelling of our story."

Salomé shook her head. "What do you mean?"

"Like they are going to take him away from me for good. That I will never see him again."

"You can't think that way. You know how superstitious we Jews can be. It will drive you mad. You'll go insane. It was only a bad dream."

"In a way, I already feel insane. This"—she swept her hand in an all-encompassing gesture—"isn't reality. It can't be. I must still be asleep, and this is a dream. I'll wake up beside Levi in our home, safe and warm beside him." The wind picked up.

Salomé nodded, her eyes shimmering with unshed tears. "I understand. All the time, I wish for this to go away. For life to go back to the way it was." She swiped at a bit of moisture that had escaped. "But we have to face what is in front of us. Life will never be what it once was. Much as we don't want it to be, this is our reality. This is true life. There is no getting away from it. Even when it's over, we will be forever changed."

Hélène nodded. "You're right. Life will never be what it once was. We will never be who we once were. All the things happening to us will transform our lives in some way or another. For good or for evil. Will we hate, or will we forgive?"

"And your answer to that question?"

Hélène resumed their stroll. "I don't have one. I can't say what's in front of us and how we will react to it, how it will affect us. All I know is that I already feel the changes. In my heart, love and hatred war with each other, and I don't know which will win."

"Just put the dream out of your mind. It's over. There's no use dwelling on what we can't change."

But all she could do was think about it. Couldn't get rid of those thoughts no matter how hard she tried to exterminate them. Hélène stooped to pick up a green leaf that stood out among all the brown ones littering the ground. As she examined it, the veins running through it, the bright color, her friend came and put an arm around her shoulders. "You're right, Salomé. Look at this leaf. When winter comes and takes its life from it, it will still bring beauty to the world. It has a purpose."

"Are you saying that's what we should be like?"

"Exactly. We don't know the number of our days, but what we do have, we must make them count."

She glanced at her expanding belly. "We are giving birth to a new generation, one that, if the heavens are gracious, will not know the pain and sorrow and torment that we do. And even here, in our conditions, we can continue to bring good and beauty to a place that is dark and ugly."

Salomé released her hold. "You ought to be a poet, *mon amie*. That is very well said."

"Merci for allowing me to talk to you about the nightmare, and merci for making me feel better. For putting things into perspective and seeing a different side to our circumstances."

"I don't think I did all that."

"You did. I'm glad I have a friend like you, especially in this unfriendly world."

A rumbling came from down the long gravel drive, around the bend and behind the tree so they couldn't see if it was more Vichy coming or someone else. In any case, they turned and hustled to the house. By the time they reached the front door, Hélène was out of breath and she was sweating.

Then the truck rounded the corner. Not Vichy, thank goodness. A delivery truck. Still, it was good to be wary of strangers, so she and Salomé slipped inside and started for the stairs as Madame Touissant came down, hunched over and coughing, not tall and elegant as usual.

"The rice truck." The director hacked, small lines radiating from her deep green eyes. "This is always a good day. And François is someone we can trust."

She understood the fear of unknown visitors, especially after yesterday.

"I saw him when I escaped Rivesaltes, but I haven't met him yet. I don't know how I've missed him all the times he's come."

Salomé took her by the arm. "Then I'll introduce you. It's good to make acquaintance with friends. You never know when you'll need them."

"Like Monsieur Laurent?" Hélène wiped the moisture from her hands onto her favorite blue-and-red polka-dotted dress.

"Exactly. We don't want too many to know what is going on behind closed doors, but those we do trust, you must know. Madame Touissant, you stay indoors and rest."

So Hélène and Salomé went to meet François. He was young, probably barely twenty years old, with a shock of white-blond hair, matching eyebrows, and blue eyes that would make anyone long for the sea.

Salomé made all the proper introductions before François returned to his truck to lug in the heavy sacks, his muscles straining under the long-sleeved shirt he wore. "This is such a happy day."

"Of course. It means we'll have plenty to eat for a good, long while." With the nightmare fading, Hélène's appetite returned.

"Oui, c'est vrai. So true. But it means more than that."

Hélène tipped her head.

Salomé lowered her voice "It's the opportunity to ferret more woman and children out of Rivesaltes."

"He's going there?"

"Right after he's finished here, or so Madame Touissant told me earlier. Though the rice is meant for us, sent by people in Switzerland for the women and children here, we only keep what we must and send the rest to the camp. As you have seen, they are in much greater need. That's how we've managed to keep so many alive there and how we've managed to get so many out."

Just how she'd escaped. "That's brilliant."

Salomé shrugged. "Madame Touissant put a great deal of thought, together with Fräulein Reiter, to come up with the scheme. From time to time, to keep the guards guessing, we whisk prisoners out using bicycles. Whichever way we choose, it's a delicate operation. Madame Touissant often goes herself." They returned to the house where Madame sat on a chair in the entryway.

"I'd like to go in your place. You're too sick." The idea sprang to Hélène's mind and leaped out of her lips before she had a chance to think it through.

Madame Touissant shook her head. "Out of the question."

Salomé tugged on her arm. "Have you gone crazy? You don't want to go back to that awful place. What if they catch you? Think about your baby."

"She's exactly right. It's lunacy, and I won't allow it." Madame Touissant tried to sit up straighter.

"I'll wear a loose dress."

"Your darker looks will give you away."

"Then I'll ride in the back."

"And take room from those we might possibly bring out? Non."

Hélène snapped her fingers. "I saw a blond wig in the storeroom as

I was moving items into the closet. At some point, you must have used it for a play or something." The older children and women were working on a production of Hamlet. Something to pass their days and provide entertainment to all.

Again, Madame Touissant shook her head. "What if something happened to you? Levi would be devastated at your loss and that of his child. Think of him. Besides, I'm usually the one to go with François. We have it down to a science."

"Just once, while you're ill. *S'il te plaît.* Just once for me to see if Levi is alive. To get the answers I desperately seek. And if he's there, to speak with him, to make sure he's doing well. To tell him I love him. Surely you've had someone in your life at some point that you've loved and lost. What would you give to touch them a final time? To express how much you care for them and the joy they brought your life?"

Madame Touissant's shoulders sagged, and her chin trembled. Hélène had hit a nerve with the usually stoic woman.

"I will wear the wig and not speak to anyone but Levi. I won't get out of the truck until François has found him. Two minutes. That's all I need with my husband. Two minutes. I'm begging you. I can see you understand. Don't deny me this chance. It might be my last one."

Madame Touissant heaved a sigh, her shoulders lifting and falling as she did so, and then she coughed. She turned to François, who had just come into the room from the pantry. "What do you think?"

"It's crazy. You must be out of your mind. But *ma mère* would be the same with *mon père*, and so would *ma grandmère* with *mon grandpère*. If you do exactly as I say, I'll take you."

Hélène's heart almost burst out of her chest, both from happiness and from fear.

To see Levi once more would be her greatest joy.

To discover that something had happened to him would devastate her.

CHAPTER THIRTY

22 August, 1955
Elne, France

As I make my way down the sweeping staircase, the marble railing cool beneath my fingers, I cannot control the memories that assault me on each step. At times, we lived in a fantasy world, one created by our own imaginations, to keep reality at bay. Other times, reality barged in and shattered our dreams.

Perhaps for a moment or two we could relax, could allow our guards to go down, could indulge in the forgetfulness of slumber, but that brief period would disappear like a cloud in the wind. A prey's rest is always interrupted by the hunter.

Cries echo throughout the now-barren rooms. Cries of women ripped from their security to face an uncertain future. Many of them never knew peace or comfort again. Cries of children who were snatched from their mothers' arms, also with an unsure future looming before them.

How I long to shut out the cries for a little while. They haunt me. They will forever haunt me. Whenever I think about this place, I will be reminded of them. Whenever I see tears or hear wails, I will remember.

Wouldn't forgetting be better? But forgetting would be to wipe their existence from the annals of history.

I sit on the bottom step, the chill of the stone seeping through my dress. Though years have passed, I can still picture each little face and hear each tiny voice. The innocent. Those who never asked for nor participated in the hatred that swept our land, our world.

It is to them that we owe the greatest debt. They deserve the greatest remembrance of all. Like chaff in a gale, they were swept away, helpless. All because of who they were.

How ugly the world could be.

But then there were acts of courage and resolve and determination. The best and most beautiful this earth could offer.

CHAPTER THIRTY-ONE

July 3, 2022
Perpignan, France

When Aiden announced he had found something, Caitlyn's heart took on a rhythm all its own. She flung the door open and rushed from her bedroom to find him ensconced in the large wicker chair in the tiny office area, his laptop open.

"What?" She leaned over for a better look. It was a website for a museum in a castle in a small town not far from Perpignan.

Aiden pointed to the screen. "See this?"

Elissa bent over for a better look. "Um, I'm catching a few things."

"See." Aiden flashed her his signature crooked grin. "Your French is already better."

"Maybe you should translate it for me so I'm extra sure I'm getting it right."

Caitlyn scanned the text. "It says that this museum in the fortress in Collioure has a section dedicated to the Holocaust and part of it focuses on the La Maternité de la Paix. Maybe they have more information there."

Caitlyn leaned forward more, almost cheek to cheek with Aiden now. "Okay, so the museum opens at ten. We have to catch our train at two, which doesn't give us much time."

Aiden set his computer on the wooden slab that served as a desk. "No time at all, unfortunately. There isn't a direct train from Collioure to Barcelona. We'd have to come back via Perpignan."

"Are you sure there's no way we can make it work?" Caitlyn picked up the laptop and studied the fortress's website and the train timetable Aiden had open in another tab.

He shook his head. "It's not too bad of a walk from the station to the museum but enough of one that it would give us thirty minutes there at the most. We can't miss that train to Barcelona. I have some flight time I have to get in next week."

"Too bad you couldn't have flown us here. Then we wouldn't have to be beholden to a train schedule." Not that he would have been able to get her on that plane. Caitlyn set the laptop down, and her shoulders sagged.

"Hey, look on the bright side." Elissa smoothed back her hair. "We can go see the château tomorrow and then come back another weekend to see the museum. I've heard that Collioure is a really beautiful village. Lots of French and Spanish people vacation there."

The days ticked away for Pops, but Aiden and Elissa were right. Even though they couldn't tour both sites before they had to leave, they could return. "Soon, though. It has to be soon. I don't want to lose the thread, because right now I have the end of it."

Aiden nodded. "That sounds like the most sensible plan. I don't know if I can accompany you lovely ladies back, because I'm really ramping up to take my final flight test in December. In about six months, I'll start getting flight assignments."

"Oh, that's so exciting." Elissa's eyes gleamed, even in the low light. "Will you take me up with you sometime? Wait, is it safe?"

Aiden laughed. "Perfectly safe, though I do recommend that you buckle up. You know, in case we do any loop the loops. They're my favorite maneuver. They don't call me Showboat for nothing. How about you, Caitlyn? Are you game?"

"I kind of have this thing about small planes." And small cars. "Big airliners are fine, but I don't know. I'll have to get back to you on that. Right now, I'm excited about going to the château tomorrow and looking forward to what we might discover."

The morning dawned clear and bright and warm as did most mornings in the Southwest region of France. The scent of baked goods hung in the air, and even frying meat from the Arabic restaurant across the street from their rental perfumed the breeze. Outside the window, birds chirped their good morning greetings to one other. The bus pulled to the stop with a hiss, loaded its passengers, and took off down the street.

As Caitlyn brushed her teeth, she caught a glance of herself in the mirror. Lindsey would hardly recognize her. In the past six months, she'd lost a good deal of weight. Mom had gotten on her case about it when they went shopping before she left for Spain.

She wasn't the same person on the inside, so why should she expect to be the same person on the outside? Losing a few pounds hadn't hurt her. Mom, however, would approve of all the French pastries she'd eaten in the past few days.

Just as she emerged from the bathroom, her hands loaded with her shampoo bottle and makeup bag, Aiden entered the apartment with a white paper sack. With any luck, he would have filled it with pain au chocolat. It was becoming her go-to breakfast.

She dropped her makeup bag on top of her backpack and went to relieve him of the carrier holding three normal-sized cups of coffee. The bus station down the road was the only place they'd discovered that didn't serve minuscule cups of joe that you could swallow in a single gulp.

"Just what I needed to wake me up. I sure am going to miss these treats you bring us every morning. How are we going to go back to the States and eat bacon and eggs for breakfast?"

"Who knows what you'll get in Africa."

Caitlyn shuddered. "Then I guess I'd better enjoy these while I can." She withdrew one from the bag and bit into it. "So good."

Aiden sipped his coffee. "I like that contented look you have on your face. Much better than yesterday."

Hopefully her cheeks weren't red. "Nothing more than a good night's sleep. It's tough to be away from home." Though not as tough as actually being there.

"Maybe your parents could visit. Mine are planning on coming when I graduate and get my post. I'll get to show them around and maybe give them a flight or two."

"Aren't you scared about the plane crashing? About having mechanical problems or something?"

Aiden shrugged. "My life is in God's hands. I've received good training, including what to do in emergencies. I'll be smart and won't fly when conditions aren't good. Other than that, I have to leave what happens up to Him. I can't live my life in fear of what might be. If I do, I'll miss out on what is."

How much easier that was to say than to do. At least she was trying. She had come here, hadn't she?

They chatted about what turns life would take for them in the upcoming months and what they had planned for their futures. "I'm not sure how long I'll stay on the field. I'll have to see what God has in store for me." Either she would love it, or she would fall to pieces.

"That's a wise approach. I've committed to four years, so I know I'm going to be here at least that long. But I'm really looking forward to meeting new people and seeing new cultures, experiencing new things. I'm excited for what the Lord has in store."

Caitlyn settled on the couch and pulled her legs underneath her. "Sometimes what He has planned for us is radically different than what we have in mind for our own lives."

"That's true, but it's what keeps life exciting."

. "I don't know if I'd characterize it like that." She sipped the creamy, sugar-sweetened brew. Just like she liked it. "*Scary* is a better word."

"Yeah, I suppose it can be. I guess that's where faith and trust come in."

"I guess."

Thirty-five minutes later, Elissa emerged from the bathroom, wearing mom jeans, the whitest tennis shoes, and a jean jacket over a white top. She'd even taken the time to curl her long dark hair.

Caitlyn shook her head. "You're going to have to learn how to do without some of those styling products and fashionable clothes when you're in Senegal."

"Ha ha. I plan on staying in the city. No roughing it for this girl."

Aiden handed her what had to be, by now, a lukewarm cup of coffee. "You do realize that even in the cities, electricity is often unreliable."

"Don't burst my bubble. Now, as for our plans for today. As soon as

I pack, we can be off."

Aiden glanced at his watch. "We'll help. We have to get moving or we won't have enough time to explore the château before we have to head back and catch the train."

While Elissa gathered all her products from the bathroom, Aiden and Caitlyn grabbed her clothes and threw them into her suitcase. When she came out to pack her stuff, Elissa gasped. "No, this won't do. I'm going to have to take it all out and start again."

Aiden grabbed the stuff from her hands, shoved it into her suitcase, and zipped it shut. "All done."

"But—"

"Nope. No arguments. We're leaving now, or we'll never get to see anything today."

"We could make two trips back here."

Caitlyn grabbed her by the arm and dragged her toward the door. "No dice. I'm leaving now, and both of you are coming with me." She peered out the window to the ground below. "Besides, our taxi is waiting. Let's go before he leaves."

"Well done, Elissa." Aiden slapped her on the back. "You managed to get him to show up at the right time and the right place."

She stuck her tongue out at him, and the three of them made their way to the street. Before long, they had ridden along the twisting, winding road, past overgrown olive groves and vineyards, and the taxi driver stopped in front of the crumbling building that had once been a grand home.

It was no longer a showstopper. Many of the windows were broken. The wooden front door was cracked and worn by weather and time.

Caitlyn shook her head. "I never expected it to look like this."

"But hey." Aiden pointed to some plants around the front door. "The garden is still well kept. See, there aren't any weeds among the flowers."

He was right. A wild assortment of roses bloomed red and white and yellow and brightened the dingy exterior without a weed among them. "That's really strange. I wonder what's going on. Someone is taking care of this."

She followed the flower beds around the side of the château and to the back of the house. Here, not only were there roses and the remnant of irises and deep purple salvias, there were herbs. A huge rosemary plant, its heady perfume filling the air, occupied one corner of the garden, surrounded by sage and other herbs. "Wow, this is something. I wonder if anyone is living here."

"We should have asked the driver." Elissa plopped on a white marble bench in the center of the garden.

"We still can. Maybe we aren't even supposed to be here if it's private property." Caitlyn turned to go find someone when she spied a small white cross in the middle of the flowers.

"You are likely some kind of relative of the people who used to live here, so I think we're fine. I can knock and see if anyone is home."

Caitlyn waved away Aiden's words. They weren't much more than a buzzing in her ear anyway. She went to where the cross was and knelt in the dirt in front of it. " 'Otto, Beloved Son. 1942.' I wonder what that means."

Aiden was soon at her side. "A child. During the war."

"Oh, that poor mother." She'd witnessed a mother's grief up close with Lindsey's mom. It was the worst kind. "I wonder whose son he was."

CHAPTER THIRTY-TWO

22 August, 1955
Elne, France

The memories, the stories contained within this house, were supposed to cheer me. That's why I came here, in part. To remember the good and dispel the ghosts that haunt me all these years later.

But that isn't how things are turning out. The good and the bad mingle together. Perhaps they aren't meant to ever be separated. How can you know happiness if you haven't known sorrow? The sweet is made all the sweeter in comparison to the bitter.

I leave the stair where I've been sitting and wander across the tiled floor, the colors in the flower pattern dulled with age. When my mind is dulled with age, will I then forget? But I don't want to throw it all away.

An unbidden sigh escapes my lips. In this open landing at the bottom of the stairs, a semicircular table still sits where it always has, now covered in years' worth of dust and grime. And on top of it, miraculously left untouched by time, is a cut-crystal vase. The light streaming from the glass dome above refracts off the sharp edges and sends rainbows across the floor and walls.

The Almighty's way of reminding His people of His goodness. Of His promises to continue sending spring and summer, winter and fall, until the end of the ages.

A remembrance that fills the sky and sometimes even the web-covered corners of an old house.

I touch the vase, almost able to smell the sweet, heady fragrance of the roses that Monsieur Laurent used to bring from the garden at his château. He had a young gardener, just a boy, really, who cared so lovingly for the flowers. After the boy lost his family, Monsieur Laurent brought him to live with him and gave him a purpose.

And Monsieur Laurent always brought a bouquet of roses each time he came, whenever they were blooming. Each rose, its petal so soft, its fragrance so heady, a promise of beauty in the midst of the worst kind of ugliness.

CHAPTER THIRTY-THREE

7 September, 1942
Elne, Vichy France

Before leaving for the trip to Rivesaltes, one she never dreamed she would be making again, at least not voluntarily, Hélène changed into a baggy muted gray dress and pinned her hair to ready it for the wig. Salomé followed her, dogging her steps. "What on earth do you think you're doing?"

"You know. You were there when I spoke to Madame Touissant. I'm going to see my husband."

"Why?"

Hélène spun to face her friend and fought to keep her mouth from falling open. "How can you ask such a question? I told you about the nightmare, about the terrible feeling I have for Levi. This might be the last chance I ever get to see him. Wouldn't you want to do the same if you had the choice? Wouldn't you want your husband to meet your son?"

"Not at the risk of all our lives."

"That's an exaggeration. I'm going to be very careful. Listen, I was in the camp for a few short weeks. The guards aren't going to remember me. Most of the women there aren't going to recall who I am. There's nothing to worry about."

"There's plenty to worry about. What is Levi's reaction going to be?"

"He'll be happy to see me." Wouldn't he? Wouldn't he want to touch her, to kiss her if possible, to see how much their unborn child had grown?

Then again, one of the last things he had told her was to take care of herself and the baby. Perhaps he would be angry that she had come. But what could she do? The rice needed to be delivered, and the women and children would be ready to make their escape. Waiting even a day or two might be the difference between life and death.

"Aren't you scared?" The cot creaked as Salomé sat on it.

The butterflies in her stomach weren't from the quickening of her child. "Of course I am. Who wouldn't be? If anyone suspects that I'm not Madame Touissant, I will put so many lives in jeopardy."

"François could go alone."

"He wouldn't be able to get the prisoners out."

"At some point, don't you think the guards are going to figure out that whenever Madame Touissant comes, women and children go missing?"

"Perhaps." That was a very real possibility. But that didn't mean they could stop the important work they were doing. "It's a chance Madame Touissant takes on a regular basis though."

"She doesn't have a child to think about. You do. If she puts her life on the line, it's only her. If you do, it's two lives at stake. You've gone crazy. Your pregnancy is making you insane, taking chances like this." Salomé's voice was almost pleading.

A few women entered the room. Bridgette, with her big-eyed infant daughter. Christine, without her two-year-old son, who was likely outside doing his best to elude the nurses. Giselle, her belly big and round. She'd give birth any day now.

Giselle approached Hélène. "We heard what you're going to do. Think this through, please. For your child's sake, if nothing else."

"And if I only think about myself and my child, what kind of person am I?" She'd done that once with devastating consequences. "There are so many who are suffering far worse than we are. They're living in deplorable conditions that may well kill them before the Vichy manage to ship them away. How can we sit here, enjoying our lives, relatively secure, while there are women and children—think about the young, innocent children—who are starving to death and dying of disease?"

Bridgette held on to her daughter so tight that the baby cried out. "And if you manage to get yourself and your child killed, all the risks Madame Touissant and Fräulein Reiter took in getting you out of the camp will have been in vain."

"And if I help more to escape, then their reward for saving me will be magnified."

"We're begging you not to do this." Salomé turned to the other women, who all added their assent.

"I need a minute to think about this. S'il vous plaît." Hélène ran from the room, down the flights of stairs, and out the front door, rounding the building until she came to the hill that sloped away from the maternity home, the last of the summer's grass brown and brittle and biting at her bare legs.

What was she doing? Was this nothing but a death wish? Non, she didn't want to die, not when she had so much to live for. Not when they all had so much to live for.

But her mind wandered back to Rivesaltes, that horrible, despicable place. A place of deep suffering. While the heat when she had been there had been brutal, the coming winter would be even more so unless they got supplies, which wasn't likely. Most of the internees had nothing but the clothes on their backs. They hadn't had room to pack heavy winter clothing in the small suitcases they had been allowed, especially when they had been instructed to also bring their own bedding.

She hadn't been able to fit in anything more than a summer blanket. The same for Levi. When winter arrived in full force, he would be so cold. It would be awful enough for a strong grown man. How much worse for the women and children?

No one should be forced to live under such inhumane conditions. Not even animals. The Germans wouldn't treat their dogs like this. Their cats sat on cushions in front of warm fires and were fed fine fish.

She remembered when she'd had a similar choice to make, one that had life and death consequences. Then she'd believed she'd chosen life, but her decision had only led to death. Almost all of her employees were dead, shot by the Gestapo. She and Levi had managed to escape the horror, had received a reprieve from the German's death sentence, but her employees had not. The raid on the factory happened so fast, they hadn't had time to neither run nor hide. Only because she was on an errand out of the building had she escaped the same fate. And what of their families? Were they still alive, or had they also been taken?

Out of desperation, fearing they would be arrested any minute, she and Levi had fled Mulhouse that very night.

Then, she had made the wrong choice, not sending them to England before the German invasion. She could have. She had all the means to make it happen, but she had begged them to stay and not abandon Papa's factory, to keep his dream alive. This time, she had to pick the right way. The way that would bring renewed hope and new life for those destined for death.

Her little one moved, and she cradled her small bump. One that was growing larger with each passing day. Levi would be so surprised to see how much she had changed. He would want to reach through the fence and touch the place where his child grew.

Is that why she was doing this? Was it to see Levi? Perhaps her motives weren't as pure as she had made them out to be to the other women. She had been taught to never be selfish but to always put others first. Maman and Papa had driven that into her head at a very early age. Sometimes their own table would be bare because they had given so much away to the poor in their community.

Her parents had brought her up to be strong and independent. To do what she could to take care of herself and of others. She did that when they died in the car crash and she assumed leadership of the glass factory. And that was just what she would do now. Though they had been gone for several years, if they could see what she was doing, they would be proud of her.

This was her battle. One way she could fight the forces that had beset them and work to free her people.

Even if it was only a few of them.

From this point on, she wouldn't turn to the right or the left. She wouldn't allow the other women to dissuade her from what she was being called to do. She could do no less.

After filling her lungs with the warm fall air, she climbed the hill and returned to the house and the room still filled with gabbing women. "Salomé, please help me put on this wig so my hair won't show underneath it."

"You're really going to do this?"

She nodded. "And I won't hear any more talk about the danger and the risk. I go into this knowing full well what might await me. But I also go in knowing that I can do no less than help those who are helpless."

The room fell silent, and Bridgette, Christine, and Giselle exited on quiet feet, until it was just Hélène and Salomé left. Her friend worked on her hair without saying a word, and the lack of conversation was fine with Hélène. Instead of running through different scenarios which all ended in a bad way, she focused on her baby. On what it would be like to hold him, to feed him, to sing to him. How he would be a joy and a blessing to both her and Levi.

Once Salomé had her hair pulled and pinned, she tugged the wig onto Hélène's head and tucked in the stray hairs. "Just don't bend over. I can't guarantee that it won't fall off if you do."

"Don't worry. I won't be foolish."

"This whole idea—"

"No more. I have to do this for Madame Touissant and Fräulein Reiter and for the hundreds of women and children still captive in Rivesaltes." And for those she had failed. "Respect my decision and support me. I'm afraid." She didn't realize it until just that moment when her hands shook.

Salomé hugged her from behind. "Regardless of my feelings, what I know is that you are very brave. Braver than any of us."

"You would all do the same if you were in my position. Don't pretend that you wouldn't."

"I couldn't. I'd probably break down crying as we were trying to get past the guards. It would all be too much. I'm so thankful I'm not a tall, graceful woman but that I'm short and rather round."

"You just gave birth to a baby. Don't be hard on yourself."

"I'm not. My mother was plump and so was my grandmother. It's how people know we belong to each other. To me, it's a badge of honor. I've carried a baby and given it life. I was never svelte, even in my younger days. This is who Ruben fell in love with and who he'll love until the end of his days."

"Well then, I'm glad that I'm tall and bear even a slight resemblance to Madame Touissant. Glad that my child isn't showing much."

"That's because of how you're carrying. And because you're so thin."

"It's my honor and privilege to be able to do this. To carry on my family legacy in some way or another. They would have never dreamed I'd be on this kind of mission, but it's what they would expect of me."

A knock came from the door. "Hélène, are you in there? I need to speak to you."

Hélène turned to Salomé and furrowed her forehead. "Is that Monsieur Laurent?"

"It sounds like him."

"I'll be right there." Hélène hugged her friend, just met yet already so dear.

"Be careful."

"I promise I will be."

Monsieur Laurent knocked again.

"I need to go."

"I wish I could say a blessing for you, but it doesn't look like he's in the mood for waiting."

"You can say it once I'm gone. I'll need it more then than I do now."

She adjusted the dark gray bow at her throat and stooped for a quick peek in the mirror to be sure the wig was still sitting right before opening the door.

He strode inside, and Salomé fled, mumbling something about having to feed her baby.

"What do you think you're doing?"

"Taking Madame Touissant's place. She's too sick to go to Rivesaltes, and François won't be able to get to the women and children to ferry them out of there. It has to be Madame Touissant, because she's the one with access to them. Besides, Fräulein Reiter will be expecting her."

"And she'll get over not seeing Madame Touissant. This is one time when François will make the rice delivery and not pick up anyone. There will be no escapes today."

Hélène attempted to duck around him, but he was too fast for her and grabbed her by the arm.

"See what I told you? No escapes."

"Let me go and do what I need to. We hear there is a woman who is close to giving birth and has been having a difficult pregnancy. She needs to be here. And there are several children who have lost both of their parents and need a safe place to come before the transports take them away. There are more and more leaving every day. Time is running out to help these people."

He softened his voice. "Don't do this. I'm concerned about you and about your unborn child."

"We'll be fine. There's no need to concern yourself on our behalf. Now, I ask that you let me go."

"Then I'll go with you."

CHAPTER THIRTY-FOUR

"What do you mean, you're coming with me?"

"I mean, I will take François' place."

"You're going to take François' place and come with me?" Hélène stood in the hall, almost nose to nose with Monsieur Laurent, sweating underneath the blond wig that was supposed to make her look like Madame Touissant, at least from a distance. "If François doesn't come as expected, it will only raise the guards' suspicions."

"Those are my conditions. Take them or leave them."

Leaving them would be her preference, but she bit her tongue to keep the words from slipping from past her lips. "And what will you do when the guards question where François is?"

"I've been told I have a silver tongue. I'll put it to good use. Now, which is it?"

"I suppose I don't have any choice, do I?" Or did she? There was still time to back out. But that wasn't how she'd been raised. Mère had always told her, when there is a need, you rise to the occasion and meet it.

"Non, you don't."

"Won't they think it strange that you, from your castle on the hill, would deign to deliver a truckload of rice to a bunch of bedraggled Jews in a camp?"

"I'm the master of the castle. I can do whatever I like. And I've decided that today, I'd like to be a truck driver. I'll tell them that, as my good deed, I gave François the day off."

Since there was no talking Monsieur Laurent out of his plan, Hélène shrugged. "Allons-y."

He held the door of both the hospital and the truck open for her, and she climbed inside. Their ride was silent until they reached the end of the lengthy gravel drive.

"How are you doing?"

She shifted in the uncomfortable seat, the springs in it needing replacing. "It's important to get those women who need medical care out of Rivesaltes. It's the worst place I've ever seen. No human should be subjected to anything like that. Especially not the innocent, be they man, woman, or child."

"I was there years ago, and I agree."

"Is that why you started the hospital?"

"I didn't. Madame Touissant was involved, along with the Swiss Aid Society. All I did was fund it. Even that wasn't much, because they raised most of the money themselves. However, the repairs to the building were more than they could afford, so I gave them money. It was the least I could do after they came from Zurich to help Spanish refugees in France. Only people who truly love the Lord would go to such lengths."

The truck bumped along the road a little farther, passing a farmer corralling a wandering cow, a stick in his hand and a straw hat on his head. "My parents were very generous with both their money and their time," Hélène said.

"They must be wonderful people."

"They were. They were killed in a car crash shortly before Levi and I got married."

"I'm sorry."

"What about your parents?"

"They were older when I was born, and so, like you, I'm also an orphan, I guess you could say. I was never supposed to inherit, as my father had an older brother and a nephew. Both died defending France. Now the castle and the land around it are my responsibility, and I want to manage it in a way that does good for others."

He turned left, onto a more main thoroughfare. They would be arriving at the camp in a few minutes. "I would like for people to like me and to think I'm a good person, though I do try to keep Jesus' words in mind."

"If you remember, I'm Jewish."

"So was Jesus. He talked about the righteous being those who do good deeds so naturally, so purely, they don't even realize they're doing good. Our righteousness comes from God, not from our works. Our works flow from our thankfulness to God for His salvation."

"Our good deeds are supposed to have such pure motives that we don't even know we are doing good?"

"Something like that. I think He meant that we do them automatically, without wondering about what others might think about us or say about us or about the awards or accolades that might come our way because of what we did."

The house where she'd grown up had been filled with citations her parents had received from governments and organizations for all the good they'd done. Framed photographs lined the walls of Père's office, showing him shaking hands with various officials as he handed them checks or cutting ribbons at hospital wards and schools named after him.

Of course, all of that was now gone. His deeds would be remembered no more. Those hospital wings and schools had been renamed something less Jewish and a lot more Gentile. "You're a good man, Monsieur Laurent. I'll try to remember what you said. I truly do want to help these people. Fräulein Reiter helped me. How can I not repay her?"

"I can't do anything more than agree with you wholeheartedly. And call me Aime. If we're going to go into the lion's den together, then I believe the time for formality is over."

"You're right. And you may call me Hélène."

"One day, will you tell me your real name?"

"Maybe. But today is not that day. It's safer for all of us if you don't know. And remember, right now I'm Madame Touissant."

"Got it." A wide grin spread across his thin but very handsome face. His features were fine, his nose long, his cheekbones high. Aristocratic, to be sure.

She had no more time to study him because they arrived at the gate to Rivesaltes. While she slunk down in her seat, covered her belly, and turned her face away from the guard, Aime rolled down his window to speak to him.

"Monsieur Laurent, what are you doing here?"

"I'm afraid François fell ill, so I offered to bring the rice delivery today. I couldn't leave Madame Touissant alone to lift those heavy bags and carry them to the warehouse."

"Of course not, though we could get some of the prisoners to assist."

"Not necessary. I'll take care of it while Madame Touissant checks with Fräulein Reiter to see if she needs anything." Aime rolled up his window and drove through the now-opened gate.

Getting in was easy. It was getting out that would be the trick.

Aime parked near the long, white concrete building that served as the warehouse. It was almost indistinguishable from the barracks. Only the open toilet buildings were any different.

And the way the wind blew today, the stench emanating from them was stomach-churning.

With his help, Hélène slid from the truck to the rocky ground, almost turning her ankle when she hit the dirt.

"Be careful. I don't want to have to carry you back here. I'll come to the women's block in a little while. Go ahead and meet with Fräulein Reiter."

She would do just that in a little while, but right now, she wandered toward the men's block, careful to skirt around the guards and to the back of the section. It was no different than the women's section. The same sterile buildings, the same awful stench of human waste and decay.

Thin men with sallow skin wandered around the yard as she approached the barbed-wire fence. "Hello?"

Several turned at her call. None of them were familiar.

"I'm searching for my husband, Levi Treves. Do any of you know him or where I might find him?"

The group of men approached her. The tallest of them appointed himself as spokesman. "If I were you, I'd keep my voice down."

"Do you know my husband? He's taller than any of you, and he has a scar on his chin from when he fell off his bicycle as a child." It was one of his most endearing features.

"What did you say his name was?"

"Levi Treves."

"And your name?"

"Noémie."

The one with the scraggly brown coat eyed her. "Oui, I know who you're talking about. Remember how he used to brag about having the prettiest wife? Said she was cultured and tall and was going to have a baby. That she'd gotten out of here."

A murmur of agreement went up between the men. "So you know him? Where is he? Can you get him for me so I can talk to him? I just want to see him for a little while."

"He was from Mulhouse, right? And worked in your father's glass factory. That's how the two of you met."

"That's him. S'il vous plaît, I would appreciate it if you would let him know I'm here."

The men shuffled their feet and studied the ground.

"What is it? What's wrong? There's something you aren't telling me." She worked to keep her voice calm. Steady and even. Maman was always unflappable. She was never nervous or upset or distracted.

Then again, her husband wasn't held in a prison camp. It was a good thing Maman and Papa weren't here. They wouldn't have survived long in Rivesaltes.

"Go get Fräulein Reiter. We'll wait for you here."

"Why would I need her? Just tell me what has happened to my husband."

"Not until she is here."

All three men crossed their arms over their chests. They wouldn't give out any information unless she was with Fräulein Reiter. Fine then. She would get her.

But she had to walk as if nothing was wrong, skirting the barracks and the guards so as not to be seen. Madame Touissant would never be in this area, speaking to the men. With each step, though, one truth drove deeper and deeper into her heart. The news about Levi wasn't good.

She came around the corner and passed Aime, who quirked a light brown eyebrow.

"I'm on my way to see Fräulein Reiter." She waved to him as if all was right. Locked her knees with each step to keep from collapsing onto the ground.

With the circle of children surrounding her, Fräulein Reiter wasn't hard to pick out of the crowd. As Hélène got closer, the children ran to her. "Madame Touissant. We've been waiting for you."

She motioned them away. As soon as they got too close or she was forced to speak to them, they would know she wasn't Madame Touissant and might well make enough of a ruckus to alert the guards.

"Go on, children. Find your tin cups, because dinner will be soon, and you don't want to miss it." Fräulein Reiter shooed them away with a wave.

That was enough to send the lot of them scurrying. Fräulein Reiter approached her, limping just a little. "Is that you, Noémie? Why are you dressed that way?" She kept her voice so quiet, Noémie had a difficult time making out her words.

"Madame Touissant is sick, and since everyone says I resemble her, I came so we would be able to get the women and children out who were scheduled to leave. Before we get to that, though, I need you to come with me. Apparently, there is news about Levi."

"I've been asking but haven't heard anything. This is good."

Hélène shook her head so hard that the wig slid a little. She straightened it. "The men won't tell me until I bring you. And I've had the worst feeling all day that something isn't right. That Levi is gone to a place where I'll never see him again."

"You mustn't believe in such superstitions. It could be good news. Perhaps he was freed or escaped."

"Then why wouldn't they tell me?"

"There's no use speculating until we hear what they have to say." Fräulein Reiter picked up the little book she'd been reading to the children and tucked it under her arm. "Let's go and find out."

They ambled together, Fräulein Reiter having to hold Hélène back every now and again from running ahead. Not that she was eager to hear bad news, but she had to know what the men had to say, whatever it was.

No one took much notice of them. It wasn't unusual for the two women to be seen together. When Madame Touissant returned from the camp, she often told Hélène about her visit with Fräulein Reiter and what information, if any, she had.

True to their word, the men still milled about near the fence. They came to it when she arrived. "We're here now. You can tell me whatever it is you must say. I'm prepared." She pressed on her stomach to keep it from jumping around, but she could do nothing to stop the palms of her hands from sweating.

Fräulein Reiter held her tight. She too expected this to be bad news. It was as if she anticipated that Hélène would faint. But she wouldn't. She'd be like Maman. Strong and stoic, no matter what happened. When her own mother, Hélène's grandmère, was diagnosed with cancer, Maman didn't cry. All she did was nod.

The tall man rubbed his pointy chin.

Fräulein Reiter took over and said what Hélène couldn't. "Tell us what you know about Monsieur Treves."

CHAPTER THIRTY-FIVE

22 August, 1955
Elne, France

I stand outside once more, overlooking the gravel driveway as the wind blows a stray strand of hair across my cheek. No matter how often I push it away, the wind will not be deterred.

During the war, there were so many who exhibited that determination. The Nazis and Vichy were not going to let anyone or anything stop them from expanding their territorial control and exterminating the Jews. What a blessing they weren't successful in either endeavor.

Then there were those who sought to do good and to help others. They refused to let anyone get in their way, even at great peril to themselves. Every time they took a breath, they were in danger of discovery by the occupiers.

Nevertheless, they undertook their jobs with little thought to themselves or to their well-being. They did what needed to be done. Because if they didn't, then who would?

It was down this very driveway that both help and harm came. Help when François drove his truck toward the house, either loaded with rice or, if he had been at Rivesaltes, with women and children. Either way, he carried precious cargo.

Even now, I hear the honking of his horn, a bright, happy sound, one that emptied the house of its occupants, all streaming toward him, eager to be fed or to greet a friend. He was one of those brave souls, ferrying food in and prisoners out. Almost as if he was thumbing his nose at the guards.

He had enough spunk that if he could have, he would.

I curve my lips into a smile. Oui, this is a much better memory, the kind I have come in search of.

I push away the pictures of other trucks that crunched the gravel underneath their tires. No happy tooting of horns with them.

Non, I cannot allow my thoughts to linger there. I cannot remember the faces peering from the back, eyes wide, the fear palpable in the air.

Unfortunately, those trucks came all too often.

CHAPTER THIRTY-SIX

July 4, 2022
Elne, France

*P*uis-je vous aider?"
The old man's voice asking if he could help them startled Caitlyn, and she toppled backward from her squat onto her backside, landing on a rose thorn.

Aiden stepped in. "Oui. This woman's name is Caitlyn Laurent."

By this time, Caitlyn had come to her feet and turned to the man whose face the sun had dried and wrinkled. Though not tall, he wasn't stooped a bit. And at Aiden's pronouncement, his clear blue eyes widened. "Laurent? Is it really?"

"My grandfather is Steven Laurent, born at the La Maternité de la Paix, and my great-grandfather was David Laurent. He came to the United States right after the war. Did you know him?"

The elderly man shook his head. "The only Laurent who was here then was Aime. I worked for him during the war."

The air around Caitlyn buzzed. "What can you tell me about him?"

"Oh, what a wonderful man he was. When my father, who was his gardener, went to fight the Nazi invasion up north and was never heard of again, Monsieur Laurent hired me and paid me the same salary. Because of him, I was able to care for my mother and my two younger sisters."

Caitlyn touched her chest. "Wow. He sounds like he was a wonderful man."

"He was a very good man. Kind and caring and always thought

of others above himself."

"But you didn't know David Laurent?"

When he shook his head, her stomach dropped. After a moment, she pointed to the cross she'd been squatting in front of. "Who is this?"

"Je ne sais pas. I wish I did know. Monsieur Laurent sent me on an errand for him in 1942. When I returned, he had disappeared. I don't know if he left of his own free will, or if he was arrested. This grave was here when I came back. Much to my great sorrow, Monsieur Laurent never visited his home again, not that I knew of. No one has lived here since that day."

"Does this château still belong to the Laurent family?"

"It has never been sold, so as far as I know, it does. But that is a legal matter, and one I'm not familiar with. All I know is that I continue to care for the gardens the best I can, and a check from a French bank comes to me each month as it has for eighty years. Somehow, I believe Aime managed to continue to make provision for me all this time."

"How old are you?"

Caitlyn elbowed Elissa in the ribs for asking such a question. The man chuckled. "Ninety-two. Just twelve when I came into Aime Laurent's employ."

"Did you know David's wife, Hélène Laurent?"

"Non. I have never heard of a woman by that name."

Caitlyn pulled a leaf from the hem of her shirt. "She was, apparently, at La Maternité de la Paix, and that's where their son was born."

"I worked here, so I didn't know the women from the hospital."

Aiden turned to her. "We don't have much more time. We have to get back and catch our train."

Caitlyn nodded. "Can I give you my phone number, and you can text me if you remember anything else? Can I text you if I have more questions?"

"Oh, I don't know about that new technology. It would have to be my granddaughter who would take care of that."

"I don't have a piece of paper."

After a few seconds of rummaging in her crossbody bag, Elissa came up with one and a pen. Caitlyn wrote out her name and number and handed it to the old man. "I didn't catch your name."

"Georges Blanc."

"It's been very nice to meet you, Monsieur Blanc. Please, have your granddaughter get in touch with me." There was still a chance her great-grandfather had been a cousin or somehow related to Aime Laurent.

He took the paper, his age-spotted hand trembling. "Enchanté. Let's hope I remember to give it to her."

Caitlyn had the same wish.

The train returning to Barcelona was filled to capacity as they made their way back to the city. Even though it had departed the Perpignan station already, Aiden was still searching for a spot in which to jam Elissa's big bag. The luggage racks were full. Since they were blocking the steps into the car, Caitlyn had gone to sit down.

She stared out the window as the train picked up speed. Scruffy trees whipped past the window along with the occasional glimpse of a cluster of houses and even a château.

Had the trip been worth it? She didn't have the answer to that question. She'd been so confident that she'd return to school with all the details about Pops' past. Instead, she didn't have a single one. She'd sent Mom a few pictures of the maternity home with an explanation of what they'd discovered.

At last, Aiden and Elissa showed up and plopped into the seats beside Caitlyn. Elissa blew out a breath and smoothed back a wild lock of hair. "That was crazy. There wasn't anywhere to put my luggage. Aiden had to rearrange everything so it would fit." She turned to him. "Maybe instead of being a pilot, you should be a baggage handler."

"No, thank you. That was enough. Next time, you aren't allowed to bring more than a backpack. Caitlyn will have to teach you how to pack."

"Ugh. I can't imagine going without my blow dryer and curling iron and all my makeup and extra clothes and—"

"Good enough. I'll show you how to make it work. And you can go with straight hair for a few days. It won't kill you."

Elissa sat back in the seat and closed her eyes. "It might. It just might."

Aiden glanced at the ceiling and shook his head. Caitlyn suppressed a grin.

Her phone dinged with a text message. Mom. She tapped to open it.

I SHOWED POPS THE PICTURE OF THE MATERNITY HOUSE. HE SAID IT LOOKED KIND OF FAMILIAR TO HIM AND THAT MAYBE THEY VISITED IT WHEN THEY WENT TO FRANCE. IT MADE HIM HAPPY. HAVE A SAFE TRIP. LOVE YOU!

Well, that was something. Maybe the photo of the château that she had sent would also trigger a memory. Perhaps they were on to something after all.

"Who was that?" Aiden leaned over his knees while Elissa snored beside him.

"Mom. Pops seems to remember the maternity hospital. He and his parents did visit the country when he was young."

"That's great. They wouldn't have gone to the hospital if it wasn't important somehow. If he was young, it was still in a state of disrepair at that time. They didn't start renovations here until the '90s."

"That's a good point. I also sent a picture of the Laurent place, so we'll see if he remembers it. Maybe deep inside his brain, he knows who Otto was. Perhaps his parents talked about the child."

"I didn't say anything at the time, and we've been busy since then, but do you think it's possible that Otto was your grandfather's brother?"

"Hmm, I didn't think of that, but I suppose it's possible. They would have had to be twins. If that's the case, though, why does Pops insist that he was born in the maternity hospital? Wouldn't he have been born at the Laurent home? Not much of this is making sense."

He rubbed the top of her hand. "Maybe the pieces will fall into place when you least expect it. If you think too hard about it, the answer might continue to elude you."

She shrugged. "Could be."

"We'll find another weekend to explore the fortress with the other museum and wait to see if Sophia finds something for us, but in the meantime, just let it simmer. And maybe your grandpa will think of something."

"That's good advice. Thanks."

She spent the rest of the trip snoozing off and on, and before she knew it, they had arrived at the Sants station, had hopped on the Metro, and were back at school.

She threw her backpack on her bed and lay down beside it. Elissa set right to work unpacking all of her belongings—all of her many belongings—and placing them into drawers with the greatest of care. "So, how do you think the weekend went?"

"Fine. It was nice to get out of the city and do a little exploring. Too bad we didn't find more information on my family, but Aiden said to just ruminate on it for a while and maybe I'll get my answers."

Elissa shut the drawer and turned to Caitlyn, a gleam in her eyes. "You know, I think he likes you."

At this, Caitlyn bolted upright. "Likes me likes me? I mean, I think he's been flirting with me, but I wasn't sure."

"Duh. I don't know how you could miss it. He's so attentive to you—"

"He helped you with your luggage today."

"—and he's always nice to you and wants to be near you. He told me how concerned he was for you after the incident on the road."

Caitlyn wasn't about to go there. "He was just being friendly, that's all. A little chivalrous. He is going to be a missionary pilot, you know."

"Oh, it's more than that. Just the way he talks about you when you aren't in the room."

"He talks about me?"

"Sure, and why not? You're a great person, and he's awfully cute and very caring, especially for a guy."

"You're sure about this?"

"Absolutely."

"It's just that I don't want to lead him on. I like him. You're right, he's a fabulous guy, but I'm not at the point in my life where I'm ready for a relationship. And who knows if we'll get posted to the same place or not."

"For pity's sake, he has a plane." Elissa widened her eyes.

"True."

Elissa shoved Caitlyn's backpack to the side and sat beside her on the bed. "What is this really about? Why aren't you ready for a relationship?"

Caitlyn stared out the window, a view of other plain but pastel-painted buildings all she could see. From down below came the noise of voices as people were out shopping or on their way to dinner. "I've seen loss up close and personal." She sipped from her water bottle to soothe the burning in her throat. "Right now, I can't deal with any more."

"Does this have anything to do with what happened on the road?"

Thankfully, just at that precise moment, her stomach churned, a rumbling noise. Elissa laughed. "You're hungry, and so am I. We missed lunch earlier. Let's go get some tapas. Sound good to you?"

"Perfect." It had gotten her out of having to answer Elissa's question, and because the plates were small, she wouldn't have to eat very much. Elissa was tiny, but she could pack away the food.

Because the area where they lived was young, lively, and vibrant, they didn't have far to go until they found a restaurant with just what they wanted. In no time, they were seated at a table along the sidewalk, combing the menu for just the right dishes to make up dinner.

"Well, hello, ladies. Imagine finding you here."

Caitlyn glanced up from the laminated menu right into Aiden's very blue eyes. If Elissa hadn't mentioned anything about him liking her, she would have thought their meeting nothing other than a happy coincidence. Now, she had to wonder if he was following her. Not in a creepy way, but still. . .

"Mind if we join you?"

"Of course not." Elissa motioned to the two empty chairs, one beside Caitlyn and one beside her. Of course, Aiden grabbed the one to her right. His friend, Brock, sat across from him.

The waitress brought out two glasses of water and two more menus. Aiden tossed his aside and leaned on the table. Caitlyn could hear Mom sing-songing, "Aiden, Aiden, strong and able, get your elbows off the table." She couldn't suppress a giggle.

"What? Am I that funny?"

She shook her head. "Nothing. It's an inside Laurent joke. Maybe I'll tell you someday." Goodness, was she flirting with him?

"Okay. Whatever. I'm glad we bumped into you. I was telling Brock about our trip and the museum in Collioure. He and a few friends went there a couple of weeks ago."

Brock didn't spare a glance from his menu. "Yeah, it was really cool. That's a neat town, really colorful and fun with plenty to see. When we toured the fortress, we weren't expecting a museum, and especially not one dedicated to Camp de Rivesaltes, but there it was."

"Oh."

The waitress came and took their orders then scurried away to care for other patrons.

As soon as she was gone, Caitlyn scooted her chair in closer to the table and directed her attention at Brock. "I thought the museum at the fortress was about La Maternité de la Paix."

"Mostly it's about the camp, what it was used for from the 1930s until the 1960s when it permanently closed. You should really see it the next time you're in the area. It's haunting and fascinating all at the same time."

"Like what?"

"Like, did you know that people escaped from there, especially women? Friedel Reiter, a Swiss Christian who lived and worked in the camp, and Eleanore Touissant, who ran the hospital, worked to get out pregnant mothers and children."

Caitlyn nodded. "I do remember reading something about that. They hid them in the trucks the food shipments came in."

"That's right. It was very risky, but they managed to pull it off a number of times."

"I wonder if they ever got caught."

Brock shrugged. "I don't remember reading anything about that. I think some rich guy who owned a castle sometimes helped."

Caitlyn froze. "Was his name Laurent?"

Brock's mouth fell open, though he quickly shut it. "Isn't that you?"

"Yes. I might be related to the guy who used to own it. Just a hunch."

"Wow. I didn't know you were loaded."

Aiden shot his friend an icy glance. "That's rude."

Caitlyn stirred the water in her glass with her straw. "And I'm not. For whatever reason, my great-grandfather wasn't as rich as the man who owned the château."

The waitress brought them their croquettes and their empanadas.

Brock filled his plate. "You might want to visit Rivesaltes and see what they have to say. But the museum at the fortress does have some stuff about the hospital."

"Tell them what it has." Aiden unwrapped his fork from the paper napkin and waved it in Brock's direction.

"Well, Aiden mentioned the cards they had at the hospital, and I know I saw some of those at the museum. Just a couple, but I distinctly remember them. It was cool how they forged identities to keep the kids safe while preserving who they really were. I only wish I had taken pictures of the ones in the display."

Elissa tossed her ponytail over her shoulder. "If you had, we wouldn't have had an excuse to go to Collioure. Now I can't wait to explore it."

A little bubble rose in Caitlyn's chest. Could it be happiness? Looking forward to something? Mom was right. It was best that she stay here. She picked up her phone and opened the calendar app. "Maybe we could go next month? We could leave at noon on a Friday and come back on Sunday. It's not a lot of time, so we'll have to cram in what we can."

Everyone agreed to it, so Caitlyn found a nice short-term rental and booked it. Brock passed his phone to her. "Here are some pictures I took at the museum. Maybe you'll find something in there that interests you. I didn't snap many, but there are a few."

She scrolled through them. The museum wasn't large, but they had a good number of displays and a few items. And then her sight snagged on a picture of a château. "This is the Laurent place." She held out the phone for Aiden and Elissa to see.

"Sure enough." Aiden took the phone from her. "Let me see if I can make it bigger." He enlarged it and squinted. "I can just make out the placard. 'Le Château Laurent, Elne, Photo from 1942.' Wow."

Caitlyn's heart beat just a little faster. She worked to draw in enough air to speak. "Wow is right. That year matches with the year on the grave. So it must have been an important one for some reason. I need to learn more about my great-grandfather."

Aiden handed the phone back to Brock. "AirDrop that to both me and Caitlyn. This is great information, though I'm not sure it gets us too much closer to finding out more about her family."

Her phone chimed as the picture came through. It might not have anything to do with Pops, but she had to find out if she was related in any way to this mysterious Laurent.

CHAPTER THIRTY-SEVEN

August 4, 2022
Barcelona, Spain

Caitlyn sat pretzel-style on her bed, her community health textbook open in front of her, desperately trying to commit the information inside to memory. It wasn't working. Instead of seeing the words about the kinds of diseases that spread in tropical climates, her mind played images of the maternity hospital interspersed with ones of the sterile white lights above her bruised and cut-up body.

Instead of seeing the little children and frightened mothers she could help with her knowledge, she saw the bright headlights heading straight for them.

She liked Elissa. While they were very different in many ways, they were also very similar. In years to come, they would remain good friends, no matter where their paths in life took them.

But she wasn't Lindsey.

It was Lindsey who should be in this apartment in Barcelona, exclaiming over the churros and hot chocolate they enjoyed for breakfast or the narrow streets of the Gothic Quarter filled with quaint shops and amazing restaurants. She should be the one beside Caitlyn as they visited the market every week for fresh vegetables and meats, spices and empanadas.

She flopped back in the bed and covered her head with her pillow, pressing hard to block all the images from her brain, all the memories from her heart. *God, take this away. Take it all away. I can't go on like this.*

WHAT I PROMISE YOU

At some point in the never-ending prayer, she must have fallen asleep, because a knock at her bedroom door woke her to a room not quite as filled with sunlight. "Just a minute." She flicked on the nightstand lamp and crawled from bed. While she made her way to the door, she finger-combed her hair and retied it in a ponytail.

"Hey." Elissa was dressed in a cute pair of jeans and a long denim jacket. "Aren't you ready to go?"

"Where, again?" She didn't have the energy to write anything on her calendar, and her mind couldn't retain information for any length of time. It might be a residual effect of the accident.

"We're meeting Brock and Aiden at Sagrada Familia and then getting dinner with them." Elissa peered into Caitlyn's room. "Aren't you done studying?"

Caitlyn shook her head. "Not really. I probably should stay here and do some more. That test tomorrow is pretty important."

"Come on, you don't want to miss this. Even though we're too poor to afford tickets to tour inside the church, we can still appreciate the outside. And we have to finish making plans for our trip to France over the weekend."

Was that this weekend already? Where had the days gone? She sighed. It might be better to get out than to stay in here and wallow in her own misery. "Give me ten minutes."

"Five. We have to catch the Metro."

"Look at you, all ready to go on time."

Elissa snorted. "Hardly. We already missed the train we should have taken. Don't worry. I texted the guys. They'll be waiting for us."

Caitlyn took a few minutes to brush her teeth, comb her hair, and refresh her perfume. And pull on a pair of skinny jeans and a loose T-shirt. She was ready in six minutes, so the two of them ran out the door and down the street to the Metro station.

The ride was only a few stops, and they exited in front of the massive, magnificent church dedicated to the Holy Family. In the midst of the crowd gazing at the ornate, multispired church, they spotted Aiden and Brock and made their way to where they were. "Hey." Caitlyn bumped Aiden with her elbow.

"Hey." He pointed to a section of the church to his left. "Tell me if I'm wrong, but are those grapes and bananas on the top of those spires there?"

She squinted against the late afternoon sun. "It sure does look like it. Why on earth would someone put fruit on top of a magnificent church that also contains gargoyles and apostles?"

"Who knows. Gaudi was an architectural genius, but a kooky genius. Maybe he got hungry while he was drawing up the church's plans."

Again, he managed to pull a smile from deep inside her. "You never know." But that didn't stop her from snapping all kinds of pictures of the unique piece of architecture that had been under construction for over a hundred years.

After about ten or fifteen minutes of acting like tourists, they made their way to one of the city's many sidewalk cafés and sat down to order dinner.

"So." Aiden plopped his menu on the table. He could decide what to eat faster than anyone Caitlyn had ever met. "Ready for the trip?"

She groaned. "If I make it through this exam. I can't seem to retain anything." She closed her eyes. If only she could retract those words. "I mean, look at where we are. Who can concentrate on school when there's so much to take in?" Good save.

"I know what you mean." Aiden sipped his water. "You should see the view of this place from the sky. I'll have to take you up one of these days."

"I've already told you I prefer to keep my feet on the ground as much as possible."

"Ah, I always bring a couple of extra parachutes. I've only had to use them a couple of times. Anyway, have you learned anything new about your family since we got back?"

"No. I haven't gotten a chance to FaceTime with Pops." She glanced at her watch. "Maybe now is good. He should be up from his afternoon nap. That way, we can all hear what he has to say, and I won't have to repeat everything a million times."

She called Mom, who answered on the third ring. In the background, *Wheel of Fortune* was on. Pops' favorite show. "Hey, Mom. I'm here with some of my friends, and we were wondering if we could talk to Pops about his memories of France."

"Sure, honey." She moved from the kitchen to the living room. Pops was in his recliner, a blanket over his thin legs. "Dad, Caitlyn wants to talk to you about France."

"Huh?"

Mom muted the TV and repeated the question. "Here, take the phone and talk to her."

"Hi there, pumpkin. You're looking good."

"You too, Pops." She kind of shouted so he would be sure to hear.

"How's Spain? And school?"

He must be having a good day if he remembered where she was and why. "It's great. Everything's going well. How are you?"

"Not so good. Your mom turned off my favorite TV show. How will I ever know what that puzzle was?"

"I'm sure you'll see it in a rerun. Did Mom show you that picture I sent? The one of the maternity home where you were born?"

"What home?"

"The one where you were born?" The weight of the stares of the pedestrians on the street sat on Caitlyn's shoulders.

"I don't remember it. My mother told me about being born in a big house."

That could be either the maternity home or the château. "Did your dad ever talk about where he grew up? Do you know what happened to his house?"

"Oh, my father was very rich before the war. His family was famous in the area. They grew grapes and olives and had many servants, but after the war, he didn't want to return. I don't know what he did with the land or the house. Maybe he sold it. I don't think I own it. He showed me a picture of it once. It was very grand."

"But you don't remember seeing it in person?"

"No, I don't know if I did. When we went back when I was a boy, we saw so much, and now it's all muddled."

"Did you ever have a brother?"

"A brother? No. Didn't I tell you I was an only child? Their miracle, my parents called me."

"Maybe a twin who died?"

"No, I don't think so. But my parents didn't talk very much about the past. We didn't do that in those days. Whatever happened in the past was in the past. You got on with your life the way it was now."

"Well, I'm going back to France over the weekend to see if I can find out more about your family."

"That would be great, honey. I'd love to know more. Wish I could go back there."

"I'll be your eyes and feet for you."

"Aw, that would be great. I'll be there with you in spirit. Love you, honey bunches."

"Love you too, Pops."

After a brief chat with Mom, Caitlyn hung up. "Well, it sounds like my family was rich after all. But it wasn't my great-grandfather that lived in that château. Maybe Aime Laurent's branch of the family had their own money?"

Aiden was staring at his phone but lifted his gaze at her words. "Now we have to work extra hard at getting your grandfather his answers. Who knows, you might just be heir to that château."

"That would be something, wouldn't it?"

"Have you had a DNA test done? If you do have a claim to the château, that would help solidify it. And you never know what you might come up with in those results."

"That's a great idea." Caitlyn pulled up the website and ordered a kit.

The four of them spent the rest of the evening chatting about exams, the upcoming trip, and what they planned to do after graduation in a few months. All about the future, not the past.

Maybe Caitlyn's great-grandparents were on to something when they decided to live in the present and not worry about what had happened to them before. Perhaps sometimes the past deserved to stay in the past.

The problem was that it wasn't as simple as it sounded. No matter how much she worked to keep the haunting dreams and awful memories at bay, they continued to invade her consciousness and her subconsciousness. They wouldn't leave her alone.

Was that what it was like for her great-grandparents? Maybe the events of the war years were too painful for them to talk about, so they kept them bottled up, not wanting to saddle their only child with all that hurt.

"Earth to Caitlyn. Come in, Caitlyn." Aiden waved his napkin in front of her face.

The waitress had arrived with their meals and set the paella in front of Caitlyn. The saltiness of the seafood and the earthiness of the saffron invaded her senses. Her mouth watered. "Sorry. I guess I was lost in my own little world. What were you saying?"

"Just that your grandfather might be on to something. The gardener told us that an Aime Laurent owned it during the war. But who owns it now? We should search the land records. That might give us more information to go on. I'll contact Sophia and see if she knows anything about that or how to go about finding out that information." Aiden picked up his fork and dug into his meal.

Caitlyn stabbed a shrimp and scooped up some of her rice. "That might be helpful. Who knows what scrap might be the lead that gives me the answers I'm looking for?"

Aiden sobered and leaned forward, placing his fork beside his plate. "Tell me, why do you want to know about your background so much? I don't think it's just for your grandfather."

She sipped her water. "The past has always intrigued me. It has a way of cropping up and affecting you when you least expect it."

"I get that." Aiden took another bite and chewed for a moment. "My dad died when I was young. I have a great stepfather, but with me about to embark on this new chapter in my life, I can't help but wish that Dad was here to see me, and I can't help but wonder if he'd be proud of me."

"He would be. You're a great guy, and I bet you're a wonderful pilot." At least he understood grief, though maybe not the way she was experiencing it. Then again, her counselor had told her that everyone went through it differently.

"Yeah, he probably would have been. It's nice to think about. So that's why you're trying to find out more about your family? To make someone proud?"

"No, just out of curiosity. Finding out what it means to be Jewish might be part of it. My great-grandmother was Jewish, but she converted to Christianity when she married my great-grandpa, so I don't know much about that part of my family. We know lots about my mom's English ancestors, including a Scottish king from a long time ago, but it would be nice to know more about Dad's."

"So you would say that understanding the past and coming to terms with whatever it holds propels us to the future?"

As she fished around the mussels for more rice, she mulled over that thought. "Yeah, I guess you're right." Before she could look to the future, she had to deal with what had happened that one night that changed her life.

CHAPTER THIRTY-EIGHT

22 August, 1955
Elne, France

I make another circuit of the yard, careful to keep my attention from wandering to a level plot of ground some distance from the house toward the long driveway. Now it's overgrown with weeds and thistles, dry grass that rustles in the breeze. Then we kept it with the greatest of care, making sure to push the lawnmower over it every week, to keep the grass green, to water the flowers we'd planted.

For it was a sacred spot.

Is a sacred spot.

Despite the brambles pulling at my pantyhose, I wander to this neglected piece of the property. The thorns prick my fingers as I pull them away, finally finding a rock. And another and another.

The sun and rain and wind have faded the paint that we so carefully applied. Even the little birds and butterflies that our brushes brought to life aren't as vivid.

Those of us who were here then don't need letters or pictures to remind us. Our hearts do that every day.

The tiny babies born too early who didn't survive. Those who entered the world too sick to draw many breaths. Those who hadn't had enough nutrition while their mothers had been in the camps, who would never feel the softness of grass beneath their feet or the warmth of the sun on their skin.

I can't cry now. Not now. Not again. I've cried too many days already, and there will be more ahead for me to cry. Today is a day of joy. Or I pray it will be.

As I turn to leave this makeshift graveyard, I speak to all the little stones now hidden by the weeds.

"I remember you. And I promise, I always will."

CHAPTER THIRTY-NINE

7 September, 1942
Camp de Rivesaltes, Vichy France

Hélène stared at the three men. "I knew it wouldn't be good news. Just tell me what has become of Levi." She leaned into Fräulein Reiter a little more. Perhaps she did need the support after all.

The tall one clasped his hands. He cleared his throat and shuffled his feet.

"S'il vous plaît, just tell me. It can't be any worse than what I'm imagining." Though as soon as Hélène said the words, she doubted their veracity.

"Your husband, Levi, was a good man."

Was. Past tense. Hélène leaned a little more on the woman at her side. "What happened?"

"A fight broke out between two men over a tin cup. It's a precious commodity."

"I know." Hélène's voice cracked. She had steeled herself for the blow, and the man continued to dance around the answer to her question.

"One was slated to leave on the train the next day. The other wanted his cup, since he wouldn't need it anymore. The first man insisted he would need it in the new camp. They started fighting, and Levi stepped in to stop them. Both men landed blows on him before he pushed them back.

"And then a guard came. He said something in German that I didn't understand, but he and a couple of other guards beat all three men with the butts of their guns and kicked them.

"I'm so sorry. All three men were killed."

Killed.

Killed.

Killed.

The word reverberated in Hélène's head. Her knees went weak, and she collapsed against Fräulein Reiter, her entire body shaking.

Her husband was gone. Dead. Never more to return. It didn't make sense.

She would never speak to him again, never kiss him or love him again, never tell him how much he meant to her again.

Her entire world imploded.

It would never be the same.

And what of his child? This precious little one became even more precious. The only bit of Levi she had left. She must take care of him and protect him from the evil in this world. The darkness and filth that permeated it.

More than that, she would do her best to protect all the children at the maternity home and all the mothers there. She wasn't the only widow. And there would be more.

She grasped the fence and pulled herself upright. The time for tears would come, but this wasn't that time. There were women and children who were depending on her. "Merci. I appreciate you telling me about Levi. There will be no Shoah for him."

"We have already said it." The tall man's Adam's apple bobbed.

"Merci, merci beaucoup. That is the kindest thing anyone has ever done for us."

"I hope you will be well. Fräulein Reiter, you'll look after her?"

"Of course I will. She'll be fine. May God go with you and bless you for your kindness to Levi."

"Pray for us. All three of us leave on tomorrow's transport."

More deportations. More suffering. More death. When would it ever end? Would it ever end? The Americans were in the war, but nothing had come of it as of yet. There was word that they were bombing Germany, but that was the extent of it. No boots on continental Europe. No true hope for freedom. Not yet.

She swallowed the football-sized lump in her throat and strode toward the women's block. Behind her came the crunch of Fräulein Reiter's footsteps on the rocky soil.

"Are you going to be okay?" Fräulein Reiter reached out to touch her, but Hélène backed away.

If she touched her again, said another kind word, Hélène would shatter into shards like pottery thrown against a stone. "I'll be fine. I have to be. We have a job to do. Let's go do it."

They returned to the truck, and Aime met them there. He wiped beads of sweat from his forehead. "I'm done. How did you fare?"

She lowered her tight shoulders, drew in a deep breath, and shook her head.

"Je suis désolé. That has to be a blow." His soft words were almost her undoing. It took every ounce of strength she possessed and then some not to break down into a sobbing heap on the orange-red ground.

Instead, she drew in the deepest breath she could manage, even though it was very shaky. "We need to get the women and children and get out of here. I'm ready to leave."

"I'll head over there with their allotment of rice, and you two can help them into the truck."

Fräulein Reiter took Hélène by the arm then glanced over her shoulder. "We'll meet you there."

As they walked, Hélène worked to free herself from Fräulein Reiter's grip, but she was having none of it. "It's okay to cry. No one would blame you if you shed a few tears for your husband. You did love him, didn't you?"

"Of course." Her answer was sharp, but that was only so she didn't break under the woman's concern. "But now is not the time nor the place. Madame Touissant would have no reason to cry. When I'm alone, in the quiet of a private space, I'll do my mourning. If I cried now, I would only draw attention to myself. What reason would Madame Touissant have to weep?"

"As long as you are going to be all right."

She would never be all right again. Her world was spinning upside down. But for now, she had a mission that would keep her focused on others and not on her own pain.

They arrived at the women's block, where Aime was backing up the truck to the warehouse that held their provisions. And, if all was in order, the warehouse also held two women and four children, with two more little ones on the way.

He opened the truck's back door in a way that would block the guards' view of what they were doing. All they should be able to see was their feet going back and forth. Aime would carry the women out. Hélène and Fräulein Reiter would be in charge of the children.

When they entered the warehouse, however, there was no sign of those who were to come with them. There was only rice and flour. Nothing more.

Fräulein Reiter moved along the edge of the building, calling in her softest voice. "It's safe now. We're here to take you away. You can come out."

No answer. No one stirred.

Hélène did the same on the other side of the building. She even slid some of the lighter sacks of grain to the side to search for those who were supposed to be there, but without luck. "Where are they?" Hélène's already cold heart froze harder.

"I'll go to the barracks and see if I can track them down. They might have gotten confused or frightened. Wait here."

Hélène stood to the side as Aime unloaded the sacks. He finished his job, but Fräulein Reiter had yet to return.

"Let's go look for them. We're not doing any good standing around here." Hélène headed out the door.

Aime stood in front of her and blocked her way. "You don't have to do this."

"I do. Right now, I can't do anything else. Excuse-moi, s'il vous plaît."

This time, Aime let her go, though judging by the breath on her neck, he was right on her heels.

Fräulein Reiter stepped from one of the barracks, motioning with wide gestures for them to come.

Hélène raced over. "What's wrong?" Even in the dying light, it was obvious that the woman was as pale as a cloudy winter's day.

"The woman we really wanted to get to the hospital because she was due to give birth soon is now in labor. And it's not a good situation.

The other woman was taken on this morning's transport and refused to be parted from her children. I didn't know that, but apparently another woman on the list passed away during the night, and she was taken in her place."

Hélène sucked in a breath. Had someone filled in for her? Another kilo of guilt weighed on her shoulders.

Right now, though, she had to focus on what was immediately in front of her. "Let's get her in the truck. What's her name?"

"Leona."

"Aime, you get Leona. I'll grab some blankets to make a soft bed in the back. Fräulein Reiter, go distract the guards. You'll need to come with us, because I don't know what to do to help a woman in labor." If only Madame Touissant were here. She would be much better equipped to handle the situation.

Hélène went with Aime to the barracks to get Leona and the others. Hannah greeted her. "It's good to see you, mon amie."

Hannah had grown thin in the time they had been apart, but Hélène didn't flinch. And didn't give her time to ask about Levi. "You too. We're here to get Leona." She had a last-minute thought. "And we have room to take a few other children too."

Within moments of issuing that proclamation, several women swarmed her, begging her to take their little ones out of this pit of misery and death. How could she choose who to bring and who to leave? She gazed at the babies thrust in front of her. Two were tiny and thin. They needed the most help. Hard as it was, she closed her eyes to the others and pointed to the mothers of the lucky ones. "Bring them around to the back of the warehouse. I'll carry them into the truck from there to keep from being seen."

Aime and one of the female prisoners positioned Leona on a blanket and used it like a stretcher to carry her to the back of the truck. They were taking a chance that the guards would see them, but that couldn't be helped. Fräulein Reiter was known for pestering them to get her way, so hopefully they wouldn't think much of her ruse.

The weeping mothers followed Hélène, threatening to open her own floodgates. "Hush. You can't appear upset, or you'll tip off the guards. Quickly, now."

By the time Aime got Leona inside the truck, Hélène had made as comfortable of a place as she could for Leona to rest and had settled the two infants on pallets of their own. Moments later, Fräulein Reiter returned and did a quick examination of Leona. "We need to go. Now."

Hélène climbed to the ground. "I'll tell Aime to drive fast but not too fast."

"Merci. Time is very important right now. If we don't hurry—"

"We will, and everything will be fine. Leona will soon have a brand-new, healthy baby." The power of positive thinking. Maman had always drilled that into Hélène's head. She relied on it now.

Aime came around to help her in, but she waved him off. "I can do it. Just get going as soon as possible. And if there's a way to avoid stopping for the guards, make that happen. No fancy talk, just fancy driving."

"I'd tease you for that, but it doesn't seem like the right thing to do now." Aime slid behind the wheel, and as soon as Hélène hefted herself into the cab and shut the door, he took off, tires spinning and spitting gravel behind them that plunked against the concrete building.

They approached the guarded gate, where Aime honked and waved but only barely slowed. The guard smiled and then scrambled to open the gate, just in the nick of time for them to avoid crashing through it. With another beep of the horn, Aime sped away from Rivesaltes and to the maternity hospital.

While the trip to the camp had gone all too fast, the return was far too slow. Hélène leaned forward on her seat, as if she could make him go faster if she did so. With each bump came a cry of agony from the back.

"Hurry, hurry, Aime. Can't you go any faster?" If she were about to give birth in the back of a truck and things weren't going well, she would want to get to their destination as soon as possible.

At long last, the truck chugged up the hill, turned onto the unpaved driveway, and pulled up to the peach-colored house. Aime flung open his door. "I'll get assistance from some of the other nurses. You help Fräulein Reiter."

Hélène pulled off the blond wig and slid from the seat, landing hard on the dry ground before racing to the back and opening the doors. "Aime has gone to get help. Tell me what I can do."

"Pray." Fräulein Reiter returned her attention to Leona. "Come on now, hang on. We're at the hospital, and we'll soon have you set up, and you'll be holding your beautiful child any moment."

"The nurses here are very good. The best." Hopefully Madame Touissant would be feeling up to helping. She would know what to do.

"That's right. You'll get excellent care here."

Within moments, Aime returned with several of the nurses. Together with him and Fräulein Reiter, they got Leona moved from the truck and into the room they had set up for deliveries. It was a sterile environment, a far cry from what she'd experienced in Rivesaltes. They even had the tools necessary to perform a Cesarean section if needed.

Madame Touissant stumbled down the stairs, wrapping a housecoat around herself, her hair sticking up in all directions. "Salomé told me what was happening."

"Are you sure you're up to this?"

"I have to help her."

Of course. Madame Touissant could do no less. She disappeared into the room, leaving Hélène pacing in the hall.

Salomé found her two hours later and offered her a cup of hot coffee. "Have you heard anything?"

Hélène shook her head and took the cup, burning her tongue on the liquid. What little managed to get down her throat soured her stomach, so she set it on a nearby table and resumed pacing. Salomé must have sensed her need for quiet because she didn't say anything, just paced alongside her.

After another hour, Madame Touissant and Fräulein Reiter emerged from the room, both covered in bloodied aprons. Hélène rushed at them. She needed good news more than anything right now. There was even a proverb about how good news was like cold water to the thirsty.

But Madame Touissant shook her head. "I'm sorry. We lost them both."

Two more deaths. Two more in addition to Levi, who had been stripped of their lives for no reason.

Hélène turned and fled the building.

CHAPTER FORTY

After she escaped from the hospital, Hélène stumbled down the stairs and across the lawn, tears blurring her vision. But she didn't stop. Even when she tripped over a root, she managed to stay on her feet and move forward.

When she was far enough away, she crumpled to the ground, sobs wracking her body. She lifted her fists to the heavens. "No! No! No! You can't do this to me. Do You hear? You can't do this! It's not fair. Why would You take Your vengeance and wrath out on innocent women and children? How could You do this to me? Why did You let Maman and Papa die in that crash? Why didn't You save my employees? Why did You take Levi from me?"

Except for the far-off sound of thunder, all remained quiet. And that was why she was a secular Jew. A Jew in blood only. All of her prayers, all of her pleas to Hashem, went unanswered.

And now He had taken from her all she had left except for her child. "Are You going to take my little one from me too?" Would that be her ultimate punishment for her sins? In the distance, lightning flashed against the darkening sky.

Soon, rain mingled with her tears until her clothes and hair were wet and moisture ran down her face, blurring her vision even more. She sat hunched over, protecting her child, protecting her heart.

"Oh, Levi, mon coeur. What will I do without you? How am I supposed to go on? How do I explain to our baby who you were, what a wonderful man you were, and what an amazing father you would have been?"

She sobbed again until her lungs ached and cried for air.

"It isn't right that you won't get to hold your only child. That you won't be here to watch him grow up and won't be here to guide him to be the kind of person who would make you proud.

"I'm a broken woman, split in half by pain and loss. From this, I will never heal. All the love and light and laughter have gone out of my life. There is nothing left for me but this child, and I don't have any idea how I'm supposed to raise him without a father."

The rain picked up, now driven by the wind, slashing her face. She shivered but didn't move, didn't have the strength to even rub warmth back into her arms. When her parents had passed away, she had believed that to be the worst tragedy she would ever endure. But it didn't compare to losing Levi and all the hopes and dreams they had for their future.

There was no future.

Only a bleak, empty expanse of time stretching in front of her. If not for her baby, she would give up and die. There would be no point in living.

At the sound of mud sloshing behind her, she turned to see Fräulein Reiter making her way toward her. "Go away and leave me alone. I'm a bitter woman, much like Mara."

But Fräulein Reiter sat beside her in the mud and wrapped a raincoat around her. "You should come inside." A bright light split the sky, and a rumble of thunder shook the ground underneath them.

"Not until what happened to Levi makes sense." She turned to Fräulein Reiter, whose coiled braids still sat neatly on top of her head, though by now she was as soaked to the skin as Hélène.

"God's ways are higher than our ways."

"I don't want to hear about God. Do you understand me? He has forsaken me in so many ways in the past few years that I've forsaken Him now."

"Mara was a bitter woman when she lost her husband and sons in a strange land. But the birth of her grandson restored joy to her. She found contentment in knowing that God kept His promises to provide a Savior, and He ended up coming through that child's line."

"Your words are nothing but nonsensical babble."

"Right now, the world is a dark place. Rain is falling, wind is blowing, lives are being destroyed. But the storm will pass. The sun will return, the grass will green, and flowers will perfume the earth with their sweet fragrance. You've always been a bright spot in our lives. Hold on to hope. Don't let go."

"I don't have any hope left to cling to. Hashem has stripped all that away. He has left me with nothing. Even if the sun returns, I will still be empty. I'll be unable to enjoy the light on my face or the smell of flowers." Hélène's teeth chattered. A branch broke away from a nearby olive tree, and the wind carried it away.

"Allons-y. It's time to go back inside before we get struck by lightning or hit in the head with flying debris." Fräulein Reiter lifted Hélène to her feet, and though she might as well stay out in the storm and die, she had no more strength to fight. She allowed the other woman to steer her toward the house.

Salomé met them at the door with warm cups of chamomile tea and towels. The two of them slipped the coat from Hélène's shoulders and helped her climb the stairs. Once in the dormitory, they stripped off her wet clothes, rubbed dry her goose-pimpled flesh, and tucked her into bed with a fresh nightgown.

They must have spiked her tea with a sleeping powder because the next thing she knew, she woke to see Salomé slumped in a chair beside her bed, sound asleep, as were all the other women in the room. She threw back the stack of blankets they must have piled on top of her and tiptoed from the room to use the *toilettes*.

Once she finished with that, she made her way to the kitchen in the basement, near the darkroom where they processed the false identity card photographs. While she had no appetite at all, she was thirsty, and a glass of water or milk, if it was available, might help her go back to sleep.

The light was already on in the windowless space, and through the open door, she spied Madame Touissant sitting at a small table in the center of the large room, holding a mug. "Come in, Hélène. Let me get you some tea."

"Stay. I'll get my own glass of milk." She took one from the open wooden shelving, found the bottle in the icebox, and poured herself some, then sat at the table across from Madame Touissant. "I hope you're feeling better, especially since your rest was disturbed."

Madame Touissant pulled her robe around herself. "I'm fine. I should be asking about you."

"My world has been shattered, and the foundation underneath me has crumbled."

"You must be numb."

"I am. When it wore off before, I couldn't stop crying. I never want to feel that way again."

"But you're human. You will. You'll have to deal with it in one way or another at some point in your life."

"Maybe. But right now, I don't want to explore those feelings."

"You're much like me. You don't let people in easily and don't allow them to know what is going on inside your head or your heart."

"Ma mère was the same way. I can't remember a time in my life when she cried. Not ever. Not when ma grandmère passed away. Through all of life's storms, she was strong and stoic in the face of the gale."

"Was that the best way to be though?"

"Je ne comprends pas."

"It's not hard to understand. Is never expressing your feelings to yourself or to others a good way to live? Is it healthy for you?"

"It's the way I was brought up, and I don't know how to be anything other than who I am."

"That's a good answer." Madame Touissant sipped her tea. "But take time to mourn what you've lost so that you don't become hardened and bitter."

"I already am."

"That isn't the Hélène I know and have come to love." Madame Touissant grasped her by the hand. "Bitterness will eat away like a cancer at your soul and leave you nothing but a shell without anything to offer anyone."

"Then that is my lot in life."

"Is that what you want to give your child? Don't you think he or she deserves the best of you, especially since it will be you raising him? I know you already love this precious little life, and when he arrives, you'll want to do whatever you can to raise him as a healthy, happy individual."

The sweet coolness of the milk coated Hélène's tongue and mouth. She took several more sips. "Of course I do."

"Then you must be filled with health and happiness before you can pour it into your child. Don't allow your anger over events and circumstances to color your world and that of your child's. He deserves love and joy in his life. And I know you can give that to him."

"How do you know so much about this?"

Madame Touissant stared at the empty wall behind Hélène, likely not really seeing the plaster. She fiddled with her teacup before taking it to the sink.

"I'm sorry if the question was too personal. You don't need to answer if you don't want to or if it's too difficult."

Madame Touissant turned around and leaned against the cabinet. "It is hard to speak about, and only a couple of people here—the nurses that came with me from Switzerland—know about this, so I'm taking you into my confidence and trusting that you won't share this with anyone else."

"Of course not. You can trust me."

"I've been married. And widowed."

Hélène gasped. "I didn't know."

"It's not something I talk about much."

"Unfortunately, I now understand that."

"My parents, very strict Christians in Switzerland—my father was a pastor—didn't approve of Hans. They said he was a bad influence on me and that his faith wasn't as strong as mine. But he loved me, and I loved him, and that was the end of that. I was determined to marry him."

"Were you happy?"

Madame Touissant nodded. "Very. I couldn't stand my parents' disapproval, so that's when I came here to establish this hospital. I'd been working with the aid society already and had my nursing license. He came with me, but that's when he started drinking. Heavily. He wasn't home much. He died a year ago in a pub brawl."

"Oh, Madame Touissant. How awful for you."

"Call me Eleanore. And oui, in a way, I lost him twice. First to drinking and second to death. I had to mourn him twice."

"That's why you don't speak about him."

"Oui. People wouldn't understand. They can't see how someone like me got involved with a man like him. Love does strange things to you. But for a while, I was happy, and it's those memories I cling to now. I'll never marry again, I know that much. But for a fleeting moment, the span of a breath, I knew pure joy."

"Levi and I had so much of that." Hélène drank more milk to help her swallow the lump in her throat. "More than a fleeting moment. There are so many happy memories for me to hang on to."

"Then that's what you must do, what you must tell your child about. Tell him what kind of man his father was and all the wonderful times the two of you shared. Tell him how excited Levi was to be a father. All of that. Share with your child as much as you can remember about your husband. That will keep him alive for both of you."

Hélène finished her milk and licked her lips. Then she picked up her glass and took it to the icebox to refill it. "I'm so glad you decided to share that part of yourself with me. Though this hospital is filled with many, many widows—too many of them—I was feeling like no one else understood."

"We do. We've had our loved ones ripped from our arms just the way you have. Some speak about it, and some can't. Be patient with yourself. This is new. There will be good days and bad. Days of joy and of grief. But you will walk out on the other side and find meaning and purpose in life again."

Back in bed, Hélène stared at the dark ceiling high above her.

Eleanore may have found a reason for life, but right now, the waters were far too murky for Hélène to see how she ever could.

CHAPTER FORTY-ONE

22 August, 1955
Elne, France

A dark cloud passes overhead, a smudge against the brilliant blue sky. Where has it come from on an otherwise sunny day? Will others follow? There's always the chance that an unexpected storm will send torrents of rain.

But the sky always clears again. It always does, though after days and days of showers and gales and lightning and thunder, it doesn't seem like it ever will.

How well I know about that in my own life. You cannot have green grass without the accompanying rain. Without it, the tender shoots will dry and crumble. There is nothing you can do to stop the rain. Nothing you can do to make the sun shine. When the storms came, I had to wait them out.

How many more storms will the Almighty send before eternal sunshine? Only He knows. How I wish, though, that He would let me know that secret. Perhaps then I would be better able to bear the bad days.

Here, we were a family. A community that loved each other and supported each other. There were many widows, many orphans who stepped through the doors. But none of us were ever alone, never truly without friends or those who could sympathize.

Yet each of us was lonely. We all had lost someone, something. Had our lives irrevocably changed. When we walked out the doors, we weren't the same people we were when we entered. Life changed.

WHAT I PROMISE YOU

The cloud passes, now sending its shadows on the village below. The sun's rays peek from behind it, then burst forth in full brilliance. I lift my face to drink them in, to bathe in their brightness and soak up their warmth, to fill myself with them and prepare for the inevitable day when the storms return.

CHAPTER FORTY-TWO

August 5, 2022
Collioure, France

O nce again, Caitlyn found herself on the train bound for France. Since this was her third trip to the country via this route, she recognized some of the landmarks. It was now familiar and comfortable. On the other hand, there was nothing ordinary about whipping through the countryside, the Pyrenees Mountains on one side, the sparkling blue Mediterranean on the other.

Caitlyn, Elissa, Aiden, and Brock had to travel past Collioure to Perpignan on the main line then catch the local train to the seaside village. Convoluted to be sure, but more views of the countryside were a perk.

At last they arrived in the small artist and tourist enclave. This time, Caitlyn had helped Elissa pack, so they weren't lugging a great deal of baggage along. Since Brock made the trip with them, he and Aiden would be in one apartment and Caitlyn and Elissa in another.

The walk wasn't too long down the hill from the station to the main part of the village. They strolled past a park and then along a narrow sidewalk beside lovely homes painted in soft pastels. The road and the sidewalk were both busy, and they curved around into the main part of town soon enough.

It was beautiful. There was another park with a monument dedicated to those who had perished in WWI. Charming shops and restaurants lined the street. To get to their rentals, they turned off the main street, down a pedestrian-only road that was narrow but bustling with more shops.

The wheels of Elissa's carry-on clicked on the uneven cobblestone street.

They came to a narrow doorway, the metal grate on it depicting a sailboat on the sea. With only a climb up one flight of stairs, Caitlyn and Elissa were soon in their flat.

Caitlyn dropped the keys and her backpack on the kitchen table. "Whew. We made it." Outside, the sky was darkening as evening set in. "I'm glad we were all able to get off a little early."

"That means we're just in time for dinner." Elissa opened the drapes across the French doors, and sure enough, the shops were closing, which meant it was time for the eateries to open.

Caitlyn's phone dinged, signaling a text from Aiden.

We found a great little restaurant on the next street over. We're starving. Are you ready?

She had to laugh. The world revolved around a man's stomach. Fifteen minutes later, they ambled down a gorgeous street, each doorway and balcony overflowing with green plants, turning what was a dry area into a lush oasis. When her breaded veal with pesto sauce on black garlic mashed potatoes arrived, her mouth watered. The weight of school and exams dropped from her shoulders.

For a moment, all was right with the world.

"Did you hear that Brock had to make an emergency landing the other day?" Aiden dug into his scallops with squid ink.

"What?" Caitlyn held her fork halfway to her mouth. "Are you okay? What about the plane?"

"Both fine." Brock shrugged. "That's the risk you take as a pilot."

But Elissa was as pale as the whitecaps on the stormy sea. "You could have been killed."

"Nah. They train us for stuff like that. You know, missionaries don't fly the most sophisticated or the newest aircraft in the world. We have to learn how to maintain our planes and what to do in case anything unexpected arises."

Elissa gasped.

"Which it almost never does." Brock savored his anchovies, a local delicacy that turned Caitlyn's stomach.

"Well, just remind me never to get into a plane with you." Caitlyn directed her gaze to Aiden. "With either of you."

"Wouldn't that be funny if one of us was assigned to fly you to your station?" Aiden grinned, his eyes gleaming, even in the restaurant's low candlelight.

Caitlyn's phone rang. She was about to ignore it, but when she saw it was Mom, she picked it up. "Hi."

"Oh good, I'm so glad I caught you." Mom was breathless. "I can't ever figure out the time difference. Anyway, don't worry, but Pops is in the hospital."

"What?" Caitlyn dropped her fork, and it clattered on the tile floor. "What happened?"

"He slipped and fell in the bathroom. He's too proud to let me help him, and Dad had a meeting at church. The floor was a little wet after his shower, and down he went."

"Is he hurt?"

"That's what they're trying to determine. It might be his hip."

"No, that's not good, is it?"

Mom paused while on the other end of the line came muffled voices. "I don't know at this point. A broken hip at his age is never a good thing."

"Do you need me to come home?"

"No." This time, Mom's answer was immediate. "Don't you dare do such a thing. Your work is very important, and you're almost at the end of your training. Pops is very proud of you, and he would hate it if you had to start from the beginning because of him. You missed the end of college. You won't miss the end of this."

"Are you sure?"

"Positive."

But everything in Caitlyn screamed to go home. Pops had been her rock after the accident. He didn't say much, but he was good at holding her hand, closing his eyes, and praying silently. At that point, words were too much for her, but his unspoken petitions to heaven were calming and healing.

She couldn't lose him too. Not after everything. Not right now. "I think I want to come home."

"Pops wants to know more about his family. Please, stay there and do that for him. Find out what you can, and then come home, if it's even necessary at that point. We don't know if he broke anything or if he's just bruised and sore."

"Did you have to call the ambulance?"

"Yes." Mom's answer was soft.

There was more to the situation than she was saying. She was holding back to keep Caitlyn from panicking, but that's just what she was doing. She pushed her chair back and left the restaurant.

The air on the street was warm and a bit salty with the breeze from the sea. Light and laughter poured out of the homes and establishments on the street. "Mom." She couldn't say anything more.

"It's okay, sweetie, it's okay." But even Mom was choked up.

"Please?"

"For him, see if you can stay. At least until we know more. He was conscious when they brought him in. He's confused, of course, being somewhere different, but I don't think he hit his head. I was right outside the bathroom door like I always am. Just say a prayer for him."

"I will." Like he had so many, many times for her.

"Okay, I think the doctor is coming, so I'd better go. I'll keep you in the loop."

"Promise?"

"I promise. I love you, sweetie."

"Love you." After she ended the call, she leaned against the cool, ivy-covered stone wall of the building. *Lord, please let Pops be okay. You know how much I need him. Don't let anything happen to him. Let him be okay. Please.* The prayer was circular, but that was all her heart could say.

A minute or two later, Aiden exited the restaurant and held his arms open to her. The small invitation was all she needed. She allowed herself to fall into his embrace, his smell manly and musky. When he stroked her hair, the dam burst, and she released the tears she'd held back for Mom's sake.

Aiden stood there and hugged her, the soft evening breeze tugging at her skirt, the noises around her fading until all she heard was her own heartbeat. He was strong and warm and just the right height for her to rest her head against his shoulder.

And he was patient. He didn't say a word while she released all the fear and pain she'd been holding in these weeks, until no tears fell and only hiccups remained. Without pushing her away, he pressed a tissue into her hand.

She stepped back and blew her nose and wiped her face. "Sorry about that."

"Why? You don't have to apologize for being human. Weeping is a very human emotion. Even Jesus cried."

Yes, He mourned a lost friend too. People had told her that more than once over the past months. "Thank you. I appreciate the use of your shoulder."

"Anytime. You can have an arm and a hand too, if you ever need them. Is everything okay?"

She nodded. "I hope so. Pops is in the hospital after a fall. That's all anyone knows. I want to go home to be with him, but Mom says he'd want me to stay here, so I'm going to try to, at least for the time being."

"This trip is perfect then. You aren't alone, and we're going to be working to find out something your grandpa wants to know."

"And me. I've found that I really want the answers to these questions as well."

"I think we've all gotten a little caught up in the mystery of it. That's why Brock wanted to come. You have him hooked. And he's a good resource. Anyway, I'll be praying for your grandpa. What can I do for you?"

Instead of reaching up to stroke his cheek like she itched to do, she stuffed her hand in her skirt's pocket. It was the nicest any guy had ever been to her. "Nothing right now. Just keep praying. It helps to know that someone can form the words even when I can't."

"You got it. Are you ready to go inside?"

She shook her head. "I think I'll go back to the apartment, if you don't mind."

"How about we take a little stroll first? We can see the water and the fortress at night. Unless you'd rather be alone."

Actually, she wouldn't. If she was, she might just pull herself further down. "A short walk might be okay."

He texted Brock then held her hand as they navigated the unfamiliar streets until they popped out on the promenade behind the beach that separated a centuries-old church and the even more ancient fortress. The reflection of village lights and the starry skies twinkled on the calm water, the rhythmic lapping of the waves on the shore lulling.

"This is beautiful." She broke the silence that had lasted the entire walk.

"It sure is. I could get used to living here."

"Won't you be based in Africa?"

"Probably. But they do have plenty of coastline there too. Someday I'd like to live in a place near water."

"That would be nice." Lindsey had always dreamed of a beach house, though they both realized how impossible that would be on a missionary's budget. Instead, they had dreamed of vacations like this.

"Are you doing okay?"

"Better now, thanks."

"In general, I mean. When I've seen you the past couple of weeks, you've looked tired."

"And here I thought you were such a sweet guy."

"Sorry."

"No, I was teasing you. Weak attempt, I guess. I am tired. The load is more than I expected. Not that I can't handle it, but I'm getting used to being away from home and everything familiar."

"I get that. It isn't the easiest life. It's not for everyone."

"Lindsey and I dreamed of this, but it's different than we imagined."

"Who's Lindsey?"

Oh dear, now she'd stepped in it. "A friend of mine."

"Did she change her mind?"

"I don't really want to talk about it."

"Okay. You have enough going on right now. I get that. Focus on your grandpa, but remember that I'm a good listener and the offer stands, just like before. I'm ready to lend an ear whenever you're ready to talk."

"Thanks." But sharing the details of that night was something she might never be ready to do.

CHAPTER FORTY-THREE

August 6, 2022
Collioure, France

Four sets of footsteps sounded against the ancient stone walls that made up the fortress in Collioure. Though outside the summer sunshine was bright and lit up the Mediterranean Sea at the base of the fortress, inside it was dark, damp, and chilly.

"This is kind of spooky." Brock drew out the word to emphasize the point, which only led to goose bumps dotting Caitlyn's arms.

While her body might be with her friends, her mind was at home with Pops. Was he doing any better today? She couldn't text Mom or Dad because it was the middle of the night, and she didn't want to wake them if they were managing to catch a few hours' sleep.

"Come on. I don't want to lose you." Aiden reached out for her.

Her thoughts must have slowed her steps, because she'd fallen behind the group. With the way the halls twisted and turned, popping out onto a balcony of sorts and then back inside, the last thing she needed was to get lost.

She hurried to him and took his hand. He squeezed hers. "How are you holding up?"

"Okay. Let's focus on the job in front of us. We have to find the museum that's here first. It would be interesting to explore all the ins and outs of this place, but we don't have the time."

"Very practical and levelheaded of you."

"I don't know if you're complimenting me or making fun of me."

"That's a compliment. I grew up around practical and levelheaded women. They're what I know and appreciate."

"I think I'm more afraid of what we won't find than of what we will."

"I get that."

"Really? I wasn't sure that sentence even made sense."

"Absolutely. If the papers aren't here, then where do you go in your search?"

"Exactly. And we don't have the time to do much more, at least not right now."

"Then let's hope we find what you're looking for."

"Here it is." Elissa's voice came from far ahead of Caitlyn and Aiden.

They picked up their pace and soon entered an open chamber. Photos and placards hung on the stone walls, a few items in a couple of small cases around the room. An arched doorway led to another similar space.

"They were over here." Brock motioned them toward the back room.

Caitlyn stepped to where he was pointing. There in the case were about a half dozen of the same kind of typed cards they had seen at the maternity hospital and a few sets of identification papers. She bent over the glass to study them.

As she did so, one stood out. ID papers for a young woman, just twenty-five years old at the time, the same age her great-grandmother would have been. She didn't know her great-grandmother's exact birthday. The name was completely different. Noémie Treves.

But what drew Caitlyn's attention was the photograph. She'd never seen one of her great-grandmother as a young woman, but there was something familiar about the woman in this picture. The slight tilt of her head. The shape of the nose. The soft smile. Could it be the same woman thirty years before any other picture of her existed?

"Look at this." Caitlyn tapped on the glass. "The age is right, though I'm not sure what my great-grandmother's birthday was. But there's something I recognize in this picture. Though I never met her, there's a resemblance to later photos I have seen."

Aiden wrinkled his nose. "A similarity in looks doesn't mean too much. They were from the same ethnic group."

"You're right." Caitlyn pulled her phone from her pocket and snapped a picture of the papers in the case. "First of all, we don't know if we have the right woman. She's the correct age, but that's about all."

She glanced at her watch. By this time, it was almost noon in France, first thing in the morning at home. Maybe Mom knew, or perhaps Pops was even up and able to answer a few questions. Able to identify the woman in the photograph. With no signal inside the thick stone walls that had survived a millennium of storms and waves and war, she stepped outside, the fresh sea air filling her lungs.

Mom answered on the first ring. "Hi. Is everything okay?"

"I'm fine. How's Pops?"

"Awake right now. He had a restless night. The nurses, of course, are in and out at all hours taking vitals and all that."

"What did they find out?"

"His hip isn't broken, praise the Lord. They kept him overnight for observation, just in case he sustained a concussion or some other type of head injury, though the CT scan was clear. He's ready to go home."

"You bet I am." Pop's voice, though muffled by the miles between them, was as strong and bear-like as ever.

Caitlyn chuckled, the knot in her stomach releasing. "That's wonderful to hear."

"Unless you spent the night with him and had to put up with his complaining." Mom's voice was light and full of laughter. She and Pops, though not biologically related, loved each other a great deal and teased each other all the time. "Your dad will be here to get us as soon as the doctor gives Pops the all clear. I made him go home and get some sleep."

"Could I talk to Pops? I have a question about his mother. We're here at the museum in Collioure and looking at identity papers that might have some connection to her."

"Sure. Hang on."

A buzzing sound followed. Mom must have been raising Pops' bed so he could sit up to talk. A moment later, he came on the line. "How's my little daisy?"

"I'm fine. Glad to hear you are too."

"Ah, nothing's going to keep me down. I just want them to spring me from this place and take me home. I have my flowers to tend, you know. The strawberries should be coming in soon."

She didn't have the heart to remind him that he had lived with them for three years since Grams had died and that it was August, long past strawberry season. "You'll be home before you know it." Good thing he remembered the past better than he did the present. "Do you know when your mother's birthday was?"

"Hmm, that's a really good question." He was probably rubbing his chin. He always did that when he was thinking, like when he was about to declare checkmate when they played chess. "When was it? December seventeenth?"

"That's Dad's birthday. I'm asking about your mom's." Unfortunately, he didn't seem to be having a very good day.

"My mom? Boys don't pay much attention to that. Do you know, Pam?"

"In the summer, I think." Mom's voice was so clear, she must've had Pops on speaker. "I remember going to her house and having a garden party to celebrate."

"That's right. Summer. We always had strawberry shortcake. With fresh strawberries. She couldn't abide the ones from the grocery store."

"Yes, we did. I remember that now."

Mom was more helpful than Pops. "That's great. So it would have been mid-June to around the beginning of July?"

"Yes, somewhere in there. Does that match with the papers you found?"

"What papers are they talking about, Pam?"

"Here, Dad, why don't you rest before the nurse comes in again?" The background noise faded as Mom took the phone off speaker. "Sorry. Being away from home is unsettling him. I hope we can get him out of here in the next few hours, but discharges always take so long."

"They do. Anyway, the birthdate on these papers is June twenty-sixth. Does that sound about right?"

"That would be in the timeframe to have strawberry shortcake. I do remember, even though your dad and I weren't married yet when she died, that it was her favorite. And Pops was right about them having to be fresh."

"Okay, that's good to know. The thing is, the name isn't right, but the photograph with it is stirring something in me. Does the name

215

Noémie Treves sound familiar?"

"No. Should it?"

"That's this woman's name."

"Then I don't think it's the right one."

"What was Great-grandma's maiden name?"

"Hmm. I have no idea. Let me ask." A few moments of muffled noises passed. "That doesn't jar anything in Pops' memory either. That's not to say he won't start talking about it in an hour or a day or two. I'll keep you posted if I hear anything more."

"Okay. In the meantime, I'm going to send you this picture and see if it triggers anything for either you or Pops or Dad."

"Sounds good. I'll be looking for it."

"Thanks, Mom. Love you."

"Love you too."

By this time, the others had joined Caitlyn on the balcony. Aiden stood beside her. "So, what did you find out?"

"Awfully curious, aren't you?"

"Hey, we're as invested in this as you are. Our families just aren't as interesting as yours."

"Well, I still don't know if Noémie Treves is who we're looking for. Oh, I should try to get a copy of my great-grandmother's death certificate. Shouldn't that list her birthdate so that we can check it against those ID papers? Maybe the certificate will even have her birth name."

"That's a great idea. What state did she die in?"

"Illinois. As soon as we get back to the apartment, I'm going to request it. In the meantime, I'll text Mom to see if she or Pops has it. Let's go back inside and look at what other information they might have."

An hour later, they had completed their tour of the fortress and were sitting at a wrought iron table along the canal with what the menu called bubble cones filled with hazelnut and chocolate ice cream. Who cared about the calories when it tasted so good? Lindsey's favorite dessert had been chocolate ice cream. She would have loved it.

"So what did you think of the art gallery inside the fortress?" Brock bit into one of the little meringue stars that decorated his ice cream.

"That was interesting." Elissa was a straight vanilla girl. "Some of the pieces were reminiscent of Monet, some of Van Gogh, and a few even of Picasso. The painter whose work was in there certainly spanned the genres."

"For sure."

Art history had never been Caitlyn's thing, so she tuned out the conversation. A short way down the canal, some men in wetsuits pushing inflatable rafts emerged from the lower level of the castle. Judging by the uniforms of those watching them, they must be from some branch of the military.

Couples strolled along the waterway, shops and restaurants lining this street. Many of them promenaded hand in hand. When Aiden had reached for hers earlier, it was so nice. Warm and comforting and strong all at once. Could there be something igniting between them?

She snuck a peek at him only to discover him gazing in her direction. They both broke off contact right away, heat rising in Caitlyn's cheeks.

Lindsey would be having a field day with this.

How much time would pass before thoughts of her friend no longer invaded her brain every hour of every day? When would time heal the pain and soften the memories? Lessen them even? Guess she would find out if and when that time came. Not that she ever wanted to forget Lindsey. She never would.

But it would be nice to forget that night.

Aiden nudged her with his elbow, bringing her back to reality. "Your ice cream is melting all over the place. I don't think you want that."

"No, of course not. I don't want to waste a single drop." She ran her pink plastic spoon along the side of the bumpy bubble cone to catch as much as she could then licked it clean.

Her phone buzzed with a text from Mom.

POPS SAID THE PICTURE DIDN'T LOOK LIKE HE REMEMBERED HIS MOTHER. MAYBE THERE IS SOMETHING FAMILIAR TO ME, BUT I DIDN'T KNOW HER UNTIL SHE WAS MUCH OLDER. SORRY I COULDN'T HELP MORE.

She shared the message with the rest of the group.

Aiden tipped his chair onto the back two legs. "Too bad that didn't lead anywhere."

"You're going to fall over." Caitlyn reached out to steady him.

"Nah. And if I do, a swim in the canal behind us might be nice."

"Don't expect me to fish you out. I'll leave it to the marines to get you."

They all enjoyed a good chuckle.

"Why don't we head to the church across the bay and see what that's like?" Brock crumpled his napkin and placed it in the cup where his cone had been.

"You like churches, don't you?" Aiden followed suit.

"You have to admit, they're kind of cool, even if we don't worship in anything near that grand."

The group agreed that would be their next stop, but as they made their way over, Caitlyn texted Sophia from the maternity home to see if she had discovered more information or if she knew anything about Noémie Treves.

Once she stepped inside the chapel, it took Caitlyn's eyes a few minutes to adjust to the dimness of the interior. Like most of the churches she'd been to in Europe, this one was elaborate, with side chambers decorated with painted and gold leaf figures depicting the lives of certain saints. Candles flickered in front of the golden altarpiece.

While the others explored, she slid into a pew and bowed her head. She didn't pray anything specific, just did her best to absorb the peace of the place.

Lindsey was in a far more beautiful setting than this, one where she could see God face-to-face. Yet Caitlyn missed her so much.

If only. . .

CHAPTER FORTY-FOUR

22 August, 1955
Elne, France

I complete another circuit around the house. Time is ticking by so slowly, the second hand on my watch moving at a turtle's pace. As I return to the side where the second-floor balcony is, I spy the little area underneath it, once paved with bricks that are now uneven. On closer inspection, many are broken.

I'd forgotten about this spot where the children would hide and play, away from the hot summer's sun. A place of shade and protection.

Some of the older girls would have tea parties here. Though supplies like dishes were precious, the cook who worked here was a woman with a heart and would allow them to borrow a few china cups. They would pretend they were in Paris, fancy ladies with fancy clothes. A few minutes of escape.

An escape we all needed from time to time. A way to forget what was happening outside of the little world we created here. Roses used to climb up the marble columns that support the balcony, their color cheering, their fragrance heady. Though we used much of the land for growing food, the beauty they'd provided was so necessary for morale, to keep us from plunging into deep despair.

I duck and make my way underneath the porch, careful not to trip on any of the uneven bricks. Once I'm seated, I pull my knees to my chest and my skirt over my knees. A few roses remain, the remnants of a bygone summer.

Just as this place remains, the remnants of a bygone era. An era that was shattered all too soon.

CHAPTER FORTY-FIVE

3 November, 1942
Elne, Vichy France

A crispness settled over the maternity home, the mornings now chilly, though with the sunshine, afternoons were rather pleasant. All of that would soon change with the coming of winter.

Hélène's child continued to grow and move, a reminder of the love she and Levi had shared. The pain in her heart was still sharper than a knife, and she often cried herself to sleep at night. There would never be a time she wouldn't miss him, never a time when he would be far from her thoughts. She couldn't speak of him without weeping.

She would always carry him close to her heart. Hide the memories of him deep in her soul.

Not too many weeks distant, and it would be Hanukkah. Last year, she and Levi had celebrated it together. They had their own festivities, just the two of them, in peace and relative comfort. While they couldn't get all the food they traditionally had, they managed to pull together quite a nice feast, including latkes and even beignets.

It was one of those recollections that Eleanore had advised Hélène to hold on to. And so she would. But for this year, it was difficult to gaze into the past and rekindle that happiness she'd experienced just twelve months ago.

And the hospital was crowded. More and more women either came from Rivesaltes or arrived on their doorstep after having escaped arrest. The raids on the hospital continued. Each time the gendarmes arrived,

Hélène hid with Margot and Beryl. They always shook with fear and were becoming more withdrawn.

All the mothers and children were. It wasn't easy to get to know someone only to have her taken back to Rivesaltes for transport to Drancy and places beyond.

Hélène's back ached, and she lay on her bed in the dormitory while the children raced up and down the halls. Rain pattered at the window, and that kept them cooped up inside today. Rainy days were the worst. Everyone was short-tempered because they were all gathered in close quarters.

The door opened, and Salomé entered, her son on her hip. He had grown so much over the past few months. One blessing in all of this mess was that Salomé was still here. Somehow, she had managed to avoid being taken in any of the raids, perhaps because she had a nursing background.

She dropped a blanket on the cold floor and set her son on top of it. He busied himself with trying to pull off his sock. "Ça va?"

"Ça va. I've been better, and I've been worse. My back is hurting pretty badly though. I can't get comfortable."

"It could be labor."

"I have thought about that. This may be my first baby, but there are so many women here who have given birth, I'm becoming something of an expert on the subject. The trouble is that it's too early. By my calculations, I have about six or seven more weeks to go."

"It may be nothing more than the baby pressing on your spine. Why don't you roll over and let me examine you. Keep an eye on Paul while I go get what I need."

Hélène sat up and scooped the baby off the chilly floor. He gurgled and pulled her hair. "Oh no you don't." She grabbed his little hand and kissed it. Was this what it would be like to hold her own child? For a moment, she forgot her grief. She had something else, someone else to think about. Perhaps this was where she would discover the purpose and joy that Eleanore had spoken about.

Salomé returned to the room. "Okay, let me see what's going on here." After she poked and prodded Hélène and completed a thorough examination, she stepped back. "You are dilating. I'm going to consult with Eleanore, but my suggestion would be for you to remain in bed. No heavy lifting, and only get up when you absolutely must."

Hélène's heart fluttered in her chest, and she struggled to keep her breathing deep and even. Panicking wouldn't help the situation. She may not know much, but she did know that. "Is the baby going to be okay?" Without warning, a fierce protectiveness overcame her. "I can't lose this bit of Levi. Without this baby, I have nothing of him. Before I left Rivesaltes, I promised him I'd take care of our child."

"Don't worry. If you stay calm, that will help. Some dilation is expected as you get closer to your due date, so this isn't a cause for concern. We want to help you do everything possible to deliver a healthy child. That's why we tell you to stay in bed. Keep your risks low."

"Ça va. I'll do as you say. I'll do whatever I have to do in order to save my baby."

Salomé squeezed Hélène's hand. "Don't worry. Everything will be fine. Soon you and I will both have our children to help us remember our husbands."

"Did you get bad news about Ruben?"

Salomé shook her head, her dark curls bouncing with the motion. "Still no word. No one ever hears from their loved ones who go to the camps. So I wait and look for whatever glimpses of my husband I can find in my son's face. Rest now. I'll send Eleanore in."

The dormitory was still after Salomé left. Even the children in the hall had quieted. Perhaps their mothers put them down for naps. This was one of the most peaceful times of the day. Hélène rolled around on the cot, not the most comfortable of all sleeping arrangements in the best of times, and even less so when the baby was growing and her back continued to hurt.

At last she found a way to lie that didn't ache too much, and she closed her eyes. Next thing she knew, a little boy bounded into the room ahead of Eleanore. He laughed and patted Hélène's cheek.

"Be gentle with Madame Treves."

Hélène leaned over and gave the tot a kiss on the cheek. "I can't believe how big Javier is getting. It's been a few days since I've seen him, and it looks like he's grown several centimeters."

"They don't stay small for long. That's why we tell mothers they must learn to enjoy each stage of their children's lives. But the question is, how are you doing?"

"I did manage to get a little rest."

"*Désolée.* We didn't mean to interrupt your nap, but I did want to check on you."

"That's fine." Hélène waved away the apology and focused on Javier, who was working to open the suitcase at the end of one of the beds.

"Non, non, *mon petit.* Leave that alone." Eleanore grabbed Javier and pulled a crayon and a bit of paper from her apron pocket and set him to coloring. Even though he wasn't yet eighteen months old, he grabbed the crayon and concentrated on scribbling blue marks on the page.

"He's adorable."

"Isn't he?" Eleanore gazed at him. There was no denying that she truly cared about each of the children under her protection, especially the orphans.

"I'm surprised you haven't found a home for Javier yet."

"You forget that he's Jewish. It's not easy to locate couples willing to take a Jewish child in the middle of war when the Jews are facing extermination."

A shudder ran through Hélène. "Of course. But one of these days he'll be a fine son for a very lucky family."

"You continue to stall on the examination."

"Salomé did a thorough job. I don't think we need to repeat it."

Eleanore nodded but proceeded to ask Hélène a series of questions. When she ran out of inquiries, she sat on the edge of Hélène's bed. "You're right. Salomé is a very good nurse, and we're fortunate to have her with us. I agree with her assessment. This may or may not be labor. I do think this baby will come a little early. He seems eager to be out in the world. Just rest and take it easy."

"What about my work with the identity cards?"

"I'll assign that duty to someone else. She won't be as good as you, but right now your baby needs to be your priority. I wouldn't be opposed to you checking her work, if you'd like."

"At the very least, I'll have to tell her my system. There's a certain way I do it so that everything stays organized. The key to running any successful company is being organized and staying on top of things."

"You're a shrewd businesswoman, and I'll be sure to send your temporary replacement in to speak with you so that she doesn't mess up your system. You've worked very hard on making it good and efficient. If I haven't said it before, I want you to know we've been very blessed that God sent you to us."

CHAPTER FORTY-SIX

20 November, 1942
Elne, Occupied France

Salomé and Eleanore and even Fräulein Reiter visited Hélène from time to time, and Margot and Beryl came for lessons on mathematics and accounting with her, but time dragged. Her forced inactivity gave her too much freedom to think. To dwell on the past.

When she was alone, she took to speaking to Levi as if he were in the room. "I wish you were taking care of me. You'd be so good and gentle and bring me whatever I want. I couldn't have asked for more in a husband. You doted on me. I should have doted on you more." A heavy weight settled on her chest.

She had been far from the perfect wife, and now the time was past for her to apologize to Levi and express to him all he'd meant to her. How happy she'd been to have him in her life and how fortunate she was to have had a husband like him. He'd forgiven her for the stubbornness that had cost her employees their lives. That was the sweetest part of it all.

A past filled with regrets lay behind her, and a future filled with uncertainty stretched in front of her.

A knock at the door interrupted her musings. Who would knock like that? The women who shared this room just entered, as did the nurses and Fräulein Reiter and the others. She pulled the blanket to her chin. "Come in."

As tall and as confident as ever, Aime entered, commanding the room. If he'd been born in America, maybe he would have been a movie star. He had that type of presence. Maybe like Clark Gable or some other actor.

"I was told you were resting and preparing for your coming baby, and I imagined that you must be quite bored."

"And you'd be correct." She pushed herself to a sitting position and smoothed her hair.

"Are you okay to be up like that?"

"I can't lie in one position from now until the baby comes. As long as I don't overdo it, Eleanore assures me I'll be fine. Besides, with each passing day, the danger grows less as the baby gets closer to his due date. But I'm sure you didn't come to talk about female things."

"Non, I did not."

For the first time, Hélène realized that he was holding one hand behind his back. Moments later he presented her with a bouquet of hothouse roses. All red, with the thorns removed. The smell was heavenly.

"They're beautiful. You didn't have to do that."

"It's my pleasure. I've enjoyed getting to know you over the past few months, and I was sorry I wouldn't be seeing you for a while. They were a good excuse for me to come."

"Do you tend them yourself?"

"Of course. Though I have a young man, still a boy really, working the garden, I wouldn't trust anyone else with Maman's prize roses. She developed a few new varieties. I even have one named for me."

"Wow, how interesting. Why don't you pull up a chair and tell me more about your mother and the greenhouse?"

So he did, and the afternoon flew by as if it had wings. They laughed about the mischief he got into as a child, how difficult his father's and cousin's deaths were on him, and his plans to possibly sell the château and use the money to start a foundation. "I just don't have the heart for growing olives and producing wine. My passion never lay there. It's just what was expected of me after they passed away."

She nodded. "How well I understand. I had the same expectations placed on me when my parents died, but at least I loved what I was doing and was happy to be involved in the business. It must be a terrible burden if you don't enjoy it."

"Oui et non. It has provided me a good living and the ability to do what I've done so far for the war effort."

"We have much in common, don't we?"

He flashed her his familiar lopsided grin. "That we do. Now tell me more about yourself."

She told him how she learned the glass-making business at her father's side and detailed her courtship with Levi and the kind of man he was. "You'd be friends, I imagine."

"He does sound like someone I would like to have known. But thank you for sharing your memories with me."

She had done that, hadn't she? She'd spoken about Levi without breaking down. When it came time to tell their child, she would be able to do it. To share with him all that his father was. She'd be able to convey the essence of him to their child.

"You must miss him a great deal."

"Oui. There is a hole in my heart that will never be filled. So many holes because of so many lost. Some I could have prevented." The words slipped past her lips without her stopping to check them. If only she could pull them back.

Aime tilted his head. "What do you mean?"

"You will never forgive me, never think of me the same, if I tell you."

"I doubt that. How could you have prevented someone's loss?"

"Many someones." Her chest constricted.

Aime touched her hand, and the gesture broke the dam that had held back her tears for years. As she sobbed, he never let go of her hand, not until he fished a handkerchief from his suit coat pocket and passed it to her.

She wiped her eyes. "Je suis désolée."

"You have nothing to be sorry for, though I gather you carry a great weight."

"We knew. Even before they invaded France, we knew what the Germans were doing to the Jews. Another factory owner told me he was going to send all his Jewish employees to England, America, Australia, wherever he could to save them.

"He begged me to do the same, but I only employed Jews. If they all emigrated, I would have no more factory, no more job, no more means of supporting myself and Levi."

"Couldn't you have góne with them?"

"Oui." She twisted the edge of the blanket around her finger until it was so tight it just about cut off the circulation. "But I didn't want to leave the only home I'd known. I was selfish."

A long moment of silence stood between them until Aime sliced through it by encouraging her to continue. So she did. "When the Nazis arrived and they cracked down on the Jews, the noose tightening around our necks, they came one night to the factory and arrested everyone. They discovered the employee lists and took even those who weren't working. Only because we were out of the factory and a neighbor told us what was happening did Levi and I escape.

"It's my fault the Nazis took my employees, all fifteen of them and their families, and condemned them to a certain death."

"How were you to know the Nazis would invade France? Could you foretell the future?"

"It was inevitable. You can't deny that."

"You did what you thought was best. In a difficult situation, you made an impossible decision. You don't even know for sure they were killed."

"I do." She covered her face, her tears coming hot and fast now. "They never made it to Drancy or any other camp. Instead, they stopped at a farm on the outskirts of Mulhouse and gunned down every one of them. Men. Women. Little children."

Aime sat on the bed and held her close while she wept like she never had in her entire life. She soaked his handkerchief and his shirt, but neither were enough to absorb all her tears. So many people dead because of her.

"It's not your fault. It's not your fault," Aime repeated for what must have been the hundredth time.

At last, she drained her lake of tears and sat back, out of his grasp.

"Is that why you wanted to go to Rivesaltes? Is that why you type the false papers?"

"Anything I can do to save even a single life. Nothing will make up for the past, but I can do better in the future. Save lives instead of condemning them to death."

She had barely dried her tears when Eleanore burst into the room. Her face was red, and she was breathless.

Aime stood so fast, he just about knocked the chair over. "What is it? What has you so upset?"

"The Germans are taking over for the Vichy. They've had enough with being the puppeteers, and now they want to be fully in charge. I've been informed that they'll be liquidating the camp at Rivesaltes.

"And they'll be closing the hospital."

CHAPTER FORTY-SEVEN

They're going to do what?" Hélène grasped Aime's hand as he stood beside her bed, Eleanore in front of them, tears shimmering in her eyes.

"Closing it." Eleanore's voice broke. "All that I've worked for, all the women and children I've helped over the years, all the money that generous people, including you, Aime, have poured into it, all gone."

"And what's to be done with us?"

"Of course the gendarmes wouldn't tell me, but we can guess. And Rivesaltes won't be the final destination. We may not even be taken there at all. They didn't give me a date, but I expect it to be very soon. Hours, days at the very most."

"Hours?" Aime's voice rose an octave.

Eleanore bit the corner of her lip and gave a single, small nod. "I don't know what to do. Where are all these women and children going to go? Who will take them in, if there's even time to arrange anything? We've worked too hard protecting them to have them fall into Nazi hands."

Aime stepped forward, requiring Hélène to release her grip on him. "I have a large, old castle that would be perfect."

"You would put yourself into so much jeopardy. And how would we be able to move everyone and all our supplies that fast?"

"I have a few automobiles, and there is François' truck. We'll go as fast as possible and do what we can."

"And if we get caught?" Eleanore pinched the bridge of her nose, a trick Hélène herself used to keep from crying.

"Then we'll entrust ourselves to the Lord's care."

Hélène stood and slipped her feet into her shoes. "From the sound of it, we don't have much time. I'll start rounding up the women and children. We have to get packed and ready to go."

Aime gave her a gentle push back onto the bed. "You can direct traffic, but you'll do it from here. I'll put the arrangements into motion."

"But—"

"None of that." Eleanore sat beside her, and Aime disappeared through the door. "This mission is about saving lives, and that includes your unborn child."

Hélène swallowed the scream that begged for release from her throat. She couldn't sit here helpless while everyone else scrambled to make the move. "It's not in my nature to sit by and do nothing."

"I've learned that about you, but you'll have to fight it. I refuse to allow you to do more than give directions. That will be help enough. If we don't have someone organizing everything, this will descend into chaos and will impede our progress in the move."

"I guess I can't do anything else," Hélène huffed.

"There will be plenty for you to do after the baby arrives. We won't be able to hide everyone at the castle indefinitely, so other arrangements will need to be made. This is only temporary."

Within minutes, the room flooded with women and their children, all chattering and clamoring. Hélène had retrieved her suitcase from underneath her bed and was busy rearranging the clothes inside, adding a few little garments she'd sewn for her baby. "Ladies, ladies, may I have your attention."

The room quieted. "Merci. We have to be quick, but we must maintain order. Pack your bags with the essentials, and don't forget what you'll need for your children. If you're not nursing your infants, be sure to get some bottles from the nursery. Pack plenty of blankets. I imagine the castle will be rather chilly. Above all, remain calm, both for your sake and for the sake of the children. There's no need to frighten them."

Though the room continued to buzz, there was more order now. Each woman, eyes wide, stripped her bed and packed her case as full as she could. Their tones were hushed but urgent. Even the children were quiet, following their mothers' instructions to gather their toys.

A short time later, Salomé came in, Paul on her hip. Her eyes shimmered with tears as she approached Hélène. "I see you've heard."

"Oui. Eleanore won't allow me to get up, but I'm trying my best to organize all I can from here."

"Do you need anything?"

"Non, you get ready to go. Knowing Aime, it won't take him long to get cars and trucks and maybe even a bus here, though we have to be careful about being too conspicuous leaving. Then again, there isn't time to lose. We can't wait until nightfall."

Salomé sat beside her and took her hand. "I'm frightened. Not so much for myself, though it scares me to think about what the Nazis would do if they arrested me. Ruben is already finding that out. But I'm most concerned for Paul."

"I know." Hélène picked at an invisible thread on her dark blue dress. "But we just have to believe that we'll be okay."

Salomé squeezed Hélène's hand so hard she almost crushed it in her grip. "I don't know how you can believe that we'll be okay. We have no guarantee of that."

"Non, we don't. All the same, we must carry on. Hashem has abandoned us, or so it seems. That's not a very trustworthy God to me. But I do trust Eleanore and Aime. They may not be as powerful as Hashem is supposed to be, but they always do their best to make sure we are as safe as possible."

"That isn't very reassuring."

"That's the best I can give you right now. Je suis désolée. I wish I had better answers for you. Maybe you can talk to Eleanore or Aime when we get settled at the castle and they'll be better able to tell you why we should trust Hashem."

"If we make it that far."

Hélène turned Salomé's head until she could stare into her dark green eyes. "We can't allow ourselves to think that way. Never." Though she herself had when she found out Levi was dead. When she had something to do, something to occupy her mind, it was easier for her to cast away those disturbing thoughts. "Negativity never did anyone a bit of good."

"In this dark world, there is no light at all." Salomé released Hélène's hand and stood. Paul squirmed in her arms. "I'd better get going. There's so much to do."

From outside the windows came the honking of a horn. Hélène forced herself to remain seated. "That can't be Aime already, can it?"

One of the women gazed out the tall, multi-paned window. "It's François, here with his truck. But it's not big enough for all of us. Wait. Two cars just pulled in. That's still not enough room."

Eleanore swept in. "We're going to take the children first, and the new mothers who are nursing."

"Hey!"

"What about me?"

"That's not fair!"

Eleanore held up her hand, but the din continued. After a minute or so, Hélène whistled, just like Papa had taught her to if she were in trouble. "We need to listen to Madame Touissant. It's not a perfect solution. Nothing about this situation is ideal. But if we go as fast and orderly as possible, we all have the best chance of getting to safety." She was about to add that the Nazis could arrive at any moment, but that would be enough to incite a panic. It was bad enough that the thought sent her heart off to the races.

"Merci, Madame Etu." Eleanore gave her a strained smile. "Allons-y." Each mother left the room, and only a few pregnant women remained.

Unable to help herself any longer, Hélène went to the window. Even though it was closed against the autumn's chill, the cries of the children and their mothers permeated the glass and broke her heart.

Nothing about this war was fair. Families were split up far too often. Some would never see each other again.

"Madame Treves." Margot and Beryl rushed into the room as Hélène turned from the window, almost unused to the sound of her given name anymore.

"What are you doing here? You need to get into the truck."

Margot stepped forward. "We're letting the littlest go first. We're big girls, and so we thought we should wait until all the babies are gone."

"You understand what's happening, don't you? You don't want to go back to the camp. Come on. I'll take you down myself. And don't worry, I'll be coming very soon."

Maxine, whose baby was due about the same time as Hélène's, stood on her swollen feet. "You should be sitting, Hélène. I'll take the girls."

They both clung to her rather round middle. She smoothed their hair from their flushed faces, then nodded to Maxine. "It's fine. I'm going to have to get up and go downstairs at some point or another. I'll just see them safely to the truck, then I'll return."

"Really, let me do it."

"We want Madame Treves." The poor girls had been through so much and had lost so much already. Now they were preparing to go to another home with more uncertainty stretching in front of them.

"I'm fine." Before Maxine could protest further, Hélène led the girls from the room and down the stairs. Though the air was cold, the sunshine on her skin was wonderful.

She walked the girls to the truck and then kissed them each on the cheek. "I'll see you very soon. Don't worry. Madame Touissant and Monsieur Laurent will take very good care of you. Perhaps I'll even be on the next truck."

With tears in their eyes, they climbed into the back, empty rice sacks still littering the floor. The truck was almost to capacity, yet there were so many remaining at the home. François had to leave now so he could come back and pick up more.

With the help of some of the weeping mothers, she shut the door and motioned for François to leave. "Hurry back."

He waved and was off.

But Aime hadn't left with him. Just as she was about to turn to go into the house, he came to her side. "I'm glad you're here. I'm going to take you to my home personally as soon as I get your suitcase."

"I can wait my turn. You shouldn't be giving me preferential treatment. It will look bad." But as she spoke, a band tightened around her middle, sucking the breath from her lungs. She couldn't hold back a moan.

"What is it?"

She waved him away, unable to speak. A minute or so went by before the pain lessened. "I'm fine."

"You're not. I'll get Salomé to come with us so you have a nurse, but we're leaving now. No arguments. If others believe it's not fair, that's too bad. Your health and that of your baby comes before what others are going to think of either one of us. Get in the car." Though he didn't shout, he was firm. There was no way she would be able to talk him out of this.

As he left to get her belongings, another pain gripped her, and she clung to the car door until it ceased. The contractions were close together. Some of the women had false labor. That was all this was. It couldn't be anything else.

Aime must have informed Eleanore that he was taking Hélène to the chateau, because she exited the building, Étienne in her arms, along with a little suitcase.

By this time, Hélène had managed to slide into the seat but hadn't closed the door yet. Eleanore rushed over and thrust Étienne into her arms. "I don't have time to explain, but I want you to take him with you."

"He should have gone with the other children."

"I know, but I couldn't part with him. I would have asked the other mothers to take him, but I couldn't bring myself to let him go."

Another contraction tightened like a vice around her middle, and Hélène moaned.

"You're in labor."

Hélène breathed through the pain as Eleanore and the other midwives and nurses had instructed. Once it passed, she managed to nod.

"I'm sorry to ask this of you, but I still want you to take Étienne. For me."

"Come with us."

"I can't. There's more to see to here. Documents I have to get rid of, and women still to be organized to leave. I'll come as soon as I can. The château isn't far, so François should be back soon. Just a few truckloads should be enough to get everyone out. But I need to make sure Étienne is safe."

Aime hurried from the building, two suitcases in his hand, Salomé and Paul right behind him.

"Hurry. Hélène is in labor." Eleanore motioned for them to come quickly.

"I know." Aime threw the cases into the trunk as Salomé climbed into the back of the car with her son. "I'll return soon."

Hélène cradled Étienne in her arms. "I'll take good care of him, you can count on that."

"Allons-y." Aime put the car into gear and sped away from the home.

When Hélène glanced over her shoulder, Eleanore stood on the front steps, tears streaming down her face.

CHAPTER FORTY-EIGHT

22 August, 1955
Elne, France

A ll these years later, that day haunts me. The day this once-beautiful building that had been a refuge, a safe haven, a fortress, became a place of terror.

The cries of the children invade my nightmares even now. Many without their mothers, frightened of what was happening, why they had to leave this place they loved, fought us. We battled to carry them downstairs. They didn't understand that what we were doing was best for them.

Isn't that the way it is with the Almighty? We push against His will for us, certain that we know better than Him. That we know what our lives should look like, the trajectory they should take.

But He is good and gracious and loving. I glance over my shoulder at the crumbling peachy lady. We believed this to be the best place for us. That if we could have stayed here, we would have survived the war unscathed.

How foolish we were. No one escaped the conflict without scars. Oui, I was an adult at the time, but even the children were touched by it. The Nazis didn't just kill people. They broke them.

But that is what today is about. A balm on the scars. Healing, perhaps even a little. Ridding myself of those nightmares. Affirming that I made the best choice on that horrific day.

A day that changed everyone's lives forever.

CHAPTER FORTY-NINE

September 6, 2022
Barcelona, Spain

While her professor was busy handing out the exam results, Caitlyn slunk down in the desk. The others in the class chattered, leaning over and whispering and sharing their papers. She didn't need to see the mark on the top of the page to know that she hadn't received a good grade.

When she was supposed to be studying, scenes of that night played over and over in her head instead. When she was taking the exam, the least cough or dropped pen was enough to distract her so much that she lost her train of thought and couldn't pick it up again.

She hadn't slept well in a good number of nights. Her head buzzed almost all the time. And she didn't need a scale to know she'd lost even more weight. Her loose jeans told her that.

No matter how hard she tried to hold it together, her life was unraveling at the seams.

Dr. Lin set the papers upside down in front of Caitlyn then leaned down, speaking in a soft voice. "Please stay after class. I'd like to talk to you."

At her words, Caitlyn's insides clenched. Nothing good could come from a professor's request to talk after everyone left. Especially when she got a—she lifted the corner of the page to peek—D on the test.

She blew out a breath. While it wasn't failing, it was far too close to it for comfort. The mission board would never approve her for the field with grades like this.

After a brief lecture, the professor dismissed the students. All except for Caitlyn, who pretended to fiddle with the zipper on her backpack. Elissa gathered her things and came over. "Let's get going. Brock has this amazing new restaurant he wants us to try."

Caitlyn painted on the smile she was getting so good at. "Go ahead without me. I have a few things I need to do. Besides, I'm not very hungry."

"What's wrong? Didn't you do well on the test? Dr. Lin is so strict. I got an A-."

At this point, Caitlyn would kill for a grade like that. "No, I just need some alone time. You understand."

"Of course." Elissa nodded, her ponytail bobbing in rhythm. "If you change your mind, text me, and I'll let you know where we are. Aiden is going to miss you."

"I'm sure, but a quiet evening sounds really good to me." Besides, she couldn't afford going out all the time. The church was paying for the school, but everything else was up to her. Since she wasn't working right now, she was living off savings.

"See you later then." Elissa bounded away, leaving only Caitlyn and Dr. Lin in the room.

The professor leaned against the front edge of her desk, and Caitlyn made her way closer.

Dr. Lin smiled a soft smile and tilted her head, her shiny black hair falling to one side. "Is there something going on I should know about?"

"Like what?"

"I don't know, but when the class began, you were one of my best students. You were focused and got wonderful grades. When we went to the hospitals, you were so kind to the patients, so sympathetic and understanding. But in the past few weeks, your grades have been slipping. You're still good with the patients, but you seem to be in a little more hurry when dealing with them."

Caitlyn bit the inside of her cheek. "I'm sorry about the grades. There's so much going on outside of school that's distracting me. I promise I'll buckle down and do better from this point on. I hope it doesn't jeopardize my ability to go on the field."

"I'm concerned about you. You're a bright young woman and very talented. You have so much to offer to the world. But answer just one question. Why are you going to the mission field?"

"I've dreamed of doing this since I was a little girl. When I was young, a missionary nurse came to our church and talked about how the clinic she worked at was changing lives for the better, both on the outside and on the inside. I want to help heal people's bodies and souls." While not the complete truth, it was the truth.

"So this is something you feel God leading you to do? You've given it plenty of thought and prayer?"

Caitlyn nodded. "Like I said, I promise to buckle down and do what I have to in order to graduate and get a posting."

"A student like you doesn't drop from getting As to getting Ds in the course of a few weeks. There's more to it. If you aren't comfortable talking to me, we can arrange a counseling session with one of the pastors here or one of their wives. I hesitate sending you to the wilds of Africa if you're struggling with something. You have to be able to handle the pressures you'll face there."

"I know." Her airway was now as constricted as her stomach. She couldn't fail, she just couldn't. If she did, she wouldn't be just letting her parents down. She'd be letting Lindsey down. And that was the last thing she was going to allow to happen.

Dr. Lin touched her shoulder. "I'll pray for you, and if you ever want to talk to me, my door is always open. Everyone has difficulties from time to time, so there's no shame in asking for help. There's nothing wrong with saying that life is getting a bit too overwhelming."

"I know. And thank you. I'm going to go home and start studying for the next exam. Is there anything I can do to make up my grade?"

"I'll look and see. But Caitlyn, remember what I said. If you need help, please ask."

"Thanks. I think I'll be fine. Just a little hiccup. I won't allow myself to get as distracted as I have been." She clutched her backpack strap and left the room, almost running out of the building.

She kept up her frenetic pace until she reached her apartment. Even then, she sprinted up the stairs and didn't stop until she was inside with the door locked behind her.

For several minutes, she stood in the small entryway catching her breath, trying to allow her racing heart to catch up. Okay, okay. This wasn't the end of the world. Like she'd told Dr. Lin, just a small hiccup. One she could overcome. If given the chance for some extra credit, it shouldn't even affect her grades that much.

She'd come too far. Too many people were depending on her.

Maybe she should call Mom. No, that wasn't fair to Mom. She'd been calling her far too much. Though Mom worked from home, she still worked and took care of Pops. Plus it was the middle of the day in Chicago. Talking to any of the pastors here or their wives was too intimidating. She didn't know any of them well enough to pour out her heart.

No, it was up to her. Her and God. Wasn't He all she needed to get over this? If she sought a closer walk with Him, she would be in a better place.

Help me, Lord, please. After a few more shaky breaths, she had calmed down enough to put her backpack away and change into some comfy flannel pants and an old, oversized sweatshirt. The words *University of Illinois* were almost faded beyond recognition. And that was why this was her favorite comfy ensemble. While it wouldn't do for the streets of Barcelona, it was fine for when she was alone in the apartment.

She hadn't been reading her Bible as much as she'd promised Mom, but now she took it and went to the gray IKEA-style love seat in the living room. But she didn't open the book. Instead, she held it and closed her eyes. *Lord, give me Your presence and peace.*

For quite a while, she sat in solitude and stillness, praying short prayers from time to time.

Hold me, Lord.

Be with me, Father.

Help me. Help me.

She imagined God wrapping His arms around her and holding her fast, like a mother hen surrounds her chicks. It was biblical, and she went with the imagery.

I need You.

As soon as she prayed that, the tears came hot and fast and unstoppable. She wept and wept until she had emptied herself of her store of tears. She was lonely and afraid. Yes, God was with her in the moment, but she missed home. She missed Lindsey.

Her phone dinged, but she ignored it. Couldn't have looked at the text if she had wanted to. If she did, she might cry more. She didn't want to be tearful and sad all the time. Here she was, facing the rest of her life, and all she wanted was to be a little girl again with little girl problems, ones that Mom or Dad could solve in a few short minutes.

Come to me, all you who labor and are heavy laden, and you will find rest for your souls.

Rest. She needed that more than anything. Still clutching her Bible, she lay on the couch, curled up, and closed her eyes.

By the time she opened them again, darkness had fallen across the city. On the other side of the street, people in the apartments had closed their shutters and settled in for the evening.

She sat up, finger-combed her hair, and fixed her ponytail, whatever good that did. When she went to put her Bible away, her phone fell, and she picked it up. There had been a message. First, though, she had better make herself presentable before Elissa came home and questioned her red eyes.

She showered, scrambled some eggs, and toasted a piece of bread. Not much of a dinner, but a dinner. Elissa would probably bring home some leftovers anyway, though there usually weren't many when they went for tapas.

When her roommate finally showed up, Caitlyn had managed to crack open her community health textbook and read a few pages. She might have even retained a few things. Maybe. Hopefully.

"Wow, studying." Elissa dropped her key on the small kitchen table. "You're putting me to shame."

"I need to. I got a D on that last test."

"Did you say you got a D?" Elissa's mouth fell open. "You never get Ds. You don't even have to study to get As."

"That's not true, and you know it. You're the smart one. If I do well, it's because I have to work hard. And I haven't been doing that lately. I need you to be my accountability partner, keeping me on track so I don't flunk out. I could never show my face at home if that happened."

"You're not going to fail. I'll make sure of that. What did you have trouble with on the test?"

"Everything." Caitlyn flopped against the back of the couch. "I studied."

"You sat with your book open while you stared into space. I caught you a few times."

"Well, I tried to study, but there was too much distracting me."

Elissa raised a perfectly plucked eyebrow. "Okay, that's your first problem. You need to find a way to shut out all distractions."

Hard to do when those came from inside your own head.

"You have noise-cancelling headphones, don't you?"

"Yeah."

"I know of some great music, or really, they're tones that you can play that are supposed to help you focus. And you have to put your phone across the room so you aren't tempted to scroll through TikTok."

"I don't even have a TikTok account."

"You know what I mean."

"Wait a minute. I got a text earlier. Let me look at it." She picked up her phone. "It's from Sophia." She opened the message.

WE FOUND MORE CARDS. IF YOU GIVE ME YOUR GREAT-GRANDMOTHER'S NAME OR YOUR GREAT-GRANDFATHER'S, I CAN SEE IF THEY'RE HERE. LET ME KNOW IF THERE IS ANYTHING ELSE I CAN DO FOR YOU.

Maybe this was it. Perhaps if she solved the riddle to her past, she would be able to get on with her future.

CHAPTER FIFTY

22 August, 1955
Elne, France

Dreams have this funny way of dying. When I was a little girl, I dreamed of the happiest of lives. Days full of sunshine and joy. Happiness that stretched into golden foreverness.

I glance at the sky, once brilliant blue, now brackish and gray. Such was my life. Nothing like the girlhood fantasies I had created for myself. Even in the best of times, those imaginings of childhood dull and fade, change and transform into something new and different.

But what we lived through didn't just change our dreams. It killed them, just as surely as the Vichy and Nazis killed us, Jews and Gentiles alike. The marble railing is smooth and chilly beneath my hands as I make my way up the outside stairs to the balcony.

For a time, I allow my heart to become as cold and as hard as the shiny white marble. But I can't allow myself to live that way anymore. It's time for me to feel again, to live again, to put away the pain of the past and create a new dream.

This one will be very different than the ones of my childhood. No more will rainbows and fairy sprinkles populate it. I'm wise enough to know that there will be raindrops along the way. Maybe even deluges.

I'm also wise enough to know that even that dream will turn and change. Nothing in this life is constant. A crack of thunder rumbles in the distance. Yes, even now the Almighty is reminding me that clouds hide the sunshine and our plans change in an instant.

But I pray for the rain to cease, just for a little while, to allow me to examine each of my memories, to face the past head on, and then to put them in a box and shut the lid.

CHAPTER FIFTY-ONE

20 November, 1942
Elne, Occupied France

Though the château had always held a presence on a hill higher than even the hospital, not only overlooking the village but the entire area, it was even more imposing as they neared. Despite the pain searing her midsection, Hélène couldn't help but stare in amazement at the very old stone building rising in front of her.

"You live here?" She managed to speak in the time between contractions.

"Oui. My family has been here for generations. The Laurent *domaine* is rather well known. The wine is sweet without being too sweet. Just right, or so they say. I am not a wine connoisseur. I'd rather help people with all our money than focus on making more."

When another pain gripped Hélène, she clutched Étienne so tight that he squealed. "Je suis désolée." She hadn't meant to hurt the boy.

"Hand him to me." Salomé reached over the seat, and Hélène managed to boost him over.

At last they reached the black iron gate that served as the castle's sentinel, François' truck waiting for them. Aime hopped out, unlocked the gate, and opened it, the hinges squeaking. Both vehicles raced through and up the long driveway to the building at the top of the hill.

Two turrets flanked either side of the pale-yellow brick castle, and ornate columns held up a portico. Banks of clear, mullioned windows winked in the bright sunlight. A balcony with a matching stone railing, not unlike the one at La Maternité de la Paix, snaked around the second story.

The outside was grand, but it didn't prepare Hélène for what the inside was like. They stepped into a foyer with black-and-white marble floors and high ceilings painted with frescos. Sweeping marble staircases swirled to both the right and left of them, up to a balcony that overlooked the scene.

François entered, not bothering to take in the building's splendor, as he was busy herding a number of children in his care.

"I have to get Madame Etu to a room and settled, but take the children to the cellar. It's quite soundproof and should provide them the protection they need."

"Is it like a dungeon?" Hélène relaxed between pains.

Aime laughed. "Hardly. There are several rooms down there, and it's heated. Simple, oui, but what we need now is safety. Madame Duval, if you can help Madame Etu to the first room to the right at the top of the stairs. Tell me what you need, and I'll get it for you."

Salomé rattled off a list of supplies as another pain tore at Hélène's middle. They were getting more intense with each one. And then, with a rush, her waters broke, soaking herself and the gorgeous floor. The floor that would be wonderful if it would open up and swallow her whole.

Aime didn't notice, or at least he pretended not to notice. Instead, he swept her from her feet, carried her upstairs, then scurried away to do Salomé's bidding. Salomé entered, Étienne in tow. The chamber was huge, with a mahogany canopy bed and dark blue papered walls with gold flecks.

It wasn't long before Salomé had Hélène in fresh clothes and tucked into bed. After a short knock, Aime entered, his arms loaded with towels and whatever else they might need.

From there, the hours passed in a haze of pain. Salomé was always by her side, mopping her forehead when the sweat trickled down and giving her tiny sips of water to quench her overwhelming thirst. Eleanore might have been there once or twice, but Hélène couldn't be sure if she was dreaming or if it was reality.

At last, with one big final push, the pain was over, and she fell into a deep sleep, one where there were no dreams of Levi. No dreams at all.

By the time Hélène awoke, sun streamed through the spotless window where someone had pulled back the heavy navy damask draperies. She yawned and tried to stretch, but that hurt a little too much.

Salomé was nowhere to be found. A heavyset woman Hélène didn't recognize occupied the upholstered chair with ornate wood carvings on the armrests and legs. A fire crackled in the oversized fireplace, and tapestries with scenes of village life covered the stone wall surrounding it.

The woman stood and made her way to the bedside. She felt Hélène's pulse in her wrist and counted off the seconds on her watch. "How are you feeling?"

"More tired than I have ever been in my entire life. And sorer than I believed I would be. But where is my child? I'd like to see him. Or is it a little girl?" Her breasts ached, her milk likely coming in, and her arms longed to hold the precious new life she'd birthed.

"I'll go see about that." Her heels clicked across the floor as she exited the room.

Hélène pulled herself to a sitting position with a great deal of difficulty. Maybe she should have asked for a brush. She didn't want to have her baby's first look at her be one that would scare him or her. Just imagine, she was going to get to hold her child.

"I wish, Levi, that you could be here to hold your baby. To stare into his or her eyes and see yourself reflected there. If only. If only."

But life was made up of "if only's." Things no one could change, no matter how hard they wished.

Levi. Her only love. Well, except for her child. The one that should be coming through the door any moment.

But it wasn't the nurse with the baby who walked through the entrance. Instead, Aime entered along with Salomé.

"Where is he? Why don't you have him with you?"

Salomé smiled, but it didn't light up her eyes. Instead, they were rimmed with red. Likewise, Aime was dour-faced and grim.

Hélène pulled her wrap tighter around herself. "What is it? Has something happened to Eleanore? Is that what you have to tell me?"

The two of them glanced at each other and shot looks that Hélène couldn't interpret.

"Don't try to spare my feelings. I have lost my home, my business, and my husband. There is no more bad news that you can bring me."

Aime sat on the edge of the four-poster bed while Salomé sat on the opposite side. She ran her hands over the fine chenille bedspread. "Do you remember anything about the birth?"

"Not really. There was so much pain. Time didn't mean anything anymore. And then the baby was born, and I went to sleep. Did someone give me something to help me rest?"

Salomé nodded. "One of the midwives did. You were exhausted. It has been two days since we moved here. Your labor was long and difficult. For a time, Eleanore was afraid that we'd lose both of you. Even after the birth, you bled quite a bit. It's truly a miracle that you're still with us."

Throughout this entire speech, Salomé didn't make eye contact with Hélène, so she turned to Aime. "There's more to this story, isn't there?"

He nodded, his Adam's apple bobbing.

"Does it have something to do with my baby, with why I haven't seen my little one yet?" Her throat constricted. That had to be it. Otherwise the child would be sleeping in his or her cradle near the fire, ready to nurse when Hélène woke up.

"Don't upset yourself. That isn't going to do you any good."

She had to restrain herself from slapping Aime. "What's upsetting me is that no one is telling me anything. It feels like you're keeping a big secret. I'm the child's mother. I deserve to know what is going on. I'm begging you, one of you, give me answers."

Aime rose from the bed and paced a circuit around it, mussing his slicked-back hair as he went, his face unshaven for at least several days. "Oui, there is something we haven't told you."

For what might as well have been a small eternity, her heart ceased beating. Or slowed to a crawl. Time remained suspended on a string, and the scene in front of her went in and out of focus. She clutched the bedsheet and the mattress, barely able to draw in a breath. "What happened?"

"You gave birth to a son."

She sank against the pillows. "Goodness, you just about gave me a heart attack. If he has six toes on each foot or big ears or even a birthmark, none of that matters. All that matters is that he's alive and well." Perhaps Hashem did hear and answer prayer.

But Salomé and Aime's expressions didn't change.

Her stomach plunged to her toes as she went cold all over. "Non, non, non. *Ce n'est pas vrai.* He isn't gone. He can't be. Tell me that you're joking, that this is all a mistake, that it's a nightmare. S'il vous plaît, tell me that nothing has happened to my son, my love, my life. All that I have of my husband."

Salomé swiped moisture from her cheek. "It was a long, difficult delivery, and he was born early and very small."

"Eleanore did all she could, but there was nothing to be done." Aime wrapped her in an embrace, but she pushed him away.

A moment later, she realized the scream she heard was tearing from her own vocal cords.

CHAPTER FIFTY-TWO

25 November, 1942
Elne, Occupied France

How Maman managed to never cry no matter what was beyond Hélène's understanding. Unless she had no heart beating in her chest, she must have cried at some point. At least in private, when Hélène wasn't around to see.

Then again, Maman didn't lose both a husband and a child to unimaginable tragedies. Losing them wouldn't have happened if not for the horrible war and if not for the horrible man standing with his arm straight and raised in front of crowds across Germany.

She hated him. She would put a bullet through him if she had a chance. Her searing white grief turned to red-hot rage when she allowed herself to dwell on all that madman had robbed from her. It was far more than her physical possessions. Those she could do without.

Going on without Levi and without their child, that was impossible.

But she kept breathing, and her heart continued beating. Salomé hardly left her side, especially that first day. Eleanore was in and out, and Aime was mostly there. They were all shrouded in mist.

A few days later, she was sitting up and waiting for Salomé to come in. Aime had been gracious in allowing her to remain in this room, the most luxurious she'd ever experienced in her entire life. But lying in bed all day and doing nothing but think about all she'd lost was not going to heal her. If she did that, she might go insane.

Salomé gave a timid knock and cracked the door.

"Come in."

"What are you doing sitting up?"

"I can't very well stay in bed my entire life."

"It's only been a few days since a very difficult labor and delivery."

"I promise to take it easy, but I can't brood forever."

"Give yourself time to heal, both physically and mentally."

Hélène went to stand. "I'm going to get to my feet with or without you. It would be nice to have your help so I don't fall flat on my face."

Salomé sighed. "There's no talking sense into you, is there?"

"That's one of the nicest things anyone has ever said about me. If you could help me to make myself presentable, I'd appreciate it."

Salomé got a basin of warm water and a bar of soap, lifted a clean dress over Hélène's head, and insisted she sit at the dressing table so she could style her hair.

"I don't know how you're even able to stand at this point." Salomé pulled the brush through Hélène's tresses.

"If I don't swim, I'll drown."

Salomé stuck in a few pins. "Oui. That's all I'm doing right now. Just dog-paddling to keep my head from going under. If I don't do that, I'll be no good to anyone."

"You do understand. I have to keep going, keep my mind and my hands occupied. It's what Maman would expect from me. What Levi would expect from me. So for them, I do it."

"Are you going to give your little boy a name?"

"Last night, lying in the dark, staring at the ceiling, it was all I could ponder. Levi and I talked about this the very day we discovered I was expecting. We were going to name him Otto."

"Otto. I like that quite a bit."

"It was my father's name. Levi said we could name our second son after his father." She bit the inside of her cheek to maintain her control.

"Monsieur Laurent buried Otto and has fashioned a small marker, whenever you are ready to see it. If you ever are."

"That was kind of him. I'll have to thank him. Now, what needs to be done around here?"

"Eleanore has been working on getting the children to orphanages and other safe homes across the region. From my understanding, Rivesaltes is now empty."

Empty. Everyone gone. "What happened to Fräulein Reiter?"

"She's here, waiting to take some children to a home in Le Chambon-sur-Lignon where the Swiss Aid Society has assigned her to work."

"I'd like to see her."

"She should be at breakfast. For the most part, the children and other women remain in the cellar. It's too dangerous for them to come out."

"Have they raided the hospital yet?"

"Not as far as we can tell."

All of a sudden, the air in Hélène's lungs rushed out. "Oh. I left the cards there. All the identity papers. The children should have them so they'll know their true names when this is over, especially those who have lost their mothers."

"Don't worry. You can go back and get them when it's safe." Salomé steadied Hélène on her feet and led her down the hall to the stairs.

The aroma of pastries baking wafted from the kitchen to welcome her. For the first time in days, her stomach rumbled. "I suppose I should eat. I don't want to, but I should keep up my strength. I have no idea where they're going to send me."

They entered a sunny breakfast room, where a long, glossy table bore several fine china dishes with little painted purple violets and gleaming silverware. As soon as she entered the room, Aime jumped from his seat to pull out a chair for her.

"You shouldn't be up." Eleanore's gaze was soft, and her eyes filled with tears.

Fräulein Reiter rushed to Hélène's side and kissed her cheek. "What an awful time you've had of it. I was so sorry when Eleanore told me the news. But I have to agree with her. You should still be in bed. It's far too soon."

"I promise not to overdo it, but I had to get out of that oppressive room." She covered her mouth, horrified with her candor.

All Aime did was quirk an eyebrow. "I understand. It's rather masculine. There's one farther down the hall papered in pink with white sheers at the windows. I'll have one of the maids make it up for you."

While she'd grown up with plenty of money and she and Levi had never wanted for anything, Aime had far more than she could imagine. Maids. Plural. Goodness. "That's very kind of you."

They spent the rest of breakfast chatting about Fräulein Reiter going farther east in France with many of the children and Eleanore possibly going with her. But no one spoke about where Hélène would go. Right now, she didn't have the strength to ask. She was surviving minute by minute.

When this miserable war was over, would she get her factory and her livelihood back? Did she even want to return to the place she and Levi had been so happy?

Those were thoughts for another day.

As soon as Eleanore and Fräulein Reiter finished their breakfasts, they made their way to the cellar to check on the women and children who would be going with them, leaving Aime and Hélène alone in the dining room.

She fiddled with the linen napkin on her lap. "Madame Duval told me that you have a marker for my son. Would you mind showing it to me?"

"Are you sure you're up to it? Perhaps you should rest awhile. We could go to the garden this afternoon."

"I'm positive." She crossed and uncrossed her ankles. "I never got to spend any time with my son after he was born. None that I remember anyway. So I'd like to do that now. I can wallow in my sorrow, or I can allow the healing to begin."

"You are one of the strongest and most courageous women I have ever met."

"I'm not. Not really. Everyone has their weaknesses and vulnerabilities. I just don't show them, but trust me, I've cried more in these past few weeks than I have in the rest of my life combined. Even when my parents passed away, I managed to remain stoic, like Maman would have wanted."

"There's nothing wrong with a few tears. They are God's way of washing away sorrow and healing us."

" 'Weeping may endure for a night, but joy cometh in the morning.' It's morning. I'm not joyful, but the time for weeping is over, at least until tonight. I'll never forget Levi and Otto. My life will never be the same without them. But for them, I'll be strong."

"Very well. You didn't eat much of your croissant."

"It was delicious. I have no idea where you get the butter to make such flaky pastry. It melted in my mouth. But my appetite hasn't returned."

"One more bite. I don't want you to faint."

She managed to lift one corner of her mouth in a half smile. "I'm not the fainting type."

"I'm sure you aren't."

He pulled her chair out for her and helped her to her feet, tucking her arm through his as they strolled toward the garden, as if they were a couple taking a turn among the flowerbeds. But she was a childless widow without anything but the clothes on her back and the few in her suitcase from a charity box. Buried among them was a photograph of her and Levi on their wedding day and one of her parents.

Underneath an olive tree was a cross constructed of wood and painted white. It gleamed in the weak sunshine.

"Now that I know his name, I'll paint it on there. I don't know his true last name though."

"And it's best that you don't include it in case the Nazis decide to search your château." She stood and stared at the simple marker and the bare ground that covered her son's tiny body. "I wish I could have seen his face."

"You'll have to ask Eleanore or Madame Duval. They were the only ones who did. By the time they brought him to me, they had wrapped him."

Each word he spoke seared another scar onto her heart. She drank in the peace of this corner of the garden. It was tucked away, the perfect, private spot for her son to rest. She memorized each bend of the tree branches and each rosebush surrounding the little memorial.

"When the war is over, we'll get him a proper marker. Move him to a Jewish cemetery, if you'd prefer."

All she could do was nod at Aime's kindness. It was sad, though, that even in death, Otto's full identity had to remain hidden. His true identity couldn't be acknowledged even when he was laid to rest.

She knelt on the ground, scooping some of the dirt into her hands and depositing it into her dress pocket.

"Why are you doing that?"

She touched her lips and then touched the rough wooden cross. "I have nothing, absolutely nothing. One photograph of my husband. None of my son. Nothing else to call my own. I don't know where I'll be tomorrow. This way at least I'll have a little bit of the soil from where my son rests. Something to carry with me no matter where I might go."

He stood back then wandered farther down the path, leaving her time alone with Otto. Words were unnecessary. Her child couldn't hear her. She simply basked in being near him, the sun warming her back, even on this chilly day. The way the château hugged the gardens, it protected them from the wind.

Je suis désolée, Levi. I broke my promise to you, to our son. I didn't take care of him. I couldn't protect him. Désolée. Désolée. She rocked back and forth.

After a while, she was tired, and when Aime returned from his walk, she motioned for him to help her stand. "I'm ready to return to my room."

"Good. It should be prepared for you. I'll send someone up with a cup of tea once you're settled."

"I'm going to be spoiled. Wherever I end up, it won't be as nice as here. I'll always remember your kindness and what a balm this was to my soul."

When they entered the house, Eleanore greeted them. "François is here with the truck and is ready to take us to the home in Le Chambon-sur-Lignon."

"Oh. I didn't realize you'd be leaving so soon."

"Within a few days, all of us will be gone, and Aime can have his house back."

"And what about me?"

"I'm working on arrangements for you. Perhaps somewhere in the area where you can be close to your son."

Hélène hugged Eleanore, the dear, dear friend that she'd become. How did she understand? "I can't begin to thank you enough for everything you've done for me these past months and for the kindness you've shown me. I can never repay you."

"There's no need. I will continue to pray for you and ask God to reveal Himself to you. To know that you've truly become one of His children, in your heart as well as in your blood, would be the greatest gift I could receive."

Hélène released her new friend. Their time together had been far too short. "I'll think about all you've said."

Eleanore held Étienne and took Beryl by the hand, Margot clinging to her sister. Hélène said goodbye to them, and they headed for the truck.

"Wait."

Eleanore turned around.

"Did you ever get the identity cards?"

"Non, I forgot all about them. I'm so glad you reminded me. Take Étienne. Margot and Beryl can go ahead and get in the truck. Aime, may I borrow your automobile to retrieve the cards?"

"I can drive."

"You're busy here. I won't be long."

He handed her the keys.

"I'll be back in thirty minutes."

Hélène snuggled with Étienne, leaned against the stone railing, and waved as Eleanore went to the car. "Be careful."

CHAPTER FIFTY-THREE

22 August, 1955
Elne, France

I stare at the balcony, its staircase twisting and winding to the ground, so much like my life. That one day changed the trajectory of it forever. Like a puff of wind, gone was my life in this house, this idyllic world I had loved. The little family we had built here scattered like the chaff.

All of that crumbled, much like the house now behind me. Cracked windows, peeling wallpaper, chipped tiles. I avoid staring at one wing of the house, now leaning to one side, about to give way.

Even in the pain and the hardship, there is a story. A story that is worth preserving because it leaves its imprint on those it affected. Those it continues to affect to this day, and I surmise, will ripple throughout the generations to come.

The story that these walls tell has no ending. The words we etched here with our lives continue to be written, not here anymore, but elsewhere, on hearts around the world. I have come, and I have listened to the first part of the tale.

There are chapters I don't know, that I perhaps will never know. I come to the bottom of the stairs and sit on the prickly grass.

Being here has brought the past back to life. I glance at my watch on my thin wrist. It's almost time. Soon, very soon, and I will hear more of the story, the never-ending story.

CHAPTER FIFTY-FOUR

September 27, 2022
Barcelona, Spain

Y ou are not going to France by yourself." Aiden's metal water bottle dinged as he slammed it onto the small kitchen counter in Caitlyn's apartment.

"I can and I will. I need this time, time to myself, to figure out a bunch of things." She circled around the four-person round table, then back the other way.

"Don't you remember the last time we went to the maternity hospital and you had that panic attack on the side of the road? I don't want that to happen to you again with no one around."

"I plan on getting a taxi both ways. Does that make you more comfortable?" Why was he being so unreasonable? They weren't a couple. He had no claim on her. As an adult, she could do whatever she pleased. Right now, being alone sounded delicious. Turning inward, examining what was going on with her. Hard, yes. But necessary.

"No, the taxi doesn't make me feel any better. A woman traveling alone makes me nervous."

"I'll be fine. I got to Barcelona by myself. I learned my way around France on my semester abroad, often on my own."

"If you're going, so am I. And you can't stop me."

She turned her back on him and stared out the window at the bustling street below. People, ordinary people, going about their day. Men with briefcases, students in ripped jeans carrying backpacks, tourists strolling down the street, stopping for selfies here and there.

Why couldn't she be ordinary like them? That was what she needed to figure out. She turned around. "Please, I'm begging you, let me do this."

Aiden took a step toward her and softened his voice. "I promise not to get in your way. I'll be there, in the shadows, in case you need me. You don't have to talk to me. If you want, you can order food and eat it in your room. We'll find a hotel so we won't share an apartment. If you don't need me, I'll blend into the background as much as possible. Besides, having a second set of eyes might help you discover something you've missed."

"Arg." Why did he always have to make good points? It galled her to have to admit it. "Fine. You win. Are you happy?"

He picked up his water bottle and sipped from it, then his grin stretched from California to New York. "Very happy. Hey, you can even pretend not to know me if you like."

She shook her head. "No, I'll acknowledge your existence. I'll even allow you to sit next to me on the train if you promise to not be a pest. But Elissa stays home this time, and Brock's not coming either. Deal?"

"Deal." They shook hands.

"What's a deal?" Elissa closed the door behind her.

"Oh. I didn't even hear you come in." Caitlyn wiped her hands on her jeans. "I'm going back to France to sift through the papers that Sophia found. But I'm only taking Aiden with me."

Elissa widened her eyes and raised her brows. "Oo. Better be careful the dean doesn't find out about this."

"*Pft.*" Caitlyn waved away Elissa's concern. "It's all aboveboard."

"I promise to be the perfect gentleman."

"Just don't tell anyone, okay? I need this time. The only reason he's going is because he wouldn't stop bugging me until I caved in."

"It's a good idea, actually." Elissa opened the refrigerator and got out a Coke. "I'd worry about you if you were alone. And my French is getting better."

"Please understand, it has nothing to do with you. I need some peace, some time away from the pressures of school and everything, to sort through a few things."

"Don't forget to take your community health book with you. We have a test next Tuesday."

"Yes, Mother. I promise."

Elissa shot Caitlyn a glance and wrinkled her nose then left, grabbing her backpack on the way.

"I'll be ready to go about noon on Friday so we can catch the train." Aiden leaned in and kissed her on the cheek, leaving the spot warm, a warmth which spread from her face to her chest. Not a bad sensation, but one she didn't have any business feeling right now.

October 1, 2022

As the taxi drew near to the maternity hospital, Caitlyn peered at it through the window. Nothing had changed in the few weeks since she'd been here. It still rose tall and elegant, the peachy color soft against the bright blue sky, the windows sparkling in the sunshine.

What a relief this must have been for the women fleeing Rivesaltes. She tried to imagine coming from such horrible circumstances to a lovely place like this, one where peace and tranquility reigned. She rolled down the window to hear sheep bleating in the distance.

Then again, there were plenty of infants and young children here, so perhaps it wasn't as quiet as she imagined.

True to his word, Aiden hadn't said much throughout the entire trip. There was still today and tomorrow to get through, but it was nice the way he was giving her space. Room to breathe. The break from school and those pressures was good.

Aiden handed the taxi driver a few euros, and they made their way across the browning lawn to the sleek glass-and-steel entrance.

"Bonjour. I remember you." Claude, the same young man behind the desk, beamed at them.

Caitlyn stepped forward. "Bonjour. Is Sophia available? She should be expecting us."

"She is. It is Saturday, not her regular working day, but I will get her. She said you would come." The man scurried away.

"How are you feeling?" Aiden stayed close to her side.

She wandered away, browsing the books and small gifts spread on a table in the foyer. "Fine. Ready to get some answers for Pops. And for myself."

"That's good." Aiden also perused the offerings.

A few minutes later, Sophia entered the room. "Bonjour. It is good to see you again. When we found the cards, the ones typed up when the women came here, right away I thought of you."

"Where were they?"

"They were in a storage box. Why? I don't know, but we have them. They will help you, I hope." She led them across the beautifully tiled floors again and down the stairs to a conference room. Overhead, the fluorescent lights buzzed and cast blue shadows across the large table that inhabited most of the space. On top of the wood table was a long, narrow box, much like the card catalog drawers Caitlyn remembered from the library in her early elementary school days.

"This is it." Sophia swept her hand over the scene as if she were a *Price is Right* model. "I don't have time now to look at them. We don't have workers to do it. But you can search and see what you can find."

"Merci beaucoup. Nous l'apprécions." Caitlyn slid an oversized upholstered chair away from the table and settled in for the task ahead.

As she left, Sophia shut the door behind her.

Aiden cracked his knuckles. "Well, I guess we get started. Remind me what we're searching for."

"Hélène Laurent. Born probably in June of 1917."

"And your grandfather's name again?"

"Steven Laurent. But his full name is Steven Henry Louis Martin Laurent. From my research, the French don't consider them middle names but multiple first names, and sometimes they're after parents or grandparents, uncles or aunts, saints, that kind of thing."

"Hmm. Didn't you say your great-grandfather's name was David?"

"Uh-huh." Caitlyn pulled the box toward herself and flipped through a few of the cards.

"I wonder why your grandfather wasn't named after him."

She gazed at him, then shrugged. "I guess it's not a hard and fast rule that children are named after their parents as long as the name has some kind of special meaning."

"Okay, makes sense. So Steven Henry Louis Martin Laurent. Born November twentieth, 1942. Got it. Hand me some of those cards so I can get started."

She grabbed a bunch of the cards out of the box, careful to keep them in order, and passed the rest to Aiden. She flipped through card after card after card. She didn't come across anyone named Hélène. None of the birthdates on the cards were near what she guessed her great-grandmother's was.

And no Steven Henry Louis Martin.

After a while, her neck ached. She stood and reached for the ceiling and did a few toe touches to stretch her back.

Aiden sat back. "Everything okay?"

"Yeah. Just need to get the blood flowing. It's all good."

"Whenever you want a break, let me know. We can run into town for a quick bite to eat."

"We have to get through these today. It's all we have. You're going to be doing more and more flying, and I really have to buckle down and study so I'm able to complete the course."

"Is that what's been bothering you lately? Are you worried about not passing?"

Like Aiden was a dentist that had stuck that pointy tool into a sensitive tooth, Caitlyn winced.

"You are."

"I thought you were going to be quiet on this trip."

His half-grin faded, and his shoulders drooped as he buried himself in the work again.

"I'm sorry. That came out wrong. I didn't mean to snap at you. I truly didn't."

"I was only asking as a friend, but you did warn me, and I overstepped. I'm the one who needs to apologize."

"You're right."

He sat up and stared at her. "About what?" He was so quiet, she almost couldn't hear him even though they sat across the table from each other.

"About my being worried about not finishing the course. About flunking out."

"Wow, that's hard."

"Dr. Lin told me a few weeks ago that if I don't get my act together, I'm not going to make it." She didn't tell him that the professor had also mentioned her emotional instability. "I've never been in a position like this. I'm not bragging, but I graduated summa cum laude."

"That's a big accomplishment."

"I just can't fail. I couldn't go home and face everyone there if I did."

"I get that. People at home have high expectations for me too. I'd be afraid of disappointing them if I didn't get my certification. But is there something else to it? Something you aren't sharing? And I'm not saying you have to. This is a share-free weekend. But if you want to talk about what's on your heart, I think I've proven to be pretty good at keeping my mouth shut."

"Not perfect." She flashed him a saucy grin to let him know she wasn't upset with him.

"Not perfect, that's for sure. Who of us is?"

"You have a point. I guess I have to forgive you. There's a lot going on in my life right now. It's been going on for a while, but this isn't the time or the place for me to go spilling my guts. We're on a mission."

"Okay." Aiden returned his attention to the index cards in front of him. "That's fair enough. Just keep my offer in mind."

"Got it." She also returned to her work. Card after card after card until her eyes burned. The years had turned the type light. Or maybe they used the typewriter ribbon until they couldn't use it anymore. The only reason she knew about that was because Grams always had a typewriter in her house and had taught Caitlyn how to use it. She had a drawer full of ribbons so she could replace the old one when it got too light.

She pulled a card out. Noémie Treves. There was that name again, the same one from the identity papers at the fortress, but she examined the rest of the card. Birthdate of June 26, 1917. That worked.

From Mulhouse. The town name triggered something in her brain. Her great-grandmother's death certificate had come in the mail just a few days ago. Mulhouse was the town listed as her place of birth.

Date of admittance was listed as August 19, 1942.

"Do you have something there?" Aiden held a card in his hand while she slid the one she had across the table.

"It's Noémie's again. The one from the fortress museum with a birthdate and birthplace that would work, but the name is wrong."

He picked up the card and studied it. Then he held it out to Caitlyn. "I think you need to take a closer look at this."

CHAPTER FIFTY-FIVE

22 August, 1955
Elne, France

I am weary, so I sit on the weather-pocked steps just outside of what had been the maternity home's front door. Oh, how many weary travelers passed through this portal, transported to a world that didn't exist beyond these four walls.

But even that wasn't enough to protect them. It was a fantasy, always a fantasy. A waking dream that a mansion in the French countryside would protect its inhabitants.

A vain and foolish notion. Mixed with the laughter and chatter are wails and cries. The home's windows and doors weren't enough to keep out the horror that was the world at that time.

Our beautiful world was shattered. Years later, we continue to pick up the pieces, trying our best to put them back together.

In the puzzle that is my life, there is a missing piece. Once I find it, perhaps the picture that the Almighty has painted for me will be complete. The colors of it will be black and gray, but there will also be splashes of pinks and greens and yellows. Bright and brilliant that stand in stark contrast to the darkness.

For that is how He paints the world. We tried to use only pastel brushstrokes, like the cheery outside of the building. Children's finger paintings tacked to the walls. Streams of sunshine cascading across bright white tile floors.

But that was unrealistic.

A dark cloud covered the beautiful peach-colored house.

CHAPTER FIFTY-SIX

25 November, 1942
Elne, Occupied France

Time ticked by on Hélène's watch, a steady *tock, tock, tock.* The truck that was to take many of them away sat nearby, a group of women and children clustered around it, clutching their meager belongings, their voices hushed. She and Aime and Fräulein Reiter and even François paced up and down the curving, tree-lined gravel drive that led to the château. Hélène's arms and legs were mush.

"You need to sit down." Aime cradled her by the waist and pointed toward a wrought iron bench near the front door.

"I do, but I'm not sure I can make myself be still." She allowed Aime to lead her to the bench, even as a wave of incredible fatigue washed over her. Étienne squirmed on her lap, and she jiggled him.

Aime poked his head inside and called for the butler to bring her a glass of water, then he came and sat beside her.

"What could be taking Eleanore so long? She could have been there and back twice over by now."

"She'll be fine. Just maybe a little trouble getting the papers from their hiding space." But Aime grabbed his tie and smoothed away all the imaginary wrinkles.

Hélène's stomach twisted. "I hope so."

Tock, tock, tock.

Aime bowed his head, and Hélène closed her eyes while he prayed loud enough for everyone gathered in the yard to hear. "Dear Heavenly

Father, protect Your servant, Eleanore, and safeguard her in all her ways. Surround her with Your angels. You see all, and You know all, and Your ways are perfect. In Your Son's name. Amen."

The prayer was nice, but it did nothing for the knot in her stomach. The butler returned with a crystal glass of water on a silver tray, and the clear, cool wetness soothed the dryness of Hélène's mouth.

"I'm going to go look for her."

At Aime's pronouncement, Hélène jumped to her feet, sloshing some of the water over the side of the glass and startling Étienne. "You can't. It's too dangerous. There are German patrols everywhere. And if they find the maternity hospital empty, who knows what they'll do to you."

"If I'm not back in fifteen minutes, send the truck. Eleanore can go another day."

In front of her, near the truck, a baby cried, followed by another. A few children chased each other around. They needed to be on their way. Then again, it was critical to those without parents that they have the records of their true identities. But it was prudent for them to leave, the only way to protect the most vulnerable. Hélène nodded in agreement with Aime.

"You rest. I'll be back before a feather dropped from the second story hits the ground."

She stood and kissed him on both cheeks. "Don't take any unnecessary risks. We need you to help get everyone out of here."

"I promise to be careful." He squeezed her hand and went to his car, already sitting in the driveway. He was wealthy enough to have more than one. Moments later, he disappeared around the bend and down the hill.

Hélène took her time lowering herself to the bench. Sitting was painful, but she was too weak to stand for long, especially with Étienne in her arms. And she didn't have the energy to pace.

Salomé came and sat on one side of her with Fräulein Reiter on the other. "How are you doing?" She touched Hélène's cheek.

"I'm fine. Just worried."

Fräulein Reiter grasped the bench's scrolled handle. "She'll be fine. Eleanore has this way of coming out of scrapes without a scratch."

The bench was cold underneath Hélène, and that sent a chill throughout her body.

Salomé helped her to her feet. "It's time to tuck you into bed for some rest."

"I want to be here when Aime returns, to hear what he has to say."

"You'll find out in due course. It's been almost fifteen minutes. I'm going to have to get going."

If nothing else, they could have a private farewell, so Hélène, with the two women by her side, went inside, climbed the stairs, stopped and tucked Étienne into his crib and had a maid watch him, and continued to the sunny room at the end of the hall.

But the mood was anything but bright. Hélène clung to Fräulein Reiter. "Merci for the help you gave to me when I arrived and for being so good to me since."

"Non, it is I who must thank you for taking such good care of Margot and Beryl. We'll pray their parents survive the war and are soon reunited with them. They're going to miss you terribly."

"And I will miss them." Hélène's voice cracked, and she covered it with a cough, then turned to Salomé.

The two of them embraced until Fräulein Reiter cleared her throat. When they parted, Hélène wiped the tears from Salomé cheeks. "Don't cry. We will always be friends. I'll stay in touch, and after this war comes to an end, we'll see each other again. Take care of Paul. He is a true blessing from above."

Salomé squeezed Hélène's hands. "And I'll be thinking about you. Take time to heal and then live a full and happy life."

A full and happy life might be out of her grasp. How could she ever find joy when everything had been ripped from her? "I'll do my best. Until we see each other again." She kissed Salomé's damp cheeks.

Then Fräulein Reiter and Salomé left the room. Instead of going to the bed, Hélène sat in the upholstered armchair near the wavy-glassed window where she could watch the truck idling in the driveway. The ladies exited the house, Salomé going to the back of the vehicle and Fräulein Reiter sharing the front seat with François.

A wave of nausea washed over her as François pulled from the driveway and started the long drive to Le Chambon-sur-Lignon. Another section of Hélène's heart tore off and blew away in the wind. Even with the extra time, she hadn't had the heart to say goodbye to Javier and all the other children she'd come to know and love. More losses to pile on top of the others.

She rested in the chair until a flash of red appeared behind the trees and Aime's car came to a stop by the front door. Waiting to see who emerged, she couldn't breathe. Aime stepped out first and went around to the passenger side.

Hélène exhaled. Good, he was going to open the door for Eleanore.

Except he didn't. He sauntered into the house, his shoulders hunched.

Hélène descended the stairs, clinging to the banister for support. By this time, Aime was almost through the foyer and heading for the parlor. "Aime."

He turned, his blue eyes bloodshot.

She faltered on the last step and had to sit. He was at her side in a flash. "Let's get you back to bed."

There was a darkness, a sadness surrounding Aime. "Not until you tell me what happened to Eleanore. Don't hold anything back."

He sat beside her, close but not too close. "When I pulled up, the Nazis were there. They must have caught Eleanore when she arrived, or they must have gotten there just after her. Whatever the case, it wasn't long before two men in their black SS uniforms escorted her from the hospital and into a car."

"Do you know where they went?"

"I couldn't say, but I did hear one of the men tell her that she was bound for Poland with the rest of her Juifs. So I need to hear you say that the others got away in time. That he was bluffing."

Hélène clutched the cotton fabric of her dress in her fist. "They did. They left, just like you told them to. But what about Étienne? He's still here. Eleanore wanted him to come with her. She loves him so much, she couldn't bear to be parted from him." Though it would have been safer for him to go with the others.

"There's a reason for the bond the two of them share."

Hélène narrowed her eyes. What was Aime saying?

From the inside pocket of his suit coat, he pulled out an envelope. Hélène's name was scrolled across it in Eleanore's flowing handwriting. "She gave this to me a few days ago and said to pass it to you if anything happened to her."

Hélène slid open the flap and pulled out a single sheet of paper that smelled like a symphony of summer roses. Her eyes filled with tears, and her mouth fell open as the words translated themselves from the page to her mind. And soul.

"Oh. Oh." The contents left her speechless. She read it over and over again then checked the name on the front to be sure the letter was hers. At last, she turned to Aime. "Do you know what this says?"

"Not exactly, but based on your reaction, I can guess. I've known Eleanore's secret since the beginning."

"Étienne has your last name. Are you. . .?"

Aime shook his head. "Non. She chose that name for him to keep him safe. Because I helped finance the hospital, I've been with her for a long time. I know what she hid in her heart."

"The sum of it is that she wants us to take Étienne to a safe place."

"Then we need to make plans to get out of here as soon as possible." He rubbed his stubble-covered chin. "We could hike over the mountains right behind us, but the snows have come, you're in no shape to make the trek, and Étienne is too small."

"And I'm Jewish, even though my papers claim I'm not."

He mussed his usually perfect hair. "I have a yacht docked at the pier in Collioure. We could drive there then take the boat into the Mediterranean and into Spanish waters."

"This time of year? Won't the water be too rough?"

"We'll have to pray that God calms the seas. He did it on the Sea of Galilee. He can do it on the Mediterranean."

"And then what?"

"We can stay in Spain, the three of us. When the war is over, I'll do my best to find Eleanore. She's sure to return to the hospital."

"There's no other choice?"

"As soon as the Germans look into the hospital's records, if they haven't done so already, I'm going to be high on their list of targets because of all the Juifs I've helped. It's not safe for any of us here. The sooner we leave, the better."

Hélène's head spun. Leave France? Leave her son buried in the garden here? "I'm not sure I can. I'm afraid." Admitting her feelings was a rare occurrence, but her heart pounded in her head so hard she had a difficult time hearing.

"I'll be with you every step of the way, and I promise to take care of you, no matter what. And Étienne too."

A weak nod was all Hélène could manage. "You're right. There's no other choice. All of our lives are in danger." She had one last chance to save just a handful of people.

"Where is he?"

"Sleeping in his crib. Or he was the last time I checked on him."

"Let me help you up the stairs. We can peek in on him, and I'll have one of the maids bring his crib into your room so he's close to you."

"Merci. I appreciate that." She reached out and touched his cheek. "You are too kind to me, a broken woman."

"Non, not broken. Just a butterfly with an injured wing."

"A wing that will never heal."

"You don't know what the Lord has in store for you."

"Hopefully nothing more bad." She stood and clutched the handrail as Aime supported her on the other side.

Just as she'd said, Étienne was snoozing in his bed, his thumb in his mouth. Every now and again, he sucked in his sleep, then sighed. Did he understand how his world had just changed? "I promise to love you and take care of you as if you were my own."

She stopped and gazed at the white ceiling, an ornate carved molding surrounding the chandelier that hung there. Could Hashem bring goodness out of disaster? Could He be using this time with Étienne to heal her, or was He setting her up for more heartache when the time came for him to leave her?

In the back of her mind, Maman scolded her for her poor posture and told her to keep her chin parallel to the floor. So she did. She would use this time to put back the broken pieces of her life. Like a shattered plate, it would never be the way it had been, but perhaps, just perhaps, it might be somewhat beautiful again.

First, though, they had to get to Spain.

CHAPTER FIFTY-SEVEN

22 August, 1955
Elne, France

There is a certain beauty in our naivety. It is a gracious gift from the Almighty that we cannot see into our future, for it would be sure to cause us unimaginable pain and deny us enjoyment in the present.

Such were those sun-splashed days at La Maternité de la Paix. I had no idea of the trials and travails that were awaiting me that day we were told the hospital was closing. At the time, I wanted to know what lay ahead, but looking back, it is so good that I didn't. Had I, there is no way I would have been able to sleep at night. No way I would have been able to feel anything but dread and apprehension.

I always knew the idyllic world at La Maternité de la Paix would someday be shattered. That what it brought us, what it represented, was as fragile as a flower in a field full of bulls.

If only I would have held tighter to that time. Oui, there were many, many moments that were difficult. Many, many times that I cried myself to sleep within the walls of the now-crumbling house behind me.

Little did I know that even harder days were ahead of me. Of all of us. For a time, we had managed to live in solitude and peace, undisturbed by the sleeping giant beneath our feet.

Then came the day that giant awakened, bellowed, and worked to pick us off like briars on his shirt.

And there were many of us that he crushed beneath his feet.

CHAPTER FIFTY-EIGHT

October 1, 2022
Elne, France

The noise of the long, bluish fluorescent light overhead only increased the buzzing in Caitlyn's head. She didn't understand what Aiden was pointing to on the card she'd handed him.

"Take a look at this."

Very, very faintly, she made out a few letters at the bottom. Either the ribbon had worn out, or time had taken its toll on the ink. Probably a combination of both.

"Can you see what it says?"

"I'm guessing it's the woman's assumed identity, but it's difficult to read."

He handed her his phone with the flashlight turned on. When she shined it on the print, she gasped.

Hélène Etu. "My great-grandmother's first name. But why not Laurent?"

"Think about why she likely came here."

"Because she was Jewish and was going to have a baby."

"And if she'd been married to your great-grandfather the entire time, wouldn't she have used his name, his Gentile name? Wouldn't she have stayed at the château with him and hidden there instead of living here with other Jewish women where there were regular raids?"

Stress and fatigue must have been clouding her thinking, because none of this was sinking in. "What are you saying?"

"I think we found your great-grandmother."

"So her name was really Noémie Treves? You believe she was unmarried when she came here?"

"Either that or had been married and was a widow. Or became one soon after her arrival. A marriage to your great-grandfather would have helped her a good deal. And it would explain why her son, if that was her son, was buried at the château."

Had Pops' parents lied to him about his birth? All this time, he'd believed David Laurent to be his father, when he very well might not have been. Or had Pops also kept the secret for some reason?

No, Pops would never do that. He would tell her the truth, especially when he knew she was coming here to find out more about his family. Then again, he'd told her that his parents were some of the most honest people he'd ever known.

A fire flamed in her chest. Her life couldn't have been built on lies. "Well, you can think what you want to think, but I know the truth. And it's not what these cards say. This isn't my great-grandmother. If it was, she would have gone back to using her true identity after the war." Her voice rang in the small room.

"Okay, okay. I didn't mean to upset you. Let's keep searching. Maybe it's a very strange coincidence. Just in case, though, I'm going to take pictures of this card. Is that all right with you?"

She nodded and drew in several deep breaths. "Sorry again. I shouldn't have gone off on you like that."

"Hey, like water off a duck's back."

She couldn't stop the chuckle that rose in her throat. "What?"

"Something my dad says all the time. It means no problem. He's weird."

"Most dads are."

They got back to work and finished combing through the rest of the index cards. As she came to the last few, her gut clenched. No other Hélènes with a birthday that would work with her great-grandmother's. It was looking more and more like Aiden was right.

She came to the end of her stack and wandered to where he was finishing searching through the last few of his. "Anything?"

He shook his head. "I'm sorry. There are no Laurents here at all.

277

The one that works, the one that makes sense, is Noémie Treves, aka Hélène Etu."

"What does that all mean? That Pops was born out of wedlock?"

"Not necessarily. How about we go back to the hotel and get something to eat. I need the internet to do a little online work."

She wasn't hungry, but if it meant they could continue trying to untangle this ever more complicated web, then she was all for it. "Okay. Let's get the taxi here."

Aiden called for their ride while Caitlyn straightened the cards and let Sophia know they were finished. "Merci beaucoup for everything you've done for us."

"Is there more I can help with?"

"Not right now, but I have your number, so is it okay if I message you if I have more questions or if I need more information?"

"Of course. Here, I will give you my WhatsApp number. If you are somewhere else, you can reach me."

As she got a piece of paper and wrote her number, Caitlyn leaned on the counter. "Do you know who owns the Laurent château today?"

"Maybe the French government? That I do not know. I think I told you before that they ran away during the war. They disappeared. Monsieur Laurent, his wife, and his child."

"Was the child a boy or a girl?"

"A boy, I think." Sophia handed Caitlyn the paper and then leaned in. "Some people, they say that the child didn't belong to Monsieur Laurent. That is what they say. Again, that I do not know for sure. But it is interesting. Why would he marry a woman with a child and then leave his home and go away? He was a very rich man."

It was interesting. Unless his disappearance wasn't voluntary.

"The stories say he came back one time but was so sad that he did not stay. But that is a story. No one knows for sure."

Pops had mentioned something about returning here once. And marrying a Jewish woman with a child would explain the disappearance. Aiden was right. They had more digging to do.

He emerged from the restroom, and they took the taxi back to the station and boarded the train for Perpignan. She closed her eyes to try to banish the headache that was attempting to bash through her skull, but the ride was far too short. All too soon, they arrived at their destination.

Bless Aiden for booking a hotel right outside the *Gare de Perpignan*. All they had to do was go under the tracks, head through the station, and cross the street. After she freshened up, she met Aiden in the lobby that had a beautiful golden-brown tile floor. He had taken up residence on a white couch and had his laptop open.

"Hard at work already, I see."

He grinned at her and scooted over so she could sit. "You know me. I never waste a minute."

Her snort was less than ladylike, but who cared. It was just Aiden.

No, he was more than just Aiden. "I apologize again for the way I've treated you the past couple of days. Weeks, maybe even. You're proving to be a good friend, and I'm glad that you insisted on coming on this trip with me."

"Like I said, duck's back and all that."

"So, have you found anything interesting?"

"I'm on the Holocaust museum website. I didn't find any Treveses that were killed during the war, but they don't have all their records online yet. To see some, you have to go to Washington DC."

"Why would you be looking that up?"

"Because it might explain matters if Noémie slash Hélène was married before. Her first husband might have been a prisoner at Rivesaltes also and died. It's possible he died there, who knows. Anyway, it's one explanation."

"Sophia told me there were whispers that my grandfather was born out of wedlock."

Aiden shrugged. "We can't discount that as a theory, but rumors so often aren't the truth. Let me see what I can pull up on French marriage certificates."

While Aiden conducted the search, she sat back and scrolled through her phone so she didn't give him the feeling she was hanging over his shoulder. What she should be doing was studying, but even though her books sat in her backpack in her room, she had no plans to drag them out anytime soon.

After fifteen minutes of watching funny cat videos, she set her phone down and leaned across her knees. "Anything?"

"Nothing. I'm coming up blank. That doesn't mean anything though. If they were married during the war, especially toward the end of it, there might not be a certificate. Life was chaos at that point. And with your great-grandmother being Jewish, it's very possible that one was never filed."

"Okay. I guess that makes sense. A little bit."

Aiden closed his laptop. "The kebab place down the street is open. How about we get some? Maybe even some falafel?"

She couldn't keep telling him she wasn't hungry, so she went along with the plan. If nothing else, a walk would feel nice at this point. They'd been sitting a good part of the day.

It was a short stroll down the street to the Arabic restaurant. Strange how many of those there were in France and Spain, but from her understanding, anywhere along the Mediterranean coast was a haven for refugees from Muslim countries. And they did bring awfully good food with them.

Instead of sitting on one of the tables along the sidewalk, they strolled down the street toward the metal sculpture of the man in the chair. She nibbled her falafel while he pulled meat from his kebab. Once they finished, they made a right turn and continued toward the Palace of the Kings of Mallorca.

"Is this a better time for you to talk about what's been eating at you? Because I noticed you literally haven't been eating much."

She shrugged. "It's not something I tell many people. I don't like to talk about it."

"I'm safe, but I can understand if you don't want to."

But the funny thing was, she might be able to talk to Aiden. He was safe. Easy. He wouldn't judge her. Hopefully not, anyway. "Okay. I'll rip the bandage off." She inhaled a huge breath. "My best friend and I were in a car accident our senior year of college and she was killed and she was supposed to be here with me."

Aiden stopped in his tracks, the large but unassuming stone palace at the end of the street. "Wow, that's hard."

All Caitlyn could do was nod. And continue walking. Aiden jogged to catch up to her.

"Were you driving?"

"No. She was, but it was the other guy's fault. We had just returned to school in Georgia and needed some groceries, so we stopped before heading to the house we were renting. We were at a T intersection, coming out from the store onto the main thoroughfare, making a right turn. We had the green light. He ran the red at a high rate of speed and plowed into her." Her airway tightened, and she couldn't get out another word, even if she wanted to.

"Hey." He tugged her to a stop. Thankfully, this was a residential street, and no one was out and about. He brushed a few tears from her face, ones she hadn't realized were falling, then drew her into an embrace. Held her while she cried.

"I didn't mean to do this." With her face against his chest, her words were muffled.

"It's okay. Let it out. I get the feeling that this has a lot to do with what's going on with you and why you're struggling at school."

"She should be here. I shouldn't be alone. This was her idea, her adventure, and that man in that car stole it from her. From us." She pushed away from Aiden. "Lindsey was the kindest, most generous person I've ever known. She kept me grounded but also gave wings to our plans. I'd known her since kindergarten." Once she started, she couldn't stop.

"I went into nursing because that's what Lindsey was doing. I wanted to be a missionary because that's what she wanted to be. I'm trying to live her life for her, but it's not working very well. I'm an actress, just pretending, and not a very good one at that."

After a while, the tears stopped. She pulled a tissue from her pocket and dried her eyes and wiped her nose the best she could. "You're going to have to wash your shirt. Sorry."

"Don't keep apologizing for things that aren't your fault. And that's how you feel about the accident, don't you?"

She walked a few paces toward the palace.

"How could it be when it wasn't even your friend's fault?"

"I saw the headlights and didn't say anything. At least I don't think I did. Some of the details are nothing but blurry images. But I should have yelled or something. Done something to get her to step on the brakes instead of continuing with her turn."

"And how do you know she would have? Maybe she was too far into the intersection already. By the time she processed everything, he might have still hit you guys."

"You don't know. None of us do."

"And you can't live her life for her. You never could, but it sounds like you were even before the accident. You followed in her footsteps all along the way."

Was that what she was doing? Living someone else's life? If so, what did she want for herself?

She had no idea if there was even a life out there for her.

CHAPTER FIFTY-NINE

November 8, 2022
Barcelona, Spain

Thanksgiving was coming soon, but it didn't feel like it in Barcelona. The sun was still warm, and the palm trees swayed in the gentle breezes. There was more rain than in the summer, but it was still a tropical paradise.

Elissa started the coffee maker and grabbed a mug from the open shelves above the sink while Caitlyn sipped at the tea in her own thermal cup. "It's going to be weird to celebrate Thanksgiving somewhere other than in the States."

Caitlyn nodded. "Sure will be. Can we even get turkeys here? I'm pretty sure there aren't pumpkins or sweet potatoes."

"Oh, no pumpkin pie." Elissa slumped over the counter. "I don't know how we're going to live."

Caitlyn threw a crumpled napkin at her. "What do you think it's going to be like on the field? Who knows what we're going to have to eat."

Elissa launched into a litany of what she thought of the entire matter, but Caitlyn tuned her out. In the weeks since she and Aiden had returned from France, all she could do was think about what he'd said. That she was living Lindsey's life and had been since long before her death.

Maybe that was why she was struggling with being here. Sure, she was homesick and still grieving her best friend, but maybe there was more to it than that. She sipped her tea and nodded as Elissa continued talking. What was it that she wanted to do with her life, truly be committed to and passionate about?

She'd always been the follower. There was the time that Lindsey had wanted to run away from home.

"But I'm scared." Caitlyn had hated the thought of being away from Mom and Dad.

"Don't be scared. New adventures are always fun. And this is going to be lots and lots of fun. You'll see. Trust me."

"I do."

"I promise you that nothing bad will happen."

"Do you really?"

"Of course."

"Where are we going to run away to?" Caitlyn's stomach still swung up and down like she was on the rollercoaster she went on at the state fair earlier that summer.

"To Matt's treehouse."

"Won't your brother be mad if we're in his treehouse? I can read the sign, and it says 'no girls allowed.'"

"He won't mind. He's just silly sometimes."

"Okay."

"Then you have to go pack."

"Pack what?"

Lindsey laughed, the sun lighting up her blond hair. She was all sparkles and shine. "Your clothes. And maybe some food."

"Oh, okay."

Lindsey left, and Caitlyn went to her room, threw some shorts and shirts and undies into her backpack along with a blanket and her stuffed dog. She couldn't sleep without Snuggles. Then she went to the kitchen and made herself a peanut butter and jelly sandwich.

"What are you doing, young lady?"

The knife slipped from Caitlyn's hand and clattered to the ground. Mom picked it up and wiped the jelly off her new hardwood floor.

"I'm just making a sandwich. Lindsey and I are running away to Matt's treehouse."

The corners of Mom's mouth twitched. "Are you really, now?"

"Yep. She promised it would be okay and we would be fine."

"You would follow that girl to the ends of the earth. Well, go if you must. I sure will miss you though. You're my little princess. What am I going to do if I'm the only woman in the house?"

Caitlyn shifted her weight from one foot to the other. "I'll miss you too, Mommy, but Lindsey says we have to have an adventure." A stray tear leaked from the corner of her eye.

"Do you want to go?"

Caitlyn rushed to Mom and hugged her legs as tight as she could. "No, Mommy, I don't want to leave you. I want to stay with you forever."

Mom smoothed Caitlyn's hair, the motion of it soothing and calming. It was one of her favorite things that Mom did. "You won't leave me forever, at least not until you're all grown-up, and even then, I'll visit you, and you'll visit me. You're my Caity-girl, and I love you. I could never do without you."

"But what about Lindsey?"

"You don't always have to do what Lindsey wants. It's okay to tell her what you'd like sometimes."

"Won't she get mad at me and stop being my friend?"

"Not if she's truly your friend. If she is, she'll want you to be happy and will do what she must to see that you are."

"Oh. I always thought I had to do what she told me."

"No. Now, if you'd like and Matt doesn't mind, you can play in his treehouse this afternoon. I'll send some Rice Krispie treats I made yesterday with you. But when you're tired of playing or it's dinnertime, you come on home. Okay?"

"Okay, Mommy. I love you."

"I love you too, my Caity-girl."

"Earth to Caitlyn. Are you in there?"

Elissa's question jolted Caitlyn back to the present day. "Sorry. Just got swept away by a memory."

"What were you remembering? It must have been good, because you were smiling, and you haven't been doing much of that lately."

"Just how my mom was always there for me, making me feel better and telling me that I didn't have to do everything Lindsey did."

"That's your friend from back home, right?"

"Yeah. She died in a car accident almost ten months ago now."

"I didn't know that. I'm so sorry. Were you with her?"

"I was."

"How awful. I'm glad you're okay now. You are okay, aren't you?"

Caitlyn took her tea to the sink and dumped it out. "Physically, I'm fine. I still miss her an awful lot. And I wish I could have done something to prevent the accident. I don't know what that might have been, but I hate that I was helpless." She couldn't say more or else she would be a sobbing mess, and she had a test to take. One she hadn't really studied for.

Elissa hugged her. "If you ever want to talk about it, you know where I am."

"That's sweet of you. Thank you. Right now, we'd better get to class. I hope I can remember all those drug names. They're a blur in my mind."

"We can go over them while we walk to campus."

But the quick review didn't do any good. She couldn't remember which drug did what or any of the side effects. Nothing was sticking in her brain these days. Not a blessed thing. She scribbled some answers, but what she wrote was gibberish.

She was the last one to leave, and instead of handing her paper to Dr. Lin, she crumpled it and threw it into the garbage can.

"Caitlyn. Wait."

Dr. Lin's command stopped Caitlyn in her tracks.

"Why did you do that?"

"Because I'm going to flunk the test anyway, so there's no point in making you grade it."

"I don't understand."

"I can't concentrate. There's not a single thing I could remember."

"What's going on?" Dr. Lin touched Caitlyn's shoulder, and that was all it took to open the floodgates again.

Through tears and sobs, Caitlyn poured out the entire story about the accident that claimed Lindsey's life and how Aiden's observations had her questioning whether she was following the right path.

Dr. Lin listened and offered Caitlyn tissues when she needed them. At last she had the entire story out, and her tears slowed to a trickle.

"Let's go to my office where we can finish this chat with a little more privacy and a lot more comfort."

Caitlyn followed her down the hall, and Dr. Lin led the way into an office with a small desk but a couple of comfortable leather armchairs that faced each other. "Can I get you some water?"

Caitlyn nodded, and Dr. Lin stepped out.

What was she even doing here? Why had she told all of that to one of her professors? For sure she was going to get kicked out now. She'd blown the test and had practically admitted that it wasn't even her idea to become a missionary.

But if she went home, she'd let everyone down, including Lindsey's parents. Before she came to Spain, they had thrown her a going-away party and had given her money to help her out. They'd told her how proud they were of her. How proud Lindsey would have been of her.

Before long, Dr. Lin returned with two bottles of water and offered one to Caitlyn. "I'm glad you felt comfortable enough with me to share your story. It took courage."

"I'm sorry to have spilled it all out." Aiden would scold her for apologizing yet again. "Thanks for listening. What's going to happen to me now?"

"First of all, you aren't in any trouble, at least not with me or the school. But I have a feeling that your soul is very troubled, that you're wrestling with quite a number of things at once."

"Yeah."

"So what would you like to see happen? Don't think about me or the school or Lindsey or your parents or your friends or anyone else. Think only about you and God. What would you, Caitlyn Laurent, like to happen?"

She picked at a hangnail for a couple of minutes while her thoughts swirled in her head. It wasn't hard to figure out how everyone else, everyone Dr. Lin had mentioned, would answer that question. But if she took them all out of the equation? That was a different story. "I'd like to figure out my life. I'd like to know who I am and where I'm going. I know what everyone else would say, but I don't know about me. I'm not sure this is what I'm meant to do."

"So it sounds like you need some time, time you haven't had, to grieve your friend and discover life for yourself. You need time to pray and think about what it is that God has in store for you."

"That sounds good, but what about what others expect of me?"

"Has trying to live up to their expectations been working?"

Caitlyn shook her head.

"The only ones who should matter are you and God. You can go to some of those other people and ask their advice, find out where your talents lie, but in the end, it has to be your decision. I'm watching a beautiful, talented young lady with so much to offer the world crumble in front of my eyes. That's no way to live."

Dr. Lin's kind words started Caitlyn's waterworks again. Would the tears ever stop?

After a while, they slowed enough that she was able to drink some of the water Dr. Lin had brought earlier.

"You've been through a tremendous trauma, Caitlyn. You don't have to rush forward with your life. Don't get stuck, but take the time you need to heal. Do you have a counselor you're seeing?"

"I was going to one at home, but I haven't been since I've been here."

"You need to be seeing someone, a professional, on a regular basis. And I think you know what your next steps need to be."

"It's going to be so hard to face everyone."

"Give them a little credit. They'll understand. If they truly love you, they'll want what's best for you. That's all they expect of you."

"Then I have to call my parents and explain things to them."

"Stop by the office tomorrow at nine. I'll be there, and I'll help you through the withdrawal process. Perhaps we can get you some credit for the work you've done to this point."

"I appreciate that."

Because leaving here and returning home was going to be one of the hardest things she'd ever done.

CHAPTER SIXTY

22 August, 1955
Elne, France

Hard things. Oh, there were so many hard things that happened here during my time at La Maternité de la Paix. There was no magic shield around us. Like the rest of the world at the time, we experienced hard things.

Babies died.

Mothers died.

Dreams died.

The Vichy and the Nazis stole so much from us. I clench my fists and pound at the air. "Why? Why did you do it? What possessed you to rip mothers and fathers and children apart? What kind of evil invaded your spirits to allow you to close your eyes to the pain you were inflicting on others?"

Only the twittering of a bird in the bare tree branch nearby answers me.

The Almighty knows. The Almighty knows. That's my head talking. But deep down, in the deepest parts of my heart that I don't allow anyone to see, my heart still hurts. It will until the day I die.

What has been taken will never be restored.

The prophet Joel talks about restoring what the locusts ate. I stare at the barren, empty, forsaken building that had once been a home, a refuge. La Maternité de la Paix is now a shell of its former self. I am a shell of my former self.

Then I turn to the drive, walk down it a way, my ankles wobbling as

I stroll in my high-heeled pumps, watching for the car to arrive.

The reason I'm here.

Not a restoration. That won't happen until I cross the river into eternity.

But maybe a gluing together of the pieces of my life the Nazis smashed.

CHAPTER SIXTY-ONE

25 November, 1942
Elne, Occupied France

The night was almost moonless. Hélène dressed herself and Étienne in dark clothing. Thank goodness Salomé thought to pack Hélène's belongings when she was in no position to do so. Though it would be difficult to see much, this was what they had to do in order to keep from being spotted by the Germans.

She sat on the settee in the parlor, soft lights casting shadows across the wallpaper with gold fleur-de-lis that sparkled. Almost magical. How could such a beautiful, serene place be so dangerous?

All day, while Aime made preparations for their trip into Spain, she rested. She couldn't return to Otto's grave. She had said her goodbyes to him and to Levi already. In her small suitcase, now battered by many treks, she had wrapped the jar that held the ground she'd scooped from the top of Otto's final resting place.

Étienne rubbed his eyes and fussed, wriggling to release himself from her grasp. She held him all the tighter and rocked him, just as she would have done for her own son. "Don't you worry, mon chéri. Everything will be fine. I promised to take care of you, and so I will. Nothing is going to harm you. I'll watch over you until I have to bring you back to where you belong."

Her words soothed him, and he nestled into the crook of her arm, rubbing his eyes again. She sang to keep him happy, a lullaby that French mothers had sung for a long time.

À la claire fontaine
M'en allant promener
J'ai trouvé l'eau si belle
Que je m'y suis baigné.

At the clear spring
Going off on a walk,
I found the water so fine
That I took a dip in it.

I have loved you for a long time.
Never will I forget you.

Beneath the leaves of an oak
I let myself dry off.
On the highest branch
A nightingale was singing.

I have loved you for a long time.
Never will I forget you.

Sing, nightingale, sing,
You who have a gay heart;
You have a heart for laughing,
I have a heart for weeping.

Tears filled her eyes as she sang the melancholy ballad, and she wiped them away as fast as possible. She had just gotten the baby to sleep when Aime came in. "Everything is ready. Allons-y. Let me carry the boy and the suitcase." He reached for Étienne.

"I can carry something."

"Non, I don't want you to tax yourself. The journey is going to be long enough, and who knows what awaits us. Save your strength for whatever situations may arise."

She understood the meaning behind his words as if he'd shouted them from the top of a mountain. What they were about to do was fraught with danger. "If something goes wrong, don't let me hold you back. Take Étienne and get away if you can."

"I'm not leaving either one of you. All three of us make it or none of us do."

Her palms were sweating, but there was nothing she could do about it right now. Instead, she nodded. Maman always said not to worry about things until the time came.

He took the boy from her arms, and he stirred in his sleep. Aime cradled him gently. Deep in his heart, he cared for this child. But she couldn't allow him to hold everything. "I insist on carrying the suitcase."

"I've got it. If you could just open the door, we can be on our way."

They had stashed all of their belongings into a single bag. One for three people. Over the past few months, she'd grown accustomed to doing without. For Aime, this would be a whole new experience.

She swung the large wooden front door open. The butler and the rest of the staff were in bed and hopefully sleeping. Aime hadn't told them they were leaving.

Together, the three of them descended the stairs, climbed into the automobile, and began their journey toward the Mediterranean. While descending the hill on which the château stood, Aime turned off the auto's engine and coasted, making as little sound as possible, his headlights off, a sliver of moonlight and the tiniest pinpricks of starlight to guide their way.

A few times, Étienne stirred in his sleep, but Hélène patted his back, and he returned to his slumber.

They had descended the hill and almost made it to Collioure when a rumble came from the road in front of them. Trucks. Several of them, by the sound of it. Aime swung off the street. "We'll have to go the rest of the way on foot. It won't be far."

Silence cloaked them once more. He took the baby from her. "We have to hurry and get far away from here before they catch up to us. Are you up to a quick pace?"

"Of course." Actually, her legs already shook, but that could be from nerves too. In any case, she wouldn't be the one to slow their progress.

There would be plenty of time to rest when they reached Spain.

They continued their trek, hurrying as much as possible. Within a few minutes, they left the cover of leafless trees behind and entered the slumbering village. Even the taverns were now closed, and along the streets, shutters were pulled tight against all the homes' windows and doors.

A shadow passed in front of her, and she jumped back. Aime gave a quiet chuckle. "Just a cat."

"I know." But her nerves were stretched as taut as strings on a recently tuned violin. From behind those shutters, anyone could peer out and watch them moving down the narrow streets and back alleys. The weight of a million perceived stares pressed on her shoulders. Her head pounded.

Aime led them in a maze down the ancient streets until they popped out near a church, the wharf to the right of them. Instead of heading straight for the boat, he turned toward the church.

"What are you doing?"

"Saying a quick prayer for us. Step inside, but you don't have to come into the sanctuary with me if you don't want to."

But she did follow him into the chapel, if for nothing else than a moment of solace and a chance to study the stained-glass windows. They were breathtaking. Each one depicted a different scene. One day, she would create something as beautiful for a rebuilt synagogue. Maybe many of them.

One was of a man standing behind a bush, his chest and arms bare. Beside him was a woman, her long hair the only thing covering her unclothed skin. That must be of the creation. Others, such as a boat on a sea with a man in white robes heading toward them must be of Jesus.

All along the sides of the church were smaller chapels, each with highly decorated figures covered in bright paint and gold leaf, candles burning in front of each one. The smell of incense and melting wax filled the air.

Aime, however, didn't take the time to admire the splendor of such a building. Instead, he slid into a pew in the back of the church, set the suitcase down, and laid Étienne beside him. Then he bowed his head. A few moments later, Hélène took her place alongside as he prayed.

"O Holy Father, be with us now, we beseech You. As You protected Your disciples on the Sea of Galilee, so protect us with Your presence.

Blind the eyes of the Germans, that they may not see us. Open our eyes and guide us, that we may know the way.

"And if it be Your will, my Lord, that we should succumb to some danger or another, then receive Your servant into Your eternal presence, that there I may fall at the feet of my Savior who has cleansed me from my sins, and that forever and ever, I may dwell in Your holy, heavenly home. In Your Son's precious name I pray, Amen."

The prayer was so beautiful and moving, Hélène couldn't help but add her own amen to his words. The supplication brought so many questions to her mind, but she couldn't ask any of them now. Not until they were safely in Spain. Until then, she would hold them in her heart.

Aime picked up the baggage and the child. "Hurry now. The boat is waiting for us, and I've put some provisions on it so you and the boy will be comfortable."

"Merci. One day, I will be able to repay you for all the kindness you've shown to me these past few months."

"No need." He led the way out of the chilly church into the even chillier night. Hashem would have to guide them because there was no other way Aime would be able to see to steer.

No more than a handful of minutes later, they were at the marina, fishing boats and a few larger pleasure crafts bobbing in the water as the waves crashed against the pier.

Aime's boat, of course, was the largest one there. That was good. Less chance of it capsizing, one of Hélène's greatest fears. She couldn't swim, and Étienne was helpless.

The pier rocked beneath her feet, and she had to bite her tongue to keep from squealing. With his hands full, Aime couldn't steady her. Instead, she locked her knees. Give her the mountains any day.

From behind them came the sound of vehicles. Aime had been correct. The Nazis weren't that far behind. If only he hadn't stopped in the church, they might be away already.

"Allons-y, allons-y." Aime set the suitcase on the dock then held Hélène by the elbow as he guided her to step over the sliver of water between the pier and the swaying boat. "Keep low."

Hélène moved as fast as she could and did what he commanded and managed to get both feet inside the boat. He handed Étienne to her and climbed aboard himself.

By now, the Nazis had loosed their dogs, who barked and snarled far too close for Hélène's comfort.

"Get below deck." Aime pointed to a set of downward-leading stairs.

"But you—"

"I need to pilot the boat. Go."

The dogs closed in, as did their handlers, shouting in German. *"Halten sie. Halten sie."*

Any moment now, they would be underway and out of the German's reach. But they didn't move. Closer and closer came the snarls and the shouts. Why wasn't Aime starting the motor? Why wasn't the boat moving away from land?

"Hélène!" Aime's desperate cry reached her.

She placed the baby in a pile of blankets, though he now opened his eyes and stared at her. "Stay here. Be a good boy. I'll be right back." With that, she fled up the stairs.

From what she could make out in the low light coming from the ever-gaining Germans' electric torches, Aime was struggling to untie the boat from the mooring. "What do you want me to do?"

"I can't get it." He almost growled the words. "There's a knot."

"Good thing Maman sent me to camp each summer." Though her hands shook because she had to lean over the edge of the boat, over the dark water, the rope was tangled but the knot wasn't all that tight. Aime must have loosened it a great deal before becoming frustrated.

She set to work on it though her arms ached. Fatigue pulled at her limbs, but she fought it off.

A loud boom, then a whiz. The Nazis were close enough to open fire. With one last twist of the rope, she freed the boat from its mooring. "Start the engine."

It roared to life, and with a jerk that almost sent Hélène overboard, they pulled away from the pier. Her heart pounded faster than the bullets whizzing past them.

Another boom and ping. Then another.

"Ah!" The boat swung hard to the left, then back to the right. "Get down!"

She flopped on the deck.

The boat jerked again.

Another couple of pings. A few unintelligible shouts from the dock.

Then the icy sea breeze pelted her face, and the salty, fishy smell of the water took over.

She came to her hands and knees and, with the boat rocking to and fro, crawled to Aime. He clutched his upper arm.

"You're hit!"

CHAPTER SIXTY-TWO

22 August, 1955
Elne, France

Pain. It was one of the ties that bound us all together here. At one time or another, each of us had experienced unimaginable pain. That's what brought us here. That's what we were all trying to forget.

I was no exception to this. My heart was forever shaped by this place, and still is, even to this very day. The pain I experienced here is why I've returned, even after vowing that I never would.

I go back inside, as restless as a jackal, not able to stay in one place for very long. I want the car to come. I don't want the car to come. Unable to make up my mind, I now take refuge where I've taken refuge so often.

So much of this home beckons to me, calls my name, echoes a whisper from the past. Once more I climb the stairs to the room where I slept. The room where I experienced so much pain, both physical and emotional. A toll that aged me well before my time.

Would I exchange all that for where I am now and what I'm doing with my life today? Oh, what an impossible question to answer. Though my life jumped the tracks and led to a different destination than I had wanted, in the end, I came to the place where the Almighty intended me to be.

Perhaps I shouldn't have returned here. Maybe attempting to recreate the past was a bad idea. I cannot undo what has been done, the decision I made that day so long ago. For the rest of my life, I will have to live with it.

Then again, the coming joy will be worth the greatest pain.

CHAPTER SIXTY-THREE

November 14, 2022
Barcelona, Spain

What was done was done. Caitlyn had met with the dean and withdrawn from school. They were gracious enough to give her a little bit of her money back, but not nearly what she had spent. When she got home, she would have to repay the people from church and everyone who had been generous enough to support her endeavors.

She had bought her tickets, and Aiden was now with her in El Prat Airport's Terminal One. The check-in area was huge with shiny, polished floors and airline counters that ran perpendicular to the entrance.

With one hand, Aiden rolled her large suitcase, and with the other, he held her hand, caressing her thumb with his. "I'm going to miss you so much. Selfishly, I wish you didn't have to go, but I understand you're doing what's best for you."

"I tried. I really did try."

He squeezed her fingers. "You did, but it was clear to everyone that it was getting to be too much, that you had to deal with the past before you could work on the future."

"Let's talk about happy things. I don't want to cry today." Although she would, when she was in private and could release the tears that had been building behind her eyes.

An airline representative came and helped them get her checked in, and they made their way toward security. All around, people bustled, some faster than others. It was easy to spot the tourists who had all the time in the world and the businesspeople who had to hustle to make their flights.

Even though that was going on all around Caitlyn, it became a background blur, and only Aiden was clear. He gave her the barest hint of a smile. "Do you mind if I keep in touch with you? I'd like to hear how you're doing and if you make any progress in finding out about your family."

"Of course. I'd love for you to call or text me anytime you want. Just remember that I'm going to be six hours behind you."

"Don't worry. I won't bug you in the middle of the night."

"I appreciate that." She stopped before she entered the line that snaked through the taped-off area that led to security. "Thank you, Aiden. You've been so good to me these past few months. I honestly don't know where I would be without you."

"I'm glad I could be there for you. All I want is for you to heal and get stronger. God is refining you in the fire, and when you come out on the other side, you're going to be more beautiful than ever."

He was going to make her cry right here and right now. "Merci, mon ami."

"I'll come and take you up in an airplane one of these days."

"You never know. I might just end up on the field after all."

"If you do it for God first and for yourself, then that's what you should do. Only for God."

She glanced at her phone to pull up her boarding pass and found an email from the DNA testing company. Her hands shook as she opened it. "I have my genetic results."

Aiden came and stood over her shoulder. "Open it."

"Here. Here it is. English and Scottish. That would be my mom's side. Her parents came here in the sixties, right before she was born." She pointed to the little pie chart on her phone. "And French, Swiss, and a little German. Mostly concentrated in Southwestern France. But do you see this? That's all of my results. There's no Jewish in there anywhere."

"Hmm, that is strange." His breath on her neck gave her goose bumps but in a good way.

"So I'm not Jewish? Noémie Treves or whatever her last name was, isn't my great-grandmother? I don't understand."

He pulled her toward a bank of chairs nearer to the check-in area. "Maybe it got diluted over the years. It did come from your great-grandparents."

"I'm so confused."

"It would explain why Noémie's card didn't have the Laurent name on it anywhere."

"You're right. Here I thought that Noémie married my great-grandfather—though I now have to question if even that's real—in order to protect herself and Pops. But something else was going on. Something I have to get to the bottom of."

"Then it's a good thing you booked your ticket so that you're flying into DC before going home. Just don't overdo it. Don't get obsessed or stressed about this. You need to take care of yourself."

"I know, but this is important. More important than ever. I still want to know if my great-grandmother was married before she married my great-grandfather. The distraction will be good for me. See, it even got my mind off of everything that's going on and why I'm flying home today."

"And missing me?" He cocked his head and wiggled his eyebrows.

"Of course, missing you." On a whim, she leaned forward and kissed his cheek.

Then he grabbed her, her heart pounding in her chest, wrapped her in his embrace, and gave her a proper kiss. Surprising and soft yet hungry and full of promise.

It didn't last long before he broke away, but it was a moment she would never forget. "That's my way of telling you that I'm really, really going to miss you and I really, really hope we get to see each other again, someday soon."

"I hope that too." She stared at the people lining up to get through to the gates. "I guess I'd better go. I want to make sure I have plenty of time to pass inspection, grab a bite of something other than airline food, and make it to my gate."

"I guess you should." He kissed her again, and she leaned into him and him back, then pulled away. "I'm never going to be able to go if you keep that up."

"In that case—"

She kissed him again, short but sweet. "That's it. No more. I'll let you know how everything goes."

"Get your grandpa tested. If he doesn't have Jewish blood, then you know for sure. It might give you more answers. And take care of yourself. Please, allow yourself some time and grace. Get better so we can have a few adventures together."

"Thank you. I couldn't have made it this far without you." She pecked him on the cheek again for good measure then wheeled her carry-on toward security. While she waited for her turn to go through, she didn't look back. The weight of Aiden's stare sat on her shoulders, but if she turned around, she would break down. With everything she had, she was holding on to her composure by the most delicate of threads.

She made it through then wheeled her carry-on down the hall toward her gate area. As fast as possible, she raced down the terminal until she found a ladies' room, where she locked herself in a stall.

And cried.

Who was she? Where did she belong? What was she supposed to do with her life?

All questions with no answers.

And here she was, leaving the city, the opportunity she had dreamed of for a long time. The opportunity Lindsey had dreamed of.

After a few minutes, she got control of herself, went to the sinks and splashed water on her face, then boarded her flight.

Her problems would come with her, but hopefully she'd be in a better place to deal with them.

By the time she landed in DC, she was bleary-eyed, only having managed a couple of hours' sleep on the plane. She made her way through border control and customs and emerged from the door toward the exit.

"Caitlyn! Caitlyn! Over here!"

Could it be? She squinted and spied a shorter, still-lean, middle-aged woman jumping up and down. "Mom?" Caitlyn ran and threw herself into her mother's embrace. "What are you doing here?"

"I missed you so much I couldn't wait for you to get home. And I wanted to be here with you, in Washington, as you did more research. What I didn't tell you was that I had Pops tested at the same time as you. We got the results a few days ago, and I know that they change everything."

They moved out of the way of couples and families reuniting. "So it's true, and not that it was so diluted in me that it didn't show up. Pops and Dad and I aren't Jewish."

Mom shook her head. "You aren't. But that doesn't change who you are as a person on the inside. God created you the way you are. It has nothing to do with your genes."

Caitlyn tucked that statement away to examine later. "I still want to go to the Holocaust museum and see what records they have for Noémie Treves. She could be the woman Dad knew as his grandmother."

"He wishes he could be here to help you with this search, but he has a big work meeting coming up, so he sent me. He really would like to know more about her, who she was and what made her tick. Why she ended up as his grandmother when she wasn't related to him by blood. At least we don't believe she was."

"First, though, I'd like something to drink at least, and maybe a little bit of sleep."

"Of course. It was a long trip. I'm so glad you're home, but for your sake, I wish you were still there. Don't worry. You aren't going to be alone on this next step of your journey. Please, though, come to me if you ever need anything or just want to talk. I'm here for you. Always. I love you and will always want what's best for you."

"So you aren't disappointed in me?"

"Far from it. So far from it that you can't imagine."

"I love you, Mom."

Together, they left the terminal and waited only a few minutes for the hotel shuttle to pick them up. Caitlyn showered and changed her clothes and emerged from the bathroom a new woman.

"Are you ready for something to eat?"

"It's not terribly late yet. Can we go to the museum now and get started?"

"Actually, I looked into research myself when I learned you were coming here. You have to go to the library in Bowie, Maryland. I've scheduled some time for us to do that tomorrow morning and for a researcher to meet us to make it go faster. She told me it was unusual for them to have a spot and a researcher available on such short notice, but I guess not many people are going with Thanksgiving coming up."

"Oh, I forgot all about that."

"Don't worry. Aunt Jennie is taking care of it this year. All I have to do is bring the sweet potato casserole."

"That's good, I suppose." She hugged Mom. "It means so much that you'd come all this way for me. The plane ticket couldn't have been cheap."

"You're worth more than a few dollars, so don't worry about it. How about we order in a pizza, and you can tell me all about whatever you want to talk about?"

"That sounds great." Caitlyn gave her mom another hug. "I'm so glad you're my mom."

"And I'm so glad to have you as a daughter. You are a blessing, and I want to see your million-dollar smile again very soon."

By the time the pizza arrived, Caitlyn had poured out most of her story, and even managed to do it without tears. When she finished, Mom patted her hand. "You know Dad and I will support you no matter what. Live your own dreams and your own calling."

"Do you think Lindsey would be disappointed in me?"

"Never, Caity-girl, never. Just the opposite. She would be so proud of you."

Caitlyn could only hope she would be.

CHAPTER SIXTY-FOUR

22 August, 1955
Elne, France

I pace back and forth across the beautiful tile floors that I have long admired, one of the house's features that I always loved the best. More than once, I wipe my sweaty hands on my skirt. My heart is skittering in my chest. Never in my life have I been so nervous.

Not even during my encounter with the Germans. I didn't have much time to think about what was happening then. This time, I've had years to ponder this moment. To dream about it. A thousand times, I've played it over in my head.

What will his reaction be? I've changed so much, he's changed so much, that I doubt he'll recognize me. I'm sure I would never have recognized him if not for meeting in this place. So much time has passed. So much life has happened.

Should I leave before he gets here, before this becomes too hard? I've asked myself this question a million times in the past week. But I've come too far. He's come too far. I can't back out now.

Each time I reach the front door, I peek outside, down the steps and across the sweeping lawn, down the lane. Nothing. No one. Silence.

Strange that it's the silence I notice. When I was here during the war, there were very few times, even in the middle of the night, when there was complete stillness. Always there was a baby crying somewhere.

Now, this place has been silent for over a decade.

Perhaps today, for one glorious moment, joy and laughter will return.

CHAPTER SIXTY-FIVE

25 November, 1942
Mediterranean Sea

Waves crashed against the boat, rocking it to and fro, and the wind lashed at them as Aime and Hélène moved farther into the Mediterranean. The darkness was as thick as a blanket, so dark that any lights shining on the shore weren't visible.

In front of Hélène, Aime clutched his upper arm. "You're hurt." She had to shout so he could hear her above the gale.

"I'm fine. Go below with Étienne."

"Where's your first aid kit?"

"Don't worry about me."

"But I am worried, and I'll continue to be until I see the wound for myself."

"You aren't strong enough to fight the wind."

She crawled closer to him. He pursed his lips and held the steering wheel with his right hand only. Every now and again, he winced.

"*You* aren't strong enough."

"I don't have much of a choice. We can't go back. We've burned that bridge."

"Then at least let me bandage you so that you don't lose any more blood. It won't do any good to have you passing out. Then where would I be?"

He flicked open a compass he'd been holding and studied it for a moment then turned the wheel to correct their course. "You'll find what you need in the galley. Top cabinet."

Crawling because if she stood the waves might toss her overboard, she reached the stairs, panting for breath. Soon she located the supplies and returned to Aime, once again on her hands and knees. "Let me see." She pulled herself to a standing position.

His dark blue shirt was torn at the bicep, and blood covered the area.

"You'll have to take off your shirt so I can properly bandage you."

"I can't." His good arm strained as he worked to keep the boat headed in the right direction. "Someone has to steer."

"Then I'll have to rip it as much as I can."

"There should be scissors in the kit."

She opened the tin box with a red cross on it, rummaged around, and located the snips, then cut a hole big enough for her to work. She was no nurse, but it appeared that the bullet had only grazed him. She completed the task of cleaning the wound and dressing it. Eleanore would have been proud. "There's some aspirin in here. Do you want some?"

He nodded, and she handed him two, along with a glass she retrieved from the galley.

"Now will you go below deck?"

"Fine." But instead of going all the way down, she sat on the top step to keep an eye on him and still be able to hear the baby if he cried. And because the walls closed in on her down there. "Have you ever sailed to Spain before?" She had to shout for him to hear her.

"All the time. I was a yachter. Won some trophies." He checked the course on his compass once again. With a groan, he turned the wheel. "You're in capable hands."

"Did you ever do it in the dark in the winter?"

"I like a new challenge, don't you?" Though his words were light, his voice was tight. That increased the tension in her shoulders.

"What will you do when the war is over?"

He focused his attention on the black sea that engulfed them. They might as well be the only three people left alive on the earth. Her teeth chattered, and she clenched her jaw.

"I don't know."

Behind her, Étienne whimpered for a moment then settled down again. At least he was able to sleep through all this chaos and commotion.

When he grew up, he wouldn't remember any of this.

"What about you?"

"Maybe return to France. Maybe create new stained-glass windows for churches and synagogues. Without Levi, I'm at a loss."

"You're resilient. You'll find your way. And you'll always have the Lord."

"Right now, it's enough to get through each day."

A gust of wind buffeted the boat. On the dock, this vessel had felt huge. Now, surrounded by nothing but water, it was tiny. But even over the howling of the wind, Étienne's cries carried, forcing her to venture into the hold of the boat.

"Oh, *mon doux garçon, mon doux garçon*." She picked him up and cradled him, rocking along with the motion of the boat. "Don't cry. I'm here, and Aime is taking good care of us. We'll be fine, just fine."

She changed his nappie, soaked in water a little of the bread they brought and fed him, and gave him a bottle. Then she rocked him again, dreaming of her child buried beneath the ground at the château. Her heart ached.

When she awoke, sprawled across the bed beside Étienne, she found one of his hands tangled in her hair, the other thumb planted in his mouth. His eyelashes brushed his fair cheeks. And something deep inside pulled at her heart.

She kissed his cheek, wetting it with her own tears while warning herself not to fall too much in love with him. It would only hurt more when the time came to return him to the place he belonged.

By this time, the rolling of the boat was gentler, more like a rocking chair than a carnival ride. Since the baby still snoozed, she covered him with a blanket, brushing a curl from his forehead. He didn't even stir.

Her legs were stiff as she made her way up the stairs. How she'd been able to sleep was beyond her, but her body, still healing from childbirth, must have demanded it. Rays of sunshine met her as she reached the top step. Morning. Glorious morning. At least now they'd be able to see where they were going.

At some point during the night, Aime had found a stool, for he now sat on it and stared straight ahead. With the calmer seas, he didn't have to work so hard to keep the boat on course.

"Bonjour."

He turned and flashed her a smile that stretched from ear to ear, his eyes sparkling as much as the light off the water. "Bonjour. Did you sleep well?"

"I did. Étienne is still slumbering. And what about you? Did you manage to get any rest?"

"Sleep, you mean? Non. Since we were out in the water without any lights, I had to be very vigilant to make sure we didn't run into any other boats or the rocky shore. But take a look for yourself." He motioned in front of him.

And there a city spread before them, a wide, horseshoe-shaped yellow sand beach in front of the packed-together, light-colored buildings that stretched flat for a while before gradually rising to meet the mountains in the background. Altogether beautiful and stunning. "Is this it?"

"Barcelona, oui. There she is, and she's never looked more beautiful."

"I've never been here before, but it looks wonderful. Perhaps a little tired from war, but aren't we all."

"C'est vrai. Here we can all rest and take a deep breath for the first time since 1940." He inhaled. "Just smell the peace and the freedom."

She did the same, but all she smelled was fish and saltwater. Still, it was somehow different. A little purer. She hugged him, and he winced. "Je suis désolée. I forgot about your arm. How is it feeling?"

"It was fine." He chuckled. "Actually, you did a marvelous job with it. I managed to keep going in the correct direction all night."

"Sounds like you may have had some doubts you didn't share with me."

"There was no sense in upsetting you. And I knew you needed the sleep. God guided us and brought us here. Though at times it has felt like He abandoned us, He never has. Nor will He ever. His promises are yes and amen." Aime turned the boat so that it headed for the port, its quays reaching fingers into the blue water.

She sat on the deck, arranging her dark wool skirt over her legs and pulling her black coat around her shoulders. "Do you truly believe Hashem is always beside us and guiding us?"

"He is."

"Then where was He when my employees were killed? When Levi

and I were arrested? When they beat my husband to death? I can't believe He was there then too."

"God is omnipresent. In all places at all times. Because He isn't constricted by a body like we are, He can be. He is always watching us. You question His presence when bad times come, and it can feel like He has left His people. But He hasn't. He has promised He never will. Sometimes, His plans for us are different than ours for ourselves."

"His plan can be for people to die in the most brutal way? Is He so cruel as to punish me so severely for what I didn't do?"

"Sometimes people die. But death is the door to life. Eternal life, where we will forever be in His presence. Never alone or forsaken. If we trust in the death of His Son on the cross for our sins, then His blood has washed us clean of all our guilt, for what we've done and what we haven't done, and guaranteed that place for us. The apostle Paul said that for him to die was gain. Heaven is even more beautiful than Barcelona."

"Merci. I'll have to think about what you have said."

"And I'm not going to leave you alone either. I'll be here for as long as you need me, until we can return to France and pick up our lives. You can count on me. Look at all the women and children you saved at La Maternité de la Paix. God has used you for good."

His words quieted some of the turmoil rolling inside her. "You're a good man, Aime Laurent. I'll never forget your kindness to me."

For a moment, his eyes softened, his gaze on her tender. Then he returned his attention to guiding the boat into the harbor.

Was that what it was like to trust in Jesus and His forgiveness and to have Him guide your life? Would He steer her ship into heaven's harbor?

Étienne's cries interrupted her musings. "He's probably afraid in a strange place with no one he knows." She rose from the varnished deck and went below to see to him.

By the time Aime pulled into port, she had the baby on top with her. He smiled and laughed with the pure joy only infants have.

Once Aime had secured permission to land and a spot to dock, they disembarked, not hunted for the first time in over two years. What a glorious, amazing experience it was. She twirled with the baby in her arms, falling against Aime.

"Be careful. I don't want to fish you out of the water."

She laughed. "If heaven is half this good, then I understand what you were talking about."

"It's infinitely better than this."

Perhaps, then, she needed to learn more about how to get there.

CHAPTER SIXTY-SIX

22 August, 1955
Elne, France

The time for looking in the mirror and searching for the past has come. I turn and stare at the once-beautiful building in front of me.

What happened here will always leave an indelible mark on my soul. But I left it in 1942, thirteen years ago now. So I close the door to that room in my heart and turn the lock, tucking the key away for if I ever choose to come back to it once more.

I face the wind and allow it to blow my hair. My future is clear and has been since that day so long ago. I made my choice then, and though I will never forget what I did, I don't regret it. After today, I will no longer dwell on it.

Because time has this way of marching on, whether we want it to or not. Just as the waves on a beach gently erode the shore over a long period, the waves of time have eroded the pain so it is now bearable.

Coming here has released some of my memories and cast them into the wind. I've allowed them to be blown far away, never to be found again. Not by me, anyway.

Some of the memories I will keep hidden, perhaps for the rest of my life. And that is how it should be.

CHAPTER SIXTY-SEVEN

November 14, 2022
Washington, DC

The librarian from the US Holocaust Museum set the archives that Mom had requested several days ago in front of Caitlyn. As she did so, she bent over and whispered, "I hope these help." Then she moved away on feet as quiet as a still winter's day.

Caitlyn wiped her hands on her jeans to get rid of the moisture on them so she didn't ruin any of the old, delicate papers. With her pulse throbbing in her neck, she opened the manila folder.

At the top of the paper was typed the words, "Prisoners of Camp de Rivesaltes, Rivesaltes, Pyrenees-Orientales, France."

Mom leaned to her right, closer to Caitlyn. "What does it say?"

"I have to look it over first." The list was in alphabetical order, and she had to turn to the third page to find the Ts. Then she scanned the list. Treves, Levi, age 25, Mulhouse, France. Birthday 5 February, 1917. Status: Married. Occupation: glassworks. Arrival date: 16 July, 1942.

Treves, Noémie, age 25, Mulhouse, France. Birthday 26 June, 1917. Status: Married. Occupation: business owner. Arrival date: 16 July, 1942.

Caitlyn could hardly breathe. "There they are. Both of them. My great-grandmother, Dad's grandmother, was married before she married David Laurent. When they arrived at the camp, they arrived together. On the same day at the same place. Wait until I tell Dad. And Pops."

"Don't rush too far ahead. They could have been siblings."

"Not born four months apart."

"Okay. Cousins then. How could she have married David if she was already married?"

"That's a valid question. We should see what we can find out about Levi Treves and what happened to him. Maybe he didn't survive." Caitlyn picked up a microfilm reel marked "Holocaust Victims in France." "Good thing you ordered this when you ordered the documents we wanted to search."

They made their way to the microfilm reader, threaded it onto the spool, and worked, churning their way through the pages and pages of documents until they came on one that said *Victims of Camp de Rivesaltes*. There were many, many names, but at last they came to one entry that sped up Caitlyn's heart rate. She tapped her fingernail on the screen.

Mom sucked in a breath.

"Treves, Levi. 30 August, 1942. Prisoner killed in fight."

"I'm glad you're here to help me with the French." Mom rubbed Caitlyn's shoulder.

"And I'm glad you learned German in college. Between the two of us, we're able to read these documents. If we couldn't, we'd really be at a loss. But what do you think about that story?"

"It's quite something, isn't it? So sad that he was killed."

"I need to call Aiden and let him know about this." Caitlyn ignored the way Mom quirked her eyebrow.

"Remember, this is a library."

"I'll put in my earbuds and speak softly. He might have some thoughts that will help us put the puzzle pieces together." She brought up WhatsApp and got Aiden on the line.

"How are you doing?"

"A little jet-lagged but not too bad. Mom is with me." Just so he wouldn't say something embarrassing, even though Mom couldn't hear him.

"Gotcha."

She filled him in on what they had discovered so far. Mom leaned over to her computer bag and pulled out her laptop.

"So she came to the camp on July 16, 1942, right?"

"Yep."

"And it was just the two of them in the register?"

"That's right."

"Okay. Processing all of this. He died on August 30. We know from the card from the maternity hospital that she was there then. Which means that she was pregnant when she was taken prisoner. Remember what we read? Men and women were separated and housed in different blocks. Blocks that were fenced off. With barbed wire."

As if poked with a cattle prod, Caitlyn sat up straighter. "Are you thinking what I'm thinking?"

"I'm thinking we should have researched Aime Laurent and the Laurent château a little more. Hang on a sec." The clicking of keys came over the line, and when Caitlyn glanced over her shoulder, Mom was also busy looking up something.

What if the little boy, Otto, who was buried on the Laurent property, was Noémie and Levi's child? Her poor great-grandmother, suffering the loss of not only her husband but also her child. No wonder Pops said she never wanted to talk about that time. It must have been so traumatic for her.

"I got it!" Aiden's shout sent her backwards in her chair.

"Hey, you're going to make me deaf. I have earbuds in."

"Oops, sorry."

Mom came alongside Caitlyn and set her computer on the small desk. "I've got it."

"Mom has it too. Let me give her one of my earbuds so she can hear what you have to say, and we can see if you guys came to the same conclusion."

Mom shifted her laptop so Caitlyn could see. What she had was an article from Yad Vashem about Aime Laurent.

Aiden's voice crackled a little on the connection, but Caitlyn managed to pick out what he was saying. "It's an article about Aime Laurent on Yad Vashem's website. You should see what it's all about. Let me tell you."

"You don't have to, Aiden. Mom has the same article, I'm pretty sure. Now give me a chance to catch up with both of you."

Aime Laurent, Righteous Among the Nations

The article chronicled how Aime had helped build and support La Maternité de la Paix in Elne, France. It gave details about the hospital they had learned when they visited. But then it went on to describe the events of November 25, 1942, and what Aime had done that had earned him the designation of Righteous Among the Nations.

And what it said stole Caitlyn's breath.

CHAPTER SIXTY-EIGHT

30 September, 1944
Elne, France

As the train pulled into the Elne station, Hélène reached for Aime's hand and gave it a squeeze as Étienne bounced on her lap. Over the past two years, he had been such a comfort to her, a protector, a great friend.

And as time healed her wounds, her memories of Levi now sweet instead of bitter, Aime was becoming even more than that to her.

Still, as she swept her gaze over the countryside, her mouth went dry. What would they find here? Facing the memories brought up by being back where Levi and Otto died was the most difficult thing she'd ever done.

Aime returned her squeeze and gave her a smile. "This doesn't feel very much like home anymore."

"C'est vrai." She turned to peer out the window as the train slowed in front of a red brick building. Where was home? Her husband and son were dead, and soon she might have to give up Étienne.

Word was that the Allies had bombed the center of Mulhouse to rubble. Because the Germans had turned her glass factory into one that produced munitions, there was likely little that was left. If she would even be able to reclaim her property.

Aime leaned over and whispered in her ear, sending shivers down her spine. "Everything will be fine, you know. We'll rebuild our lives. Together. Perhaps in America, where it will be better. Away from the destruction." It would be so easy for her to fall into his arms and allow him to kiss her troubles away.

"So many have lost so much. I suppose we should be grateful for what we have."

"Even if it's two small apartments in Barcelona's cramped Gothic Quarter and jobs in shops?" He tipped his head and gave her that half-grin she was coming to adore.

She had found employment, crafting small pieces of stained glass. It was something, at least. A kind older neighbor kept Étienne during the day. "It's more than so many have. So many don't even have lives at all." She sighed to help wash away the lump in her throat.

"You're right." Aime reached over and tickled Étienne, who squealed in delight. "Isn't she? Hélène is a very wise woman."

Long ago, she'd shared her true identity with him, but he insisted on keeping up the charade, just in case. And that was fine with her. Noémie was dead and gone. Everything that made her who she was had disappeared. So it was fitting that she had discarded the name and adopted a new one.

The train's brakes screeched, and it came to a halt. Aime jumped up and grabbed their bags as Hélène led Étienne toward the doors. As this wasn't a big town where many would be getting off, they didn't have much time to disembark before the train moved on.

The trip from Barcelona wasn't long, but still she stretched her legs and arched her back.

"Train! Train!" Étienne pointed at the last car just disappearing around a bend in the tracks.

Trees hid the hill where La Maternité de la Paix sat, but the mountain where Aime's château was stood above it all.

The building wasn't as proud as it had once been. Something was different. Something was wrong.

Beside her, Aime gasped. So she hadn't been seeing things or going crazy. "I'm sure it's not as bad as it looks from here."

"There's nothing green on the hillside. My grapevines. The house. What did they do?"

"We have our lives, remember? That is what's important." She kept all traces of harshness out of her voice. Every loss was a blow.

"Oui, oui. How easily I forget. Even if there is nothing left, it can't compare to what they snatched from you."

"Your loss is no less real than mine. The Germans stole so much from so many. None have escaped without damage. No one's life will ever be the same."

Hélène led the toddler by the hand while Aime carried their two suitcases to the hired car that would take them to La Maternité de la Paix. So much had happened since she had first arrived there a little over two years ago. Everything had changed.

And yet, Hashem was showing His goodness to her. Though her flat was small, barely enough room for her and Étienne, they made do. Her job provided them with food and clothing. Aime helped where and when he could.

They almost missed the turnoff for the hospital. Briars and brambles had taken over and had obscured the drive. They left the car and made their way toward the home. She clutched the boy a little tighter and slowed her steps.

Aime matched her pace until they were almost not moving. She raised her shoulders and inhaled, then turned the corner, the hospital coming into view.

The shutters hung at odd angles, and almost all the windows were broken or cracked. The paint peeled, and there was no longer a front door. The grass was tall, and the garden overrun by weeds.

What had once been a happy place where children laughed and women sang, was no more. She turned to Aime. "Let's go. There's nothing for us here. We need to see what has become of your château. And then perhaps head for America, if we can. First, though, we must find Eleanore."

"We have to start over, both of us. Why not make a clean break and begin again somewhere new?"

They returned to the car they had hired, and Aime gave instructions for the driver. Just as they were about to pull out of the driveway, someone called Hélène's name from behind.

She turned to find a very thin dark-haired young woman running and waving her arms. *"Arrêt! Arrêt!"* When the car ground to a halt,

Hélène jumped from the seat and ran into Salomé's arms. "Mon amie, mon amie? Comment vas-tu?"

"I'm well. I can't believe I found you. Almost every day I've come, watching and waiting for you."

"You're living in the area?"

"Oui. Paul and I are here. My husband. . ."

Too often that was the story they heard these days. "Je suis désolée."

"We aren't alone, are we? Is that Aime with you? And Étienne?"

"Oui. We've been in Barcelona."

"All this time, I wondered what had become of you and how you were faring. But I can see that you look well. You've gained a little weight. And there's a lightness about you that wasn't there before."

Aime joined them, wrapping Hélène in a side embrace.

Salomé's eyes went wide. "Are you. . .?"

"Not yet. But soon we will marry, once things here are settled. And then we will probably go to America."

"That's so far away."

Hélène nodded. "But it's for the best. We just need to know what happened to Eleanore."

"Oh." Salomé's face fell. "I saw her on a list of names of those who perished in Auschwitz."

Hélène's knees went weak, but Aime was there to support her and hold her upright. "When?"

"Soon after she arrived in January of 1943."

For a moment, Hélène stood in stunned silence, attempting to get her heart to accept the words her ears heard. "I can't believe it." She trembled, and Aime held her tighter. "Then there truly is nothing left for us here."

"I understand." Salomé wiped away the tears Hélène couldn't cry. "If I had the means, I might be tempted to go as well. But I will be returning to my secretarial job in Perpignan in a few weeks, and we are rebuilding our lives here. I will miss you though. All this time, I had hoped we would end up in the same place."

Hélène hugged her dear friend. "War may have separated us, but I will always think of you as the sister I never had. You and Paul hold a special place in my heart. That will never change, even with an ocean between us."

They spent an hour or so sitting on the balcony, reminiscing, talking about Eleanore and the others as Aime and Paul and Étienne played on the grass below them.

After a while, the conversation switched and centered on what the future held. Both of them had moved on from the past, the current of time carrying them further and further away from the most difficult and most painful parts of their lives.

At last, Aime climbed the steps, the boys racing up ahead of him. "Those two have more energy than ten of me." But he laughed at their antics and tousled their hair.

Hélène went to him. "I suppose you are ready to go to the château?"

He nodded.

"What about your family's property?" Salomé picked up her tired-out son.

"For now, I'll keep it and use the revenue it generates to fund different causes. Perhaps help other Europeans settling in the United States. No matter what, Hélène and Étienne and I will be together."

She intertwined her fingers with his, stood on her tiptoes, and placed a light kiss on his lips. "This home brought us peace for a season, but now we must set our faces toward a new future. And keep the promise I made to Eleanore two years ago."

CHAPTER SIXTY-NINE

January 10, 2023
Downers Grove, Illinois

Caitlyn sat in the comfortable gray chair, her water bottle on a small wood table to her left, Dr. Harris in a similar chair across from her. Raina, as Dr. Harris insisted Caitlyn call her, wasn't too much older than Caitlyn herself, which helped make her more approachable. And the fact that she was a Christian was another plus.

Outside the large window on Caitlyn's right, snow floated on the air currents, coating the trees in glittery white.

"Tell me how the holidays went." Raina sat back and tugged her brown and pink cardigan sweater tighter around her shoulders. It was chilly.

"Hard. It's been a year now. One year that Lindsey has been gone. And so much has changed."

"How did you handle Christmas and New Year's?"

Caitlyn closed her eyes and took a deep breath. "Half the time I was in my room crying. The other half I was trying to convince myself and everyone around me that I was fine, things were fine, and it was a happy holiday."

"Why do you think you put on that mask?"

"What mask?" Caitlyn furrowed her forehead.

"The one you show the world. I've seen it myself. It's a smiley-face mask. Your everything-is-fine-so-don't-talk-to-me-about-it mask."

"I do that?"

"Yes, you do. Think about that for a moment."

Memories surfaced of her having cookouts with her college friends that last semester of school when they all lived in the same cul-de-sac. She laughed and went along with whatever they planned. In fact, she was the one who suggested they go hang gliding because that's what Lindsey had wanted to do. They'd had such a great time, but inside, Caitlyn was crying.

Even when she got to the missionary school, she and Elissa and the others tried all the restaurants, saw the Antoni Gaudi architectural sites, including Sagrada Familia and Güell Park, which he designed. They spent an evening at the magic fountain and laughed the night away as they sat at the taverna having tapas.

"I guess I do wear a mask. I try to pretend it's all good. Who wants to be around someone who is, as my mom says, a Debbie Downer?"

"That's true, but you also have to acknowledge your feelings and what happened. You said it was a long time before you were able to share about the accident with your roommate in Spain."

"She still doesn't know the full story."

"Why is that?" Raina tucked a strand of her curly blond hair behind her ear.

Caitlyn studied her counselor's silver disk earrings swinging back and forth. Why couldn't she tell Elissa what had happened, all of the gritty details? "I guess I wanted to spare her the gruesome crime scene photos."

Raina twirled the pen in her hand.

"But I did tell one other person. I told him everything."

"Who?"

Caitlyn twisted a ring on the middle finger of her right hand. Back and forth, back and forth before she inhaled. "Aiden. This guy I met there. This really great guy. He knows more about it than just about anyone. But he's going to be a missionary pilot, and the more I think about it, the more I think I'm not cut out to be a missionary nurse."

"Okay. You have time to decide that. You aren't in a position to make life choices right now. But why do you think it's so hard for you to tell people the accident details?"

Caitlyn jiggled her foot and stared out the window at the snow. Yes, they had shown her compassion. Everyone did. But very few knew the entire story. "Aiden doesn't, but I'm afraid if I told people everything, they would hate me."

"Why? Is there something you aren't telling me? I read the police report."

"I know you did. And no, what I've said to you is pretty much what I remember about that night." Caitlyn stood and paced in front of the window.

"Then why would they hate you?"

She stopped in her tracks and spun to face Raina, the lump in her throat swelling by the second. "Because I couldn't do anything to prevent it. I should have done something, and maybe I could have saved Lindsey."

"What could you have done?" Her counselor's voice was soft and calm.

Caitlyn paced again for several minutes as she ran various scenarios through her head. Ones that she had been running for the past year. And she was no closer to an answer than she was a year ago. "I don't know!" She fisted her hands. "I don't know! That's the entire problem. There had to be something, but I don't know what it is."

"Do you know why that's the case?"

Caitlyn shook her head.

"Because there was nothing you could do."

"If I had turned the wheel or, or. . ."

"Nothing, Caitlyn, nothing. It wasn't your fault. Has anyone ever blamed you?"

Again, she shook her head.

"Then you have your answer."

"Her parents and brother are always so nice to me."

"Because they know there was nothing that could have been done to prevent it. God chose that time to call Lindsey home."

"Why in such a horrific way? Why would He take her like that?"

"I'm not God, and I would never try to get inside His mind. It's too great for me to fathom. But His ways are perfect, and He had His reasons."

By now, tears streamed down Caitlyn's cheeks. "Why did He take her? I needed her." She plunked into the chair.

"Look at you. You're young and smart and talented. Despite this tragedy, you graduated college with highest honors. You went on to study abroad for the second time, this time without knowing anyone there. That takes some guts."

"I only went because it's what I thought Lindsey would want me to do."

"For whatever reason, you did it. How do you view yourself?"

Caitlyn dabbed at her damp cheeks with a tissue. "I don't know what you mean."

"Weak or strong?"

"Weak. I need people. I rely on people. I relied on Lindsey."

"Maybe a little bit too much? Is that possible?"

"I don't know. Maybe." That conversation she'd had with Mom when she was seven popped into her head again. "Mom always thought I did."

"Is it time for you to stand on your own two feet?"

"I don't know if I can."

January 21, 2023
Downers Grove, Illinois

Caitlyn jiggled her keys in her hand as she made her way from the hospital to the parking garage where her car was. The job she had working on the geriatric floor was actually pretty good. She loved her patients, though it was often heartbreaking, as many of them were facing end-of-life illnesses. But she enjoyed talking to them and to their families and getting to know them.

She swung by the house to pick up her mother, tired as she was from a long week of work. Mom slid into the seat beside her and pecked her on the cheek.

"Mom, do we really have to go get your friend from the airport? Why can't Mrs. Unger just take an Uber or have her husband pick her up?"

"Her husband is on a business trip. And I just appreciate having you along, especially so late on a Saturday night. The older I get, the more I hate driving in the dark."

Caitlyn shrugged. She didn't have anything better to do tonight, so she might as well go to O'Hare. Not that it was her favorite place to drive, but it wasn't too bad. Maybe Mom was testing her to see if she freaked out driving at night, since that was when the accident happened. While she did grip the steering wheel tighter and kept her focus sweeping all over the road, she managed it pretty well. Could keep her panic to a minimum.

Mom relaxed in her seat and chose her movie soundtrack playlist. "Do you think Dr. Harris is helping you?"

"Yeah, I do. She's getting me to see that I couldn't have done anything to save Lindsey, because God was calling her home. And the accident was in no way my fault. I wasn't doing anything to distract Lindsey, and she did have the right of way. But it hasn't been easy to put away that guilt. Sometimes it rears its ugly head, and I fall into that trap again."

"It's going to take time. You have to allow that for yourself. Although it's not good to wallow in grief, there has to be some sorrow as you come to terms with what happened and how it has affected your life."

Caitlyn put on the blinker to merge from the on-ramp onto the highway. "Hmm, you sure you aren't a psychologist?"

"Pretty sure. Just a mom who has lived long enough to see a thing or two. Life experiences make us wise."

"I feel like I'm healing a little bit at a time. The pain isn't as sharp as it was, and I'm sleeping better."

"You're eating better too, which makes me very happy. I know it hasn't been easy, but I'm proud of you for admitting you needed help and for getting it."

"Yeah. I couldn't go on like I was. That was no kind of life. It's time for me to forge my own way."

They chatted about plenty of things during the thirty-minute trip, including wanting to discover who Pops' biological mother was. "It's just a little frustrating. If it wasn't one of the Jewish women at the home, who was it? And how did he come to be in Great-Grandma's care? It's beyond frustrating that we don't seem to have any DNA hits on that side of the family. No connections I'm making, anyway."

"I know, and who Pops' mother was is a big question, and a very good one to ask. But whether or not you get the answers, that doesn't change who you are today."

"Doesn't the past affect our future?"

"In some ways, yes, it does shape it. In other ways, a past that is so far past doesn't define us. It might give us some grounding, a place to start, but it doesn't change who God made us to be. He's the one who shapes and molds us, not someone who gave birth to my father-in-law eighty years ago."

What Mom said was true. Whoever Caitlyn's great-grandmother was didn't change who she was today. Her immediate past did have a hand in how she lived, but the distant past was no more than an echo.

"So what do you think of the wedding gown that Brenna chose?"

"Oh, that cousin of yours. She wants to make a splash, doesn't she?"

They continued their conversation with normal talk about her cousin's upcoming wedding and Caitlyn's new job at the hospital not far from where they lived. Which she was enjoying quite a bit, much to her surprise.

Soon she had to concentrate on the exit for O'Hare and getting to the right place. "American Airlines. There's the pickup spot there. See it?"

Caitlyn glanced over her shoulder and slid into the spot. "Is she here?"

"She says she is, and she needs help with her bags. Can you give her a hand?"

With a sigh, Caitlyn got out of the car and went to the curb. She didn't see Mrs. Unger, but there was a young man, curly blond hair so much like Aiden's, with his back to her. She was about to ask Mom if she was sure they were in the right place when the guy turned around. "Aiden?"

That wonderful, goofy grin stretched from cheek to cheek. He let go of his bag, opened his arms, and she ran into them. He smelled of leather and warm wood, a delicious, homey scent.

She squeezed him. "What are you doing here?"

Mom called out the window. "Are you surprised?"

"Did you know about this? What about Mrs. Unger?"

"As far as I know, she's sound asleep at home. So yes, I did know about this."

"Why are you here?"

Aiden kissed the top of her head. "Because I missed you. Is that allowed? Our FaceTime calls and late-night texts weren't doing it for me. I had to see you in person."

"I'm so glad you came. How long can you stay?"

"I'll get my posting soon, so a few days."

"That's all?"

"Yeah. We'll have to make every minute count."

Her heart fell to her feet, and she stepped out of his embrace. "Oh." This was temporary. Soon he would be gone, committed to what he was going to do. Not like her, not knowing which direction to move.

"We have so much to talk about. I want you to tell me how things are going, and I think we have a few things to figure out. It sounded like you're ready to have that talk, so that's why I'm here."

Mom raised the hatch, and Aiden slid his suitcase in before getting in the car with Caitlyn. "It's so nice to meet you, Mrs. Laurent. Thanks again for arranging the surprise. I think we got her."

Caitlyn laughed. "You sure did. And here I was grumbling in my mind the entire way here why we had to make this trek on a Saturday night."

They chatted on the way home, Mom asking Aiden the usual questions about his family and his plans for the future. Those hadn't changed. So Caitlyn would have to cherish these moments they had together. They were soon to come to an end. A relationship between the two of them wasn't in the cards.

Everyone was tired, especially Aiden, so once they got home, they called it a night, but they were all up and ready for church the next morning. It wasn't until that afternoon that Aiden and Caitlyn managed to get some alone time when they bundled up and braved the biting cold for a walk.

He held her mitten-covered hand in his own. Almost as good as hand warmers. "So how are you really doing?"

"Good. It will be a long process, maybe even a lifelong process, but I'm making progress. I'm not obsessing over the accident and my role, or lack of role, in it. My nightmares are far fewer. And I don't cry every day."

"I'm glad to hear that." He filled her in on what had happened at school after she left and how he was ready to get to work.

"That's exciting. I'm sure you're looking forward to doing what you've always wanted to do."

"I am, but I'm not."

She pulled him to a stop and moved to face him. "What do you mean?

Whenever we've spoken about this, you're always so eager to fulfill your mission, to do what Christ has called you to do."

"Okay, brutal honesty?"

"That's the best kind. Most of the time."

"Since you've been gone, I've been questioning if flying missionaries is what I really want to do."

"What? I can't believe what I'm hearing."

"What's pulling at me more than anything is you."

"Me?" Her heart fluttered.

"You. When you left, I realized how empty I was, how I was developing feelings for you."

"I'm a mess, Aiden. I don't think anyone wants anything to do with me right now."

"That's not true. You're beautiful and funny and caring and kind and I could go on and on. The point is, I'd like to have you in my life for a long time to come."

Little bubbles tickled her stomach.

"Do you ever see yourself on the mission field?"

Those little bubbles popped, her short-lived joy deflated in an instant. "I'm really happy working with older patients. I've found my passion, and I'm content. The only thing missing in my life is you."

He pulled her close, or as close as he could when they were both bundled like Eskimos. "We'll figure something out, I promise you that."

Promise me. Promise me.

The words rang in Caitlyn's head. "Wait a minute. I have somewhere we have to go. Right now."

"Now?"

"Yes. I need to take you there. I need to go there."

Within ten minutes or so, Caitlyn was driving them to the cemetery where Lindsey was buried.

"Why there?" Aiden turned off the music that had been blaring when she started her car.

"Your words about promising me we would find a way triggered a memory. I can't believe I never thought about it until now."

"Something about Lindsey?"

"Yes." They arrived at the cemetery. Not many people were out on such a frigid day, and there was no one else anywhere near the gravesites. Most of them were buried under snow, but Caitlyn knew just where Lindsey's was.

They hiked a little way through the plots, only a few of them with markers that stood vertical instead of horizontal. She came to one and brushed the snow from it.

LINDSEY GREEN. OCTOBER 1, 1999–JANUARY 5, 2022. BELOVED DAUGHTER.

Caitlyn shivered, and Aiden pulled her close, his chest against her back. "What did you remember?"

"After the collision, Lindsey was still alive for a minute or two. I pleaded with her to be okay. She was bleeding so much. I've always thought she said, 'Live my life for me.' But that's not what she said. She told me to live my life. 'Promise me,' she said. 'Promise me.' She wanted me to live *my* life. I've had it wrong this whole time. I've been living her life, not keeping the promise I made to her to live mine."

"That's a big breakthrough."

"It is. She was such a true friend that her last words were meant for me, her last thoughts were of me." Caitlyn's throat tightened, but she wouldn't give in to the tears. "I promised her I'd live my life, and I'm going to do that from now on. You know, Africa is only a hop, skip, and a jump from southern France. Eleanore went to France from Switzerland to open that maternity hospital, and it served so many women and children, saved so many of them from death, including the woman I knew as my great-grandmother."

"What are you saying?"

"I've found my passion, and it's helping the elderly. Taking care of them in their declining years. Would it be possible for you to be based in France? I know you'd be gone for long periods of time, but I think I'd like to start a geriatric home there. The French government provides pensions, but I'd like for it to be a Christian place, one where the elderly can go and be surrounded by people of a similar faith. Maybe one where some of them would come to faith."

"There would be a great number of hurdles to overcome to make that a reality."

"That doesn't matter. We could be together, and we could both be living our passions and serving on the mission field at the same time."

"You won't miss your parents?"

"Something fierce, but I have a feeling they'll make a hundred little excuses to come to France."

"Does that mean we're going to have a hundred children?"

She gave him a playful swat and sauntered away, turning to glance at him over her shoulder. "You, sir, are getting ahead of yourself. And if you think I'm having a hundred children, then this relationship is over right now."

His laughter, while maybe a little out of place in a graveyard, rang through the chilly air. "We'll see about that. We'll just see about that."

"A hundred children may have been Eleanore's dream, but it's not mine. I'd like a hundred men like Pops in my life. Maybe even you."

CHAPTER SEVENTY

January 23, 2023
Downers Grove, Illinois

Caitlyn wove her way through Monday afternoon traffic with Aiden by her side. "I'm so excited for you to meet Pops. Since his fall, his memory has gotten pretty bad, but maybe we'll catch him on a good day. We're blessed to have found this facility for him. Taking care of him while trying to work was getting to be too much for Mom."

"I like your mother. And your father. They're great people. No wonder they have such a fabulous daughter as you."

If Aiden kept this up, she'd have to switch off the car's heater and turn on the air conditioning.

"Pops is a safe person to talk to. He doesn't remember what I tell him, so I can pour out my heart to him. He just smiles and nods and pats my hand, calling me a good girl. That's why I love him. He's been that way since before dementia stole so much from him."

Once they arrived at the memory care facility and signed in, they made their way to Pops' room. "Hey there," Caitlyn said. "Have you had your dinner yet?"

"Oh, yes. Come in." Pops sat in a wheelchair, age spots covering what had once been strong hands, though he sported a head full of white hair. He had to be wearing three shirts and two sweaters, and an orange and green afghan that Grams must have crocheted in the seventies lay across his lap. "We had roast beef and mashed potatoes. It was delicious. Gert always makes the best meals."

The distinct odor of fish permeated the place, so it was more than likely that they hadn't had roast beef. But Caitlyn played along. "Grams sure is the best cook in the country. No one can make mashed potatoes as velvety as she can."

"You are so right. Now pull up a chair and introduce yourself."

"I'm your granddaughter Caitlyn." They had this same conversation every visit. "And this is Aiden. My. . .friend."

Aiden shot her a sideways glance, and she shrugged.

"My granddaughter, you say?"

"Yep."

"Well, aren't I the lucky one, to have such a beautiful granddaughter. And you're all grown-up. How did that happen when I'm so young? Grams doesn't like getting old."

"No, she doesn't. Did you know I've been to France?" She also asked this question every week. Most of the time, it didn't elicit much of a response from him.

"France, is that what you said?"

"It is. Aiden and I were in Perpignan and Elne."

"Ah, Elne. That's where I was born, you know."

"Yes, I know that. I visited the maternity home there."

"La Maternité de la Paix. Paix means 'peace' in French. My parents taught me just a little bit of the language. I didn't like it."

This was more information than he had ever given her. Maybe she'd finally caught him on a good day, a day where he was a little more with it. "What was your mother's name?"

"Hélène. My, she was a beautiful woman. Not as beautiful as Gert, but beautiful nonetheless. Tall and regal almost." He turned and pointed to a piece of stained glass hanging on the wall behind him. "She made that, you know. All my life, I remember her working in the studio my father built her, creating these beautiful works of art."

"I didn't know that." She had never seen the piece before. Perhaps it had gotten put away in the attic. But now she and Aiden went to examine it. The piece was of a beautiful hillside town, capped with a château. "Do you think that's Elne?" she whispered to Aiden.

"Very possible. If that's the castle, it was magnificent in its day."

"No wonder my great-grandfather fell in love with her." She turned to Pops. "Do you know what year your parents married?"

"During the war some time. I'm not sure. That was a long time ago. She didn't talk about the past very much. Neither did he. You don't know what war does to people, how it changes them. What she saw, what she experienced in the camp was horrible. But Madame Touissant saved her life."

"That's the woman who ran the hospital, right?"

"Yes. I met her once, did you know that?" His afghan slipped from his lap, and she went to fix it. "Thank you, dear. You're such a nice nurse."

Between her work with older patients and visiting Pops so often, she didn't allow his forgetfulness to get under her skin. He wasn't doing it on purpose. It was sad, that was all.

"You were telling me that you met Madame Touissant once? So you were in France?"

"Yes. I think I was about twelve or thirteen years old. I can't remember. It's hard when you forget things like that. But my mother had this jar of dirt from France. I broke it when I was little, and she cried. She almost never did, and I hated that I made my beautiful mother cry." His dimming eyes shimmered.

"Tell me about Madame Touissant." She couldn't allow him to get too far off topic, or he might never get back on it.

"We drove to a house on a hill. Not Papa's house. No, we went there later. We saw a little grave there, and Mom told me that was my brother. He was born there, at Papa's house, but he was too early. Madame Touissant helped Mom, but they couldn't save such a small baby. The war was going on, you know. And it was a long time ago."

So they had been right. Otto was Noémie's child. Noémie and Levi's child. What a shame that he didn't survive. Her great-grandmother had faced two devastating losses.

She would have understood Caitlyn and what it was like to have someone you loved very much die. It was bad enough when it was a friend, but it must be so much more devastating when it was a husband and child.

Aiden squeezed her hand. He understood what this information meant.

But that didn't answer whose child her grandfather was. Not Noémie's, that was for sure. Not any of the other Jewish women at the maternity hospital. "What else do you remember about that trip and about meeting Madame Touissant?"

He stared out the window, icicles glistening in the weak sun. His eyes glazed over, and his face softened, some of the many wrinkles disappearing as he was transported back in time.

"Madame Touissant was at the house on the hill. Such a beautiful house with a glass dome for a ceiling. The paint was peeling, and some of the windows were broken, but it was a lovely place.

"She was tall like Mom, and she wore her hair in an old-fashioned German way, you know, with the braids coiled on either side of her head. But she had kind green eyes. Tears. There were tears in her eyes when she greeted me. Called me by my name.

"Mom pushed me forward and told me to say hello and be polite. I thought Eleanore would shake my hand, but instead, she reached out and wrapped me in a hug."

Pops turned toward her, his green eyes wide. "I remember." His voice was nothing more than a whisper. "She uttered just a few words. That's all she said to me. I don't think I remembered until now. *Mon fil. Je t'aime.*"

My son. I love you.

CHAPTER SEVENTY-ONE

22 August, 1955
Elne, France

As the wind swirls my full skirt around my calves, I glance at my watch, the thin black braided band encircling my wrist. Any moment now. Oui, I came here to reconnect to this house and to listen to all the stories, good and bad, that it had to tell.

More than that, though, I came to reconnect to some of the people who had comprised these stories, who had filled these rooms, and who had left their mark on it. Any minute now and my life will come full circle.

I press on my stomach, a little rounder with advancing years. We've made an agreement, that I not reveal my true identity to him. How difficult it will be to control myself and not blurt out the love I have for him, the love I've always had for him from the very moment of his conception. But that love compels me to hold my tongue and keep silent, to remain a woman in the shadows, someone he may not even remember meeting.

Difficult as that is, as much as it tears my heart from my chest to contemplate, it's for the best. We lost so much time, time that can never be regained. The war and the years and an ocean separated us and forever changed our relationship.

He now has a wonderful life. It's a very different one than the one Hans and I would have given him, but God's ways are perfect and often beyond our understanding. Because I love him more than I love my own life, I must give him this one last gift—a home, a family, an abundance of happiness.

I must keep my promise.

Over the years, there were times I walked to the sea's edge, ready to throw myself into its waters and allow it to consume me, just as my grief had almost done. Something, Someone, always stopped me before I acted. For that, I will be forever grateful. My life may not look like what I once dreamed it would be, but it's good.

The puttering of a car's engine draws me from my musings. I inhale and then exhale little by little, clasping my hands together to stop them from shaking. I have to bite the inside of my cheek to keep the tears at bay, and I haven't even seen him yet.

Non, for his sake, I cannot allow him to see me weeping. I'll only frighten him, and that's the last thing I want. If he remembers any of this, I want him to recall me as the nice lady with the pretty smile, not as the crazy woman who cried the entire time.

I pat my pocketbook where the treat waits for him and then, as the car approaches and grinds to a halt, I force my lips into a smile and turn around.

Out of the black Renault steps a woman with dark brown hair and hazel eyes that take in the entire scene in one swoop. There is memory behind that scan, the walls speaking to her as well. Next is a man, tall as ever, gray now distinguishing his temples, and he closes the middle button of his well-cut black suit.

Last is a boy, his hair the same color as mine, his chin very similar to Hans'. He's entering adolescence now, no longer the infant I have envisioned in my mind for these past twelve years. Even though I don't know him anymore, my heart swells with pride.

I am part of him, and he is part of me.

My eyes may not recognize him, but my heart knows him in an instant.

Étienne.

My boy.

The child I birthed. The child I had to give up because of my arrest.

Beaming, Hélène runs to me and throws herself into my arms. "Eleanore, is it really you? I can hardly believe it, after all these years. We thought you were dead."

"I'm so glad to have found you." I squeeze her hard, my only way of thanking her for all she's done for Étienne these long years.

"If we had known. . ."

"There was no way. I was reported to have died, and so that's what everyone believed." I release my hold on her and step back so that I can stare into her eyes, as if I might divine her feelings by doing so. "If I had known my name was on that list, maybe it would have changed things."

She sobers, the smile falling from her face and the shine in her eyes dulling. "Before David—Aime—and Étienne—we call him Steven—get here, we have to talk. You said in your letter that you want us to continue raising him as our own. Seeing him now, you haven't changed your mind, have you?"

Oui, oui, I have, I have. But I don't say the words. Only too well do I know the pain of turning your back and walking away from your child. I did so over a decade ago so that Étienne could have the life he deserved. "By taking him away from you, what kind of mother would I be? He's growing. You and Aime are the people he knows as his parents. How could I ever disrupt that? How could I ever ask you to do the very thing that tore my heart out of my body?"

She kisses me on both cheeks. "We love him so much, you know. He is our gift from our heavenly Father. God never blessed us with a child. Merci beaucoup isn't enough to express all that your sacrifice has meant to us."

"I'm glad he was able to be a comfort to you."

"More than that." She turns around for a moment and motions Aime and Étienne forward. "He is our greatest joy. When everything else was ripped from us, in the end, we had each other."

I dig my fingernails into the tender flesh of my palms, the pain in my heart much greater than in my hands.

She touches my cheek. "I understand the ache of missing a child. Of losing the greatest love of your life. Your selflessness and your sacrifice don't go unnoticed. Every night when David and I go to bed, we thank God for what you've done. As soon as Salomé wrote to us that you were alive, we prayed for a chance to tell you that. And for this."

Aime and Étienne come to her side, Aime's lopsided grin as endearing as ever. He grasps me by my shoulders and kisses my cheeks. Étienne scuffs his black shoes—new, judging by the shine still on them—in the gravel.

"He doesn't speak French, just a few words." Hélène gives him a small nudge and switches to English. "Steven, this is Madame Touissant. She knew your father and me when we lived here in France during the war." Her English words are smooth and flowing. Almost too fast for me to catch.

He gazes at me, his blond hair cut close to his scalp, and offers his hand for me to shake. Polite. Instead, I pull him close and wrap him in a hug. "It is nice to meet you." My English isn't as good as Hélène's. The years it has sat in disuse have eroded it. *"Mon fil. Je t'aime."*

"Enchanté."

I step away. Ah, so he does speak a little French. Hopefully nothing more than that single word, so that I haven't given away my secret. I switch to English. "Do you like France?"

"It's nice. Dad says he used to live in the big house on the hill, and that his family still owns the land. Maybe someday I'll come back and build an even better house."

I try in vain to keep my heart from fluttering. To have my son so close would be a dream come true. But I can't allow my hopes to run away with reality. "Do you want to build houses?"

"That'd be neat."

I glance at Hélène, unsure of what must be a colloquialism. She shrugs and answers in French. "It means that he likes the idea. He works hard in school, so anything is possible for him. We'll keep encouraging him and see what God has in store for him."

That was the third or fourth time she had mentioned God in the short while we'd been conversing. "Tell me about your faith."

A hint of pink rises in her cheeks. "I have you to thank for that. And Aime. When my life was at its darkest, you both shined the light on my Savior. Men may fail, but God never does. He brings beauty. He keeps His promises."

And now a tear does leak from my eye, and I do nothing to stop it. "He does do that, doesn't He? My heart is so full right now, not only knowing that you have come to faith, but that my son is being raised in a household of faith. That means more to me than anything."

"I read that promise you made to him, that if you couldn't raise him, you would find someone who would love him and who would love the Lord even more. Merci for choosing me to be that person. One thing I don't understand though. Why did you keep his identity a secret?"

"It's as I explained in the letter. My work was dangerous. If the Vichy or Nazis had discovered his identity, they would have had no qualms in killing him."

"They could have taken him, believing him to be Jewish."

"Non. That's why I gave him Aime's last name. And he doesn't look at all Jewish."

Hélène nods. "I understand doing whatever you had to do for your child. But I hurt for you. Why don't you come to America with us? You can watch Steven grow up and be part of his life."

I turn a quarter of a turn and stare at what had once been a beautiful home, now decrepit, stark against the steely gray skies. For a long moment, I drink in the sight of her. That was a long-ago dream, one that was part of my life for a season, a season that has now come and gone.

As has my season with my son, however short it had been.

Hélène loops her arm through mine, and together we stroll to the far side of the building, the drying grapevines stretching down the hill's slope from us.

"You haven't told him anything, have you?"

"Non." She shook her head, her hair cut and curled in the latest style. "I didn't know what to say to him or what your reaction to him would be."

"It's a generous offer." I sigh, the wind carrying my breath away with it, all of it commingling. Why did life have to be so difficult? Why is the war still affecting our lives more than ten years after it has ended? "I can't leave France, and I couldn't bear to spend time with Étienne and not share my story with him. It would be too hard."

"Perhaps in time. . ."

I wave her words away. "Allow him to lead his life and enjoy the only one he knows. Don't muddle it for him. He deserves every happiness in the world, not the confusion such a revelation would bring. It's enough. I got to meet him once again. I'm keeping my promise to him. I will always treasure today in my heart."

She grasps my arm with amazing strength. "I feel so selfish for taking him from you."

I stop and spin her to face me. "It is not selfish, what you are doing for him. There were many years I wouldn't have been able to care for him. It took me a long while to get back on my feet after my time in the camp. I needed you to look after him. And you're doing a wonderful job."

"How can you bear it?"

"Margot and Beryl are with me."

"They are?" She widens her eyes. "I'd love to see them again."

"They're at the house making dinner, and I want you all to come. Both have grown into beautiful young women who are working with me to establish maternity hospitals in Africa. You wouldn't recognize them."

"Then you truly are happy?"

"Content. At peace. And now, seeing you, my heart is full."

"I promise to continue to do the best I can for Steven, to give him all the love of two mothers."

I let go of some of my French reserve and hug her. She embraces me once again, and together we weep for all that we've lost and all that we've gained.

And the walls of the building have yet another story to tell.

LA FIN

AUTHOR'S NOTE

Separating fact from fiction is something I love to do when I read a historical novel, and you must be wondering what is real and what is not in this story.

In May 1940, when the Nazis invaded France and the government surrendered, eight million people fled to the south of the country known as Vichy France. The Germans set up a puppet government there, and though they did arrest Jews and other political prisoners, the area was relatively safe. By the summer of 1942, however, the Nazis were putting increasing pressure on the Vichy government to step up their arrest of Jews. They'd had enough of dealing with the Vichy and took control of the entire country on November 11, 1942. This is very simplified, and the true workings were extremely complicated. The thickest book in my library is on Vichy France.

Camp de Rivesaltes was a prison camp near the town of Rivesaltes in the far southwest corner of France, almost to the Spanish border. During the Spanish Civil War in the late 1930s, many crossed the Pyrénées Mountains into France to find refuge and were held at the camp. Some remained there even after May 1940 when the Vichy began to use it. In September of 1942, Camp de Rivesaltes became the only transit camp for all of Southern France. From Rivesaltes, prisoners were taken to Drancy and then to Mauthausen or Auschwitz.

When the Nazis began putting pressure on the Vichy, they tightened restrictions at the camp. On August 26, 1942, there was a wave of roundups of Jews, and from August until November 1942, over 10,000 were transported to Drancy. Rivesaltes was a huge camp, but soon only two blocks were set aside for Jews, and finally only one block was allocated for their housing. On August 18, 1942, barbed wire was erected there for the first time, and on August 25, more guards were added. Even the children were not exempt, and on August 31, the Jewish children in the care of relief agencies were ordered to the camps.

Friedel Reiter was a real Swiss nurse and member of the Swiss Red Cross who voluntarily lived in the deplorable conditions at Camp de

Rivesaltes in order to help the women and children there. Somehow, she managed to spirit out a good number of women, some on bicycles in the dark of night. This was, in part, thanks to the laissez-faire attitude of the French guards. Because of the timing of the story and the tightening of restrictions at the time, I had to invent a plausible way for Friedel to get the women and children out, and so I created François.

After the closing of the camp in November 1942, Friedel moved to a children's home in Chambon-sur-Lignon, where she married the man who ran the home, August Bohny. She was recognized as Righteous Among the Nations in 1990.

There really was a maternity hospital in the village of Elne, not far from Rivesaltes. It was used during the Spanish Civil War and then during WWII. Elisabeth Eidenbenz was the daughter of a pastor in Zurich, Switzerland. After teaching for a while, she joined Asociación de Ayuda a los Niños en Guerra and went to Spain and then France to aid Spanish refugees. The conditions expectant mothers were living in were appalling, and she bought a run-down mansion and turned it into La Maternité Suisse d'Elne. After the fall of France, she was forced to join the Swiss Red Cross to maintain neutrality and continue aiding pregnant women. Approximately 550 babies were delivered at La Maternité Suisse from the late 1930s until 1944. For the most part, her neutrality protected the hospital, but there were occasional raids, and some of the women didn't survive.

Elisabeth lived to be almost one hundred years old and never married or had children. She considered the children of La Maternité Suisse to be her children. She was recognized as Righteous Among the Nations in 2002.

Although I have the hospital closing in November of 1942, it actually remained open until 1944. I needed it to close earlier for dramatic effect. There were benefactors who contributed money to the home, but Aime is completely fictional, as is his estate.

Margot and Beryl are based on two girls, Hannah and Hilda Krieser, that Friedel saved from a transport. They were older, sixteen and twelve, and Friedel got them passes to work as teachers in a home in Pringy, France, not far from the Swiss border. One day, French gendarmes entered the home and took the girls, returning them to Rivesaltes, where their parents were about to board a transport. Friedel protested that the gendarmes had no right to take the girls, because they were on neutral Swiss territory. She pestered the guard so much that he finally told her to take the girls and get them out of his sight, to hide them until the transport left. Friedel gathered several other children—some parents refused to be parted from their little ones—and hid them as well. After three days, she managed to get them out of the camp and back to Pringy and other homes. Hannah and Hilda's parents were murdered in Auschwitz.

I took some liberties with the contemporary storyline, though I endeavored to be as factual as possible. To my knowledge, there is no missionary school in Barcelona, though it is a fascinating city with amazing tapas. In 1883, architect Antoni Gaudí was put in charge of a new project, Basílica i Temple Expiatori de la Sagrada Família (Basilica and Expiatory Church of the Holy Family, or Sagrada Família). He completely changed the design, and construction is ongoing. Yes, there really are grapes and bananas on some parts of the exterior of the church. I couldn't believe my eyes when I saw them.

My friend and I stayed in Perpignan for part of my research trip to France and Spain, and we stayed in the same spot Caitlyn, Elissa, and Aiden did, right across from a kebob restaurant with the Perpignan train station at one end of the street and the huge metal sculpture of a man in a chair at the other. *Le Petit Train de Perpignan* is a real attraction that gave us a great overview of the city, and we really did eat at a restaurant nearby, one of the few open at that time of the day. Yes, restaurants in France are open between about noon and two p.m. for lunch and then don't open again until at least seven thirty p.m. for dinner.

We also spent time in the very quaint and beautiful town of Collioure, which is much like I describe it. We ate at the same restaurant as in the story, enjoyed bubble cones while watching Marines take their rafts from the canal next to the fortress into the Mediterranean, and toured the church. The fortress is ripped from my experience there, including the art and the museum, although I didn't see any of the cards that play such a pivotal role in the story. From my research, Elisabeth and her staff did change the names of the children to protect them but preserved their identities so they would never lose them. How they did that was something I invented.

Train travel is a great way to get around this part of Europe, and we got very good at taking them everywhere we went, though I learned the hard way not to drag big suitcases along. The section where Aiden has to rearrange the luggage on the train so Elissa's suitcase will fit is, unfortunately, something that happened to me. A huge thanks to the young man who helped me. I hope my French was adequate to express how deeply I appreciated him. The stations at Perpignan and at Barcelona were just as I portrayed them.

ACKNOWLEDGMENTS

Books don't magically appear in an author's head one night and transfer themselves to the bookstore the next day (oh, how I wish!). There are so many people who had a hand in turning *What I Promise You* into what you hold in your hands.

Thank you to Becky Germany and the entire team at Barbour Publishing, including Shalyn Sattler and Laura Young. You are the best to work with, and I appreciate the hard work each and every one of you do.

What would this book be without my terrific editor, Ellen Tarver? Probably still a hot mess with the same people named fifteen different names throughout the course of the book! Thank you so much for all you did to clean this up and make it readable. I love working with you.

Tamela Hancock Murray, my fabulous agent, I would never have been this far in my career without your love, support, and cheerleading over the years. It's been a journey, but I've loved taking it along with you. Thank you for championing me and always answering my phone calls.

Merci beaucoup to author Elizabeth Musser. When we got talking when I interviewed you for my podcast, who would have thought we'd find we had so much in common, including a mutual love for France. God surely put us together. Thank you for fixing my French. No wonder the people there enjoyed so many good laughs when I spoke their language!

In addition to the young man on the train, I owe a great debt to the people of France. They were nothing but kind and accommodating. Thank you to the people in the bus station for getting us on the right bus to Camp de Rivesaltes. Merci to the man behind the desk at the camp who didn't laugh when I asked for two tickets but graciously sold them to me and then gently recommended that I might like a headset with an English narrator as we toured the grounds.

Merci to the people at La Maternité Suiss d'Elne for your knowledge, your guidance, and for calling a taxi so we didn't have to walk along that highway back to the village. While I didn't have a panic attack like Caitlyn, my friend and I did yell to each other, "Suck in your butt!" as we stood on the almost non-existent shoulder. To the owner/waiter at the Ô

Petit Chez Nous Restaurant in Collioure, merci for being patient with us and for explaining in detail everything on the menu. The food was fantastic. Caitlyn might not have finished hers, but I cleaned my plate!

And gracias to the hotel clerk at the Hotel Lloret Ramblas in Barcelona for your kindness and helping us figure out the metro system. Another gracias to the hotel clerk at Sallés Hotel Ciutat del Prat. We would never think poorly of your city because of one unscrupulous taxi driver. You were so good to two weary travelers.

I cannot say thank you enough to my very dear friend, the sister of my heart, who accompanied me on this journey. Lisa, you were so very good to me and took exceptional care of me, especially that day in Elne when I wasn't feeling well. Thank you for reminding me to eat and drink, for the wonderful charcuterie dinner you made for us, and for willingly allowing me to drag you around Spain and France. We had some adventures (I won't mention the door and suitcase fiasco!), and I'm so glad I got to share them with you. You're the best, sweetie, and you deserve the best. I love you!

To my family, there aren't enough words to express how I feel about all of you. Doug, Alyssa, and Jonalyn, thank you for holding down the fort while I went globetrotting. I pray that there are adventures that await us in the future. Thank you all for seeing me through my deadline and for being willing to eat lots of pizza and chicken nuggets. I have the best family in the entire world, and I wouldn't trade any of you for any amount of money. Honestly. Even when I threaten it! I love you all dearly. You are my world.

Thank you, all my readers, for taking the time to read Noémie and Caitlyn's stories. I appreciate all of you more than you can know. Your encouragement has kept me writing. I pray that the story has touched your heart in one way or another. You have many choices these days for how to spend your free time. Thank you for choosing to spend it with Noémie and Caitlyn.

To my launch team, who helped catapult this book into the work, I owe you a great debt of gratitude. Merci beaucoup. Without you to spread the word about its release and to share your excitement about it, my job would be infinitely more difficult. You are a true blessing to me.

And to my Lord and Savior, Jesus Christ, thank You for blessing me with this gift of storytelling and allowing me the ability and resources to use that gift. I pray that through Your Spirit, my words may touch hearts and that You will receive all the praise and glory.

Liz Tolsma is the author of several WWII novels, romantic suspense novels, prairie romance novellas, and an Amish romance. She is a popular speaker and an editor and resides next to a Wisconsin farm field with her husband and their youngest daughter. Her son is a US Marine, and her oldest daughter is a college student. Liz enjoys reading, walking, working in her large perennial garden, kayaking, and camping. Please visit her website at www.liztolsma.com and follow her on Facebook, Twitter (@LizTolsma), Instagram, YouTube, and Pinterest. She is also the host of the Christian Historical Fiction Talk podcast.

Other Barbour Books by Liz Tolsma:

The Pink Bonnet (True Colors series)

The Green Dress (True Colors series)

The Gold Digger (True Colors series)

The Silver Shadow (True Colors series)

Picture of Hope (Heroines of WWII series)

A Promise Engraved (Doors to the Past series)

What I Would Tell You (Echoes of the Past series – book 1)

ECHOES OF THE PAST

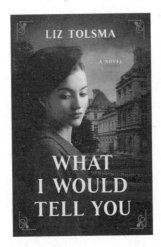

What I Would Tell You

AWSA 2023 Golden Scroll winner
for Historical Novel of the Year
Book 1

Tolsma uses split time storytelling and DNA testing to uncover a family's courageous story that was lost to the horrors of WWII.

When college student Tessa Payton takes a DNA test for fun, she never imagined it would change everything she knew about her family and send her on a journey to uncover a mystery in her ancestry lost to the horrors of WWII. Will what she discovers change what Tessa believes about herself and her faith? In 1940s Greece, Sephardic Jew Mathilda Nissim is angry that her people have not stood up to their invaders, so she continues printing her newspaper in secret, calling them to action. She trusts no one to help them—not even God. But is her resistance futile with generational consequences?

Paperback / 978-1-63609-459-5

Christian Fiction for Women

Christian Fiction for Women is your online home for the latest in Christian fiction.

Check us out online for:

- Giveaways
- Recipes
- Info about Upcoming Releases
- Book Trailers
- News and More!

Find Christian Fiction for Women at Your Favorite Social Media Site:

 Search "Christian Fiction for Women"

 @fictionforwomen
